Pulaski County Public Library
12...
Winamac, IN 46996
574-946-3432

A DOOMED FERRY RIDE . . .

Denny withdrew a short black gun, not much bigger than Matt's water pistol, and pointed it at Bonnie.

Bonnie stared at the gun. She didn't know what kind it was, only that it was aimed at her heart. A small gun could be just as deadly as a large one. Fear crashed against her like ocean waves.

Denny wouldn't get away with it; Bonnie was positive of that. As soon as Denny shot her, Matt would scream and run upstairs for help—and what would Denny do then? Shoot Matt, too?

OTHER BOOKS BY PEG KEHRET

Cages

Danger at the Fair

Don't Tell Anyone

Horror at the Haunted House

I'm Not Who You Think I Am

Nightmare Mountain

Searching for Candlestick Park

Spy Cat

The Stranger Next Door

Terror at the Zoo

ABDUCTION!

ABDUCTION!

PEG KEHRET

PUFFIN BOOKS

PUFFIN BOOKS
Published by the Penguin Group
Penguin Young Readers Group,
345 Hudson Street, New York, New York 10014, U.S.A.
Penguin Group (Canada), 90 Eglinton Avenue East, Suite 700, Toronto,
Ontario, Canada M4P 2Y3 (a division of Pearson Penguin Canada Inc.)
Penguin Books Ltd, 80 Strand, London WC2R 0RL, England
Penguin Ireland, 25 St Stephen's Green, Dublin 2, Ireland
(a division of Penguin Books Ltd)
Penguin Group (Australia), 250 Camberwell Road,
Camberwell, Victoria 3124, Australia
(a division of Pearson Australia Group Pty Ltd)
Penguin Books India Pvt Ltd, 11 Community Centre, Panchsheel Park,
New Delhi - 110 017, India
Penguin Group (NZ), Cnr Airborne and Rosedale Roads, Albany,
Auckland 1310, New Zealand (a division of Pearson New Zealand Ltd)
Penguin Books (South Africa) (Pty) Ltd, 24 Sturdee Avenue,
Rosebank, Johannesburg 2196, South Africa

Registered Offices: Penguin Books Ltd, 80 Strand, London WC2R 0RL, England

First published in the United States of America by Dutton Children's Books,
a division of Penguin Young Readers Group, 2004
Published by Puffin Books, a division of Penguin Young Readers Group, 2006

10 9 8 7 6 5 4 3 2 1

Copyright © Peg Kehret, 2004
All rights reserved

THE LIBRARY OF CONGRESS HAS CATALOGED THE DUTTON EDITION AS FOLLOWS:
Kehret, Peg.
Abduction! / by Peg Kehret.—1st ed.
p.   cm.
Summary: Thirteen-year-old Bonnie has a feeling of foreboding on the very day
that her six-year-old brother, Matt, and their dog, Pookie, are abducted, and she
becomes involved in a major search effort as well as a frightening adventure.
ISBN: 0-525-47294-0 (hc)
[1. Kidnapping—Fiction. 2. Brothers and sisters—Fiction. 3. Fathers and sons—
Fiction. 4. Seattle (Wash.)—Fiction.] I. Title.   PZ7.K2518Ab   2004
[Fic]—dc21 2003063531

Puffin Books ISBN 0-14-240617-1

Printed in the United States of America

Except in the United States of America, this book is sold subject to the condition that
it shall not, by way of trade or otherwise, be lent, re-sold, hired out, or otherwise
circulated without the publisher's prior consent in any form of binding or cover
other than that in which it is published and without a similar condition
including this condition being imposed on the subsequent purchaser.

The publisher does not have any control over and does not assume any
responsibility for author or third-party Web sites or their content.

For my daughter, Anne Konen,
love always

ABDUCTION!

CHAPTER 1

Denny Thurman stuck the black wig on his head, pulling it snug above his ears. He put on the brown shirt with the fake UPS logo, buttoned it over his T-shirt, and tucked it into his brown pants. Last he pressed a false mustache on his upper lip, pushing hard to make it stick.

He smiled at himself in the mirror. His own mother wouldn't recognize him.

The temporary rose tattoo on his left biceps showed below his sleeve, but the slight bulge of the handgun in his shoulder holster was barely noticeable under his shirt.

Denny hurried downstairs to his car, feeling nearly as excited as he did when he placed a bet. An hour later, he stopped the car in the alley behind his ex-wife's house and put on thin plastic gloves. He got out but left the engine running, in case he needed to drive away quickly. He looked both ways, saw no one, and walked to the gate that connected the garage to the fence.

He reached over the top of the gate, feeling for a latch. Good. No lock. He opened the gate and stepped into the yard. One hand rested in his pants pocket, the fingers wrapped around a small plastic bag containing a piece of broiled steak. With luck, the dog would come to him without the bribe. If that happened, Denny would have a steak sandwich for dinner tonight.

He wished he could remember the dog's name, but Denny had never paid attention to the dog—he didn't care for animals—and six years was a long time. By now it might be a different dog.

Denny's eyes swept across the small yard: neatly mowed grass, a swing set, sunbursts of yellow tulips in full bloom, a bird feeder and birdbath. No dog, though. Surely Anita would have a dog; she had been crazy about dogs, and so had Bonnie. They both petted every mutt they met, acting as if each was the grand champion of all time. Anita even kept dog biscuits and a leash in the car, in case she saw a stray in need of help.

The dog must be inside. Denny would have to pry open a door or window. He hoped the house wasn't wired with an alarm system.

Denny walked toward the house but stopped before he reached the screen door. His eyes swung to the corner of the house, to a metal flap at ground level. A dog door! If he could coax the dog out the door, he wouldn't have to break in, after all, and wouldn't risk setting off an alarm.

Denny stood outside the dog door and whistled. "Here, dog," he called. "Come get your steak." He whistled again.

When no dog appeared, Denny pulled off a piece of the steak, pushed the door flap inward, and tossed the meat inside.

Soon the flap pushed outward, and an elderly black-and-white terrier waddled out. The once-dark muzzle was gray, and the dog walked stiff-legged, as if his knees didn't bend well anymore. It's the same dog, Denny thought. He must be over one hundred in dog years by now. Denny wondered if the dog would remember him.

"Hey, dog," Denny said.

The dog blinked, looking around as if unsure where the sound had come from. He's almost blind, Denny realized.

Denny held the steak toward the old terrier. The dog sniffed, wagged his tail, and came closer. When he tried to take the meat in his teeth, Denny pulled it away. He put the steak back in the bag and shoved it into his pocket. He had the dog; why waste the steak?

He removed the leash from his other pocket, looped it around the dog's neck, and tugging gently, led him out the gate. The dog followed willingly but couldn't jump into the car; Denny had to lift him into the backseat.

Before he shut the door, he unbuckled the dog's collar and read the ID tag. *Pookie,* it said, then a phone number. That's right; Pookie. Denny remembered now. Foolish name for a dog. The ID tag clinked against a rabies tag and a King County dog license as Denny tossed the collar into the weeds beside the alley.

He opened the driver's door and slid behind the wheel. He glanced at himself in the rearview mirror, to be sure the wig and mustache were still in place. Satisfied with his appearance, he drove slowly out of the alley and headed for the school, removing the gloves as he drove.

The dog whined and pawed at the back of Denny's seat.

"Too late to cry," Denny said. "You're the bait now, Pookie, my boy. You're the insurance to make sure Matt gets in the car without calling for help."

CHAPTER 2

Bonnie hadn't thought about the dream in years, which was fine with her.

She remembered it when her best friend, Nancy, said, "Last night I dreamed I jumped out the window during math, landed in the ocean, and rode off on a sea turtle."

"I can never recall my dreams," Bonnie said as she pulled on her Mountain Middle School shorts and T-shirt for PE class. "Except for one. I used to have it a lot."

"You had the same dream more than once? Mine are different every night."

"This one was a nightmare. The first time I had it was the night my dad died."

"What was it about?"

Bonnie leaned down to tie her shoes, surprised by the chill she felt. "It's hard to explain."

"Try me."

"In the dream I'm lost on a huge prairie, acres and acres of grass higher than my head. I spend the whole dream running, calling out for help that never comes."

"Just grass? No vicious lion chases you? You don't fall into a pit full of poisonous snakes?"

"I know it doesn't sound scary, but whenever I had the dream I always woke up crying, with my heart pounding." Each time she had felt as if a heavy black fog hung over her bed, seeping through the blankets into her skin and making it impossible ever to feel happy again. Bonnie shuddered, remembering.

"You were four when your dad died, right?" Nancy said.

"Right. The thing is, I didn't know about death until it happened. I'd heard the word, but I didn't think it had anything to do with me. I never expected it to happen to my family, to my daddy."

"Most four-year-olds wouldn't."

"My grandma tried to help me understand, but she made me more scared than before."

"What did she say?" Nancy asked.

"She told me, 'Everyone dies, but usually not until they're very old.' She meant to comfort me, but I thought Daddy was old. When you're four, twenty-six seems ancient."

"Small wonder you had nightmares."

The girls left the locker room and began jogging around the gym with their classmates.

"Grandma talked about heaven and angels and how it was a tragic accident," Bonnie said, "but I focused on, *Everyone dies*. Everyone included my mother, who was the same age as Daddy. That night, I dreamed I was lost on the prairie."

"You were afraid you'd be an orphan."

Bonnie spoke softly. "I've never told anyone about the dream before. Mom used to come into my room when I'd wake up crying, and she'd ask what I had dreamed, but I always pretended I couldn't remember. At first I was superstitious about it, afraid if I told the dream it would come true. Later I worried there was something wrong with me for having the same bad dream over and over. I didn't tell Mom because I didn't want to go to the doctor. I was scared I'd get a shot."

"You don't need a master's degree in psychology to figure out that nightmare," Nancy said. "It's the classic fear-of-loss dream. You lost your dad, and you were afraid your mom would die, too. Perfectly normal. They'd march you straight to a kiddie shrink if you *didn't* have dreams like that when a parent died. Do you still have it?"

"No. I had it a lot at first, and then it gradually came less often. It stopped when I was eight or nine."

"So you are now a well-adjusted thirteen-year-old who has overcome a terrible loss and gotten on with her life. No more nightmares."

"You, on the other hand," Bonnie said, "are a serious mental case who secretly yearns to escape from school and ride away on a sea turtle."

"You got that right," Nancy said.

Although Bonnie smiled, the familiar cold ache settled in her stomach. It didn't happen often anymore. To be honest, whole weeks went past when she never thought about her dad at all, but when she did think of him she felt as if she had a hole in her heart, like some vital piece of herself was missing.

Remembering how suddenly she had lost him always made her feel vulnerable. If tragedy could knock on her door without warning once, it could arrive again.

She wished she hadn't told Nancy about the dream. Now she felt anxious and edgy, as if some unexpected disaster were about to strike her family.

You're being paranoid, Bonnie told herself. Mom's at work; Matt's in kindergarten; Pookie's probably asleep in a patch of sunshine on the rug. It's an ordinary morning, and everybody's safe. Still, the vague feeling of dread stayed with her.

CHAPTER 3

It had been simple for Denny to learn Matt's room number. After he found Anita's address in the telephone directory, he called the school district office and asked which school kids in that area would attend. Next he had called the school and said he was Matthew Sholter's uncle.

"I want to send balloons to his classroom on his birthday," Denny had said, "but I don't know which room he's in."

The student who had answered the phone looked up Matthew Sholter and then told Denny everything he needed to know, including what time all-day kindergarten started and let out, and where Room 27 was located. She called the boy Matt, rather than Matthew. Useful information.

Jefferson School sat on the corner of Milton Street and Seventh, a sprawling one-story structure that had overflowed its quota of children years ago and now depended on portable buildings to house the extra students.

For the last three days, Denny had parked in front of the school every afternoon, in the line of cars that arrived to pick up children who spilled out the doors like popcorn from a popper promptly at two thirty-six.

Until now Denny had left the school by himself. Today he would have a passenger.

Denny glanced at the car's clock. Two twenty-three. He was right on schedule.

The first day Denny had wondered how he would know which one was Matt. It seemed impossible that he wouldn't know his own son, but one kid looked pretty much like the next to Denny, and he'd never actually met Matt or even seen any pictures of him. He hadn't wanted to, until recently.

Maybe the kid resembled him. Tim and Thomas, Denny's nephews, looked a lot like Denny's brother-in-law, Winston, so Matt would probably look like

Denny. The boy might be a real chip off the old block, Denny had thought, and I'll know him the second I see him.

He had watched the children rush outside, but none of them seemed even slightly familiar. Maybe Matt was absent. As Denny watched the children line up for the school buses, or head to the waiting cars, he saw Bonnie join a small blond boy in the second bus line.

Denny hadn't seen Bonnie since the divorce, but she had been six or seven during his brief marriage to her mother, so he recognized her instantly. She was taller, of course, and more slender, but she still had thick, curly brown hair and a lopsided smile. The boy showed Bonnie a drawing, and she gave him a thumbs-up.

Denny stared at the boy with Bonnie. He wore a Donald Duck T-shirt and jeans. That must be him, Denny thought. That's Matt. My son.

The same scene repeated the next day, and the next, as Denny parked near the school, watched for Matt, and made his plans.

After the second day, Denny knew which boy was Matt, even before Bonnie came.

Matt always arrived first and got in line. Then Bonnie dashed across the playground and rode home with him. The trick would be to coax Matt into the car quickly, without alarming the bus driver or the other kids, and drive away before Bonnie got there. He planned to wait outside Room 27 and intercept Matt the second he emerged.

Denny had come back to the school one night and walked around, deciding where to park so that he wouldn't be seen by the other parents or the bus drivers. That's when he saw the notice on the front door: ALL SCHOOL VISITORS MUST SIGN IN AT THE OFFICE AND GET A VISITOR'S BADGE.

He couldn't take a chance on being stopped for not wearing a badge, but he didn't want to sign in, either.

Denny had soon figured out what to do.

Now he was finally putting his plan into motion. He had rehearsed the whole thing in his mind so many times that when he began to do it for real, he felt as if he were merely repeating actions he had already taken.

Instead of parking where the parents lined up, he stopped on the side street, close to the door Matt always came out. He opened the trunk of his car, then took out a clipboard and a cardboard box addressed to the school library. Carrying the box under one arm, he walked around to the front entrance, past the flagpole, and into the school office.

"UPS," he said to the woman behind the counter. "I have a delivery for the library."

The woman glanced at his brown uniform. "You

need to sign in, please," she said, "and wear a visitor's badge. The library is down the hall, on your left."

Denny scrawled UPS on the sign-in ledger, thanked the woman, hung a badge around his neck, and walked out of the office. Instead of heading for the library, he went straight for the door at the end of the hall, the one next to Room 27.

Then something happened that Denny had not planned for—a lucky break he had never imagined as he mentally rehearsed this day's activity.

The door of Room 27 opened, and Matt stepped into the hallway. He closed the door behind him and headed straight toward Denny.

"Matt," Denny said.

"I'm going to the bathroom," Matt said. He held a piece of yellow paper toward Denny. "I have a hall pass."

"I was coming to get you out of class," Denny said. "You're supposed to come with me. Right now."

The boy shook his head, frowning.

"It's an emergency," Denny said. "Pookie got hurt, and I'm taking him to the vet. Your mom wants you to go along so Pookie won't be so scared."

Matt's eyes grew wide. "Pookie's hurt?"

"He got hit by a car. I stopped to help, and when I called the number on Pookie's tag, your mom asked me to get you and then take Pookie to the vet. She's going to meet us there." Denny held out his hand to Matt. "We have to hurry!"

Matt shook his head again, putting his own hands behind his back. "I don't know you," he said. He took a step backward. "I'm not supposed to go anywhere with someone I don't know."

"You're right to be cautious," Denny said. "It shows you're a smart kid. But I checked in at the office; see my visitor's badge? That's how I knew where to find you. If you walk outside with me, you can see my car from the playground. You'll see I'm helping Pookie."

Denny went out the door, holding it open for Matt.

Matt followed Denny out the door to the playground.

Denny pointed. "That's my car," he said. "Pookie's in the backseat."

Matt looked toward the green sedan. He saw the dog's nose pressed against the side window of the man's car.

"Pookie!" Matt said. "How bad is he hurt? Are his legs broken? Is he all bloody? Is he going to die?"

"He might, if we don't get him to the vet right away. Pookie's scared. He needs you to ride along to the vet, so he won't be afraid." He extended his hand again.

Matt hesitated, glanced again at the dog, took the man's hand.

Together they ran across the playground toward the street.

While the boy climbed in beside the dog, Denny tossed the box and the clipboard into the trunk, his heart thumping in triumph. His plan had worked perfectly. The woman in the school office never suspected that a fake UPS logo had been stitched on last night by Denny himself. Matt had seen the dog in the car and left the school without a whimper.

As Matt hugged Pookie in the backseat, Denny started the engine and drove away, being careful to stay within the speed limit. The last thing he needed was to get pulled over for a traffic violation.

He rounded the corner as the first school bus pulled into the drive. The car clock said 2:34.

CHAPTER 4

By the time Bonnie got to her last class of the day, her mood had brightened. Friday afternoons always felt full of promise, even if she had no special plans for the weekend.

As she finished her math assignment, Nancy slipped her a note.

Can you leave baby brother with your neighbor and go to the mall with Sharon and me after school? Mom's driving us. We're going to try on shoes and get free makeup samples.

Bonnie sighed. She would love to go shopping with Nancy and her sister, but she wasn't supposed to ask Mrs. Watson, her neighbor, to watch Matt unless it was an emergency. She wrote *I have to stay with Matt. Lucky me. Bring me some samples—my face needs all the help it can get.* She passed the note back to Nancy.

Bonnie often wished she had an older sister instead of a younger brother. Sharon helped Nancy with homework and hairstyles, taught her the latest dances, and let Nancy listen to her CDs. Best of all, Nancy never had to be in charge of anyone but herself.

Last year, in sixth grade, Bonnie and Nancy often hung out together after school. They'd go to the library or talk with their friends for a little while before they walked home. Matt was in day care then, and Mom picked him up after work, so Bonnie didn't have to worry about him.

This year, with Matt in all-day kindergarten, Bonnie had to hurry from the middle school to the adjoining elementary school as soon as the final bell rang. She rode the bus home with Matt and took care of him until Mom arrived.

Bonnie knew it was important to watch Matt after school; she knew she saved Mom a lot of money each month. She also knew it was a pain.

Matt always wanted to practice pitching a baseball, with Bonnie as the catcher. If she didn't catch for him, Matt threw a tennis ball against the garage door for hours at a time. *Thwack! Thwack! Thwack!* Each *thwack* left a faint, round green spot from the tennis ball's fuzz. The Sholters had the only house in town with a polka-dot garage door.

The final bell rang at two thirty-six. Bonnie could never figure out why it wasn't two-thirty or two forty-five. An example of adults setting rules that don't make sense.

Bonnie slipped her backpack on and hurried toward the school library. She had two books due and didn't want to owe a fine. After dropping the books off, she headed across the ball field toward Matt's school.

She arrived as the lines of students began boarding the yellow school buses. Her eyes darted from front to back of the second bus line, but she didn't see Matt. She went to the bus door and called in to the driver, "Is Matt already on the bus?"

"Haven't seen him," the driver replied.

Bonnie frowned. Wouldn't you know it. The one day she didn't come straight to the bus, Matt wasn't there. Maybe he had stayed after school to help Mrs. Jules.

She rushed to Room 27. Mrs. Jules was pinning new material on a bulletin board.

"Do you know where Matt is?" Bonnie asked. "He isn't in the bus line."

"He got a hall pass to go to the bathroom a few minutes before school got out. I let him leave because he said he couldn't wait and when he didn't come back to class, I assumed he went straight to the bus."

"He isn't there," Bonnie said.

"I'll look in the boys' restroom," Mrs. Jules said. "Sometimes Matt stands in front of the mirror pretending he's pitching a baseball, and he forgets the time."

Bonnie nodded. Matt did that at home, too. It drove her nuts when she was waiting to use the bathroom herself.

Mrs. Jules cracked the restroom door and called, "Anybody in there?" When there was no answer, she went in. Seconds later she came out. "He isn't there. Let's check the bus again."

This time Bonnie boarded the bus, looking at all the passengers. Matt wasn't there. As soon as she got off, the doors wheezed shut. The first bus in line pulled out of the school driveway; Bonnie's bus followed.

"You check the playground," Mrs. Jules said. "I'm going to the office to alert Mr. Quinn."

Bonnie nodded. She rushed to the playground and looked at the monkey bars, the ball field, and the basketball court. No Matt.

She ran to the office where Mr. Quinn, the principal, was speaking over the public-address system, alerting all teachers that Matt Sholter had not boarded his bus.

"If you see Matt," Mr. Quinn said into the microphone, "bring him to the office immediately." He clicked off the mike and turned to Bonnie. "Has he ever done this before?" he asked.

Bonnie shook her head, no. "Once he was late because he goofed around with his friends, but Mom scolded him, and since then Matt has always gone straight to the bus. He gets there before I do."

"Maybe he went home with a friend today, and your mother forgot to tell you."

"Mom would never forget," Bonnie said. "She always makes sure we know what we're supposed to do after school."

"Let's call her, to be sure," Mr. Quinn said. "Do you know her work number?"

Bonnie gave it. Her insides felt hollow as she listened to Mr. Quinn ask for Mrs. Sholter. A few seconds later, he identified himself and said, "Matt didn't get on the school bus today and we can't find him. Did he go home with a friend?"

He talked another minute or so. When he hung up, he said, "She's on her way. Matt was supposed to go home as usual."

"I don't like this," Mrs. Jules said.

Apprehension crawled up Bonnie's arms and across the back of her neck.

"Let's not panic yet," Mr. Quinn said. "I've had situations before where a youngster gets in trouble at school and doesn't want to go home, or they get invited to play at a friend's house and forget to call. Sometimes, especially with the kindergartners, they get on the wrong bus. Then they have to ride the whole route before they're brought back here. One student fell asleep on the bus and wasn't found until the driver had already parked in the bus barn."

Bonnie could easily have disputed each of Mr. Quinn's theories. Matt never got in trouble at school, and he wasn't allowed to go anywhere with a friend unless Mom had arranged it. Certainly he wouldn't have boarded the wrong bus; they had ridden bus number two all year. She didn't argue with the principal, though. It was Mr. Quinn's first year at this school, so he didn't know Bonnie. She knew he was only trying to make everyone feel more optimistic.

While Bonnie looked out the office window, hoping to see Matt approach, Mr. Quinn called each of the bus drivers.

Matt was not on any of the busses.

The black fog of Bonnie's old dream seemed to hover at the edge of the school yard.

CHAPTER 5

Puppy kisses! Puppy kisses!" Matt said.

The old dog, wriggling with happiness, slurped the boy's face.

How disgusting, Denny thought as he watched in the rearview mirror. He had never understood why some people act as if their dogs were part of the family. Besides getting unsanitary slobber on the kid's face, the mutt was probably shedding all over the backseat.

"Pookie doesn't act hurt," Matt said. "Are you sure he got hit by a car?"

"He feels better because you're here," Denny said. He stuck two fingers inside the wig and scratched his scalp. It was too warm to have an extra head of hair.

"Why are you going this way?" Matt asked. "Pookie's vet isn't this way."

"We aren't taking him to the vet. You said the dog is okay."

"Then where are we going?"

"Home."

"Home isn't this way, either."

"I know where I'm going," Denny said. "This is a shortcut." He glanced in the rearview mirror again. The boy stared back, one hand fingering his earlobe.

The boy's nervous, Denny thought. I need to put him at ease, but how?

Denny had no idea what to say. He didn't know anything about kids. What should he talk about? He tried to think how Celia and Winston handled their boys.

Denny leaned over, opened the glove compartment, and felt inside. He picked up a large chocolate bar and tossed it into the backseat.

"Here you go," he said. "Something to munch on."

"I'm not allowed to eat chocolate," Matt said.

"You are now."

"Really?"

"Yep. When you're with me, I make the rules and I say every kid needs some chocolate now and then. Go ahead. Take a bite."

"Won't I get hives?"

"Hives? From a candy bar? No way."

Matt ripped the wrapper open and took a bite. "Yum," he said. "It's good." He took another bite.

Pookie whined.

"Pookie wants some," Matt said.

"So give him a piece."

"Mom says chocolate is bad for dogs."

"Well, that shows how much she doesn't know. Would you want to eat nothing but dog food all the time?"

"No."

"Neither does Pookie."

Matt broke off a piece of chocolate and gave it to Pookie, who swallowed it whole and immediately begged for more.

"He likes it," Matt said. "So do I."

"Of course you do. Everybody likes chocolate. Chocolate is one of life's great pleasures."

"Want a bite?" Matt asked.

"No, thanks. I had my own candy bar a little while ago." Denny smiled, congratulating himself for thinking of the candy.

Imagine a kid who never eats chocolate bars.

Anita had always worried too much about health.

Once when he'd given Bonnie a sip of his beer, Anita acted as if he'd tried to poison the girl.

As he drove, Denny glanced frequently at Matt, who continued to share the chocolate bar with the dog. Denny felt no surge of fatherly affection, no pride because this handsome boy was his son. He felt only relief that he had succeeded in getting Matt away from the school without being questioned.

Although he'd been prepared to use his gun if a teacher had tried to stop him, he was glad it hadn't been necessary. A school shooting would have brought every cop in the county swarming toward the scene; a kid who didn't go home after school would attract far less attention. No one had seen him take Matt; he would not be connected to the missing boy.

"I need to go to the bathroom," Matt said.

"We'll be home soon."

"I have to go really bad. I was on my way to the bathroom when I met you, remember?"

Denny tried to think of a safe place to stop. He didn't want someone to notice the dog and the kid, and then remember later what kind of car they were in. "You'll have to wait," he said.

"I can't. I'm going to wet my pants."

"Hold it! I'll find a place."

"Could we stop at McDonald's to use the bathroom?" Matt asked. "Mom does sometimes."

"I'll stop at Marymoor Park. It has a public bathroom." People walk their dogs around Marymoor all the time; nobody would pay attention if Denny stopped there.

A loud retching sound came from the backseat.

"Pookie's going to throw up," Matt said.

Denny slammed on the brakes and pulled the car on to the shoulder, but before he could get stopped, Pookie gave back the chocolate he'd eaten.

"Yuck," Matt said. "Pookie barfed all over the seat."

Denny swore. "Keep the dog on the floor," he said as he pulled back on to the road and continued toward Marymoor.

"It stinks in here," Matt said. "I think I'm going to be sick, too."

"No! Roll your window down and breathe the fresh air."

Matt put the window down and stuck his face in the breeze while Denny drove into Marymoor Park, ignored the parking-fee sign, and stopped near a playground.

Three empty cars waited in the parking lot. Denny parked as far from them as he could. He didn't think

Anita would have reported Matt missing yet, but he was taking no chances. The fewer people who saw Matt with him, the better.

"You go to the bathroom," Denny said. "I'll clean up the mess."

Matt ran up the sidewalk to the restrooms.

The leash still hung from Pookie's neck. Denny lifted the dog to the ground, then led him to a large sign that gave park regulations. After making sure no one was watching, Denny wound the end of the leash around one of the wooden signposts and tied it with a double knot. Pookie sat beside the post.

Denny went into the men's room, grabbed a fistful of paper towels, and held some of them under the faucet. He could hear Matt singing inside one of the stalls. "Come straight to the car when you're done," he said.

"Okay."

As Denny started out of the building, a trio of young women emerged from the women's restroom. Talking and laughing, they paid no attention to Denny as they walked toward their car, but he lingered next to the building until they drove away before he returned to his own car.

Denny cleaned up the seat and threw the towels in a trash can. He removed the school's visitor badge from around his neck and tossed it in the trash, along with the gloves. He unbuttoned the brown shirt and discarded it, then yanked off the wig and the false mustache and stuffed them in the trash. He added the clipboard, but the empty box didn't fit; he put it back in the car.

He had wondered where to get rid of his disguise. This park was perfect—a public spot, well used. Soon other people would dump their litter bags and toss their empty coffee cups and even put soiled diapers into that same trash can. When it got emptied, nobody would sort through the contents. It would all go straight into the garbage truck, and there would be no evidence that Denny Thurman had ever been here.

Denny got back in the car, eager to leave. He could hardly wait to see Winston. For years, his brother-in-law had showed off his two boys.

The last time they'd been together, Winston had suggested Denny had no children because he never stayed married long enough to father a child. "You'll never have kids," Winston had said, "because your wives file for divorce on the honeymoon."

Furious, Denny had determined to find his own kid and prove Winston wrong.

It had been easy to learn Anita had given birth to a boy. The library offered old newspaper records on microfiche, and he knew approximately when the baby would have been born.

He read all the birth announcements for that month and quickly found the notice for Matthew Lee Sholter.

A week after he read the birth notice, Denny moved to a bigger apartment and made plans to take the boy to live with him. He would laugh in Winston's face and claim he had known about his son all along.

Denny knew Anita would never give Matt up, not even for a visit. There was no point asking her. If he did, it would tip her off that he wanted Matt, and then he'd be a prime suspect when Matt disappeared. The only way to get his son was to abduct him.

Tomorrow Denny would see his sister and brother-in-law and their boys. They lived on Bainbridge Island, in a house near the beach. Winston and Celia frequently invited him to join them for a weekend, but Denny usually made up excuses not to go. The two noisy kids got on his nerves, and Winston's endless bragging about the little monsters irritated him.

Even worse, Celia always tried to change Denny's lifestyle. Once she had dragged him to a doctor, and now she nagged him constantly to take the medication the doctor had prescribed.

She didn't know the doctor had also recommended Denny start counseling and take an anger-management class. Well, forget that. Denny didn't need some stuffed shirt with a string of medical degrees messing with his head. He'd thrown the pills away and refused to see the doctor again.

This time he looked forward to seeing his sister and her husband. This time Matt would be with him. Celia might even be too shocked to nag.

Denny started the engine. What was taking the kid so long in there?

A flatbed truck with some heavy equipment on it pulled into the parking lot, and a burly man jumped down.

Denny tapped his fingers on the steering wheel impatiently. He had hoped Matt would be out of the men's room before anyone else went in.

The truck driver walked along the side of his rig, checking the tie-downs.

Come on, Matt, Denny thought. Get out here!

The truck driver jogged off down the path, without looking at Denny. When he reached the sign where Pookie was tied, he gave the dog a pat and kept going.

Finally Matt came out and headed toward Denny's car. Denny opened the front door on the passenger's side. "Sit up here with me," he said. "It doesn't smell as strong."

Matt climbed into the front seat and buckled his seat belt.

He looked at Denny and gasped. "You changed your hair," he said, "and you shaved off your mustache." One hand nervously fingered his earlobe. "You're wearing a new shirt, too."

"Smart kid. Very observant."

"You look a lot different."

"Do you think I look like you?" Denny asked as he backed out of the parking space.

"No."

"Do you know who I am?"

Matt shook his head no.

"I'm your dad."

Matt's eyes narrowed. He examined Denny for a few seconds, then asked, "What's your name?"

"Don't you know your own dad's name?"

"I know it. My mom told me."

"My name's Denny Thurman."

"Oh."

Denny could tell Matt recognized the name.

"You had on a wig before, didn't you?"

Denny didn't answer.

An uneasy feeling crept over Matt as he thought about everything this man had told him. Something was wrong here, and as soon as he got home, he'd tell Mom exactly what had happened.

Denny left the parking lot and headed out of Marymoor Park toward Highway 520. He glanced once in the rearview mirror, but he couldn't see the dog.

Good-bye, Pookie, he thought. Good riddance.

CHAPTER 6

It had been less than ten minutes since the school buses left, but it seemed like forever to Bonnie. *Where was Matt?*

"Who are Matt's friends?" Mr. Quinn asked.

Bonnie and Mrs. Jules named four children from Matt's class. Mr. Quinn called each of their homes. Twice he got an answering machine and left an urgent message. The other two times, a woman answered, questioned her child, then reported the child hadn't seen Matt after school let out.

"Maybe someone gave him a ride home today," Mr. Quinn said. "Perhaps a neighbor or somebody else Matt knows saw him in the bus line and offered to drop him off. Maybe he's home right now, waiting for you."

Bonnie called her own number, although she knew Matt wouldn't be there. They always rode the bus home together unless Mom made other arrangements in advance. Always.

The answering machine clicked on. "Matt," Bonnie said, "if you are home, call the school right away." She read the number off the telephone base.

Bonnie hoped her mom would get there soon.

"Did Matt have a problem today?" Mr. Quinn asked Mrs. Jules. "Did you send a note home?"

Mrs. Jules said, "He didn't get in trouble in class. He rarely does. Matt's one of my easiest boys, except for his tendency to think about baseball too much."

Something's happened to him, Bonnie thought. Maybe the anxious feeling that started in PE hadn't been because of remembering the dream; maybe it was a premonition.

Was Matt going to disappear from her life without even a chance to say good-bye, the way her dad did?

Mr. Quinn turned to the school secretary, Mrs. Williams. "Were there any visitors at school this afternoon?" he asked.

Mrs. Williams picked up the sign-in sheet and glanced at it. "One parent came to take a sick child home. The regular volunteer who listens to the first-graders read was here, and we had a delivery for the library."

"Nothing unusual," Mr. Quinn said.

"Nothing unusual," Mrs. Williams agreed.

Matt's cheeks started to itch. He rubbed them, one hand on each side of his face. The more he rubbed, the more his cheeks itched. They felt hot, like two glowing coals. His chest itched, too, and he stuck one hand up his T-shirt to scratch.

"I think you were wrong about the candy bar," he said.

"What do you mean?"

"I've got hives."

Denny looked at the boy. His face was puffy, especially around his eyes.

"I itch all over," Matt said. "I need to take one of my pills."

"What pills?"

"The green ones that I take every morning."

"Vitamin pills?"

"No. I take a vitamin pill, too, but now I need the kind I get from the doctor, for my allergies."

Matt kneaded his ears. Denny frowned, watching him. Pink blotches bloomed on the boy's face and neck. Whoever heard of a kid being allergic to chocolate? Still, Matt did look as if he had scrubbed his face with poison ivy. Small bumps like mosquito bites rose on the blotches. Matt's lips seemed swollen.

"Did you ever get hives before when you weren't home?"

"Once I got them at school when I traded my snack for another kid's cupcake."

"What did your teacher do?"

"The school nurse gave me an allergy pill. Mom had taken some in to the nurse on my first day, in case I ever needed one."

Denny gripped the steering wheel tighter. Nervous perspiration began to soak his T-shirt. He couldn't take the kid to a doctor. No way. "What happens if you don't get a pill?" he asked.

"The hives last longer and itch more. The pill makes them go away."

"You'll have to itch, then."

"I'll take a pill as soon as we get home. I know where Mom keeps them."

"Forget the pills. We're not going there."

"You said we're going home."

"We are. We're going to my home, which is now our home. You're going to live with me from now on. We'll have a great time, me and you."

Matt shook his head. "I don't want to live with you."

"Too bad."

"I want to call my mom."

"Hey, this was her idea. She said to be a good boy and do what I say."

"What about my clothes and my toys and my blankie?"

"She's going to mail everything to you. The pills, too. Not that you'll need your old clothes or toys. I bought everything new for you—a PlayStation with lots of games, and a DVD player and a bunch of movies and a Game Boy."

Matt stared at the man. "Are you rich?" he asked.

"You better believe it, kid. I hit it big last week, so once you get to my place, you can have anything your little heart desires."

Matt thought about that. Mom wouldn't let him have a PlayStation because she thought most of the games were too violent. He had a few movies but not DVD movies. He wondered if Mom really knew where he was going and about all the computer games.

His father's name was Denny Thurman, but how did Matt know that's who this man was? He'd never seen his dad; he didn't know what his dad looked like. Maybe this man was only pretending to be Denny Thurman. "How do I know you're really my dad?" he asked.

"What? My own kid wants to see identification?" Denny pulled a wallet from his hip pocket, then tossed it to Matt. "All right. If you don't trust me, look at my driver's license."

Matt flipped open the wallet and peered at the driver's license, wishing he could read. The photo was this man's face. The license must say Denny Thurman; if it didn't, the man wouldn't show it to him.

Denny scowled while the kid examined his driver's license. This was not going the way he had planned. Not at all. Tim and Thomas never got red spots on their faces. They didn't question everything Winston said.

Matt closed the wallet and handed it back.

"Satisfied?" Denny asked. "Convinced I'm not lying to you? I'm really your dad?"

Matt nodded, but he didn't know what to think. This man really was his father, yet he knew not everything the man said was true. Mom would never have sent Matt to live somewhere else without talking to him about it first, and she certainly wouldn't have let him go without his clothes or his allergy pills.

Something didn't add up. First the man said Pookie was hurt when Pookie wasn't, and now he wasn't going to take Matt home. A terrible suspicion formed in Matt's mind. Had he made a horrible mistake when he got in this car?

Matt rubbed his face some more. He didn't like this man, even if he was his dad. "What about Bonnie?" he asked. "Is she going to live with us?"

"She isn't my kid. You are."

"Bonnie will be mad when she finds out Pookie came with me."

"We don't care what Bonnie thinks. Forget about her."

"I don't want to forget Bonnie. I want to go home."

"Be quiet," Denny said. "You're giving me a headache."

The uncertainty flowing through Matt's mind jelled into conviction. He should never have gotten into the car with this man, whether Pookie was there or not.

"I'm going to sit in back with Pookie," Matt said. He unbuckled his seat belt and started to climb over the seat. He stopped, looking down at the floor. "Pookie's gone!" he cried. "He isn't here!"

Denny shrugged.

"He must have jumped out when we stopped at the bathroom," Matt said, "and we didn't see him go. We have to turn around!"

"Forget it."

"*Forget it?* We can't drive off and leave him behind."

"Sure we can."

"Pookie's old," Matt said. "He can hardly see."

"Calm down. He's fine."

"He isn't fine! He's loose at the park. We have to go back and get him. He'll get hit by a car!"

"He won't get hit. I tied him to a post."

Matt glared at Denny. "You left him at Marymoor Park on purpose?"

"Stupid dog stunk up the whole car."

"That wasn't his fault. You're the one who said to feed him chocolate." He put his hand on Denny's arm. "You have to turn around! We can't leave Pookie by himself!"

"Let's get something straight here," Denny said as he pushed Matt's hand away. "I call the shots. I make the decisions, not you, and the sooner you learn that, the better off you'll be."

"Pookie will be scared. He won't know where he is."

"The dog's lucky I left him at the park. I could have got rid of him."

Matt's voice was only a whisper. "What do you mean?"

Denny pulled his T-shirt up, revealing the gun.

Matt stared. He'd never seen a real gun before.

"Zip your lip about the dog, understand? The mutt was nothing but trouble."

Matt shrank into the seat, leaning against the door, as far from Denny as possible.

They rode in silence for a minute.

"I bought a bunch of board games," Denny said. "Stuff like Monopoly. I used to play Monopoly when I was a kid."

"You said I could have anything I want at your house," Matt said.

"That's right. You got it made, kid."

"I want Pookie."

Denny gave Matt a disgusted look. "Correction: You can have anything you want except a dog."

Two tears trickled down Matt's cheeks, making shiny trails across the red blotches.

"What are you sniffling about? Any normal kid would be thrilled to get every new toy and game."

"Why did you bring Pookie if you don't like him?"

Denny didn't reply.

Let the kid figure it out for himself.

CHAPTER 7

Bonnie ran out of the school office when she saw her mom's car. Mrs. Sholter stopped in the bus zone, jumped out, then put an arm around her daughter's shoulders as they hurried inside.

"He didn't come to the bus," Bonnie said, "so I went to his room and he wasn't there. We've looked everywhere."

Mrs. Jules explained about the hall pass and how she'd checked in the boys' bathroom. Mr. Quinn told about calling the bus drivers and Matt's friends. Other teachers said they had searched the classrooms and the playground.

"We need to call the police," Mrs. Sholter said. She

took a phone from her purse and dialed 911. Everyone in the office listened to the call.

"The police are coming," she said when she hung up.

Teachers wove in and out of the office, asking if Matt had been found yet. Several walked back through every room in the school again, checking closets, restrooms, and the cafeteria for any sign of the missing boy. By the time the police arrived, the staff felt positive Matt was not on the school grounds.

The policeman, Officer Calvin, asked the same questions Mr. Quinn had asked, plus a few more.

"Would he have left the school grounds by himself? To buy candy, perhaps?"

"Absolutely not," Mrs. Sholter said.

"Would he have left with someone else—maybe accepted a ride home?"

"No," Mrs. Sholter said.

"He always rides the bus with me," Bonnie said.

"Did anyone other than staff come to the school this afternoon?"

Mrs. Williams said, "A parent picked up a sick child, a volunteer came to hear the first-graders read, and a package was delivered to the library."

"I didn't get any package today," Mrs. Payton said.

Everyone turned to look at the librarian.

Mrs. Williams picked up the sign-in sheet. "A delivery man came at two twenty-five, with a box for the library. He signed in and took a visitor's badge, and I told him how to find the library." She frowned. "He didn't sign out, though. I didn't notice before; he never signed out." She counted the badges in a small box next to the sign-in sheet. "He didn't return the badge, either."

"I never got a delivery," Mrs. Payton repeated.

Officer Calvin asked, "What company was the deliveryman with?"

"UPS," Mrs. Williams said. "He said he had a package for the library and—"

"Are you sure he said UPS?" Officer Calvin asked. "Was it the regular driver?"

Mrs. Williams ran one hand nervously through her hair. "I didn't recognize him, but he said he was from UPS. He carried a box and a clipboard, and he had on a brown UPS uniform."

"Did you see his truck?" the officer asked.

"I didn't look for his truck."

"Would someone call UPS, please?" Officer Calvin said.

Mr. Quinn looked up the UPS number and called. It took a while to get a live person on the line, but when he did, he explained what had happened. He gave the school's address. Then he put one hand over the telephone mouthpiece and whispered, "She's checking."

A moment later he said, "Are you certain?" Then, after a pause, he said, "Thank you. Yes, I'll let you know."

Even before Mr. Quinn hung up, Bonnie knew from his expression what he was going to say.

"UPS had no delivery scheduled here today," Mr. Quinn reported.

Mrs. Williams covered her mouth with one hand, her eyes brimming with tears.

"This isn't your fault," Mr. Quinn said. "You had no reason to suspect the man wasn't who he said he was."

"He lied," Mrs. Jules said. "Maybe he came here to try to steal a child and he saw Matt alone."

Bonnie's throat felt tight, the way it always did when she came down with a bad cold.

Officer Calvin said, "It appears Matt was by himself at the wrong time."

Mr. Quinn pounded his fist on the countertop. "We tried to have good security," he said. "We tried to prevent something like this. We even had an assembly on what to do and say if approached by a stranger."

"It's hard to prevent every possibility," the officer said.

"Matt *knows* not to go anywhere with a stranger," Mrs. Sholter said. "We talked about it many times. He's been told to scream and run away if anyone tries to take him."

"None of the staff noticed anything unusual," Mr. Quinn said. "Nobody heard Matt yell."

"He would never leave with someone he doesn't know," Bonnie insisted.

The police officer shook his head. "Even kids who know better sometimes get tricked," he said. "The man probably lied to him, and Matt believed what he was told."

"Are you saying you think Matt went willingly?" Mrs. Sholter asked.

"It happens, even with kids who've been taught all the right things. The trouble is, we can't figure out in advance what some crook might say."

"I can't believe Matt would do that."

Bonnie couldn't believe it, either.

"I'll need a photo of Matt as soon as possible," Officer Calvin said, "and a full description, including the clothes he wore today. I believe this case warrants issuing an Amber Alert."

"What's that?" asked Bonnie.

"Matt's description will be broadcast immedi- ately on the emergency alert network. It's the system used for severe weather emergencies such as torna-does or a volcanic eruption. An Amber Alert will get Matt's description out to the public instantly with messages on the highway reader boards and on radio and TV. Thousands of people will be looking for him within an hour."

"Thank you," Mrs. Sholter said.

"I wish we could broadcast a description of the abductor or the vehicle Matt left in. More than once a motorist has spotted a car that police were looking for and called to report its location. But a good description of the boy might be enough."

Mrs. Sholter opened her wallet, took out a picture of Matt, and handed it to Officer Calvin.

"When was this taken?" he asked.

"Two weeks ago."

"Good. You wouldn't believe how many parents don't have a recent picture of their kids. One woman gave me a snapshot taken at her daughter's third birthday party; the girl was ten years old when she disappeared."

Bonnie said, "Mom's always taking pictures of us, for our scrapbooks and to send to our grandparents."

"We'll put Matt's picture on the TV news and give it to the papers. Pictures work. People see a photo of a cute kid like this, and they pay attention. They look for him."

"I always thought the police waited twenty-four hours to declare a person missing," Mr. Quinn said.

"An adult, yes. Adults often leave home voluntarily without telling anyone. In a case like this, with a child, the faster we move, the better. We don't use the Amber Alert often, but I think it's justified today."

"What can we do to help?" Bonnie asked.

"First tell me what Matt was wearing."

Mrs. Sholter said, "Jeans, a blue Mariners T-shirt, and white shoes—the kind with heels that light up when you walk."

"As soon as I call this in, I'd like to bring a police dog to your home and let him sniff Matt's clothes—maybe the pajamas he slept in last night."

"Of course," Mrs. Sholter said. She gave the address.

Bonnie could tell Mom was struggling to keep her emotions under control. Her voice sounded tight, and she kept fingering the strap on her shoulder bag.

"Do you want to ride with me?" the officer asked. "Or would you like me to follow you?"

"I'll drive; you can follow me," Mrs. Sholter said. "I'll need to have my car."

"Is there anything more any of us can do?" Mr. Quinn asked.

"Please stay here," the officer said. "Another officer will be here shortly, to question everyone and to get a description of the man who claimed to be with UPS."

Mrs. Williams said, "I know exactly what he looked like. He had curly black hair and a mustache and there was a tattoo of a flower on one arm—a rose, I think. I'd recognize him, or his picture."

"Why would anyone take Matt?" Bonnie asked.

"Because he happened to be there," Officer Calvin said. "A crime of opportunity."

Bonnie and her mother rode home without talking. The police car followed. Usually Mrs. Sholter parked in the garage, but this time she pulled up in front of the house. Officer Calvin parked behind her. She opened the front door and motioned for the police officer to come inside as a second squad car parked behind the first one.

"The Amber Alert has gone out," Officer Calvin said. Then he introduced Detective Morrison.

"I have a canine partner," Detective Morrison said. "I'd like to bring him in, and let him smell clothing Matt wore recently."

"You'd better shut Pookie in the kitchen," Mrs. Sholter told Bonnie. "He's still asleep, but he might smell another dog and get in the way."

"Pookie's your dog?" Officer Calvin said.

"Not much of a watchdog, I'm afraid," Mrs. Sholter said.

"He's old," Bonnie explained. "He doesn't see or hear very well, but he's a great dog."

Detective Morrison went out to get her K-9 dog.

Bonnie headed for Pookie's basket in the kitchen. When it was empty, she looked under the dining-room table and in her bedroom. She checked all of Pookie's favorite napping spots, then checked the backyard. She whistled and called.

Bonnie rushed back into the living room. "Mom!" she said. "Pookie's gone!"

CHAPTER 8

Pookie's gone?" Mrs. Sholter repeated, as if she couldn't possibly have heard correctly.

"I looked in his bed," Bonnie said, "and under the table where he likes to sleep, and then I looked in the backyard. He isn't here."

"Could he have gotten out of the yard accidentally?" Officer Calvin asked. "Is there a gate that might have been left open?"

"There is a gate," Mrs. Sholter said, "but we only use it when we put the trash can in the alley for the trash collector."

"The gate's closed," Bonnie said. "I checked."

"Might someone have let him out on purpose? A neighbor, perhaps? Does Pookie bark a lot?"

Bonnie could follow Officer Calvin's thoughts. "Pookie hardly ever barks anymore," she said. "If someone came in the yard, he probably wouldn't even notice."

"If he did, he'd wag his tail and hope to get petted," Mrs. Sholter said.

Detective Morrison returned with a German shepherd. "This is Spike," she said.

"The family dog is missing," Officer Calvin said.

Bonnie saw the two police officers exchange a glance, the significant kind of look adults give each other when they know something the kids don't know.

Fear had flickered at the edge of Bonnie's mind all morning, but it had been a dull fear, without a name. As she looked at Pookie's empty bed, a sharp, specific fear wrapped around her. Matt was missing, and so was Pookie. What if they never came home? She might never see her brother or her dog again. The tears Bonnie had successfully held back at school now spilled out.

"Do you think Pookie's disappearance is connected to Matt's?" Mrs. Sholter asked the police.

"It might be," Detective Morrison said.

"Let's make sure the dog isn't here," Officer Calvin said.

A thorough search of the house and yard turned up

no Pookie, nor did it yield any sign the house had been broken into.

Bonnie and her mom called Pookie, both in the alley and up and down the sidewalk in the front of the house, in case he had somehow been let out. Pookie did not come.

"Let's have Spike smell those pajamas," Detective Morrison said. "Then I'll take him over to the school."

Bonnie led everyone upstairs to Matt's bedroom. "He keeps his pajamas under his pillow," she said.

"Don't touch them," Detective Morrison cautioned. She lifted the pillow. Matt's pajamas were scrunched into a ball, as usual.

When Mrs. Sholter saw them, she started to cry.

Detective Morrison led Spike toward the bed and pointed.

The dog sniffed the pajamas.

"Matt," said Detective Morrison. "Find Matt." She put Matt's pajamas in a bag and took them with her. She and Spike returned to their car and drove away.

"Does anyone else have a house key?" Officer Calvin asked Mrs. Sholter.

"Bonnie has one."

Bonnie held up the chain she wore around her neck; the key dangled from the chain.

"We also have one hidden outside. We put it there after I accidentally locked myself out."

"Let's see if it's still there," Officer Calvin said. "I hope you don't keep it under the doormat. Thieves look there first."

Bonnie and her mom went out the kitchen door, followed by the police officer. Bonnie counted five fence boards from the corner, then picked up a small rock from the base of the fence. The extra key was taped to the bottom of the rock.

"It's here," she said.

"Who else has a key?" Officer Calvin asked. "Your husband?"

"I'm single."

"Ex-husband?"

Mrs. Sholter leaned against the fence as if her legs were too weak to hold her up. "My first husband, Bonnie's father, was a firefighter who died when a burning roof collapsed on him. I married again two years later, but the marriage was a disaster and I filed for divorce after only three months. Seven months later, Matt was born."

"What is Matt's father's name?"

"Denny Thurman."

"Is this where you lived with him?"

"No. I bought this house two years ago."

"Has there been a recent disagreement about Matt's custody or visitation rights or support payments?"

"Denny has no visiting rights," Mrs. Sholter said, "and I didn't ask him to pay child support. He wouldn't admit the baby was his; as soon as he found out I was pregnant, he vanished, and I haven't heard from him since."

"Then you don't think he might have taken Matt?"

"No. He doesn't like kids; that was one of our problems."

"I didn't like him, either," Bonnie said. "I was glad when he left."

Officer Calvin nodded as if to say *I don't blame you.*

"We all make mistakes," Mrs. Sholter said. "Marrying Denny Thurman was the biggest mistake of my life. The only happy result was Matt."

"We'll check him out. A high number of abducted children are taken by the noncustodial parent."

"Not this time," Mrs. Sholter said. "He doesn't even know if I had a boy or a girl."

"Do you know where he lives?"

"The last I knew, he was living in Reno, but that was six years ago. He always moved often, to get out of paying his gambling debts."

"Would Matt recognize him, maybe from a picture?"

"No."

"Can you think of anyone at all who would want to take Matt? Is there someone Matt would know, someone he'd go with willingly?"

"He'd know lots of people—neighbors or friends or people from church—but he would not leave school with any of them unless I had told him it was okay."

Bonnie said, "If the same person took Pookie, how did they get in? Matt doesn't have a house key, and the one under the rock is still there."

"I think he took Pookie first," Officer Calvin said. "He might have used the dog to get Matt to go with him."

"Then it *wasn't* a crime of opportunity," Mrs. Sholter said. "Matt didn't happen along at the wrong time by accident. If whoever took Matt came here first and got Pookie, then that person set a trap specifically for Matt."

"It's one possibility," Officer Calvin said.

Who would do that? Bonnie wondered. She couldn't think of a single person who would commit such a crime.

"We'll check the house for fingerprints," Officer Calvin said, "and call the animal shelters."

"Pookie is microchipped," Bonnie said. "If he gets scanned, the scanner will show our number."

Officer Calvin called the police station and gave

Pookie's description. "Please call the humane society, PAWS, animal control, and the other shelters," he said. "Have them notify us immediately if anyone brings in such a dog."

Bonnie didn't expect that to happen, though. Dogs brought to shelters by someone other than their owners are usually strays. Pookie had not wandered away accidentally; he had been stolen.

This, Bonnie thought, is worse than any bad dream I ever had.

She hugged herself, trying not to shiver.

CHAPTER 9

Matt stared out the car window, fighting nausea. He always got carsick easily, and now his stomach rumbled from the chocolate he'd eaten. He closed his eyes and breathed slowly.

He knew he should stay alert. He should try to figure out where he was, so when he got a chance to call home, he could tell his mother how to find him.

Matt intended to call as soon as possible. This man couldn't watch him every second. When Denny fell asleep or went to the bathroom, Matt would sneak to the telephone and call Mom.

He knew Denny had driven across the Evergreen Point Floating Bridge, but Matt hadn't recognized anything else. He didn't go to Seattle very often; he knew only major landmarks such as the Space Needle and Safeco Field.

He pressed his forehead against the cool window glass and kept his eyes shut until the car stopped.

They were at the end of a driveway next to a small office building. Denny opened the trunk and lifted out a cardboard box. Matt watched him stomp the box flat, then carry it to a Dumpster at the end of the driveway.

Denny got back in the car and drove off. This time Matt looked out the window, but he still didn't recognize anything. Soon Denny drove into a large apartment complex. The car slowed, going over a series of speed bumps. Rows of buildings, each with adjoining carports, lined the driveway. The road turned several times, but the buildings they passed all looked the same.

The car clock said 4:48. Tears puddled in Matt's eyes. Mom got off work at 4:30; she got home at 4:45.

I should be home now, Matt thought as he rubbed his itchy arms. I should be playing with Pookie or eating an apple. I should be telling Mom about the movie we saw at school today or throwing my ball at the garage.

Sometimes the three of them took Pookie for a walk before dinner or went out together to buy groceries or run errands. Whatever Mom and Bonnie were doing, Matt wished he were doing it with them.

The car stopped in one of the carports. "Hop out," Denny said. "We're home."

Matt followed the man up a flight of stairs and watched as he unlocked an apartment door. Inside, he saw dozens of new computer games and toys. A scooter leaned against the wall next to the door, and stuffed animals covered one end of the couch. A stack of unopened board games towered on an end table. Matt recognized Clue and Candyland. The living room looked like a toy store.

Matt looked around for a telephone but didn't see one.

"Want to watch a movie?" Denny asked.

"No. I want to call my mom." Matt expected Denny to refuse. He had decided Denny was lying; Mom didn't know where Matt was. He figured he'd have to call when Denny didn't know.

"Okay," Denny said.

"I can call her?"

"Sure. She probably wants to talk to you, too, and I need to let her know you got here safely. What's the number? Save me looking it up in my book."

Surprised, Matt gave the phone number. Maybe

Denny hadn't lied. If he had, he'd never let Matt talk to his mom.

Denny took a cell phone out of his pants pocket and punched all the numbers except the last one. Instead of seven, he hit "off." He held the phone to his ear, turning his head so Matt could see his face as he talked.

"Hello," he said. "Is Anita there?"

He paused, as if listening. Then he said, "What? Who is this?" He looked shocked. "What happened?" he asked. "When?"

After a few seconds, he said, "Oh, no!"

Matt pulled on his earlobe. Denny was hearing bad news.

"That's terrible!" Denny said.

"Is that Bonnie?" Matt asked. "I want to talk to her." He reached for the phone, but the man shook his head and motioned for Matt to be quiet.

"This is Denny Thurman," the man said, "Matt's father. I picked up Matt at school today because Anita wanted him to stay with me for a while. I called to let Matt talk to her." He paused again. "Anita planned to send some of Matt's clothes to me, and his allergy pills. Can you mail them?" He gave an address. "Thank you," he said. "Yes, I'll tell Matt."

Denny put the phone back in his pocket, then turned to Matt.

"Your next-door neighbor answered the phone," Denny said.

"Mrs. Watson?"

"Right. Mrs. Watson."

"Why did she answer our phone? Where's Mom?"

"I have some sad news," Denny said. "Your mother and your sister died in a car wreck this afternoon."

Horror crept up the back of Matt's neck. "Mom's dead?" he whispered. "Bonnie, too?"

"Afraid so."

Matt sat down, his mind whirling like the Spinner ride at the county fair. Was Denny telling him the truth, or was this another trick, like when he said Pookie was hurt?

"What happened?" Matt asked.

"A little while ago, they headed for the grocery store," Denny said. "Someone ran a stoplight and hit their car."

Disbelief wedged in Matt's throat like dry cracker crumbs. His voice cracked as he forced out the words, "Did anyone call nine-one-one? Did the ambulance come?"

"An ambulance came and the police came, but they were too late. They did CPR, but your mom and

Bonnie were already gone. Dead at the scene. The other driver died, too."

Matt felt as if he'd been punched in the stomach and had the wind knocked out of him. Head bent, he hugged himself and rocked gently. I'll never see Mom again, he thought. Or Bonnie. Mom will never again tuck me in at night or call me to get up in the morning. He took quick, shallow breaths, trying to wrap his mind around the unbelievable.

I'm a genius, Denny thought. What a flat-out brilliant idea! The kid had bought the story hook, line, and sinker. The one problem Denny had worried about— that Matt would call home when Denny wasn't watching—was solved.

Matt said, "Did Mrs. Watson call Grandma and Grandpa?" They'll come to get me, he thought, and take me to Arizona to live with them.

"Mrs. Watson hasn't been able to reach your grandparents."

"They're on a trip."

"Right. Mrs. Watson said she thought they were traveling."

Grandma and Grandpa often traveled in their RV. They liked to visit new places and learn about the local history. Mom had told him they were leaving, but Matt couldn't remember where they were headed this time.

"They have a phone in the RV," Matt said. "I don't know the number, but it's probably in Mom's directory."

"Your neighbor is trying to find it."

It's all true, Matt thought. The accident really happened. Why else would Mrs. Watson be at his house, trying to call Grandma and Grandpa?

"Mrs. Watson says she'll send your things as soon as she can."

Matt nodded, too shocked to care about his clothes or his allergy pills or even his blankie.

"It's a good thing you came with me today," Denny said, "or you'd be dead, too."

Matt shuddered. He wanted to cry, but his tears had dried up into a hard, little ball deep inside his head.

Matt had memorized his phone number long ago. Mom had drilled it into him when he was only three. "If you are ever in trouble," she said, "call home, even if it's the middle of the night." Matt knew how to place a collect call, in case he was out of the local area and had no money.

None of that knowledge would help him now. He had no one to call. Why dial his own number if Mom and Bonnie would never be there again?

With Mom and Bonnie dead, Matt had no choice but to stay with Denny until he could talk to Grandma and Grandpa. Matt was sure they would come for him as soon as Mrs. Watson told them what had happened, but when would that be?

Denny put soap on his hand and scrubbed off the temporary rose tattoo. Whistling cheerfully, he got out bread, mustard, and a jar of pickles. He took the bag of steak from his pocket and sliced it into thin strips. "I'm hungry," he said. "Do you want a sandwich?"

Matt shook his head no.

"I have peanut butter, if you don't want steak."

Matt shook his head again. How could Denny think about food when Mom and Bonnie were dead? Matt had never known anyone who died, but he knew when it happened the person was gone forever and you never saw them again for the rest of your life.

Bonnie once told Matt, "The day my dad died was the worst day of my life. It was the worst day of Mom's life, too."

Matt had nodded, but he hadn't really understood. Now he knew what she meant. This was the worst day of his life.

The phone rang. Matt went closer as Denny answered, hoping it was Grandma.

"Celia!" Denny said. "Glad to hear from you. I'm looking forward to coming over in the morning." After a pause, Denny said, "Oh. Well, sure, next weekend will work. I wouldn't want to come when the boys are sick."

Denny hung up, disappointed. He would have to wait a whole week to introduce Matt to Celia and Winston. For the first time ever, Denny wanted to see his nephews, and now the little brats had stomach flu.

He sighed and slathered steak sauce on his sandwich. The phone rang again. Denny said, "Hello."

"It's Bronco. You owe me five grand."

Hearing the familiar sandpapery voice on the phone made Denny's stomach knot up. How had Bronco gotten his new phone number?

"Hey, no problem, man," Denny said, trying to sound calm. "I've got your money. I would have brought it to you today, but I had some personal business to take care of. I'll bring it tomorrow."

"I need it tonight."

"Well, sure, I can get it to you tonight. It'll take me a while to get there; I've moved."

"I know. I'm parked in front of your new place right now."

Denny swallowed. How had Bronco learned his new address so quickly? He wiped the perspiration from his upper lip. "I'll be right down."

"I'm waiting."

Denny's hand shook as he clicked the phone shut.

He took an ice-cream carton out of the freezer, removed the lid, and pulled out a thick wad of money. He'd won big on the horse races last week—big enough to pay Bronco off with some left over—but he shuddered to think what would have happened tonight if he had not had the cash. He knew a guy who had run out on Bronco once without paying what he owed. The guy's house had burned down, and the cops never caught the arsonist.

As he counted out five thousand dollars, Denny saw Matt's eyes get huge. The boy looked stunned.

He's a cute kid, Denny thought, with those big brown eyes and thick blond hair. Winston and Celia would love him. Denny paused, looking at Matt, and a slow smile curved across his face.

Why hadn't he thought of this at the start? From now on, the boy was his ticket to financial freedom.

After Winston and Celia met Matt, Denny would explain he urgently needed money because he was going to raise his son himself. He'd mention allergy pills and clothes. He'd say the kid needed braces on his teeth.

Denny's grin spread. His money problems were solved! Winston and Celia were suckers for kids, and they had no other nephews or nieces. Once they met Matt, they'd be glad to help out.

His sister and brother-in-law had money up to their eyebrows. Winston had started his own business, something to do with computer software, while he was still in college and had sold it for millions eight years later. Then, instead of leading the easy life, Winston had started another company. It, too, was a success.

"You're a workaholic," Denny had said.

"Better than being a bum," Winston had replied.

Denny put the ice-cream container back in the freezer with steady hands. Thanks to Matt, he'd never have to fear the Broncos of the world again.

Matt watched Denny stuff the money in his jacket pocket. He had never seen so much cash. Denny had told the truth when he said he was rich.

"I'll be right back," Denny said. "Make yourself at home."

Matt sat on a wooden chair and looked at his lap. His head ached. He itched all over. Worst of all he felt a deep sorrow unlike any emotion he'd experienced before.

I don't like Denny Thurman, Matt thought. I always thought if I ever met my dad I'd like him a lot, but I don't like this man. He isn't even sad! Mom and Bonnie got killed, but he's acting as if Mrs. Watson told him Mom and Bonnie were on a vacation.

Matt longed to bury his face in Pookie's fur and cry.

He wondered if Pookie was still tied to the post or if someone had rescued him by now. Poor old Pookie. He must be so afraid.

Matt felt cold inside, as if he'd swallowed a big chunk of snow and all his blood had turned to ice water. He didn't think he would ever feel warm or safe or happy again.

CHAPTER 10

After the police left, Bonnie said, "I'm going to call Nancy and my other friends. They'll let all the kids know to watch for Matt."

"I don't want you using the phone," Mom said. "Matt might call and get a busy signal. I want to keep the cell-phone line open, too. He memorized both numbers; I know he'll call if he can."

"Is it okay if I use Mrs. Watson's phone?"

Mom nodded.

Bonnie ran next door. Mrs. Watson didn't answer the door, so Bonnie continued down the street to the Largents' house. She told Mrs. Largent what had happened.

"Make as many calls as you want," Mrs. Largent

said. She plucked her toddler from his playpen and held him tight, as if she feared he would disappear next.

Bonnie dialed Nancy's number, but Nancy wasn't home. Of course she isn't, Bonnie thought; she went shopping with Sharon.

She left a message: "Hi, it's Bonnie. Matt is missing, and so is Pookie. The police came with a police dog, and they're searching at the school now. Don't call me because Mom wants to keep the phone line open. I'll call you again when I can."

She felt surreal, as if she couldn't possibly be speaking the words she said. She reached two other friends, who both promised to spread the word.

"I'll alert the other neighbors," Mrs. Largent said.

"Thanks." Then, not knowing what else to do, Bonnie returned home.

Twenty minutes later, Nancy and her mother drove up. "What happened?" Mrs. Tagg asked as Bonnie let them in.

Mrs. Sholter quickly explained.

"I thought you went to the mall," Bonnie said.

"Sharon has a bad headache," Nancy said, "so we decided to go shopping tomorrow. We came here as soon as we heard your message."

"What can we do?" Mrs. Tagg asked.

"I don't know," Mrs. Sholter said. "I can barely think."

"Do you need anything?"

"Maybe the police need help looking for him around the school," Bonnie said.

"We'll go there," Mrs. Tagg said. "Come on, Nancy."

"Can I go with them?" Bonnie asked. "I might be able to help."

Mrs. Sholter hesitated. "Right now, I don't want to let you out of my sight," she said.

"I'll go crazy waiting here, doing nothing."

"I'll stay with her," Mrs. Tagg said, "unless you want her here."

"You can go," Mrs. Sholter said to Bonnie, "but please don't be gone too long."

As they drove to the school, Bonnie told of Pookie's disappearance and the visit from Spike. For once Nancy didn't offer an opinion or make a joke.

Four police cars lined the school driveway. Mr. Quinn, some teachers, and several other people stood near the flagpole, listening to a police officer. As the girls and Nancy's mother joined the group, they heard the officer give directions for searching the neighborhood.

Before he had finished, Detective Morrison and Spike came around the corner of the building. Bonnie hurried over to them, followed by Nancy and Mrs. Tagg.

"Did Spike pick up Matt's scent?" Bonnie asked.

"Yes. He finds it near the side door, then cuts across the playground to the street." She pointed. "Spike stops at the curb and can't find the scent again. We've repeated the search three times with the same results. Matt apparently left the school via that door, then got in a vehicle that was parked on the street."

Nancy took Bonnie's hand.

Bonnie clung to her friend, glad for Nancy's presence. "What happens now?" she asked. "The teachers and others are planning to search this area, but there's no use looking for Matt around here if he was driven somewhere else."

"We still want a door-to-door search of this neighborhood. Someone might have noticed a vehicle parked here. Someone might have glanced out a window and seen Matt and the person he was with as they walked across the playground, or maybe someone walked past as they drove away. We might get lucky and get a description of the vehicle or the abductor or both."

At the word *abductor*, Bonnie's blood ran cold. What a horrible word, she thought. An ugly name for a terrible person.

"The searchers are starting out," Mrs. Tagg said. "Do you still want to join them, Bonnie, or do you want me to drive you home?"

"Join them," Bonnie said. "I'll do anything I can to help find Matt."

CHAPTER 11

"Let's stop at Marymoor Park," Fred Faulkner suggested. "We can walk the path and stretch a bit."

His wife, Ruth, shifted in her seat. "Good idea," she said. "My arthritis is bothering me."

"We used to drive half a day without stopping," Fred said. "Now these old joints stiffen up if I don't get out every hour."

"At least we still go on outings," Ruth said. "Not like some of our friends, who sit at home day after day and get bored with themselves."

"Life's too short to waste any of it," Fred said. "We've been having good times for more than seventy years. No point in getting bored now."

Ruth smiled, and patted his knee. "I did enjoy seeing the Mount Vernon tulip fields," she said.

"Acres of color—and no charge to look at such beauty."

"Maybe there'll be some children on the play equipment," Ruth said. She enjoyed watching the little ones climb and run; it reminded her of when her own girls were small.

Fred pulled into Marymoor Park and stopped the car. After putting a dollar in the parking-fee box, he and Ruth both stretched and headed toward the restrooms.

When Ruth came out, Fred was waiting for her. "Come and see what I found," he said.

Ruth followed her husband to a sign at the side of the restrooms.

"Oh, look at you!" Ruth approached the terrier who was tied to the signpost. "Aren't you a sweet thing?" She let the dog sniff her fist before she petted it. The dog wagged his tail and licked Ruth's fingers.

Ruth looked around. No children climbed the slide; no parents pushed the swings. "Who does he belong to? Is there someone in the men's room?"

"There's nobody else here," Fred said. "We're the only car in the lot."

"Someone drove off and *forgot* their dog?" Ruth said. "How could they?"

"Maybe somebody was walking him, and the dog got tired, so they left him here while they finish their walk."

"I'd be afraid someone would take him."

"Maybe the owner wanted to get rid of him. Maybe he's been abandoned."

"No! Oh, who would do such a thing?" She patted the dog's head. "He isn't wearing a collar," she said. "No license. No ID tag."

"No way to contact the owner," Fred said.

"I can't believe anyone would purposely leave a darling dog like this," Ruth said. "Let's stay here with him for a while, until they come back."

"He looks like an old-timer," Fred said. "He'd probably like to walk around a bit, the same as we did. No telling how long he's been sitting here." He untied the leash from the post, and the dog walked along the path beside him. The tail never stopped wagging.

"We still have half a sandwich left from our lunch," Ruth said. "I'll get it." She took a wicker basket out of the trunk, opened it, and unwrapped half a peanut-butter sandwich.

When Fred returned from walking the dog, Ruth put a piece of sandwich on her palm and held it out. "Here you go," she said. "Here's a treat for you."

"Thanks," Fred said as he reached for the sandwich.

"Not you. The dog."

The dog took it eagerly, smacking his jaws as the peanut butter stuck to the roof of his mouth.

Ruth broke the rest of the sandwich in pieces and the dog gobbled all of them. He nudged her hand, hoping for more.

"He's starving," Ruth said. "He probably hasn't eaten for days."

"He isn't starving," Fred said as he ran his hands down the dog's sides, digging his fingers through the thick fur. "I can't feel his ribs. He's clean and he's been brushed recently and his nails are trimmed. He's been neutered, too. Someone has taken good care of this dog."

"Not good enough."

"Now, Ruthie, you mustn't jump to conclusions. His people will probably drive up any minute with an explanation."

"I wonder what his name is," Ruth said.

A car drove in.

"Here they come now," Fred said.

A couple and two young boys got out and headed for the playground. The boys raced ahead of their parents; none of them paid any attention to Ruth and Fred or to the dog.

"Must not be their dog," Fred said.

Ruth heard music and looked down the path. Three teenage boys with a boom box glided past on Rollerblades. They glanced at the dog but didn't stop.

A van arrived next, followed by a car pulling a trailer loaded with bicycles. The couple in the van got out to walk; the others rode off on their bikes. None of them showed any interest in the dog.

Forty-five minutes and many passersby later, Ruth said, "We've waited long enough. If this dog was left here accidentally, he would have been missed by now."

"We can't leave him here," Fred said. "Look how cloudy his eyes are. I don't think he can see much."

Ruth smiled. "It looks like we have a new friend," she said as she opened the back door of the car.

The dog put his front paws on the seat and tried to jump in, but didn't make it. "He needs a boost," Ruth said.

Fred gave the dog's backside a shove, and the dog scrambled into the car.

"An old arthritic dog will fit right in with us," Ruth said. "I need a boost myself now and then."

"We should leave a note on the signpost," Fred said, "in case someone comes looking for him."

"Hmmph!" Ruth said. "Anyone who would go off and leave a wonderful dog like this tied to a post doesn't deserve to get him back."

"Now, Ruthie. The dog might belong to a family, and one of the kids tied the dog there and the parents won't know he isn't with them until they get home. They could be frantic, worrying about what happened to him."

"Oh, all right," Ruth said. She rummaged in her purse for some paper and fished out a grocery receipt. She wrote on the back: FOUND: DOG—Call 425-555-3268.

"Shouldn't we say he's black and white?" Fred asked. "An older terrier with cloudy eyes?"

"Absolutely not. If someone calls, they'll have to describe him. I'm not giving this dog to just anybody."

Fred took the receipt to the signpost where he'd found the dog, but there was no way to attach it. He went back to the car. "Do you have any tape?" he asked.

"No."

"What about a pin?"

Ruth dug in her purse some more and finally came up with a small sewing kit with a needle in it. Fred put the needle through the receipt and then jabbed it into the wooden signpost.

"Such flimsy paper won't last ten minutes if there's rain or wind," he said as he got back in the car, "but it's the best we can do."

"I've decided to name him Monty," Ruth said. "We'll need to stop on the way home to buy a collar and some dog food. I think we still have Max's ball."

"It's been a while since we had a dog to walk," Fred said. "Remember how Max always woke us up early?"

"It'll be good for us to have a dog again. We'll go out for walks every day whether we feel like it or not. Monty will keep us limber. The best arthritis medicine in the world is a dog."

Fred smiled at his wife. "Rescuing a dog sure beats sitting around getting bored with ourselves," he said.

"You bet it does."

It was nearly six-thirty by the time they arrived home with their purchases. Ruth folded an old blue blanket for a dog bed. Fred filled a cereal bowl with dog food and another with water. Monty slurped the water enthusiastically, spilling some on the floor.

"Do you want to sit and watch the local news?" Fred asked as Monty sniffed all around the house.

"No," Ruth said. "I'm going to heat up some soup for us, and then I want to walk Monty around the outside of our house before it gets dark. If he ever got out by mistake, I want to be sure he knows which house is his."

"I'll walk with you," Fred said. "There's never any

good news anyway. It's always murder and arson and missing children."

"Then why do you watch?"

"Maybe I won't anymore. Maybe I'll walk Monty before dinner every night."

"The good news today," Ruth said, "is that we got a dog!"

CHAPTER 12

The search teams came up empty. No one living around the school had seen Matt or the person who took him. No one had noticed a vehicle parked at the curb where Spike kept stopping.

After an hour of knocking on doors, Mrs. Tagg said, "I think I should drive you home, Bonnie. Your mother will worry if we stay longer."

Bonnie didn't want to quit, but she knew Nancy's mom was right.

When they got to Bonnie's street, Mrs. Tagg couldn't find a place to park. Television crews clogged the front yard; a news helicopter circled overhead. A spokesman from the police department was trying to create order out of the chaos.

"You can drive up the alley," Bonnie said, "and drop me off by our back gate."

"I had planned to come in," Mrs. Tagg said, "but it's clear your mother doesn't need any more visitors."

Bonnie and her mom, along with Officer Calvin, were interviewed by reporters from two newspapers and three television stations. Bonnie found it hard to talk about Matt and Pookie without crying. It was especially difficult when a reporter asked, "Do you think your brother ran away?"

"No!" Bonnie said.

"Maybe he ran off and took the dog with him," the reporter said. "The largest percentage of missing kids are runaways."

Bonnie wanted to scream, "He didn't run away! Quit saying that!" But she knew media help was important, so she tried hard to be pleasant. "He had no reason to run away," Bonnie said. "Matt was happy at home."

"Matt was abducted from his school," Mrs. Sholter said. "Less than fifteen minutes elapsed between when his teacher saw him and when Bonnie reported him missing."

"A police dog picked up Matt's scent in the doorway of the school," Officer Calvin said, "and followed it across the playground to the street. It stopped there, indicating Matt got in a vehicle at that point."

This silenced the reporter with the runaway theory, but it gave Bonnie chills to think of Matt crossing the playground and climbing into a car. She found it hard to believe he would have done such a thing after Mom had warned both of them repeatedly not to ever go anywhere with someone they didn't know. Yet that must be what he had done.

When all the reporters and photographers finally left, Bonnie felt as if she'd run a twenty-mile marathon. The phone rang often as the word spread among their friends. Each time, she answered quickly, hoping it might be Matt.

At eleven p.m. Bonnie and her mom sat together and watched themselves on the Channel Seven news.

Mr. Quinn and Mrs. Jules appeared briefly on the newscast. They said Matt was a good student; everyone liked him. Matt's friend Stanley, looking scared, told how he and Matt had played on the monkey bars during recess.

The screen showed a highway reader board on Interstate 90, with Matt's description in bright lights. The announcer explained the Amber Alert and urged viewers to call 911 if they thought they saw Matt.

The story moved to Jefferson School, where nearly a hundred volunteers still searched the neighborhood for any clues. One man, who said he didn't know Matt, explained why he was there.

"I have a little boy myself," he said, "and I know how I'd feel if somebody took him. I'm here because I want to help."

Then the camera focused on Bonnie and her mom.

Bonnie felt as if she were viewing a movie, watching an actress who looked like her. The look-alike girl talked about her brother and her missing dog. She held up a picture of Pookie while her mom held one of Matt. Mrs. Sholter begged whoever had taken her son to return him unharmed.

"Please bring my dog home, too," the TV Bonnie said, her voice ending in a high squeak as she fought back tears.

The camera zoomed in on the picture of Matt.

"Anyone with information about the missing boy or his dog is urged to call nine-one-one or local police." A number flashed on the screen, followed by a commercial.

After her mom turned off the TV, Bonnie felt numb. She wanted this nightmare to be over.

The police had set up a special telephone system so any calls coming in to the Sholters' number would be monitored by the police. "You may get a ransom demand," Detective Morrison said.

"Ransom!" Mrs. Sholter waved her hand around the modest living room with its worn furniture. "Why would anyone think I can afford to pay a ransom?"

"People who abduct children aren't the great brains of the world," Detective Morrison said. "Clear thinking is not required in order to commit a crime."

The night dragged on. A police car remained parked in the Sholters' driveway. Using their computer, Bonnie and her mom made posters with Matt's picture on them. MATT IS MISSING the posters said.

Mrs. Jules had called earlier to say all the teachers would go out at daylight the next morning to hang posters around town.

"Don't use your own phone number," Detective Morrison had said. "Use the police number, so you don't get any calls from wackos."

"Wackos?" Bonnie said.

"People who call, even though they haven't seen the missing child."

"If they haven't seen him, why would they call?" Bonnie asked. "What would they say?"

"Oh, happy things like 'If you watched your child properly this wouldn't have happened.' One woman used to call every time a child disappeared and claim she'd seen the child's body floating in Lake Washington."

"Gross!"

"People can be cruel. Use my number. Better yet, use the toll-free hotline for the National Center for Missing and Exploited Children. Someone's there to answer the phone twenty-four/seven so you'll be sure not to miss an important call. They know exactly what questions to ask." She had written the number and handed it to Bonnie.

"Are you sure the center knows about Matt?"

"We gave them all the information this afternoon. His picture's already on their Web site. We've also asked for help from the Washington State Patrol's Missing and Exploited Children's Task Force."

Bonnie added information about Pookie to each poster. Knowing other people were trying to find Matt made his return seem possible.

At midnight, Bonnie's mom insisted she lie down for a while. Bonnie knew it was pointless to go to bed; she'd never fall asleep, but she lay on top of her bed in the dark, listening for the phone as tears trickled into her ears.

At six the next morning, Mrs. Jules and Mrs. Payton came to get the posters. "Every teacher at Matt's school and yours, Bonnie, will distribute these," Mrs. Jules said. "There are dozens of other volunteers, as well. We'll make more copies as we need them."

It helps, Bonnie thought, to know the teachers are giving up their Saturday for this.

"We plan to blanket the entire Puget Sound area with posters," Mrs. Payton said.

Mrs. Jules left her cell-phone number. "Call as soon as he's found," she said.

At seven, someone else knocked on the door. Hope surging, Bonnie ran to open it. Mrs. Watson stood on the step holding a pan of warm cinnamon rolls.

Mrs. Watson's curls had a bluish tinge and she always smelled faintly of lilacs. Three years ago when Mrs. Watson turned eighty, she announced she would count backward on future birthdays. Now if anyone asked her age, she said, "Seventy-seven."

"I thought you might need some breakfast," Mrs. Watson said.

"Come in, Mrs. Watson," Bonnie said.

"Is there any word about Matt?"

"No."

Bonnie had eaten nothing the night before; the fragrant rolls smelled delicious. Although cinnamon rolls were her favorite treat, especially Mrs. Watson's homemade cinnamon rolls, she felt guilty for wanting one. How could she think about food when her brother and her dog were missing?

"You have to eat," Mrs. Watson said, "to keep up

your own strength. You won't be any help to the police otherwise."

Mrs. Sholter poured two cups of coffee and invited Mrs. Watson to stay. Bonnie got herself a glass of orange juice to go with her roll. The prism in the window sent rainbows dancing across the tile floor. Maybe that's a good omen, Bonnie thought. Rainbows are a sign of hope. On the other hand, she'd seen rainbows yesterday morning, too, and look what had happened.

"I saw on the news that Pookie's gone, too," Mrs. Watson said.

"The police think someone might have taken Pookie first and then used him to entice Matt to go with them."

"That gives me the all-over shivers," Mrs. Watson said. "It means the person who took Matt came here, too."

Bonnie knew Mrs. Watson was upset in part because she lived so close.

"I wish I'd stayed home yesterday, instead of going to my book club," Mrs. Watson said. "I might have seen or heard something. Maybe Pookie barked."

After Bonnie finished eating, she said, "I'm going to look around outside some more."

Every inch of the yard had been examined the day

before, but she was too antsy to sit still. As she crossed the yard, she looked at the polka-dot garage door. I'd give anything, she thought, to hear a tennis ball hitting the door again.

She went out the back gate then walked up the alley to the corner. When she returned, she spied something red deep in the weeds next to the fence.

When she pushed the tall weeds back, she saw Pookie's collar. She reached for it, then withdrew her hand. The police might find fingerprints on the collar.

Bonnie raced inside. "I found Pookie's collar!" she said. "It's in the weeds out in the alley."

Mrs. Sholter quickly called Officer Calvin. "Don't pick it up," he said. "I'll be right there."

Bonnie returned to the alley. She wanted to be sure nobody else found the collar and took it. Officer Calvin arrived soon and, wearing gloves, carefully picked up the collar and dropped it in an evidence bag.

"So whoever took Pookie went out the back gate," Bonnie said. "They must have parked in the alley and thrown his collar away so he couldn't be identified by our phone number."

"That's as good a theory as any," Officer Calvin said.

"Pookie was probably out in the yard," Mrs. Sholter said, "which explains why nobody broke into the house. Pookie used his doggie door, then the man opened the gate and took Pookie."

Bonnie imagined the scene. Dear old Pookie, plodding outside to do his business, then falling asleep in the sunshine. When the man entered the yard, Pookie probably licked his hand.

"Of course we don't know it was a man," Officer Calvin said. "A woman might have taken Pookie."

Bonnie wondered if a woman might have taken Matt. She knew sometimes women who can't have a baby freak out and steal someone else's baby, but she didn't think they stole six-year-old boys.

Officer Calvin had brought a computer-generated image of the man who had come to the school, pretending to work for UPS. "The secretary gave a detailed description," he said, "especially of his hair, mustache, and tattoo."

Bonnie stared at the drawing, examining the man's eyes and his curly dark hair. She had never felt hatred toward anyone, but as she looked at the drawing she felt such intense dislike for the man that her feelings shocked her.

Mrs. Sholter glanced at the drawing, then covered her face with her hands and turned away, as if she couldn't bear to look.

"Do either of you recognize him?" Officer Calvin asked.

"No." Bonnie and her mom spoke at the same time.

"This image went out last night via e-mail and broadcast faxing," Officer Calvin said. "It's now in the hands of law-enforcement agencies all across the country. The school secretary says it's a good likeness, and the rose tattoo is an excellent clue because it's specific. People notice such things and remember them. Of course we don't know for certain the UPS impostor took Matt."

Officer Calvin doubts everything, Bonnie thought, even the obvious facts. She supposed it was good the police considered all possibilities, but only one scenario made sense: a man dressed as a UPS delivery man stole Pookie, drove to the school, and talked Matt into going somewhere with him. Who had done it? Why? Where were Pookie and Matt now?

Bonnie looked at the drawing again, barely resisting the urge to rip it into pieces.

Since the police were now monitoring the Sholters' phone, Bonnie and her mom left the house together and spent the day distributing more MATT IS MISSING posters. They checked in with Officer Calvin frequently, but there was never any news.

By the time they returned home, Bonnie was worn out. She ate, took a shower, and went straight to bed.

Two hours later, she woke trembling and drenched with sweat. She had dreamed of running alone through tall grass, calling for help.

No, Bonnie thought. I can't start having nightmares again. Matt isn't gone forever, and I'm not alone. Dozens of people are helping us, people we don't even know.

Bonnie longed to have Pookie on her bed again, pawing at the blanket and making little whimper sounds in his sleep.

As her heart rate returned to normal, she remembered reading Nancy's note and wishing she could go to the mall instead of watching Matt. Had Matt been lured away from school at that exact moment? Had he climbed into a car as Bonnie wished she didn't have to take care of him?

CHAPTER 13

On Sunday, the Sholters' house seemed full of what wasn't there. Everywhere Bonnie looked she expected to see Matt or Pookie. She put fresh water in the dog dish, as she did every morning. She set three cereal bowls on the table for breakfast, then put Matt's bowl back in the cupboard.

Even the sun glinting off the prism didn't seem cheerful. Bonnie reached for the milk carton without glancing at the rainbows on the floor.

That afternoon Bonnie made smaller MISSING flyers on the computer. She put Matt's picture on them plus his name and age. She added: *Favorite food: macaroni and cheese. Loves to play baseball.* She put a description of Pookie, too, and said he was also missing.

She used the phone number Detective Morrison had given her.

Bonnie printed the flyers, getting four per sheet of paper. She used red paper because red was Matt's favorite color, but his picture didn't show clearly, so she switched to white paper. She didn't need to please Matt; she needed to find him.

"Pictures work," Officer Calvin had said.

She printed fifty sheets, or two hundred flyers. Nancy helped her cut them.

"I'll give some to everyone at school tomorrow," Nancy said. "I'm sure they already know about Matt, but they can pass the flyers on to people who might not know."

"Thanks," Bonnie said. "Mom said I can take them to the grocery store and hand them out to people shopping."

"What about other towns?" Nancy said. "Whoever took Matt might have gone away from here. I could mail some to my Aunt Judy and Uncle Frank in Richland. I know they'd give out the flyers."

"Good idea. The police are using a national organization for missing kids, but we need to reach people who don't know about that group."

Nancy took a stack of flyers. "I have to go home now," she said. "It's my grandma's birthday, and we're having a party for her. We don't feel like having a party—we'd rather help try to find Matt—but we invited Grandma's friends weeks ago. I'll give all of them one of the flyers."

"Thanks."

"Mom says if Matt isn't found today, I can come over and help again tomorrow, as soon as I get home from school."

Bonnie promised to call if there was any word. After Nancy left, Bonnie thought, Nancy's right. The person who took Matt could have gone anywhere. Matt might not be in Washington State now. Matt could be in Florida or New York or anywhere.

The police had alerted the airport, but what if Matt's kidnapper took a short flight before the word got out? Maybe he flew a private plane. Maybe they took a bus or Amtrak. Matt might be in a car right now, speeding across Iowa.

The possibilities were endless. Bonnie looked at the stack of MATT IS MISSING flyers. They seemed like such a small thing to do in the face of a huge problem.

Bonnie took a deep breath. My flyers may be small, she thought, but they're better than doing nothing, and Matt might still be in the Seattle area. His abductor could be holed up somewhere, waiting for the furor to die down.

She filled a bag with flyers, got on her bike, and headed for the grocery store. One of the clerks gave Bonnie permission to stand at the door and distribute the flyers.

"I saw you on the news last night," the clerk said. "I hope they find your brother real soon. Your dog, too."

In between shoppers, Bonnie had time to think. The Internet was the best way to spread information quickly. She decided to write an e-mail about Matt to all the names in Mom's address book. She would ask everyone to watch for him and to send her message to all the people on their e-mail lists. She could include the Web site that had Matt's picture. Hundreds more people all over the country would instantly be looking for Matt.

The idea was too good to wait. Bonnie left her post at the store and went home to send the e-mail right away. As she turned her bike onto her street, she saw a van from one of the TV stations parked in front of her house. Bonnie's mom was talking to reporters again.

Bonnie's pulse raced. Had Matt been found? She pedaled faster. Mom stood on the porch alone.

If Matt had been found, he would be there with her. Was there bad news? The small seed of fear that had lurked all day in the back of Bonnie's mind quickly blossomed into panic.

As soon as she reached her own house, Bonnie dropped the bike at the curb and listened to Mom's words: "If anyone sees Matt, please call the police immediately." It sounded like a rerun of yesterday's news conference.

Bonnie noticed her mom's eyes were puffy and red. She probably cried half the night the same as I did, Bonnie thought. She retrieved her bike, rode it around to the alley, and put it in the garage.

When the media people left, Mrs. Sholter told Bonnie, "My boss called. He's offered a ten-thousand-dollar reward for information leading to Matt's safe return."

"Wow!" Bonnie said.

"Most people are good," Mrs. Sholter said.

She's right, Bonnie thought. There are bad people in the world, people who steal children and dogs, but there are lots more good people. Dozens of people—maybe even hundreds—were walking the streets today, searching for Matt.

Detective Morrison came to the door. "We heard from someone who thinks he saw Pookie."

"Did he see Matt?" Bonnie asked. "Was Matt there?"

"No. He didn't see Matt."

"Was Pookie running loose or was he with someone?" Mrs. Sholter asked.

"He was with an elderly couple."

"An elderly couple? Are you sure it was Pookie?"

"The caller thinks it was Pookie. He saw them late Friday afternoon."

"Where?" Bonnie asked.

"He was Rollerblading with friends at Marymoor Park, and he saw the dog with a man and woman, both about seventy years old, who stood near some restrooms. The caller didn't notice what kind of vehicle they were driving, but the time would be about right."

"Did he talk to them?" Bonnie asked.

"No. At the time he had no reason to pay attention to the couple or the dog. Then he saw Pookie's picture on television and thought the dog he saw Friday afternoon was the same, so he called. Of course, he could be mistaken; the dog he saw might not have been Pookie."

There she goes again, Bonnie thought. The police didn't seem to believe anything until it was proven.

"We have officers at Marymoor Park right now," Detective Morrison said, "looking for anything useful. The young man who called remembered exactly where he saw the dog."

"If it was Pookie," Bonnie said, "why wasn't Matt there, too?"

"Perhaps he was," Mrs. Sholter said. "That's what the police are trying to find out."

Matt might have been in the bathroom, Bonnie thought, where the boy on Rollerblades didn't see him, or he might still have been in the kidnapper's car.

"Marymoor Park isn't very far," Bonnie said. "Why would the person have gone there?"

"If an elderly couple had Pookie," Detective Morrison said, "I'd like to know where they got him."

"I wonder what their connection is to the man who was at the school," Bonnie said.

"Someone has to notice a small boy and a dog who suddenly show up where they didn't live before," Mrs. Sholter said. "Whoever took them might be able to pretend Matt is a visiting relative, but Pookie's not easy to conceal—he has to go outside regularly. Matt and Pookie together will be hard to hide."

"They may not be together," Detective Morrison said. "Matt's abductor might have given the dog to someone."

"Such as the couple in the park," Bonnie said.

"It's also possible Pookie's disappearance and Matt's aren't connected."

"Pookie's picture has been on TV and in the newspaper," Bonnie said. "Who would keep a dog they know was stolen?"

"Not everyone watches the news or reads the papers," Detective Morrison said.

Bonnie sank into a chair. "It keeps getting worse and worse," she said.

"We'll find Matt and Pookie," Mrs. Sholter said. "We have to find them."

Detective Morrison nodded. "It may take a few days."

Bonnie didn't think she could stand it if it went that long with no word.

"The abductor might try to disguise Matt," Detective Morrison said. "His hair could be cut differently or even dyed a different color. He's probably wearing new clothes by now."

"Maybe they'll dye Pookie's hair, too," Bonnie said.

"I doubt anyone would dye the dog's fur," Detective Morrison said, "but they might shave it off."

"Everyone is looking for a shaggy dog," Bonnie said.

"I know."

"Maybe the man kept Matt, but gave Pookie to the old couple," Bonnie said. "Maybe they're his parents or his grandparents."

"You should go into police work," Detective Morrison said. "You think like a cop. More likely, the person who took Pookie dumped him after he served his purpose of luring Matt into the car."

"Whoever found him thinks he was a stray," Bonnie said.

"Do you know anyone who works for UPS?" Detective Morrison asked.

"No," Mrs. Sholter said.

"Did you in the past?"

"No."

"I thought the man at the school wasn't really a UPS deliveryman," Bonnie said.

"He wasn't. I'm trying to find out where he got the uniform. Maybe he used to work for UPS, or a relative works for them. Maybe it wasn't a real uniform. Anyone could buy a brown shirt and embroider UPS on the pocket. If he wore matching brown pants, he'd look authentic."

"There are so many possibilities," Bonnie said. "How can you sort through everything?"

"I can't," Detective Morrison said. "I start with what seems most important, the most likely to provide a solid lead, and follow through on that. Other officers do the same, one idea at a time."

"We appreciate all you're doing," Mrs. Sholter said.

"By the way, the police in Reno say your ex-husband left there four years ago, leaving twelve unpaid traffic tickets but no forwarding address."

Mrs. Sholter made no comment.

Usually Sundays flew past much faster than school-days, but this one dragged on. Every time the mantel clock struck the hour, Bonnie thought, Another hour without Matt. Another hour without Pookie.

Two women who worked with Bonnie's mom brought a casserole and some potato salad. "You have to eat," they said, "and we didn't want you worrying about what to fix."

Not long after they left, Nancy and her parents arrived with a platter of fried chicken and half a cake. "The cake's left over from Grandma's party," Nancy said.

Matt's friend Stanley and his dad brought a big bowl of macaroni and cheese. Stanley still looked scared.

"This is Matt's favorite meal when he's at our house," Stanley's dad said. "We thought you should have some ready to warm up as soon as Matt gets home."

"Thank you," Bonnie said as she took the bowl.

"Will you have Matt call me as soon as he gets home?" Stanley asked.

Mrs. Sholter promised she would. Then she put the macaroni and cheese in the freezer, to save for Matt's homecoming.

Mrs. Largent, pushing her toddler in his stroller, brought over a pan of lasagna. "When I made our dinner," she explained, "I made extra for you."

When everyone had left, Bonnie looked at all the food and said, "This is what people always do when there's been a death in the family—they bring food." She burst into tears.

Mrs. Sholter hugged her daughter. "It's what people do for each other in any time of trouble. I took a salad to Mrs. Watson after she had surgery, remember? And you baked cookies for Nancy when she broke her ankle."

Bonnie wiped her eyes.

"It's kind of our friends to bring food," Mrs. Sholter said. "They want to help, and it's one of the few things they can do."

She got two plates and handed one to Bonnie. "We may as well eat it while it's fresh."

Bonnie put some potato salad and a piece of chicken on the plate. She hadn't realized how hungry she was until she started to eat. Everything tasted wonderful.

As she bit into a piece of cake she said, "I wonder what Matt is eating."

"Even getting kidnapped probably hasn't dulled Matt's sweet tooth," Mrs. Sholter said. "If he were here, he'd be trying to see how much cake he could eat before I made him stop."

Bonnie smiled, a bittersweet smile. She remembered scolding Matt only a week ago, because when she went to the freezer for some strawberry ice cream, it was all gone. Mom didn't buy ice cream often, and Bonnie was furious when she discovered Matt had eaten the whole quart.

"You little pig," she told him. "Other people like ice cream, too, you know."

For a few seconds, Matt looked ashamed and pulled on his earlobe, the way he always did when he was anxious. Then he dropped to all fours and grunted and snuffled like a pig until Bonnie had to laugh and couldn't stay mad at him.

Oh Matt, she thought. I'd gladly let you eat all the ice cream, if only you were home again.

CHAPTER 14

"Are you going to take me to school today?" Matt asked.

"School?" Denny looked blank.

"It's Monday. I go to school on Mondays. I'm supposed to be there by eight-fifteen."

"Not today. You won't be going to school for a while."

"I'm almost done with kindergarten. I have to finish so I can graduate to first grade."

"You don't have to go back. You've already graduated. You'll start first grade in September."

Denny hadn't thought that far ahead—he hadn't thought beyond the weekend visit with Winston and Celia—but he knew he couldn't enroll the kid in school anywhere in the Northwest. He wished he could. It would get the boy out of the apartment every day.

Denny's nerves jangled when Matt sat around with those big, sad eyes watching everything Denny did. The only thing worse was when the kid pretended to throw a baseball. He actually held an imaginary ball, then pretended to throw it as hard as he could. It was weird.

"What am I going to do until September?" Matt asked. "It's boring here. All you do is watch boxing and horse racing on television and talk on your telephone. I don't have anyone to play with. You should have kept Pookie."

"Boxing and racing are not boring, kid. I make big bucks on the boxers and the horses."

Denny's phone rang, ending the discussion.

On Saturday and Sunday, Matt had listened carefully to all Denny's conversations because each time the phone rang, he had hoped it would be his grandparents. Now he didn't bother to eavesdrop because Denny only talked about numbers and money. Sometimes the calls made Denny excited; often they made him angry. Once he threw the phone across the room, then kicked the refrigerator so hard that the grille fell off the bottom.

Matt wished he could see Mrs. Jules and his classmates. He wanted to tell Mrs. Jules how sad he felt
about Mom and Bonnie. Mrs. Jules would be sad, too.
He wanted to sit in the story circle and finish his project about windmills and play on the monkey bars with
Stanley. Even if he had to go to a different school, it
would be better than being cooped up in this dumb
apartment all the time. He couldn't even practice his
pitching. He didn't have a ball.

"You could buy me a ball," he suggested, "and we
could play catch."

"Forget it," Denny said.

"I could throw a tennis ball against the back of the
carport."

"I said, forget it! You aren't going outside."

Matt remembered all the times after school when
Bonnie had caught balls for him. "Zinger!" she would
call, which meant Matt should throw as hard as he
could. Matt would take aim at Bonnie's mitt, then
throw with all his might.

Matt's throat felt tight. Bonnie would never again
be the catcher while Matt practiced pitching.

Stanley's dad played catch with Stanley all the time.
Why wouldn't Matt's dad play with him?

Matt recalled once last year when he had asked
Mom about his father.

"Your dad and I made a mistake when we got married," she had said. "We thought we loved each other, but we didn't. We didn't know each other well enough."

"Why doesn't my dad ever come to see me? Stanley's parents got a divorce, but he stays with his dad lots of times. Is it because my dad doesn't like me?"

"Of course not," Mom had said. "He doesn't even know you. If he did, he'd love you to pieces, the same as I do, and Grandma and Grandpa do, and Bonnie, and Mrs. Jules and everyone else who knows you."

At the time, Matt had believed her, but now he thought she had been wrong. His dad didn't love him to pieces. His dad didn't even like him.

Matt closed his eyes and silently recited the list he'd made of all the fun things he'd done with Bonnie. Remembering good times helped get him through this bad time.

Bonnie stayed home from school on Monday, and her mom stayed home from work. They talked to reporters, trying to say something different to keep the story in print and on the air even though there was nothing to report.

Bonnie spent an hour at the grocery store handing out flyers. A light drizzle dripped from the gray sky, matching Bonnie's gloomy mood. She wished it would either rain hard or clear up. It was as if the clouds had cried all their tears and now could squeeze out only this faint mist.

At noon, the Office of Emergency Management called off the Amber Alert.

"Why?" Bonnie asked.

"The Amber Alert is most helpful when we have a vehicle description," Detective Morrison said. "By now Matt's photo is on TV and in the newspapers; the public is aware of his disappearance, so using the emergency services is no longer necessary."

Detective Morrison had other disappointing news. The search of Marymoor Park had found no evidence that either Matt or Pookie had been there.

"A crew cleaned that restroom on Saturday," she said. "They emptied the trash cans and picked up any litter from the ground before they mowed the grass. It was a long shot there would be anything linked to Matt, but still it seems incredibly bad luck for the cleaning crew to go there that particular day."

Ever since the report that Pookie had been seen at Marymoor Park, Bonnie had hoped Matt had been there, too, and that he would have left a clue. Matt was smart; he knew how to print his name and he knew his numbers.

Bonnie had fantasized that the police would find MATT and a license number scratched in the dirt with a stick or written in soap on the restroom mirror.

As she listened to Detective Morrison, Bonnie's hope was erased by disappointment. Matt might have been too scared to think about leaving a clue. Maybe his abductor hadn't left him alone long enough for Matt to write his name. Perhaps Matt had never been near Marymoor Park. It might have been some other dog who looked like Pookie.

On Tuesday, Bonnie's grandma and grandpa arrived from Arizona. Usually Bonnie loved it when her grand-parents came to visit, but this time was different. Grandma cried a lot; Grandpa looked old and tired. Instead of playing gin rummy and working a new jigsaw puzzle together—as they usually did when Grandma and Grandpa visited—Bonnie put up posters, checked all the animal-shelter Web sites for Pookie, and tried to think of new ways to find Matt.

Since Matt had twin beds in his room, Grandma and Grandpa always slept there while Matt used an inflatable mattress on the floor in Bonnie's room. This time the extra mattress stayed rolled up in its bag, making Bonnie's room seem empty.

The days blurred together like scenery viewed from a fast-moving car. Each day, Bonnie and her mom and grandparents traveled farther from home with their stack of posters, hanging them as far south as Centralia and as far north as Bellingham.

Detective Morrison called or came by every day. One day she said, "I heard from a truck driver who says he saw Pookie tied to a post at Marymoor Park last Friday."

"What about the old couple?" Bonnie asked.

"He didn't see them, just the dog. He described the same area we've already searched, so the report doesn't help."

Another day she said, "We traced Denny Thurman to California. He's been married and divorced twice since you left him."

Mrs. Sholter shook her head. "I wish I could have warned those women," she said.

"We talked to his most recent ex-wife. She said Denny had no kids and no job. From the sound of it, he's still a compulsive gambler. He was convicted once for assault and served six months in prison. The court-appointed psychiatrist called him an antisocial personality who doesn't care who he hurts as long as he gets what he wants. His last known address was in Los Angeles, but he isn't there now."

Assault! Prison! The words sent ripples of horror down Bonnie's spine. She had once lived in the same

117

house with Denny Thurman. He was Matt's father!

"When he wins, he rents a nice place," Mrs. Sholter said. "He eats in good restaurants and buys an expensive car. When he loses, the car gets repossessed. He stays in the nice house or apartment without paying rent until he gets evicted, and then he moves on."

"His fingerprints are in the system. Too bad the only prints we got from your house, gate, and Pookie's collar were the two of you. Does he have any family?"

"An older sister, Celia. I never met her, but Denny talked about her a couple of times. They weren't close, and Denny disliked her husband. His first name was Woodson or Weston or something like that, but I don't remember their last name and I don't know where they lived."

Mrs. Sholter watched Detective Morrison write this information down, then added, "I really think you're wasting your time trying to find Denny. He had absolutely no interest in his child."

"People change," Detective Morrison said, "and we don't have a whole lot of other folks to look for in this case."

No suspects, Bonnie thought, and no clues. How would they ever find Matt?

Bonnie and her family watched the local newscasts and read the papers, hoping there would be articles reminding people to look for Matt, but there weren't. Since there were no new developments in the case, it had been replaced by more recent events.

"It's as if nobody cares anymore," Bonnie said. "We're the only ones who talk about Matt."

"They care," Mrs. Sholter said, "but when there's nothing new to say, the story isn't going to get media attention."

On Thursday afternoon Bonnie said, "Tomorrow is one week since we saw Matt. It seems more like a month."

"Or a year," Mrs. Sholter said.

"Maybe the TV station could make a story out of the fact he's been gone a week," Bonnie suggested. "That would get people looking for Matt again."

"Great idea!"

Mrs. Sholter called the reporter who had broadcast the first story about Matt and asked if she would show the pictures of Matt and Pookie again, on the one-week anniversary.

The reporter agreed.

CHAPTER 15

Fred Faulkner pounded the last nail into the fence board. He straightened, rubbing his aching back. The old terrier plodded toward him, tail wagging.

"All done, Monty," Fred said. "No more missing boards. You can go outside whenever you want without being on the leash."

The dog wagged his tail and followed Fred into the house.

"The fence is fixed," Fred said.

"Good," Ruth said. "Now when Monty needs to go out after dark, he'll be safe and we won't have to go with him."

Fred eased into his favorite chair. "I'm worn out,"

he said. "I'm going to sit here awhile, and watch the news."

"Would you like some coffee?"

"Are there any cookies to go with it?"

"Dinner will be ready soon."

"A man gets hungry, working outside. A cookie won't spoil my appetite."

Ruth disappeared into the kitchen, then returned with a mug of coffee and a chocolate-chip cookie.

"Only one?" Fred said.

"I'm fixing spaghetti. You can eat cookies after dinner."

She went back to the kitchen.

The dog sat next to Fred's chair, laid his head on Fred's knee, and stared at the cookie. Yawning, Fred clicked on the TV and pressed MUTE until the commercials ended. He yawned again. Maybe he'd close his eyes and take a little snooze before dinner.

He pointed the remote at the TV to turn it off, and then froze. The screen showed a picture of the dog who sat beside him.

"Ruth!" Fred yelled as he turned the sound back on again.

She came running. "What is it? What's wrong?"

Fred sat upright in his chair, staring at the TV.

"You know how they always have teasers at the start of the news, to try to get you to stay tuned? Well, one of those teasers was a young girl holding a picture of Monty."

"Are you sure it was him?"

"Of course I'm sure. I know my own dog when I see him."

"But why would—"

"Shhh. The news is starting."

They sat through a report about the budget crisis in the state government, and a story about a ten-car accident on Interstate 5. The weatherman said, "Will the cold front continue through the weekend? My forecast, coming up." Next came pictures of an apartment fire in Oregon.

"Come on!" Fred said. "Tell us about Monty!"

As he said it, Monty's picture appeared on the screen again, along with a picture of a small boy. "Stay tuned for an update on the disappearance of six-year-old Matt Sholter and his dog, Pookie," the announcer said. Another commercial came on.

Fred and Ruth looked at each other.

"Pookie?" Fred said.

The dog's tail thumped the floor.

Ruth felt sick to her stomach. The spaghetti sauce no longer smelled good.

The newscast resumed with a report of an increase in car thefts from local park-and-ride lots, followed by a grinning couple who had won the state lottery.

Finally the announcer said, "One week ago today six-year-old Matt Sholter was abducted from his elementary school. That same day, the Sholter family's dog, Pookie, vanished from their yard. Police believe the dog may have been stolen and used as a decoy to get Matt to go with his abductor. There are no suspects in this case and no clues to the whereabouts of Matt and his dog. Anyone with information is asked to call . . ."

Ruth grabbed a pencil and wrote down the number as the camera focused on a woman holding a picture of a boy, and a girl holding a picture of the dog.

"It's Monty, all right," Ruth said. "We found him a week ago today."

"It wasn't his family who left him tied at Marymoor Park. It was whoever stole him out of his yard."

"Oh, that poor woman," Ruth said. "Losing her boy and her dog."

As the news went on to the next item, Fred clicked off the television. He leaned down and scratched behind the dog's ears. "We have to give him back, Ruthie," he said.

"I know." Fighting back tears, she picked up the phone and dialed the number.

Bonnie, her mom, and her grandparents watched the Friday newscast together.

"Someone, somewhere, has to know something," Mrs. Sholter said. "Matt and Pookie can't vanish without a trace."

Twenty minutes after their segment of the newscast ended, the telephone rang. Bonnie answered.

"I had a call from someone who says she and her husband have Pookie," Detective Morrison said. "They saw his picture on the television news a few minutes ago. It was the first they knew about the case. Everything the woman told me fits—her description of Pookie and when they found him. You're about to get your dog back."

Bonnie clutched the telephone as goose bumps slithered down her arms. "What about Matt?"

"She had no information about Matt, only Pookie."

"Where is Pookie now?" Bonnie asked. "Where does this woman live?"

"She and her husband live near Pine Lake. They're bringing him to the station," Detective Morrison said. "I'll come with them to your house."

Bonnie cupped her hand over the mouthpiece and

called to her mother and grandparents in the kitchen. "Somebody found Pookie!" She spoke into the telephone again as the others rushed into the living room. "Where did they find him?" Bonnie asked.

"He was tied to a post at Marymoor Park, the area we've already searched. It seems the skater who called was right; he did see Pookie there with an older couple. These folks are both seventy-four. When nobody came for the dog, they thought Pookie had been abandoned by his family."

"He was abandoned," Bonnie said, "but not by his family."

"The people who found him are Fred and Ruth Faulkner," Detective Morrison said. "We should arrive in about an hour."

Bonnie hung up the phone. "Pookie's safe!" she cried as she hugged her mother. "He's coming home!"

Forty-five minutes later, Detective Morrison parked in front of the Sholter residence, followed by another car. Bonnie, who had been watching out the window, dashed outside.

"Pookie!" she said as she looked through the window into the backseat. "It *is* him," she called back to her mother and grandparents, who had followed her out of the house. "It's really Pookie!"

A gray-haired couple got out. The woman opened

the back door of the car. Pookie scrambled out and pushed his head into Bonnie's arms. She dropped to her knees to hug him. Pookie's tail waved back and forth like a flag at the Fourth of July parade. He made happy little yips as he licked Bonnie's face.

"I guess there isn't any doubt," Ruth said.

Mrs. Sholter introduced herself. "I can't thank you enough for bringing Pookie back to us," she said.

"He's a fine dog and we love him dearly," Ruth said, "but when we saw you people on the TV news, we knew what we had to do."

"Please come inside," Detective Morrison said, "and tell me again exactly where and when you found the dog."

Ruth and Fred told their story, being careful to put in every detail they could remember. While they talked, Bonnie sat on the floor with her arms around Pookie.

When Fred told about using a needle to put the FOUND DOG notice on the signpost, Detective Morrison said, "Either it blew away or the cleanup crew tossed it out, not knowing it might be important."

"Thank you for taking good care of Pookie," Bonnie said.

"We enjoyed having him," Ruth said.

"I've been so scared," Bonnie said. "I thought he was lost and hungry, or he'd been hit by a car."

"May I give you something for your trouble?" Mrs. Sholter asked.

Fred looked insulted. "It was no trouble," he said. "No trouble at all."

"At least let me pay you for the dog food and the new collar and whatever else you bought for him."

The Faulkners refused to take a penny. "Monty—I mean Pookie—gave us a lot of pleasure last week," Fred said. "We'll miss him."

"I wish Pookie could talk," Bonnie said.

"So do I," said Detective Morrison.

"Come along now, Ruthie," Fred said. "We need to get on home."

Ruth's voice quavered as she said good-bye to the dog.

"You may come to visit anytime you want," Mrs. Sholter said. "Pookie would love to see you again, and so would we."

"I hope you find your boy soon," Ruth said.

Detective Morrison walked with the Faulkners to their car. As they got in, she told them, "Many of the local animal shelters have special programs to help senior citizens adopt a dog or cat at little or no charge.

You might want to call the Humane Society or PAWS or Pasado's Safe Haven. There are always good dogs at the shelters who need a home."

Ruth wiped her eyes on her handkerchief as Fred started the engine. "Not as good as Monty," she said.

CHAPTER 16

Matt's days crept slowly by. He missed Mom and Bonnie and Pookie. He wondered where Mom and Bonnie were now—in a graveyard someplace? He cried himself to sleep every night.

Denny placed and received calls all day long and late into the night. He said things like, "Two grand on Dandy Dancer to show," or "Five hundred on Bradshaw in seven."

Grandma and Grandpa didn't call.

Some days Denny was wildly happy, singing and urging Matt to play with his new toys; other days Denny practically snapped Matt's head off for walking through the room.

On one of the good days, he brought Matt a tennis

ball, then had a fit when Matt threw it against the back of the couch. He said the thump of the ball on the couch got on his nerves.

He often left Matt alone but never for more than an hour or so. When Denny was gone, Matt always practiced his pitching by throwing the tennis ball as hard as he could at the back of the couch, over and over. Matt wished he could be outside at home, throwing against the garage door. Better yet, he'd like to practice again with a real baseball, pitching to Bonnie.

One day when Denny was laughing and excited, he asked Matt what he'd like to do. "Something special," Denny said. "Something you always wanted to do. Ride to the top of the Space Needle? Visit the zoo?"

Matt didn't have to think long. "I want to go to a Mariners baseball game," he said.

Denny thought for a moment. "You got it," he said. When he came home that afternoon, he showed Matt two tickets. "We're going Saturday afternoon," he said. "After the game, we'll take the ferry to Bainbridge. You're going to meet your Uncle Winston, your Aunt Celia, and your cousins, Thomas and Tim."

"I have cousins?"

"Two boys, your age. Their house is right on the beach; we'll stay there overnight."

For the first time since he'd learned about Mom and

Bonnie's accident, Matt felt a glimmer of happiness. He was going to a game at Safeco Field! He was going to a sleepover with two boys his own age. He would take his new mitt; maybe the boys liked to play catch. Maybe he would even snag a fly ball at the game.

As the week wore on, Denny's crabby times came more and more often. On Friday afternoon he put all the movies and the DVD player in a big box. He put Matt's new baseball glove and the Walkman in the box, too.

"What are you doing?" Matt asked.

"Taking these back. They're no good."

"What's wrong with them? I haven't even caught a ball in the mitt yet. I'm going to take it to the ball game tomorrow."

"Don't argue with me! I'm returning all this stuff and getting a refund." Denny's eyes flashed with anger as he stomped about. He unplugged the PlayStation and grabbed all the video games, tossing them in the box.

Matt said no more. He had quickly learned not to talk during Denny's bad moods. He knew Denny didn't like him any more than he liked Denny, and sometimes Denny acted furious with him for no reason. Most of the time Matt felt as if Denny wished Matt were any place except in his apartment.

Denny had not hurt Matt, but Matt sensed that it could happen. Denny's anger flared easily, and Matt knew Denny always carried the small handgun he'd shown Matt in the car. The gun made Matt uneasy even though Denny never mentioned it.

Mom had warned Matt about guns. "Never pick one up," she told him. "If a friend shows you a gun, leave. Call me, and I'll come to get you."

Mom wouldn't like Matt living with someone who took a gun everywhere, but Mom wasn't here to object. He couldn't call her; she couldn't come to take Matt home.

"I'll be back in a little while," Denny said. He carried the box out, slamming the door behind him.

Matt looked around the room. He didn't care about losing the movies; he hadn't liked most of them anyway. Instead of animated Disney films and other G-rated movies, Denny had bought movies with lots of fighting and killing and car crashes. Matt covered his eyes during the car-crash scenes; they made him think about the wreck that killed Mom and Bonnie.

He didn't mind losing the PlayStation, either. It frustrated him because he couldn't read the directions, and Denny never took time to show him how to play. When Matt tried to do the games on his own, he didn't get far; he suspected they were intended for people older than six.

None of the board games had been opened because Denny wouldn't play them with Matt, and it was no fun alone.

He wished he could have kept the baseball mitt, though. He had worn it when he practiced pitching. When Denny was home and Matt couldn't throw the ball, he still kept the mitt on his hand for hours, pretending to pitch for the Mariners. He had planned to take it with him to the game tomorrow.

A new worry seized Matt. What if Denny returned the baseball tickets, too? What if they didn't take the ferry to the beach house tomorrow?

Matt went into Denny's bedroom and looked on the dresser top, where he had seen Denny drop the tickets. Lottery tickets with their numbers scratched off littered the dresser. He saw no baseball tickets.

Matt decided if Denny didn't take him to the ball game, he would run away.

I can't run away without money for food, Matt thought. He dragged a chair over to the refrigerator, climbed up, and opened the freezer section. I won't take all the money, he decided. If I only take part, he might not notice it's gone.

He listened for the front door to click open as he

took out the ice-cream carton and started prying off the lid. He didn't want to think about what would happen if Denny came back and caught him stealing money.

When the lid popped off, it slipped out of his hands and dropped to the floor. Matt scrambled off the chair, grabbed the lid, and looked inside the carton. Empty!

Matt climbed back on the chair and looked in the freezer, thinking he'd opened the wrong ice-cream container, but it was the only one.

He couldn't believe it! A few days ago, Denny had put a thick stack of money in here. What had happened to all of it?

This explained why Denny took all the toys back; he needed the money he'd paid for them.

Matt replaced the empty carton in the freezer and returned the chair. He couldn't run away when he didn't have any money. He'd starve.

Matt sat on the couch and played the list game. He closed his eyes and tried to remember everything he could about his mother and his sister and his dog.

He said the lists to himself every night before he went to sleep. He had made up lists of the stories Mom had read to him, the songs she sang, her clothes. He had one list of all the games Bonnie played with him. His favorite was when she pretended to be a catcher and he was a pitcher who threw fastballs.

"Ninety-eight miles an hour," Bonnie would say when she caught a ball. "Another zinger!" It used to make him laugh, but remembering made him sad. He always ended up crying when he played the list game, but he knew it was important not to forget his family.

Mom liked flowers, Matt thought, and music. She taught me the words to lots of songs like "Down by the Station, Early in the Morning" and "I've Been Working on the Railroad." She liked to drink tea and do cross-stitch. Best of all, she liked to have Matt sit on her lap while she read *Little Bear* or *Officer Buckle and Gloria* or *Blueberries for Sal* to him.

Bonnie liked to make beaded bracelets and run races with her track team and play her clarinet in the school band. She let Pookie sleep on her bed. Bonnie liked cinnamon rolls and ice cream.

Matt wished he hadn't eaten all the strawberry ice cream the last time they had it. If he had known Bonnie was going to be killed in a car wreck, he would have left the ice cream for her and not eaten a single spoonful.

Pookie's list was shorter: He liked to be petted, and he liked chew toys, and he liked to sleep in the sun.

Matt always put Pookie last in the list game because he hoped he might get Pookie back someday. Pookie wasn't killed in the crash. Maybe some nice people found Pookie at Marymoor Park, and someday Matt would see them walking him on a leash, and Matt would run to Pookie and hug him, and Pookie would be so excited and happy that the people would know he was really Matt's dog.

Denny returned, talking on the phone as he entered. He seemed calmer, but Matt pretended to be asleep.

Denny shook his shoulder. "I bought pizza," he said.

Matt opened his eyes and sniffed the cheese-and-tomato smell. "You said we couldn't afford pizza anymore."

"I got my money back for all those games. One clerk didn't want to give me a full refund on the opened movies, but I made such a stink, she caved in."

Matt was glad he hadn't been there. "Are we still going to the baseball game tomorrow?" he asked.

"I said we were going, didn't I?"

"I thought maybe you took the tickets back."

"I promised my kid we'd go to a ball game, and I always tell the truth. Besides, they're not refundable."

"And then we're going to ride the ferry and meet my cousins?"

"Your cousins and your aunt and uncle," Denny said. "There's only one thing."

"What?"

"You're going to have black hair and wear glasses tomorrow."

"I am? Why?"

"Because Thomas and Tim have dark hair, and they wear glasses. This is a family reunion and everybody's supposed to look alike for the pictures."

"Oh."

Denny opened a drawer and removed a small pair of eyeglasses with wire rims. "Here. Try them on."

Matt put the glasses on and looked through the lenses. "Everything looks the same," he said.

"It's clear glass. It won't change the way you see."

"How's my hair going to get black?"

Denny grinned. "Shoe polish. We'll do it in the morning."

The next morning Matt watched in the mirror as Denny applied black shoe polish to Matt's blond hair. Denny stroked it on slowly, careful not to get any color on Matt's ears or neck.

"This is how the movie stars get ready," Denny said.

Matt giggled. He looked so different, even Stanley wouldn't know him. When all his hair was black, Matt put on the glasses. "I don't look like me," he said. The red-and-gold Hawaiian-print shirt Denny had bought him was unlike anything in Matt's closet at home. Matt never chose shirts with buttons. He liked the new pants, though, with their deep pockets on both legs.

"Now all you need is a new name," Denny said.

"What's wrong with Matt?"

"Not a thing. But all the other kids have names that start with *T*—Thomas and Tim. You need a *T* name, too."

"For always?"

"You're going to be Travis."

Matt thought about that. "I'll be Travis for the weekend," he said. "Then I want to be Matt again."

He didn't understand why Denny wanted him to be exactly like his cousins. Mom had always said every person is unique and we should celebrate our differences, but Matt didn't say so. He didn't want to take any chance on making Denny angry today. Matt would have dyed his hair pink and called himself *Doofus* if that's what it took to go to a Mariners game, a ferry ride, and a sleepover with two other boys.

CHAPTER   17

Pookie slept with Bonnie Friday night. Even though he hogged the bed and snored, Bonnie wanted him where she could touch his fur anytime she felt like it.

Getting Pookie back had renewed her hope that Matt would come home, too. Of course she had never totally given up, but as the days went by, her optimism had faded.

The worst moment had come when she read on a Web site that seventy percent of abducted children who are murdered get killed within three hours of when they were taken. Three hours! Bonnie had cried, and that night she'd had the prairie dream again.

Now Pookie's familiar doggie smell comforted her as she lay in bed. For the first time since Matt's disappearance, she fell asleep quickly. She awoke once in the night because Pookie had a dream and his paws kept twitching against her side. Bonnie smiled as she talked to Pookie and petted him.

When Pookie went out his doggie door the next morning, Bonnie stood in the yard, too, even though it was raining. She knew the danger to Pookie was over, but she wasn't quite ready to let him be outside by himself.

She took the frayed brown "dog towel" from its hook and wiped Pookie's paws. Before she could rub down his back he shook vigorously, spraying droplets across the laundry-room floor.

As she came through the kitchen, she heard Mom on the telephone. "To be honest," Mom said, "we forgot all about it, but I agree it would be good for Bonnie to see her friends and do something fun. Hold on; let me ask her."

She held the phone away from her mouth. "It's Nancy's mom," she said. "She wants to know if she can pick you up for the baseball game."

"The Mariners game is today?"

"It starts at one o'clock. Mrs. Tagg is driving Shelly and Kristi—and Nancy, of course. She can pick you up at eleven."

"It doesn't seem right for me to go off to a Mariners game when Matt is still missing."

"I know, honey," her mother said, "but there's nothing more you can do to help Matt today, and we already bought your ticket. I think you should go."

"All right. I'll go." How odd, Bonnie thought, that I forgot about the Mariners game. When her track coach had arranged to get tickets at the group price, Bonnie had been thrilled. She had never seen a game at Safeco Field, and it would be great to go with her teammates—thirty-four girls plus the coach and two parents.

"How could I have forgotten about something that seemed like such a big deal?" Bonnie asked her grandma.

"Because losing your brother is a bigger deal," Grandma said. "But I'm glad you're going, honey. You've done everything you can to help Matt. It's time you let your life start again."

"Catch a fly ball for me," Grandpa said. Then he gave Bonnie twenty dollars for a hot dog or cotton candy or whatever she wanted to buy at the game.

"Thanks, Grandpa."

"I wish I could go with you," he said. "I'll watch the game on television and think about you. Wave if you see a TV camera."

Mom insisted Bonnie take their bird-watching binoculars. "It's fun to see the players up close," she said.

When Bonnie first got in the van with her friends, she felt awkward, as if she'd been away far longer than a week. But when she told them about getting Pookie back, everyone cheered and asked lots of questions. Bonnie relaxed. The other girls told her what had happened at school that week and then they all sang "Take Me Out to the Ball Game," at the top of their lungs.

By the time Mrs. Tagg parked, the morning's drizzle had stopped. They strolled past outdoor stands selling peanuts, T-shirts, Cracker Jacks, hot dogs, and various souvenirs. The smell of grilled sausages tempted Bonnie, but she decided to wait and spend her money inside.

They walked alongside Safeco Field, admiring the huge pictures of the players on the outer walls of the stadium. Crowds lined up at the gates. Two people held up hand-lettered signs: NEED TICKETS.

"Programs!" called out a man on the corner. "Get your official souvenir programs!"

The girls posed in front of a sculpture of a huge baseball glove while Nancy's mom took their picture.

Mrs. Tagg cautioned them to keep their ticket stubs

so they could easily find their seats again if they needed to leave during the game. As soon as she went through the turnstile, Bonnie tucked her stub in her jeans pocket. She didn't plan to miss any of the game, though. She intended to watch every second of her first major-league baseball game.

They rode the escalator to the three-hundred level. Most of the girls bought something to eat before they found their seats, but Bonnie was too excited to feel hungry.

Her first glimpse of the field took her breath away. Green grass, mowed so it created a pattern; crisp white lines around the batter's box and along the baselines; a huge lighted scoreboard. It looked even better than it did on TV.

Vendors moved up and down the aisles hawking cotton candy, soft drinks, beer, and frozen malts. The peanut man used gestures to communicate with fans several rows away, then expertly flipped the bags of peanuts over his shoulder to the waiting customers. Money passed from person to person until it reached the vendors.

From their seats on the first-base side, the girls had a view of the Mariners' dugout. Bonnie aimed her binoculars at the players.

The retractable roof was closed because of the rain earlier in the day, but after the girls settled in their seats, the clouds blew away and the roof began to open.

Bonnie laughed as she recognized the music being broadcast: "Let the Sun Shine In." She watched the huge roof slide into itself on its track until blue sky covered the playing field. She would have to tell Grandpa how it worked. He liked mechanical things, and that roof was amazing.

It felt good to be with her friends and to think about something besides her brother. Then she felt guilty for having fun at Safeco Field when Matt, who loved baseball more than anything, was still missing.

What if he's never found? Bonnie thought. For the rest of my life, will I feel ashamed every time I start to enjoy myself?

She pushed the gloomy thought away, turned to Nancy, and said, "I hope the Mariners hit a home run today."

Matt sat on the kitchen floor, watching the digital clock on the oven. Denny had promised they would leave for the ballpark at eleven, and as eleven o'clock passed and then eleven-thirty, Matt's disappointment grew. He wanted to see batting practice. He wanted to walk around Safeco Field and look at all the souvenir stands before the game began.

Denny kept making phone calls and checking things on the computer as the clock numbers flashed toward noon. Matt grew more and more nervous that they wouldn't get to the game at all.

When Denny finally said, "Let's go," Matt rushed to the car, forgetting to put on the glasses. Denny made him go back to get them.

By the time they got to Safeco Field, all the parking places on the street were already taken. Denny got angry at the fees charged by the parking lots.

"That's highway robbery," he said. "Fifteen bucks to let my car sit for a couple of hours. I have half a mind to go back home. You can watch the game on television."

"We already have the tickets," Matt said.

Denny drove farther and farther away from the stadium, looking for a free parking spot. He didn't find one, so he parked in front of a business with NO STADIUM PARKING signs posted on the building. A few other cars had parked there, too. "I'll take my chances," Denny said. "They can't tow everybody."

As they approached Safeco Field, Matt heard "The Star-Spangled Banner" being sung. He walked faster. "We're going to miss the first pitch."

"There'll be plenty of other pitches."

Inside the stadium, Denny led the way through crowds of people buying refreshments. Although Matt wished he could have popcorn or an ice cream, he didn't ask for any because he didn't want to wait. Overhead television monitors showed the game had already begun.

Their seats were on the second level, past third base toward the outfield. By the time Denny found the correct aisle and then their row, the Mariners were up to bat in the bottom of the first.

In the second inning, Denny's phone rang. When he began talking loudly, people nearby gave him annoyed looks until he walked up the aisle to have his conversation on the concourse.

He didn't return until the third inning. Matt hoped he would stay this time. It was more fun to watch a ball game *with* someone, even his dad, who didn't care about baseball.

The girls sitting on the other side of Matt giggled and acted rowdy; they paid no attention to Matt or the Mariners.

The cotton-candy vendor walked past. Matt wished Denny would offer to buy some, but he didn't.

Denny left for another phone call in the fifth inning and stayed away so long, Matt grew nervous. One part of him cheered for the Mariners while another part worried about Denny.

What if Denny came back in one of his angry moods? He might want to leave before the seventh-inning stretch when the Mariner Moose drove his quad around the field. Stanley had told Matt about that, and Matt really wanted to see the Moose do it.

Matt had figured out that Denny's phone calls always involved winning or losing money. When Denny won, he was happy. He ordered pizza and bought Matt new toys. When Denny lost, he got angry and nothing Matt did pleased him. The last two days, Denny must have lost a lot. Matt remembered the empty ice-cream carton.

He looked anxiously down the aisle. What if Denny didn't come back? He didn't like living with Denny, but at least Denny gave him a place to sleep and food to eat. Without Denny, Matt might end up like the homeless man he'd once seen standing beside the freeway exit, holding a sign—HUNGRY. NEED MONEY FOR FOOD.

Mom had told him if he was ever in trouble to tell his phone number to a police officer or other adult, but she had also said, "Don't talk to strangers." The only police Matt saw were down on the field, where fans weren't allowed, and Matt didn't see any adults he knew. Besides, his phone number wasn't any good now that nobody lived in his house.

Matt nervously fingered one ear, pulling on the earlobe.

Bonnie stood at the entrance to her section, waiting for Nancy. Between innings, they had gone to the restroom together and then to a souvenir stand, where Bonnie bought a Mariners baseball. Now Nancy wanted to buy some nachos.

"I'll wait for you where I can see the game," Bonnie had said when she saw the long line at the food stand. "I want to watch the Mariners bat."

She pointed her binoculars at the Mariners on-deck circle. Mom was right; it was fun to see the players up close. She watched the first baseman walk to the plate, then smack the ball on the first pitch and send it sailing high into the second-deck stands beyond third base.

Bonnie followed the foul ball with her binoculars. Half a dozen fans scrambled to catch it. One of them spilled his drink all over the woman in front of him as he lunged for the ball.

Bonnie chuckled as she watched the successful fan hold the ball in the air while his friends cheered.

She scanned the crowd around the man with the ball. As she moved the binoculars from left to right, she suddenly stopped and reversed direction.

She stared at a boy who was pulling on his earlobe, exactly the way Matt always did when he was nervous. Bonnie's scalp prickled as she blinked and adjusted the focus. The boy was Matt's size, but he had black hair and he wore glasses. He had on a gaudy shirt with buttons up the front; Matt disliked buttons and wore only pullover shirts.

She didn't think the boy was Matt, but there *was* a resemblance, especially around the eyes. Detective Morrison had said whoever took Matt might change his appearance.

Bonnie looked to see who sat next to the boy. There was an empty seat on one side of him. On the other side, a pair of teenage girls jumped and danced as they held up a sign, clearly hoping the fan camera would put their picture on the big screen. Behind the boy, a young couple with a sleeping baby ate hot dogs.

It can't be Matt, Bonnie thought. Nobody was making that boy sit there by himself. If Matt had been left alone at Safeco Field, he wouldn't sit calmly and watch the baseball game. He would tell an usher or the parents of those girls sitting beside him who he was. He'd say he had been abducted and needed help. He would give an adult his phone number and have them call Mom or ask someone to call the police.

Bonnie let the binoculars dangle from the strap. A train whistle filled the air as a train passed Safeco Field. Bonnie tried to concentrate on the batter.

The boy only looks like Matt because I'm thinking so much about him, Bonnie told herself. She remembered riding in the country last summer. Each time she saw a DEER CROSSING sign, she looked so hard for deer that she imagined every large rock or tree stump was a buck or doe.

Was it going to be like that with Matt? Every time she saw a boy Matt's size, would she imagine it was him whether it made sense or not?

Still . . .

She peered through the binoculars once more. The boy kept pulling on his ear. Bonnie decided to go closer and then look again. She moved the binoculars until she saw which section the boy sat in. She turned and walked down to the concourse.

She didn't want to tell Nancy or the rest of her group where she was going; no point getting everyone all excited when she was sure it couldn't really be Matt.

She found Nancy still waiting in line for her nachos, and said, "I saw a friend of my mom's, and I'm going to go talk to him for a few minutes. I'll see you back at our seats."

Then she went down to the second level and walked as fast as she could around the concourse until she reached the third-base side of Safeco Field.

CHAPTER 18

Denny pressed the phone to one ear and covered his other ear with his hand, straining to hear through the crowd noise.

"Bronco tells me you paid him."

Denny recognized Hank's voice; his stomach did somersaults.

"Right," Denny said. "Right! And I'll pay you, too."

"Today." Even with the noise around him, Denny caught the threat in that one word.

"I can't get the money out of the bank until Monday," Denny said. "I'll pay you then."

"I've heard that before."

"I'm not stringing you along, Hank, I swear. I'll bring your money first thing Monday morning."

"I'll probably regret this," Hank said, "but you have until Monday noon. After that, no excuses."

"I'll be there," Denny promised. He put the phone in his pocket and paced nervously. Winston and Celia were his only hope, but the last time Denny had tried to borrow from them, Winston had said, "Get yourself some help for your problems first. Stop gambling, and learn how to get along with people so you can hold a job."

Denny had sworn he would do so even though he knew he didn't have any problem. He could quit gambling anytime he wanted to; he'd had a string of bad luck, that's all, and the only people he didn't get along with were the jerks of the world, who seemed to be everywhere. They had the problem, not him.

Celia and Winston often urged Denny to "get some professional help." Once, after Denny threatened to shoot a driver who cut him off in traffic, Celia had given him a phone number to call. "You need help to control your temper," Celia said, "before you hurt someone."

Denny's blood boiled as he remembered how Celia and Winston had jumped all over him when the other driver was at fault. Denny had thrown the number away.

It would be different today. Celia and Winston would be sympathetic when they found out Denny needed the money for Matt. They knew how much it costs to raise kids.

He'd say he needed it to buy clothes and a bed for Matt. He'd say he had custody of the boy and needed cash to take Matt to the doctor and to buy allergy medicine. He'd say he had an interview next week for a real job with a steady paycheck because more than anything he wanted to take good care of his boy.

They'd agree to help this time instead of lecturing Denny to change his ways.

But what if they didn't? What if Winston and Celia said no? What if Celia threw a fit because Denny had never paid back the last loan? What if they had somehow found out about his time in prison?

Hank and his partner could get mean. If Denny didn't come up with the cash by Monday, he would have to hide out for a while. The money from the merchandise he'd returned wasn't nearly enough to pay off Hank, and he'd already spent part of it on Lotto tickets.

He watched people buying refreshments, then read the posted prices. Six bucks for a beer! Cash flowed all around him, but Denny's pockets were nearly empty.

He had to get enough money from Winston and

Celia not only to pay off Hank but also to place some bets on next week's races. He had a hot tip on one race; he'd have big bucks soon. Winning felt better than anything else in the world.

He fidgeted, watching the people, resenting the easy way they purchased hot dogs and drinks. Why should foolish fans in baseball caps be able to afford what he could not?

He itched to talk to Winston and Celia, hit them up for a loan, and tuck the check safely in his pocket.

When he got home tomorrow, Denny would prepare to move. His rent was already a week overdue; he had to leave before the landlord came to collect. Children weren't allowed in the complex; the landlord would notice Matt.

He'd pay Hank Monday morning, then hit the road. The money from Winston and Celia would give him a fresh start. Maybe he and Matt would go back to Reno, where the gambling was good.

A new idea struck him. He could say Matt needs surgery and there's no insurance on him. Surgery is expensive; at least ten thousand dollars. With that much money, he and Matt could fly to Reno. He'd use one of his fake IDs for the plane.

Excited by this surefire plan, Denny rushed back to his seat. They would leave right now, catch an earlier ferry, and give Winston and Celia more time to get over their shock about Matt before Denny asked for the money.

Denny sat beside Matt and said, "Come on, kid. We're going."

"Now? The bases are loaded and the game is tied."

"We have to catch the ferry. Let's go."

Reluctantly Matt stood and followed Denny. Just then Matt heard a sharp *crack!* as the bat hit the baseball. A grand slam!

The crowd exploded. Matt cheered and clapped as he watched the players round the bases.

"Quit stalling!" Denny grabbed Matt's arm and pulled him along.

Don't get your hopes up, Bonnie told herself. This isn't a mystery novel. You aren't the brilliant girl detective who saves her brother from the crook.

She walked as fast as she could, dodging fans carrying cardboard trays full of food. The concourse was so crowded she wondered if anyone was still watching the game until a huge roar arose from the stadium.

From the television monitor, she heard Dave Niehaus, the Mariners announcer, shout, "Get out the rye bread and mustard, Grandma. It's grand salami time!"

A grand slam! The crowd was going crazy. The first Mariners game of my life, Bonnie thought, and I'm missing the best part, because I'm on a wild-goose chase after a kid with black hair and glasses who looks a little bit like my brother.

But she didn't turn back.

When she was one aisle from where the boy had been sitting, she decided she was close enough to get a really good look at him without actually confronting him. She walked up to the seating area and turned her binoculars toward the seats one section to her left. She moved them back and forth, but didn't find the boy.

She scanned the crowd again, more slowly, and saw the two girls who had sat beside the boy. The girls were still jumping and screaming. This time there were two empty seats beside them. The boy was gone.

Maybe he's using the restroom, Bonnie thought. She returned to the concourse area and looked in both directions, but it was hard to spot a small boy amid so many adults.

Bonnie hesitated. Should she go talk to those girls— ask them if the boy had told them his name? Little kids are friendly; he might have talked to them.

Of course if Matt had dyed hair and glasses and new clothes, he probably had a different name as well. Whoever had taken him wouldn't let him use the name

Matt Sholter anymore. But Matt would never go along with such a pretense unless his abductor was there with him, making him pretend to be someone else. Nobody had been forcing that boy to do anything.

I should forget it, Bonnie thought. I saw a kid pulling on his ear the way Matt does, and I got all excited, but it wasn't him, so I need to return to my own seat before Nancy's mother worries about me. Probably lots of kids pull on their ears. It's a habit, like nail biting or knuckle cracking.

She started back toward the first-base side. As she walked past the escalator that leads to the street, she glanced down. On the moving steps one flight below, she saw the black-haired boy, riding down. Directly behind him was Denny Thurman.

Shock zapped through every nerve in Bonnie's body. She recognized Denny immediately, even though she had not seen him since she was seven. It *is* Matt, Bonnie thought. Detective Morrison was right; Matt's dad took him!

Bonnie clutched the escalator railing, feeling the smooth rubber slide beneath her hands while her heart beat *rat-a-tat-tat,* like the snare drum in a marching band. She had only a moment to decide: run to a phone and call the police—or follow Matt and Denny down the escalator.

What if Denny had parked in the lot directly across from the stadium? Or on the street only a block or two away? He and Matt could be in a car and gone before the police found them.

Bonnie stepped on the escalator.

Much as she longed to shout "Matt!" and rush down the escalator to hug her brother, Bonnie stood still, riding down quietly. Because Matt wasn't trying to escape, Bonnie assumed Denny had somehow threatened him if he ran or called for help.

She didn't want to endanger Matt. All she wanted to do was keep Denny and Matt in sight long enough to get a car license number, or if Denny and Matt got on a bus, she would get the bus number. Then she would call the police, and they would find the car or be waiting when Denny got off the bus.

Matt and Denny stepped off the escalator on the ground floor and headed toward the exit.

Bonnie easily kept Denny and Matt in view because few people were leaving the game early. Why would they, when the Mariners had come from behind with a grand slam?

Matt stopped to tie his shoelace. When he straightened up, he looked around, wanting one last look at Safeco Field. Even though he had to leave before the game ended, it had been exciting. He had especially liked seeing the Moose dance on the dugout, and the computer hydroplane race on the big screen, and, most of all, the Mariners' grand slam. Maybe he could come again sometime; maybe next time Denny would sit with him and watch the action, and they could stay to see the Moose ride around the field. Maybe he would get another mitt.

Matt heard the crowd yelling again. He glanced at the escalator and found himself staring up at his sister. He blinked and looked again. His whole face lit up.

"Bonnie!" he shouted. He pointed up at her. "Look, it's Bonnie!" He waved his hands over his head, jumping with excitement.

Denny whirled around. His eyes met Bonnie's, and his face froze into a mask of fear and hatred.

Bonnie turned and began running back up the down escalator.

She heard Matt's panicked shout, "Don't leave me!"

Bonnie stopped, remembering what the court psychiatrist had told Detective Morrison about Denny: *He doesn't care who he hurts as long as he gets what he wants.* What would Denny do if she ran? She couldn't leave Matt alone with him while she sought help.

Bonnie turned back, feeling trapped as the escalator carried her closer to Denny and Matt.

When she stepped off the escalator, Matt flung his

arms around her. "You're alive!" he cried. "You didn't die in the accident."

She held him close. Despite her anger at Denny, tears of joy stung her eyes. Matt was okay.

Then his words sank in. "What accident?" she asked. "Of course I'm alive." As she looked over the top of Matt's black hair, she saw Denny unzip his sweatshirt partway, then slip his hand inside.

"I have a gun," he said softly. "Say one word to anyone, and your brother will be dead."

Bonnie clutched Matt and stared at Denny. "If you shoot a gun here, you'll never get away," she said. "A thousand people will hear it go off."

"Wrong," he said. "I have a silencer on it."

Bonnie assumed that meant the gun wouldn't make noise when it was fired.

"I have plans for Matt today," Denny said, "and if you want him to live, you'll help me keep them."

"What are the plans?"

"You don't need to know. Just do what I tell you to do."

Still clinging to Matt, Bonnie nodded agreement.

"The two of you are going to walk out of this stadium in front of me," Denny said. "You won't talk to anyone or try to signal for help or do anything to suggest we are not a happy family."

"He does have a gun," Matt whispered. "He wears it on a strap across his chest."

Bonnie wondered how Denny had made it through the security check at the gate with a handgun under his sweatshirt. Mrs. Tagg's tote bag full of peanuts and granola bars had been thoroughly searched and her water bottle confiscated. Well, it didn't matter how he'd smuggled a gun into the ball game. What mattered was preventing him from using it.

She put her hand on Matt's shoulder and walked with him toward the exit. Denny Thurman stayed directly behind them.

"What about Mom?" Matt asked. "Is she alive, too? Did she get well after the accident?"

"Mom wasn't in an accident."

"She wasn't? Denny talked to Mrs. Watson and she said—"

"Be quiet!" Denny said angrily.

Bonnie looked at her brother's face, glowing with happiness, and understood why he had sat alone in the crowd without asking for help and why he had never called home. Denny must have told Matt that she and Mom had been killed. Even though they were in terrible trouble, Matt looked happy because this danger mattered less to him than learning his mother and sister were alive.

Poor Matt, she thought. He must have felt so sad and alone. She wondered if he had nightmares.

They exited the stadium near the sculpture of the baseball mitt, where Bonnie and her friends had posed for a picture. They walked past the stadium to the corner where a motorcycle policeman was ready to direct traffic at the end of the game. A few other people stood on the curb, waiting to cross the street.

Bonnie stared at the police officer, willing him to look her way. *This is Matt!* she wanted to shout. *This is the boy who's been missing! Help us!*

"Don't say a word," Denny whispered.

Bonnie tried to make eye contact with the officer, but he only blew his whistle and waved for the people to cross the street.

The wind picked up and dark clouds covered the sun again. Bonnie buttoned her coat.

As they stepped off the curb, Bonnie reached for Matt's hand. For the last few months he had objected when Mom or Bonnie tried to take his hand, claiming, "I'm not a baby anymore. I know to watch for cars."

Today he slipped his hand quickly into Bonnie's. His warm fingers intertwined with hers, and when they reached the other side of the street, neither Bonnie nor Matt let go.

By the time they'd walked a few blocks, the other

pedestrians had turned up a side street or had reached their cars and driven away. Denny, Matt, and Bonnie kept walking. Bonnie wondered if they were headed for a car or if Denny lived in downtown Seattle and was taking her home with him.

"I have to go to the bathroom," Matt said.

"Not now," Denny said.

"Now," Matt insisted.

"You'll have to wait. The car's only a few more blocks."

"I can't wait. I have to go bad."

Bonnie's thoughts raced faster than the traffic speeding along the freeway behind them. We need to be where people will notice us, she thought. Taking Matt to the bathroom might be their only chance to get help.

"There's a restaurant across the street," Bonnie said. "He could use the bathroom there."

Denny stopped walking, as if he were thinking it over.

"I have to go bad," Matt said.

"You wouldn't want him to make a mess in your car," Bonnie said.

"I wouldn't . . ." Matt began, but Bonnie squeezed his hand hard, and he didn't finish the sentence.

"Okay," Denny said. "Okay, we'll go in the restaurant, but remember what will happen if you say anything. I'll do the talking." He led the way across the street.

A banner over the restaurant door said WELCOME MYSTERY FANS! Inside, every table was full; people laughed and talked. A waiter in a white jacket with a stethoscope hanging around his neck walked past carrying a tray of drinks.

A woman in a long red evening gown, a rhinestone tiara, and a gold streamer across her chest that said MISS CLUELESS, asked, "Are you here for the mystery meal?"

"No," Denny said. "My son is desperate to use a bathroom."

The woman smiled. "Sure. The men's room is that way." She pointed.

"Make it fast," Denny said, "and don't talk to anybody."

"You'd better take him," Miss Clueless said.

"He can go by himself," Denny said. "We'll wait here."

Bonnie knew Denny didn't trust her. He was afraid if he went into the restroom with Matt, Bonnie would ask for help, and he was right.

"You should go with him," the woman urged. "We're having a solve-the-mystery party, and there are a lot of odd things happening." She leaned closer and whispered so none of her customers could hear. "There are two actors headed toward the men's room right now and they're going to stage a fake robbery. Your son would be terrified."

"I'll take him to the ladies' room," Bonnie said.

"I can't go in the girls' bathroom," Matt said.

"Yes, you can." She squeezed Matt's hand, holding her breath and hoping Denny would say yes. Maybe a customer would be in there, and Bonnie could tell the woman who she was. Someone in the restroom might even have a cell phone, and Bonnie could call the police.

Denny looked at Bonnie, his eyes narrow. "Come right back," he said, "and don't talk to anyone." He put his hand inside his sweatshirt as he spoke. "Do you understand?"

Bonnie nodded. She understood perfectly.

"Ladies' is right down the hall," said Miss Clueless.

Bonnie walked that way, with Matt beside her.

There was no one else in the restroom. Matt went in a stall.

Bonnie squirted liquid soap on her index finger and wrote on the mirror: HELP!! Denny Thurman kidnapped

That's as far as she got when the door opened and

two matronly women entered. Bonnie felt faint with relief.

"You have to help me," she told the women. "My brother was abducted, and now the man's making me go with him, too. He's out there right now waiting for us, and he has a gun." The words tumbled from her lips as she pleaded with the women. "Call the police! Tell them where we are. Tell them we're with Denny Thurman."

The two women smiled at each other, clearly delighted by what Bonnie said. "A clue in the ladies' room," one said. "I didn't expect that!"

"Let's go tell the boys," the other woman said. "We can freshen our makeup later."

"This isn't a clue!" Bonnie said. "This is real! Call the police!"

But the women, laughing, went back out. One spoke over her shoulder to Bonnie as they left. "You did a fine job, dear," she said, "and you're so young to be an actress!"

CHAPTER 19

Bonnie's hand shook with frustration as she finished writing her soapy message on the restroom mirror. *HELP!! Denny Thurman kidnapped Matt & Bonnie Sholter. Gun.*

She no longer believed any of the customers would take her plea seriously. Not today, when the restaurant was hosting a mystery meal where the diners try to solve a fake crime. Her only hope was for an actress to see the message and realize it wasn't part of the mystery script.

Behind her, Matt came out of the stall.

"Why didn't you back me up?" Bonnie demanded. "Why didn't you tell those women I wasn't acting?"

Matt look embarrassed. "I didn't want anyone to

see me in the girls' bathroom." He pointed at the wall behind Bonnie. "Let's climb out the window," he said.

Bonnie eyed the window—a narrow rectangle of frosted glass high on the wall above a radiator—and wondered if she could squeeze through it.

"It's worth a try," she said. She climbed on the radiator, reached up, and turned the window latch. When she pushed on the window frame, the bottom moved outward.

The opening was only about a foot wide. Matt could probably get through it, but she wasn't sure she would fit.

"You first," she said as Matt scrambled up and stood beside her on the radiator.

She bent over, with her hands on her knees. "Stand on my back; I think you'll be able to reach the window."

Matt climbed on Bonnie's back, then stood up and grabbed the window frame.

"Hurry," she said. "You're heavy!"

Matt swung one leg up and through the opening, then the other leg. He slid down the outside of the building and dangled for a moment, still grasping the ledge with both hands. "It isn't too far down," he said.

Rubbing her back, Bonnie straightened up. "Let go!" she said. "If I get stuck, don't wait for me. Run away! Get help."

He released his grip and dropped to the ground. "I'm okay," he called. "You can do it, too, Bonnie. You'll fit."

Quickly Bonnie pulled herself up. By sucking in her breath and scraping her back on the top of the opening, she squeezed through. She dropped down beside Matt.

They stood beside three garbage cans in a short, narrow alley on the back side of the restaurant. At the end of the alley, cars drove past on the street that ran along the side of the building.

"We could hide in the garbage cans," Matt said.

Bonnie shook her head. "Let's run for it," she said. "We'll flag down a car and get help."

Together the children bolted toward the street.

Parked vehicles lined the curb. Bonnie and Matt stepped between two parked cars into the street, then waved frantically at an approaching white Toyota.

The Toyota's driver frowned at them and kept going.

Denny paced nervously back and forth beside the hostess station. What was taking those kids so long? They should have been back by now.

The noise level in the restaurant continued to increase. A man rushed out of the restroom claiming he had been robbed at gunpoint, which put the whole place in an uproar. Denny's head started to ache.

When Miss Clueless returned, Denny said, "My kids haven't come out of the restroom. Could you check to see if they're all right?"

Miss Clueless, looking annoyed, headed for the ladies' bathroom. Instead of going all the way in, she opened the door, poked her head in the anteroom, and called, "Anybody here?" No one answered.

A few seconds later she returned. "They aren't in there," she said. "Maybe you missed them and they're waiting outside."

Denny put a hand on her arm. "Are you sure?"

"Of course I'm sure. If you don't believe me, go look for yourself. The ladies' room is empty." I'm too busy to babysit his kids, she thought. This guy wasn't even a paying customer.

Denny rushed past her down the hall and pushed open the door of the women's bathroom. As he stepped into the anteroom, a woman came toward him on her way out.

Denny stopped.

The woman screamed.

"Sorry," Denny said as he backed away.

"Peeping Tom!" the woman said. "For shame!"

"I'm looking for my kids," he said. "The hostess said nobody was in there."

"I can see why," she said. "It's freezing in here. I just came in, but it's too cold to use the facilities. The toilet seat would feel like an ice cube. If you're one of the actors, tell the manager to have someone close the window and turn on the heat."

Denny looked over the woman's shoulder at the open window. "No!" he said. He dashed out of the restroom, brushed Miss Clueless out of his way, and opened the door. He ran out, looked both directions, then raced to the corner, where he turned and ran alongside the building until he reached the alley. From there he could see the open window, but he did not see Matt and Bonnie. He ran down the alley toward the other street.

A dark green van came toward the frantic children.

"Help!" Bonnie shouted as she waved at the van. "We need help!"

The van stopped for a red light. The windows, both front and rear, went down and three teenage boys looked out.

"What's the problem?" the boy in the backseat asked.

"Take us with you," Bonnie said. "We'll explain after we get away from here."

The boys looked at one another.

"Please!" Bonnie said. "You have to help us."

The driver said, "We don't have to do anything. My old man would kill me if I picked up hitchhikers."

"They're kids," one of the other boys said. "Maybe they really need help."

"Maybe they're working the streets, and as soon as we unlock the doors, a gang of carjackers shows up and gets in with them."

"There's no gang," Bonnie said. "My brother's dad has a gun and he's making us go with him. Please, please, let us in! You don't have to take us far; drive us to the nearest police officer and we'll get out."

"There are cops all over, directing traffic," the boy in back said. "We'd only have to take them a few blocks."

"We don't have time to argue," Bonnie said. She tried to open the rear door of the van, but it was locked.

"Hey! You there!" Denny's voice came from behind them. "You leave my kids alone!"

Matt started to cry.

"He's trying to kidnap us," Bonnie told the boys. "He stole my brother, and now he's trying to take me, too."

Denny reached the van. "You young punks," he said. "I ought to turn you in to the cops, trying to lure children into your car."

"We didn't do anything," the driver said. "They waved for us to stop."

"You expect me to believe that?" Denny said. "I let my kids out of my sight for two minutes, and some pervert tries to snatch them."

"He's lying," Bonnie said. "If you won't help us, at least go tell the police what we told you. He abducted us."

"She's lying," Denny said. "She stole money from her teacher and now she's trying to run away."

The three boys gaped at Bonnie.

The light changed; the driver behind the van honked his horn.

"Get out of here before I decide to teach you a lesson," Denny snarled. "How would your parents react if you're arrested for trying to molest a child?"

The windows shot up.

The van sped away.

Bonnie's hope of getting rescued went with it.

Denny glared at her. "I told you not to talk to anyone."

Bonnie didn't answer. Beside her, Matt continued to cry softly.

Bonnie expected Denny to march them back to the other street where they had been walking, but instead he raised his hand and hailed a passing taxicab.

"Get in," he said.

"What about your car?" Matt asked.

"I'll get it tomorrow. We're going to miss the ferry if we waste any more time."

They piled into the backseat of the cab. Bonnie hoped the cabdriver would remember them later. When she didn't return to her seat at Safeco Field, she knew a huge police search would ensue. Maybe the cabbie would recall a crying boy and a scared girl and an angry-looking man. Maybe he would tell the police where he dropped them off, and what the man looked like.

Bonnie realized Denny looked nothing like the police sketch of the man suspected of taking Matt. That man had dark curly hair and a mustache; Denny was blond and clean-shaven. Bonnie wondered if he had a rose tattoo on his arm.

Heavy traffic blocked the streets. As the cab crept down First Avenue and idled at red lights, Bonnie tried to figure out how to escape. If only Denny didn't have a gun. She could have screamed in the stadium or run to the traffic cop or asked Miss Clueless to call for help. If Denny wasn't armed, she and Matt could even jump out of the cab right now, while it stopped at a red light.

But he did have a gun and he'd threatened to use it on Matt, so Bonnie kept silent and stayed in the taxi.

When they reached the ferry terminal, Bonnie slipped her hand in her pocket, withdrew her ticket stub from the ball game, and laid it on the seat. It wasn't the greatest clue in the world, but it was the best she could do. She hoped the driver cleaned out the cab after every fare.

Denny asked the cabdriver to wait.

"I'll have to leave the meter running," the driver said.

"No problem," Denny said.

"Aren't we going on the ferry?" Matt asked as they walked up the ramp beside a nonworking escalator.

"We're going," Denny said.

"Then why did you have the cabdriver wait?"

"So I didn't have to pay him. By the time he realizes we aren't coming back, we'll be gone."

What a mean trick, Bonnie thought.

In the terminal, Matt paused by a huge antique clock, but Denny said they didn't have time to look at it. He went straight to the ticket window and bought three tickets for Bainbridge Island.

"You barely made it," the ticket person said. "Walk-ons will start boarding at gate two in a few minutes."

As Denny paid for the tickets, Bonnie stood behind him and waved at the ticket seller to get her attention. When the woman looked at her, Bonnie mouthed the word *help*. She pointed at Denny, then made a "gun" with her thumb and pointer finger and pretended to shoot Matt.

The startled woman looked from Bonnie to Denny, then back at Bonnie. Bonnie quickly dropped her hand as Denny took his change. They continued past the ticket booth. As they walked away, Bonnie glanced once over her shoulder. The woman in the ticket booth stared after them.

Please, Bonnie thought. Please, please call the police and tell them which ferry we're on.

Denny draped his arm across Bonnie's shoulder, his fingers digging into her arm. "Smile," he said, under his breath. "Act happy."

Bonnie gritted her teeth and forced a smile.

"I wonder how long the cabbie will sit there," Denny said, "before he figures out we aren't coming back."

They joined the crowd waiting to board. College students chattered about their classes; one man had an assistance dog; a woman pushed a baby stroller.

A sign beside the door said ATTENTION in red letters. It warned people to report suspicious activity to any ferry worker.

I did, Bonnie thought. I warned the ticket seller.

She looked behind her and saw a man in uniform

cross the lobby near the big clock. The bright green vest that he wore over the uniform said SEATTLE POLICE.

Bonnie held her breath. Had the ticket seller called the police already? Was the officer coming to talk to her right now? She pretended to scratch her shoulder so she had a reason to keep looking back.

Instead of entering the room where ticketed passengers waited to board, the police officer stopped to chat with a man who was mopping the floor.

"Your attention please! Walk-on passengers to Bainbridge Island may now board at gate two."

Bonnie and Matt, with Denny at their heels, joined the crowd that filed down the ramp and on to the huge white-and-green ferry. In the middle of so many people, Bonnie felt all alone.

The last few cars drove aboard. Attendants in lime green vests with orange stripes directed the drivers where to park, and put blocks of wood in front of the tires of the cars nearest the front. Soon the ramp raised and the ferry backed away from the dock.

Denny took the first vacant bench seat and had Bonnie sit next to the window, with Matt in the middle next to Denny. He fidgeted and kept glancing around. After only a few moments, he said, "There are too many people in here. We're going down to the car deck."

They descended two flights of stairs, to the deck closest to the water. The ferry wasn't full; only half the parking spaces held cars, and they were all at the other end, facing the direction the ferry was going.

Gulls swooped beside the ferry, their raucous cries riding high over the noise of the engines and the churning water. Bonnie watched the Seattle skyline grow smaller as the ferry moved west.

Under other circumstances she would have enjoyed picking out Seattle landmarks: the Pacific Science Center, the Space Needle, the grain terminal. Huge orange cargo cranes, the kind used to load containers onto barges or freighters, stood guard all along the waterfront.

She could see the curved tops of Seahawk Stadium and Safeco Field. Was the Mariners game over yet? Were Nancy and her mother and the rest of the track team frantically searching for her?

I should never have followed Denny by myself, Bonnie thought.

I knew he was dangerous. What was I thinking? Instead of getting on the escalator, I should have run to the nearest concession booth and asked an adult to call the police. By the time Denny walked to his car, the police would have been there. Denny would be under arrest by this time and Matt would be on his way home.

Instead, Mom was probably getting a call right about now telling her Bonnie was missing, too. Poor Mom. She was already stressed-out, and so were Grandpa and Grandma. They would really fall apart over this latest development.

What am I going to do? Bonnie wondered. How can I get us out of this mess without being shot?

CHAPTER 20

Miss Clueless longed for the mystery to be solved so she could sit down. Her feet were killing her and this outfit made her look ridiculous, especially the banner with that stupid name on it.

On a normal day, she wore flat heels and a comfortable skirt and blouse to work, but for the Mystery Meals she always had to wear the red gown, the banner, and high heels. She worked harder, on these days, too. The Mystery Meals brought in crowds, so in addition to her hostess duties Miss Clueless helped clear the tables between courses.

As she piled dirty dishes on a tray, a pudgy woman with frizzy red hair tapped her on the shoulder.

"There's a message written on the mirror in the ladies' room," the redhead said. "It gives some names and says they've been kidnapped."

"Not again," said Miss Clueless.

"Since we're supposed to solve a murder, not a kidnapping, I thought I should tell someone, in case it's a real message."

"It's not real," Miss Clueless said. "Customers often plant phony evidence as a way to throw the others off track and give themselves a better chance to solve the mystery first."

"Oh," the redhead said. "That's a relief. I thought for a moment it was an actual plea for help."

"I'll take care of it," Miss Clueless said. She headed for the women's bathroom. Some people would do anything to solve the mystery and get their meal free.

The last time someone had left a fake clue on the mirror it was written with lipstick, and it had taken Miss Clueless fifteen minutes of hard work to get it off. Thank goodness whoever wrote this message had used soap.

She took a wad of wet paper towels and scrubbed away the words. The message came off easily.

She rubbed the mirror with dry towels and inspected her reflection. No trace of any soapy words.

She threw the towels in the trash container, then returned to the hostess station.

A cold wind blew across the open car deck, but Denny insisted they stay there.

"Where are we going?" Bonnie asked.

"We're going to meet our cousins," Matt said.

"We don't have any cousins."

"Yes, we do. Denny's sister has two boys my age, and we're going to stay overnight with them."

Bonnie realized Matt might have cousins she knew nothing about. Mom had told Detective Morrison that Denny had a sister.

"You have to call me Travis tonight," Matt said, "because all of the boys have names that start with *T*."

Bonnie gave Denny a disgusted look. "How are you going to explain us to your sister?" she asked.

"Matt—er, Travis is my son. That's all the explaining I need to do."

"No, it isn't. What about me? I'm not your child." To herself Bonnie added, *Thank goodness*.

Denny said nothing.

Anger spurred Bonnie on. "If your relatives have watched the television news this week or glanced at a newspaper, they will know Matt was abducted. Mom's been on every channel, pleading for his return."

"She has?" Matt said.

"She has, and her picture's been in all the papers." Bonnie looked at Denny. "Since you and Mom were once married, surely your sister would recognize Mom. Unless she's completely stupid, she'll put two and two together when you show up with Matt."

"Celia and Winston never met Anita. They lived back East, and we got married on the spur of the moment."

"Has *my* picture been in the paper?" Matt asked.

"Your picture is in store windows all over the state of Washington," Bonnie said. "It's in the newspapers and on TV. Your face is everywhere, including the Internet."

"Wow!" said Matt.

"He looks different now," Denny said. "No one will recognize him."

"I recognized him."

"You're his sister."

"I'll make a deal with you," she said.

Denny didn't respond.

Bonnie kept talking. "When we get to Bainbridge Island, you keep going, but let us reboard the ferry and go home. I promise we won't tell anyone where you are. You'll have a head start—a chance to get away."

"No way. You'd break your promise the minute I was out of sight."

"Suit yourself. Either you let us go home, or as soon as I see your sister, I'm telling her what happened. All of it. I don't think you'll shoot Matt or me in front of your sister and your nephews."

Bonnie hoped she sounded more confident than she felt. She knew it was risky to threaten Denny, but she didn't want to wait until she could ask Denny's sister for help. For all she knew, Denny's sister and brother-in-law were as bad as he was, and the two cousins were young punks on drugs. Denny's relatives might help him instead of helping her and Matt, even if they knew the truth.

"Celia won't believe you," Denny said. "I'm her brother. She knows I wouldn't lie to her."

Bonnie rubbed her hand across Matt's head, then showed Denny the streak of black on her palm. "It'll be easy to prove you dyed his hair," she said.

"Shut up!" Denny wiped his hand across his brow.

Bonnie couldn't keep quiet. He looked nervous; maybe she could convince him to let her and Matt go. "All your sister has to do is call the police. They'll verify everything I say."

Denny had never liked Bonnie when he was married to Anita, and he liked her even less now. How dare she interfere when he was on his way to Bainbridge with the perfect reason to ask for money. He was so close to pulling off his plan; he refused to let Bonnie spoil it.

He'd had an incredible losing streak since he took Matt. Eight days ago, he'd been riding high with more cash than he could stuff in his pockets. Now desperation chilled him more than the icy wind. Denny hated this feeling of impending disaster. He hated being broke, hated knowing the Hanks and Broncos of the world knew exactly how to track him down.

Even if his luck turned again so he could eventually afford to pay Hank, it would be too late. He'd be a marked man. He'd seen how Hank's anger worked: Pay up promptly or be the victim of a "hit-and-run accident" that wasn't an accident at all.

Denny needed money—*a lot* of money—and he needed it fast, before Monday morning. With Matt, he could get it. Without Matt, Denny was doomed to running from Hank and his henchmen.

His plan had worked fine until Bonnie showed up. Now this annoying girl with the big mouth threatened to ruin everything.

If he let Bonnie talk to Celia and Winston, he would never get the money he needed. Not only would they refuse to pay, they'd probably call the cops.

Denny could almost hear his righteous sister:

"You've gone too far this time, Denny. Kidnapping is a crime. I'm going to have to turn you in."

This time Denny would be in prison a lot longer than six months. The prosecutor would learn about Denny's previous conviction and his unregistered firearm. Denny couldn't afford a defense attorney. He'd be stuck with the public defender, who would treat him like scum and be secretly glad to lose the case.

Denny's head pounded. Tension headaches always made him sick, and now the up-and-down motion of the ferry increased his nausea.

He looked around. He and the two children were alone on the lower deck. The cars were empty; all the passengers had gone upstairs to the warm lounge area.

He glared at Bonnie. Loathing made his eyes narrow, as if by squinting at her he could make her disappear. Matt had agreed to do everything Denny said; why wouldn't the girl cooperate? She had wrecked it all.

Denny could think of only one solution. He had to get rid of Bonnie before the ferry docked.

Shove her overboard.

Pretend it was an accident.

Even if she screamed as she fell, no one would hear her cries over the noisy engine.

Wait. Denny took a deep breath and tried to think calmly.

What if Bonnie could swim? Other passengers might see the girl splashing in Puget Sound and call for help. The events played out in Denny's mind.

"Girl overboard!" the person would yell, and everyone would rush to that side of the boat to gawk.

The captain would stop the engine. Someone would throw Bonnie a life preserver and she'd hang on and get pulled back to the ferry, or some hero-type would dive in and keep her afloat until one of the small lifeboats could be launched to rescue her.

If Bonnie got plucked from the frigid water, the captain and crew and all the passengers would see a dripping-wet kid, shaking with cold, and hear her accuse Denny of kidnapping and attempted murder. She'd tell everything, *yak yak yak*, and Winston and Celia would see Denny on the nightly news as he was being led off to jail.

Denny cringed at the imagined scene. He couldn't let it happen. He refused!

I'll shoot her before I push her into the water, Denny thought. If she's dead, she'll sink right away.

CHAPTER 21

Detective Morrison dreaded this visit. How could she tell Anita Sholter that her daughter was missing? This was the hardest part of police work: breaking bad news to good people.

Detective Morrison and Spike had rushed to Safeco Field as soon as the call came in. A security guard, so upset he was barely coherent, had dialed 911 to report a girl had vanished from the ballpark.

At first Detective Morrison assumed it was a typical lost-child case and she wondered why Seattle Police were alerting her. Kids often get separated from the group they came with but usually they're reunited quickly, with no harm done. It's easy to get turned around in crowded places. Happens all the time.

Detective Morrison had been on her first break of a busy day when the call came, and her ham sandwich seemed more interesting than a kid who went out the wrong exit at the ballpark. She only half listened to the report—until she heard the name of the missing girl.

She concentrated on the words coming from the police radio: "This girl is the sister of six-year-old Matt Sholter, who vanished from his school eight days ago."

Detective Morrison dropped her sandwich and ran to her squad car. En route to Safeco with her siren screaming, she learned Bonnie had left her seat in the sixth inning and never returned.

When Detective Morrison arrived, she found a group of girls, plus a few adults, milling nervously around the private office of a Safeco Field official. She recognized Bonnie's pal, Nancy. Two Seattle Police Department officers were already questioning the group.

"Bonnie told me she saw someone she knew, a friend of her mom's," Nancy said. "She said she was going to talk to him and would meet me back at our seats, but she never came."

Someone she knew. Detective Morrison had wondered all along if the person who took Matt was someone he recognized—a family friend or a former neighbor, someone whom Matt would go with because he didn't consider the person to be "a stranger," as he'd been warned against. Had Bonnie now been lured by the same familiar person?

Detective Morrison felt sick to her stomach. Bonnie was a smart, capable girl. She would never willingly leave the ballpark, even with someone she knew, without first telling the people she had come with. It flat out would not happen. Which meant Bonnie had left against her will.

After questioning Bonnie's team and the chaperones, the three police officers left, each with an urgent assignment. Detective Morrison offered to do the worst task of all—inform Bonnie's mother—because she already knew Anita Sholter.

The rain began again as Detective Morrison drove out of downtown Seattle and headed east across the Mercer Island Bridge. By the time she stopped in front of the Sholter house, her mood matched the dismal weather.

With a heavy heart, Detective Morrison rang Anita Sholter's doorbell.

Mrs. Sholter took one look at the detective's face and knew she brought bad news. "Come in," she said.

"It's Bonnie. She told her friends she saw someone she recognized and would be back in a few minutes. She never returned."

The color drained from Mrs. Sholter's face. "Bonnie's gone?"

"She's missing. As soon as Seattle Police got the call, they ordered roadblocks around the whole district. They're checking every car in the parking garage. Those who parked on the street will be searched before they leave the area."

Mrs. Sholter nodded as if she understood, but Detective Morrison knew the woman was too shocked to pay full attention.

"Bonnie left the others during the bottom of the sixth inning," Detective Morrison continued. "They didn't report her missing until the game ended, nearly an hour later. Until then her group thought she was watching the game with the friend she'd seen. They didn't start to worry until the crowd began to thin out. Then they looked for her, and realized she wasn't coming back to her original seat."

"So Bonnie could have left the area before the roadblocks went up," Mrs. Sholter said.

"Correct."

"Do you think the same person who took Matt managed to take Bonnie?"

"We can't be sure, but it's awfully suspicious. It makes me wonder again if Matt recognized his abductor."

"If the same person was after Bonnie, he must have followed her to the Mariners game. How could someone have stalked her like that? Where was Matt while this happened?"

Chills crept up Detective Morrison's arms. Was Matt dead and now the killer had come for Bonnie? Was this revenge on Mrs. Sholter by someone with a twisted mind and an old grudge?

"We don't know if Matt is still with his abductor," Detective Morrison said. Then, seeing Mrs. Sholter's stricken look, she added, "The kidnapper could have left Matt locked in somewhere, or had someone guarding him. Or maybe Matt was there. Maybe Bonnie saw him and followed him."

Bonnie's grandpa, who had listened to the whole conversation, said, "Perhaps the abductor used Matt as a decoy, to get Bonnie to go with him, the same way he used Pookie to trick Matt."

"You think Matt was at the ball game, in plain view of thousands of people?" Mrs. Sholter said. "Surely someone would have recognized him. Besides, if he had been out in public, he'd have screamed for help, and if Bonnie had seen him she would have called the police immediately."

Detective Morrison nodded. Mrs. Sholter was right. On the other hand, if Bonnie had not left the ballpark voluntarily, it meant she had been kidnapped. How could that happen to a thirteen-year-old girl in a crowded baseball stadium?

"Bonnie would never have left the game without consulting Mrs. Tagg," Mrs. Sholter said.

Detective Morrison knew this girl, knew this family, and she knew in her bones that Mrs. Sholter spoke the truth. Bonnie could be trusted to do the right thing.

What had happened? What in the world could have seemed so important to Bonnie that she would go against everything she'd been taught? Especially now, with her brother missing.

Grandpa said, "Whoever she went with had a weapon and forced her to leave the stadium."

Grandma said, "She wouldn't have gone otherwise."

Detective Morrison believed they were right. "There's no point speculating what happened," she said. "The important thing now is to find Bonnie as fast as possible. I'll need a picture of her."

It was like watching a rerun of a horrible movie where she stood in the Sholters' living room, asking for a photo of a missing child.

This time was worse because she knew the child personally. Knew her and liked her.

Throughout her nine years on the police force,

Detective Morrison had purposely maintained a detachment from the people she served. She knew if she let herself get emotionally involved in the cases she worked, she would burn out and not be able to continue.

Over the last week, however, Bonnie's loyalty to her brother and concern for her dog had touched Detective Morrison. The girl had distributed flyers, checked Web sites, knocked on doors, given interviews, and sent e-mails. She never gave up.

Bonnie Sholter was more than another missing person; she was a missing friend. When Mrs. Sholter handed over a picture of her daughter, her second child to vanish in eight days, Detective Morrison's heart broke for the woman.

No one should have to endure what this family was going through.

CHAPTER 22

The wind whipped Bonnie's hair around her face as Matt huddled against her. She slipped her hands in her jacket pockets to keep them warm, and found the souvenir baseball she'd bought at the Mariners game.

"Here," she said, handing the ball to Matt. "I bought you a present at Safeco Field."

Matt's eyes lit up when he saw the blue-and-green ball with the Mariners logo on it. He turned the ball carefully around and around in his hands. "Thanks," he said. He carried the baseball to a small patch of sunlight where the colors looked brighter.

Bonnie warily watched Denny, who stared at her as if she were his worst enemy. She wondered what he intended to do.

She knew she had angered him when she said his sister would believe her and not him. Even though it was true, Bonnie realized it might not have been smart to say so. She needed to keep him calm, not get him all worked up.

Denny stepped toward her, his hand inside his sweatshirt, presumably on the gun. When he was only about two feet away, he said, "You're going to walk as close to the edge as you can." He kept his voice low, but Bonnie saw Matt, who was now off to the side and behind Denny, stop examining the ball and pay attention.

"Why?" Bonnie asked. "What are you going to do?"

"I'm going to take my son to visit my sister and brother-in-law, without you there to interfere. Back up."

Bonnie stepped toward the rear of the ferry.

Matt, his eyes on Denny, began inching toward the stairway, but Denny looked over his shoulder and snapped, "You stay where you are and keep quiet or you won't live to meet your cousins."

Matt stopped.

Bonnie reached the yellow rope that stretched from side to side, preventing people from walking too close to the back edge of the boat. She looked at Denny.

"Duck under the rope and keep going."

Bonnie went under the rope. A few feet farther, a

strong mesh of rope blocked her from reaching the end of the ferry. She stopped with her back to the mesh.

"Climb over," Denny said. He now stood next to the yellow rope.

"I'm a strong swimmer," she said. "Even if you make me jump, I'll survive. Someone on the upper decks will hear me yell, and see me in the water."

"You won't be swimming," Denny said, "or yelling." His voice was hard as steel. His hand stayed inside his sweatshirt.

Beads of perspiration broke out on Bonnie's lip. She glanced at the stairs, hoping other passengers would come down to their cars, but no one came. The deck remained empty except for her, Denny, and Matt.

When she looked up, however, she saw two men watching through a window on the deck above. One of them pointed at her.

They see me, she thought. Even if they don't realize what's going on, they'll know I shouldn't be out here on the end of the boat. They'll tell a ferry worker, and someone will hurry down to make me get back where it's safe. I have to stall until that happens.

"Climb over the barrier," Denny said. "Now!"

Bonnie looked into his eyes and saw the face of a madman. He's going to fire the gun, she thought. As soon as I get to the edge of the deck, he's going to shoot me and let my body topple into the water.

Clyde Wallace and his brother, James, stood at the back end of the ferry's lounge, in the small outdoor smoking area. Through the window that shielded them from the wind, they looked down at the rear of the ferry.

"Hey!" James said. "Look at that girl down there. She's climbing over the rope."

"What's she doing?" Clyde asked. "She shouldn't go out there. It isn't safe."

"I hope she doesn't jump in the water. A guy leaped off the Tacoma Narrows Bridge a couple of months ago. Tried to kill himself and ended up paralyzed."

"She won't jump. It's a kid, showing off."

"Maybe it's a dare," his brother said. "The guy with her sees where she is. He doesn't seem concerned."

"He's old enough to know better," Clyde said. "I have half a mind to notify one of the ferry workers."

"Oh, don't get involved," James said. "We might have to stay and give a statement or something, and we'd be late getting home. My wife'll have a fit if I'm not there before her parents come to dinner."

"The girl is almost to the edge of the ferry."

"And we're almost to Bainbridge. The girl will come back on this side of the rope as soon as people start downstairs to get in their cars."

Clyde snuffed out his cigarette. "I suppose you're right," he said. "Let's go back inside."

Denny withdrew a short black gun, not much bigger than Matt's water pistol, and pointed it at Bonnie.

Bonnie stared at the gun. She didn't know what kind it was, only that it was aimed at her heart. A small gun could be just as deadly as a large one. Fear crashed against her like ocean waves.

Denny wouldn't get away with it; Bonnie was positive of that. As soon as Denny shot her, Matt would scream and run upstairs for help—and what would Denny do then? Shoot Matt, too? She shuddered.

Even if Matt got away and brought help and Denny was caught, it would be too late to save Bonnie.

She had to take action now, before Denny pulled the trigger.

Bonnie's mind flew in all directions, trying desperately to think of a workable plan. She glanced up again, but the two men had left; no one was watching.

"Keep going," Denny said. "Move!"

Bonnie lifted her left leg over the mesh rope and put her foot down on the other side. The edge of the ferry was only a couple of feet behind her. Trembling, she clung to the top of the mesh, one foot on either side.

Denny held the gun steady.

Over Denny's shoulder, Bonnie saw Matt move closer. His eyes showed his horror as he stared at the gun. He held the baseball against his chest.

Matt has a strong arm, Bonnie thought. He practices pitching all the time. Could he throw the ball hard enough and accurately enough to save her?

If he threw the ball at Denny and missed, Denny would be even more angry. He would shoot Bonnie instantly and then might turn the gun on Matt. Bonnie didn't want to endanger Matt to save her own life, yet she thought her idea could work. Matt was already in danger, and time was running out.

"You brought this on yourself," Denny said. "You always did talk too much."

"Zinger!" Bonnie yelled.

"What?" Denny said.

Matt froze. *Zinger* was the word he and Bonnie used for his hardest, fastest pitch.

Please, Matt, Bonnie thought. Please figure out what I'm asking you to do, and do it!

Bonnie lifted her right foot over the mesh rope. If she kept moving she hoped Denny would stay focused on her and not notice if Matt came closer.

"Zinger!" she shouted again. The wind lifted the word and carried it back toward Seattle, toward home and school and Mom. Bonnie wished the wind would pick her up, as well, and let her fly like a kite away from this cruel man and his lies.

She stood on the far side of the mesh now, gripping it with both hands. The wind was stronger out here, and the sea spray blew against her, dampening her hair and clothes. She tasted salt from the seawater on her lips. Or was it tears?

She looked straight at Matt and screamed, "Zinger!"

Matt understood Bonnie's message. Could he do it? With his heart racing, he gripped the Safeco Field souvenir ball in his hand. He saw the gun in Denny's hand but decided it was too small to be a good target.

Matt pretended he was in a ball game. The strike zone was Denny's back, and Matt knew he had only one chance; he couldn't miss.

"Good-bye, brat," Denny said.

Bonnie heard a click as Denny removed the safety catch. She stuck her left foot back, feeling for the deck, but she felt only empty space under her shoe.

She dropped to her knees and ducked her head, making herself into a smaller target. Hurry, Matt, she pleaded silently. Hurry!

Matt raised both arms over his head, his eyes focused on Denny's back. He gritted his teeth, lifted his left leg off the ground, and threw the baseball with every ounce of strength he had.

Thunk! The ball hit Denny hard, at the base of his neck.

Denny cried out in pain. He dropped the gun, fell to his knees, and clutched his neck with both hands. The gun landed on the deck and slid toward Bonnie.

Bonnie leaped over the mesh rope, rushed forward, and grabbed the gun. She turned toward the back of the ferry and flung the gun as hard as she could. It sailed over the mesh rope, far beyond the end of the boat, and splashed into the water.

"Run!" Bonnie yelled at Matt, but he was already halfway up the stairs, screaming for help.

Bonnie jumped over the yellow rope as Denny straightened up. He lunged for her and caught her by the ankle. She fell forward, getting slivers in her palms when she landed on the wooden deck. Bonnie kicked, struggling to get away from his grasp. His fingers dug in, bruising her skin.

With his weapon gone, she wasn't afraid of him any longer, and she fought with all her might, but he was too strong for her. He got to his feet, then grabbed her arms and yanked her upright.

"Help!" she shouted. "Help!"

Footsteps thundered down the stairs.

"That's him!" Matt yelled. "He has a gun!"

Denny clamped his hand across Bonnie's mouth and held her arms behind her so that it looked as if he still had the gun pressed to her back.

"Stop where you are," Denny said, "or the girl won't leave this boat alive."

The ferry workers and passengers who had followed Matt down the stairs stopped. For a moment no one moved or spoke.

"Who are you?" a man asked. "What do you want?"

Bonnie heard Denny's rapid breathing, smelled his fear, felt his fingers pressing against her lips.

"He's going to shoot her," Matt sobbed. "He's going to kill my sister!"

Bonnie forced her mouth open as wide as she could, then bit down hard on Denny's middle finger.

"Hey!" he said, and moved his hand just enough that Bonnie could speak.

"The gun's gone!" she yelled. "I threw it overboard!"

The adults surged forward, quickly overpowered Denny, and dragged him away from Bonnie. Two ferry workers pushed him facedown on the deck, then held his arms behind his back as the others reached for Bonnie.

Several voices spoke at once.

"Are you all right?"

"Did he hurt you?"

"Do you need a doctor?"

"I'm okay," she said, but her knees shook as she was led upstairs.

Bonnie and Matt were taken to a room marked PRIVATE. CREW ONLY. There they told the ferry captain and other workers what had happened.

The captain notified police on Bainbridge Island. "The police will board the ferry as soon as we dock," he told the children, "and take Denny Thurman into custody."

Next he let Bonnie call her mother.

"Hi, Mom," Bonnie said. "I'm okay, and so is Matt. We'll be home soon." Her mother, of course, had a hundred questions, so the conversation took a while. Then Matt wanted a turn to talk. By the time they finished, the ferry was docking.

No passengers or vehicles were allowed to leave until the police had boarded. A few minutes later Bonnie and Matt saw Denny get led to a waiting police car, his wrists handcuffed behind him.

Tears of relief trickled down Bonnie's cheeks as she watched. At last, the ordeal was over.

As the police car drove away, Matt said, "I always

thought it would be cool if my dad showed up, but it wasn't. I don't like him. He's a mean, rotten pickle-puss, and I wish I didn't have a dad."

Bonnie put an arm around Matt's shoulder. She'd spent years feeling cheated because her dad was gone, but she knew she was luckier than Matt. Her father was dead, but she had memories of a kind man, an honorable man who died a hero.

Matt would remember Denny.

Hard as it was to be without her dad, Bonnie still had pride in him. Matt would never have that.

"When you grow up," she told Matt, "you'll be a good man. You won't be anything like Denny."

"How do you know?"

"Because you're a good kid now. How you act is way more important than who your parents are."

"I'll act like Mom," Matt said, "and you."

A police boat docked next to the ferry, and two officers came aboard for Bonnie and Matt. "You get a private boat ride back to Seattle," one of them said. "It will be faster, and you can tell us what happened while we travel."

Officer Calvin met them in Seattle and drove them home while they told their story again.

A crowd of reporters and neighbors had gathered to welcome them. When Bonnie and Matt got out of the squad car, a cheer went up. Mrs. Sholter ran to greet them, followed by their grandparents, Detective Morrison, and Pookie. Pookie yipped and ran in circles around Matt.

Officer Calvin gave a statement to the reporters. Matt was declared a hero for bonking Denny with the baseball, and Bonnie was credited with being the brains behind the scheme.

Before they all went inside, Bonnie and Matt answered questions from the press and posed for more pictures.

One of the ferry workers had retrieved the Mariners ball for Matt, and he clutched it happily, demonstrating to the reporters exactly how he'd held it and how he wound up to throw his "zinger."

CHAPTER 23

Matt and Bonnie's safe return topped the news on every local channel Saturday night. Throughout the Northwest, television sets showed the missing boy and his sister reunited with their mother.

Bonnie, Matt, their mom, and their grandparents watched the reports together while they ate the macaroni-and-cheese that Stanley's dad had brought a week earlier. Mrs. Sholter had taken it out of the freezer as soon as she learned Matt and Bonnie were safe.

Pookie snoozed through the broadcast, even the part about him.

In a downtown apartment, Miss Clueless took off her banner, her red evening gown, and her high heels.

Wearing her comfy flannel bathrobe, she munched on salted peanuts as she turned on the TV.

Her jaw dropped in disbelief when she saw Denny in handcuffs being led from a squad car to the police station. That was the cranky man with the kids who had used the bathroom at the restaurant!

She stared at the TV screen, remembering how restless and angry the man had been, and how he'd rushed out of the restaurant when he learned his kids weren't in the bathroom.

A chill went up her arms as she recalled the red-haired woman who had reported the writing on the mirror. She had shrugged the woman off, positive the message was written by someone trying to send the other guests down the wrong path.

She tried to think exactly what the message had said. At the time she had only paid attention to removing it, not to the words themselves.

There had been names: Bonnie and Matt and Denny—the same names now being mentioned on the news.

Guilt spoiled Miss Clueless's appetite as she remembered her actions. She set down the dish of peanuts. Those poor children! They might have been killed because of her.

Across Lake Washington, a woman in Bellevue saw

the news, grabbed the phone, and dialed her friend. "Shelly!" she said, when the friend answered. "That girl in the bathroom who asked us to help her wasn't an actress!"

"What?" the friend said. "How do you know?"

"Turn on your TV," the woman said. "The girl had been abducted at gunpoint! Her brother, too!"

"You're kidding," said Shelly.

"I wish I were."

South of Seattle, in Kent, Eddie Gilden, the teenage driver who had stopped to talk to Bonnie and Matt, was eating lemon pie with his parents when he saw the reports.

Those kids in the street were telling the truth, Eddie realized. I could have saved them, but I drove off and left them with their kidnapper.

Eddie put down his fork, remembering how the girl had begged him to help. He and his pals had debated whether to look for a police officer and tell what had happened. "I don't think we should get involved," Eddie had said.

"Neither do I," the boy in back said. "That guy looked mean. He might remember your license plate and track you down."

"If he's mean," the third boy said, "maybe the girl

gave us the straight story. We should tell the cops about those kids and let them decide what to do."

In the end, the three boys drove home without disclosing the incident to anyone.

As he watched the news report, Eddie said nothing to his parents. He couldn't bring himself to call the other boys who had been in his car, to see if they'd seen the news. If he avoided them for a few days, maybe nobody would mention the two children who had pleaded for a ride.

The ticket seller at the ferry terminal was driving home from work when she heard the news on the radio. She gasped when she heard Bonnie's voice describing what had happened on the ferry. The girl said she'd tried to alert the ticket person, but the woman didn't understand.

That isn't true, the woman thought. I knew exactly what the girl meant, making her fingers into a pretend gun and all, but I didn't think it was for real.

She had watched the man and the two kids walk away; nothing in their manner seemed out of the ordinary. The man even put his arm around the girl's shoulder, like a loving father. She considered dialing 911, but then other customers came to buy tickets, and by the time she had a free moment again, she had con-

211

vinced herself that the girl had merely been playing a joke. She never made the call.

With a lump in her throat, she listened to the rest of the radio report. Those children needed my help, she thought, and I turned away.

In their tidy home near Pine Lake, Ruth and Fred Faulkner cheered when they heard Matt and Bonnie were both safely home. They cheered again when the news coverage showed Matt running to his mother's arms. They cheered even louder when the camera zoomed in on Matt hugging Pookie.

"There's Monty!" Fred said.

"Oh, he looks so happy," Ruth said. "See how his tail is wagging? He's glad to see that boy again." She wiped tears from her cheeks.

Detective Morrison went off duty and got home in time to watch the ten o'clock news with her husband. She missed part of what Bonnie said because Spike, who was also off duty, kept playing with his loudest squeaky toy. Detective Morrison didn't mind. She'd heard it all in person and she figured Spike deserved some playtime.

One reporter interviewed the kidnapper's sister. Detective Morrison held Spike's toy so she could hear that part.

"I didn't know Denny had a child," Celia said. "He

never told me. He's mentally unstable and blames others for all his troubles. I've tried to get him into treatment, but he would never go. I apologize to the Sholter family for my brother's behavior."

"Apologies aren't going to be enough," Detective Morrison said. "The prosecutor will throw the book at Denny Thurman."

"Woof!" said Spike, and got his toy back.

The next afternoon, Mrs. Sholter baked three loaves of her special banana bread and took them to the police station where Detective Morrison and Officer Calvin worked.

"Here's a treat for all the officers who helped me get my children back safely," she said. She also took a large rawhide bone for Spike.

At two o'clock, the teachers from Jefferson School joyfully hit the streets, taking down the MATT IS MISSING posters.

Fred and Ruth Faulkner drove to the humane society Sunday afternoon. Faces aglow, they announced, "We're here to adopt a dog."

They didn't get one, though. They got two. When they found two older dogs who had lived together since they were puppies, Ruth and Fred couldn't bear to split them up.

"Old dogs are harder to place," a humane society worker told them. "Everyone wants a cute little puppy."

"Nothing wrong with getting old," Fred said.

"We'll each have a dog to walk," Ruth said. "It'll be good for our arthritis."

"That's right," Fred agreed, "and we'll never sit around getting bored with ourselves."

Matt and Bonnie spent Sunday afternoon playing cards with their grandparents and talking about their adventure to the many friends who called or stopped over.

"I shouldn't have believed Denny," Matt told Stanley. "Even after I saw Pookie in his car, I should have run back to class and told Mrs. Jules what Denny said."

"Bad guys lie," Stanley said.

"I should have screamed my head off," Matt said.

After the visitors left, Grandma and Grandpa decided to pack for their flight home the next day.

When Bonnie asked Matt if he wanted to practice his pitching, his smile would have lit up Safeco Field.

Bonnie crouched next to the garage and caught the balls Matt threw to her. After a few warm-up tosses, she called, "Give me a zinger!"

The two children grinned at each other. They both knew that for the rest of their lives, the word *zinger* would be a special bond between them.

How could I ever have wished for a sister instead of Matt? Bonnie wondered as the fastball streaked into her glove. She decided to buy him a "welcome home" present—a whole quart of strawberry ice cream, all for Matt.

On Monday in PE, Nancy said, "Last night I dreamed I jumped on a magical trampoline and bounced through a hole in the clouds. I think it means my life is dull and I'm searching for excitement."

"I think it means you should write fiction," Bonnie said. "Nobody has dreams like yours."

This time, talk of dreams didn't bother Bonnie. With her brother safe, she had slept soundly Saturday night and again Sunday night.

"Do you want to go to the mall with me and Sharon after school?" Nancy asked.

"I can't," Bonnie said. "Mom went back to work today, so I have to go home."

"Lucky you."

Yes, Bonnie thought. Lucky me. I get to ride the bus home with my brother, and pet Pookie, and catch the baseball while Matt practices his pitching.

She could hardly wait for two thirty-six.

Pulaski County Public Library
121 S. Riverside Drive
Winamac, IN 46996
574-946-3432

THE DESIGN OF INSTRUCTION AND EVALUATION

Affordances of Using Media and Technology

Edited by

Mitchell Rabinowitz
Fran C. Blumberg
Fordham University

Howard T. Everson
The College Board

GOVERNORS STATE UNIVERSITY
UNIVERSITY PARK
IL 60466

 LAWRENCE ERLBAUM ASSOCIATES, PUBLISHERS
2004   Mahwah, New Jersey   London

LB 1028.38 .D47 2004

The design of instruction
and evaluation

Copyright © 2004 by Lawrence Erlbaum Associates, Inc.
All rights reserved. No part of this book may be reproduced in
any form, by photostat, microform, retrieval system, or any other
means, without the prior written permission of the publisher.

Lawrence Erlbaum Associates, Inc., Publishers
10 Industrial Avenue
Mahwah, New Jersey 07430

Cover design by Kathryn Houghtaling Lacey

Library of Congress Cataloging-in-Publication Data

The design of instruction and evaluation : affordances of using media and technology / edited by
Mitchell Rabinowitz, Fran C. Blumberg, and Howard T. Everson.
   p. cm.
  Includes bibliographical references and index.
  ISBN 0-8058-3762-0 (cloth : alk. paper) — ISBN 0-8058-3763-9 (pbk. : alk. paper)
   1. Instructional systems—Design. 2. Learning, Psychology of. 3. Educational technology.
 I. Rabinowitz, Mitchell. II. Blumberg, Fran. III. Everson, Howard T.

LB1028.38D47 2004

        2004043288
          CIP

Books published by Lawrence Erlbaum Associates are printed on acid-free paper,
and their bindings are chosen for strength and durability.

Printed in the United States of America
10 9 8 7 6 5 4 3 2 1

Contents

Part III   Affordances of Software

INTRODUCTION:
The Design of Instruction and Evaluation: Psychological Foundations

Mitchell Rabinowitz

This book is about the design of instructional and evaluation systems and the use and promise of media and technology within such systems. Successful design is a consequence of an interaction between art and science. Artistically, there are ways to present information that are pleasing and engaging. However, the artist might design a system that looks good, but does not work. In his book, *The Design of Everyday Things*, Norman (1988) presented a number of really interesting manufacturing designs that do not work (the contexts illustrated in that book are not instructional ones). Scientifically, I argue, there is a body of knowledge and principles that have been empirically tested that informs the design of instructional systems. However, the scientist might design instruction that should work, but is boring to interact with. Each is enhanced by the other. The chapters in this book are related more to the science than the art side, and they discuss and provide examples of some of these knowledge bases and principles that are relevant to the design issue.

In 1993, I edited a book entitled *Cognitive Science Foundations of Instruction* (Rabinowitz, 1993), which was also related to the topic of the design of instructional and evaluation systems. The premise of that book was that the study of psychology provides the scientific underpinnings of successful design that improves learning. In this book, we continue with that premise. However, the psychological perspective presented within this volume significantly differs from that presented in the earlier volume given the developments and advancements within the field of psychology.

In this Introduction, I briefly overview three different perspectives on how psychology should inform the design of instructional and evaluation systems: the behavioral, cognitive, and affordances perspectives. I do not present these perspectives as alternatives. Rather, I suggest they represent a development process in the advancement of knowledge and understanding. The cognitive perspective represents an advancement from the behavioral, and the affordances perspective represents an advancement over the cognitive perspective. Although not necessarily accepting the premises of the preceding, each still builds on the foundation already developed.

PSYCHOLOGICAL FOUNDATIONS

The Behavioral Perspective

The behavioral perspective emphasized the role of the environment in determining behavior. The basic assumption was that people (and other animals) learned to respond to environmental input in certain ways on the basis of contiguity and reinforcement (Hulse, Deese, & Egeth, 1975). This perspective posits a causal connection involving events in the environment, activity in the mind, and ultimately behavior (Flanagan, 1991). The behavioral assertion is that an event in the environment *causes* something to happen in the mind, which then *causes* some behavior to occur—If A, then B, and then C. If the contiguity of these events occur regularly or lead to positive consequences, an association among A, B, and C is formed. The implication of this assertion is that if you knew or controlled A and an individual's learning history, you could predict or create C. To manipulate behavior (learning, in this context), there was no reason to investigate B or the mind. The behavioral perspective never suggested that the mind was not part of the equation—just that you did not need to study it to predict or manipulate behavior. Thus, the mind became a *black box* in which information went in and behavior came out; what occurred in the black box was irrelevant. The primary emphasis was the relation between the environment and behavior. Thus, designers of instructional systems who adopted this perspective paid attention to setting up the environment and manipulating the consequences of different behavioral responses. The designs of teaching machines, programmed instruction, and behavior modification were a direct result of this orientation (Glaser, 1976; Skinner, 1968).

The Cognitive Perspective

Historically, the emphasis on cognitive processing arose as a reaction to the behaviorist dogma, which emphasized the prominent role of the environment in determining behavior. Although there was extensive empirical evidence showing that people learned to respond to the environment, research also showed that the assumptions underlying the behavioral model were incorrect and that the model could only predict and account for a limited amount of behavior (Gardner, 1985). These studies showed that people did not respond in a direct causal way to that environment—they responded to their representation or perception of the environment. Hence, it was necessary to study how the mind processed information and the processing constraints the mind impose. Consequently, we had the cognitive revolution and the development of information-processing models of learning.

The consequence of adopting this cognitive perspective was the development of instructional programs on the use of cognitive strategies. As Perkins and Grotzer (1997) stated, ". . . we often do not use our minds as well as it appears we could" (p. 1125). These programs were very successful (e.g., Pressley & Woloshyn, 1995). The chapters in the Rabinowitz (1993) edition were also written with this perspective in mind and illustrate a number of successful implementations of this perspective.

The contrast between the behavioral and cognitive perspectives can be seen as a contrast between external and internal influences, in relation to the learner, on learning and performance. Whereas the behavioral approach emphasized the role of the environment (external to the individual) in determining behavior, the cognitive approach represented an advancement over the behavioral approach—it was not just an alternative that was deemed to be more appropriate. Specifically, the latter incorporated many ideas and empirical data from the behavioral research and added the mind into the equations. The cognitive approach clearly emphasized the role of information processing (internal to the individual) in determining behavior.

Bringing Back the Environment— The Affordance Approach

I guess I have learned—during the intervening 10 years from the publication of my first book to this current book—that the definition of cognition offered earlier (the study of the mind) is too limiting. Cognitive psychology is not just the study of the mind—it is the study of the mind in interaction with the environment. One of the basic premises of the cognitive approach is that behavior is explained and manipulated by understanding how information is processed. Information can be defined in reference to knowledge and/or representation (internal to the person) or it can be defined in terms of the affordances within the environment (external to the person). Both sources of information—in combination and interaction—contribute to understanding learning and behavior.

The term *affordances* was first introduced by J. J. Gibson (1977). Gibson defined affordances to mean features offered to the individual by the environment. Affordances exist relative to the capabilities of an individual—independent of the person's ability to perceive it and independent of the person's goals. The construct of affordances was later introduced by Norman (1988) to the manufacturing design community. As illustrated in the chapters within this book, the construct of affordances is now part of the instructional design community.

The affordances approach, like the behavioral approach, clearly emphasizes the role of the environment and factors external to the individual. However, the environment is presented in different ways in the two approaches. In the behavioral approach, the environment is there for the person to react to and receive feedback from. The environment does not necessarily constrain or determine a response, but rather offers the opportunity to the individual to respond. In the affordances approach, it is presented as something that constrains or determines processing. It interacts and has a causal impact on the individual's processing capabilities. Once again, I perceive the addition of considering the affordances of the environment, in interaction with the cognitive processes of the individual, to be an advancement and evolution within the cognitive approach—not an alternative to it. The chapters in this book illustrate this perspective.

OVERVIEW OF THIS VOLUME

Affordances of Media

The first few chapters in the book start out by discussing the affordances of media and how, when, and why to use media as a component of instructional systems. In chapter 1, Fisch compares and contrasts the affordances and demands of three different types of media: TV, magazines, and interactive computer software. When should each be used? For what populations? For what purposes? Does each have the affordances to be equally effective in varying circumstances? Fisch suggests that there are both similarities and differences among the different types. As a consequence, the use of each type assumes certain competencies on the part of the user. For example, using magazines assumes that someone knows how to read; relying on TV does not. The different media also afford different types of interactions and lead to different types of activities and cognitive processing. Fisch argues that an understanding of the features of each of these types of media and how they interact with the cognitive capabilities of the audience or user is essential to develop effective instructional media.

In chapter 2, Calvert takes a similar perspective, but limits her analysis to audiovisual media; the type of media often viewed on TV, films, and, more and more, in computer software and on the Web. What are the formal features or forms that direct the audiences' attention? That signal importance? That enhance memory and comprehension? Calvert presents an extensive analysis of these features as well as data that address how these features interact with the viewers' cognitive processing. Calvert argues that knowledge of these features and their consequences are essential for developing effective educational TV.

In chapter 3, Mayer takes a similar tack when looking at the design of multimedia—specifically, the combination of pictures and words. What are the consequences of different presentations of multimedia? Mayer presents some basic principles for the design of multimedia after investigating and presenting how different features of the presentation interact with the cognitive resources and processes of the learner.

Affordances of Technology

In the next set of chapters, we move on to discuss the affordances of technology—computers and the Internet. As is discussed, computers offer a wide range of affordances, but one does not have to do with the features of the computer, but rather the affordances of the activity of using the computer. Computers afford a motivational effect; students seem to enjoy interacting with them. In chapter 4, Guavain and Borthwick-Duffy look at the opportunities for learning and development that occur as a consequence of participation in an after-school computer club for elementary school children. They were interested in looking at the relations between cognitive processing and the sociocultural settings. They look at the constraints and enabling aspects of this informal learning environment on the development of computer skills.

In chapter 5, Kafai, Ching, and Marshall look at the affordances of a specific activity—collaborative software design on the engagement within the learning process and the learning outcomes. They address the hypothesis that learning within project-based contexts provides students with rich learning experiences and affords different opportunities for collaboration. It is not absolutely necessary to use a computer to investigate this, but the use of the computer affords the opportunity to engage in specific types of projects. The authors present a "software design project," where fourth and fifth graders are asked to create instructional software to teach astronomy. They examine the relationships between the student's individual contributions to this collaborative effort and the consequent learning of science, programming, and planning skills.

In chapter 6, Bennett discusses the affordances that the Internet offers toward the design of high-stakes evaluation tests such as the SAT. He presents a presentation of the features of the Internet and then asks, what do these feature afford for the development of assessment? He suggests "the *potential* to deliver efficiently on a mass scale individualized, highly engaging content to almost any desktop; get data back immediately; process it; and make information available anywhere in the world, anytime day or night." He discusses the consequences of these affordances throughout the chapter.

The final chapter in this grouping is chapter 7, by Fletcher. Fletcher actually discusses the affordances of the computer and how it influences software design and the development of instructional media. He discusses the potential of computers to interact individually with users, give individual feedback, and enhance dialogue and feedback, to name just a few. He discusses the potential of the computer to enhance instruction by paying attention to these features and presents data on the efficacy of computer-based instruction.

Affordances of Software

The chapter by Fletcher actually presents a very effective bridge to the next set of chapters—that is, the use of specific software. In chapter 8, Blumberg, Torenberg, and Sokol look at the features and affordances of computer-mediated communication software and the consequent effects on classroom activity and learning. These communication systems allow for the development of asynchronous learning contexts—anytime, anywhere. Blumberg et al. present an analysis of how this software was used with graduate-level courses and the resulting consequences on the academic interactions among the students and teachers.

The last two chapters—chapter 9, by DiPaolo et al. and chapter 10 by Everson—are both about the development and implementation of intelligent computer tutoring systems. DiPaolo et al. investigate the use of hints within tutoring systems. To accomplish this, they analyze the features of different types of hints, the features of the subject matter, and features of the software. Everson addresses the importance of developing accurate models of students' knowledge within computerized tutoring systems. One of the interesting things about these two chapters, however, is that although they present that the ultimate goal of this work is the improvement of student learning, their immediate goals are the designs of the tutoring systems. The interesting implication of looking at the development of the design of the systems is that the authors have to address the affordances of the learners; they need to analyze how students perceive, understand, and react to the system and integrate theses affordances into the design. In this instance, the student is the external factor, and the processing of the tutor represents the internal factors.

CONCLUDING COMMENTS

I set out in this Introduction to distinguish among three perspectives on the psychological foundations underlying instructional and evaluation design—the behavioral, cognitive, and affordances perspectives. The behavioral perspective emphasized the role of the environment in influencing learning—a factor external to the learner. The cognitive perspective emphasized the role of cognitive processing and constraints in determining learning—factors that are internal to the learner. I present that the affordances perspective is an advancement over both; it addresses how the environment and affordances within interact with the cognitive learner and the affordances within to determine learning. The chapters in this book present insights into this interaction.

References

Flanagan, O. (1991). *The science of the mind*. Cambridge, MA: MIT Press.

Gardner, H. (1985). *The mind's new science: A history of the cognitive revolution*. New York: Basic Books.

Gibson, J. J. (1977). The theory of affordances. In R. E. Shaw & J. Bransford (Eds.), *Perceiving, acting, and knowing*. Hillsdale, NJ: Lawrence Erlbaum Associates.

Glaser, R. (1976). Components of a psychology of instruction: Toward a science of design. *Review of Educational Research, 46*, 1–24.

Hulse, S. H., Deese, J., & Egeth, H. (1975). *The psychology of learning*. New York: McGraw-Hill.

Norman, D. A. (1988). *The design of everyday things*. New York: Basic Books.

Perkins, D. N., & Grotzer, T. A. (1997). Teaching intelligence. *American Psychologist, 52*(10), 1125–1133.

Pressley, M., & Woloshyn, V. (1995). *Cognitive strategy instruction that really improves children's academic performance*. Cambridge, MA: Brookline Books.

Rabinowitz, M. (Ed.). (1993). *Cognitive science foundations of instruction*. Hillsdale, NJ: Lawrence Erlbaum Associates.

Skinner, B. F. (1968). *The technology of teaching*. New York: Appleton-Century-Crofts.

I

Affordances
of Media

1

Characteristics of Effective Materials for Informal Education: A Cross-Media Comparison of Television, Magazines, and Interactive Media

Shalom M. Fisch
MediaKidz Research & Consulting

The past 10 to 15 years have seen an explosion in the availability of commercially produced informal education materials for preschool and school-age children. Pioneering educational television series such as *Sesame Street* and *The Electric Company* have been followed by television programs on subjects such as mathematics, science, literacy, and history. At the same time, the children's magazine business has expanded. For example, by the late 1990s, children interested in science could choose among magazines such as *Contact Kids*, *Owl*, *Discovery Kids*, and *National Geographic for Kids* on a monthly basis. Dozens of educational CD-ROMs and electronic toys are now available for a broad range of age groups, including product lines such as *Jump Start*, *Reader Rabbit*, and *Leap Frog* that include materials for both preschool and school-age children. The rapid growth of the World Wide Web provides immediate access to an even greater pool of resources.

There are many reasons for this expansion of educational media. One of the most important, certainly, lies in the rapid technological advances that have led to the growing availability of VCRs, cable TV, home computers, and the Internet. Another lies in governmental legislation and initiatives, such as the provision of government funds for making computer technology accessible in schools and libraries, or the Federal Communications Commission's (FCC's) 1996 decision to strengthen the Children's Television Act of 1990 by requiring television broadcasters to air at least 3 hours of programming designed for children per week (e.g., Schmitt, 1999). Still another lies in commercial realities; the youth market has become big business in recent years, and the financial success of properties such as *Barney & Friends* has encouraged numerous producers to enter the field of educational media.

3

Whatever the explanation, however, the net result is that, whereas the biggest issue in using educational media once lay in finding appropriate media in the first place, a greater issue today lies in choosing among the available options. For creators of educational media, this issue is manifest in identifying characteristics to build into their materials so as to make them maximally effective. For adult users of educational media (e.g., parents, teachers), there is a parallel concern: finding standards by which to identify and select the materials that will be most beneficial for their children.

Various attempts have been made to address these needs for producers, researchers, parents, and teachers. It is interesting to note, however, that in most cases each attempt has focused on only a single medium with little or no reference to others. For example, Flagg's (1990) excellent book on formative research for educational technology makes virtually no mention of print, and an equally fine volume on formative research for interactive media (Druin, 1999) does not draw explicitly on the large body of research on educational television that has been built over the past 30 years.

To some degree, of course, this can be attributed to the fact that each new medium presents its own particular issues, challenges, and constraints. Yet I would argue that there are at least as many commonalities across educational media as there are differences, and the lessons learned in one medium can often be applied to others as well. To best understand this point, it may be helpful to distinguish between what I refer to as *format issues* and *content issues*. Format issues grow out of the nature of users' interaction with a particular medium and the requirements/constraints inherent in that use. For example, pacing can be seen as a format issue because reading is self-paced, but viewing a television program (in the absence of a VCR) is not. In contrast, content issues pertain to users' interaction with a particular type of content independent of the medium by which it is delivered. For example, the factors that determine the difficulty of a question in a mathematics game are likely to be similar regardless of whether the game is presented via print, a CD-ROM, or a television game show. Broadly stated, commonalities across educational media frequently pertain to content issues, whereas differences more often lie in format issues (although there are, of course, exceptions to this rule).

This chapter reviews research on several forms of media intended for use in informal education outside of school: television, magazines, and interactive software (including online). The focus is on characteristics of these media that have been shown to contribute to their effectiveness, with an eye toward both commonalities and differences across media.

DIFFERENCES ACROSS MEDIA: FORMAT ISSUES

Even when a particular educational subject or message is similar across different media, some of the factors that contribute to the effectiveness of that educational content will nevertheless differ as a function of the medium by which it is delivered. Each medium carries its own strengths and weaknesses, and each presents its own constraints on the ways in which educational content can be conveyed. These types of issues pertain to format rather than content, and they can be conceptualized as relating to either the prerequisites for users' interaction with a particular medium or the factors that make the material accessible to or usable by its target audience.

Nature of the Interaction

Literacy. One of the most intuitively obvious factors of this type is the degree to which the medium requires users to be able to read. Clearly, if children cannot read (or do not have the assistance of someone who can), their ability to access the information in a printed magazine is severely impaired (cf. Cherow-O'Leary, 2001). However, even preliterate children typically can access most or all of the information in an age-appropriate, educational television program.

Interestingly, even within the domain of interactive media, the degree to which literacy is required can vary between interactive materials delivered via a CD-ROM versus materials delivered online. Often, much of the instruction necessary for engaging in a game or activity in an educational CD-ROM (particularly one designed for young children) is presented in the form of verbal instructions that are spoken by a narrator or on-screen character. Yet, as Revelle, Strommen, and Medoff (2001) observed, the situation is different for interactive materials delivered online. Online sound files can take considerable amounts of time to download, which can discourage use of the materials. For this reason, rather than relying heavily on spoken dialogue, designers of online materials often rely much more heavily on written text (which can be downloaded relatively quickly) to deliver instructions and information. Thus, the ability to read (or the presence of an accompanying reader) can be a stronger prerequisite for the use of online materials than for a CD-ROM.

Need for Parental or Adult Involvement. A related point is the degree to which adult involvement is needed for various educational media to be used effectively. In dealing with young children, literacy again becomes an important consideration here. For example, pre-readers require the involvement of an adult or older skilled reader to gain the full benefit of a magazine. Indeed, one survey of 2,000 families that subscribed to *Sesame Street Magazine* found that, on average, parents and children spent between 1 and 1.7 hours reading each issue of the magazine together (CTW Magazine Research Department, 1993). Similarly, the *Sesame Street*-based games and activities on the SesameStreet.com Web site (www.sesamestreet.com) also have been designed for joint use by preschool children and their parents, who can read the directions and guide their children through the activities (Revelle et al., 2001). In these media, one of the major roles played by adults is simply to make the educational content accessible to children in the first place.

By contrast, although there are also benefits to be gained from children's joint viewing of educational television with their parents (e.g., Reiser, Tessmer, & Phelps, 1984; Reiser, Williamson, & Suzuki, 1988; Salomon, 1977), the benefits to be had from these media are not as absolutely dependent on parental involvement. Children can also learn important skills and information from viewing educational television programs by themselves; the role of the adults in this case is not so much to make the educational content accessible to children as it is to enrich it, elaborate on it, and extend the learning after the children have turned off the television.

Pacing, Advancement, and Review.   A third major difference among educational media lies in the fact that, unlike print or interactive media, broadcast television is not self-paced. Readers can choose to slow down their reading when they encounter a difficult passage of text, and users of interactive software can spend as much or as little time as they wish on a particular game or activity. However, viewers of broadcast television cannot control the speed of the incoming information. Instead the processing that underlies viewers' comprehension of television must be employed in such a way as to fit the pace of the television program (Eckhardt, Wood, & Jacobvitz, 1991; Fisch, 2000).

Similarly, when children fail to comprehend a piece of information, different media lend themselves more or less easily to "repair strategies" that might correct the problem. For example, research on text comprehension has shown that readers routinely re-read material that they have difficulty understanding (Pace, 1980, 1981). Such review is not possible when watching a program on broadcast television (although it is more possible in watching a videotape on a VCR).

Thus, in some ways, the cognitive demands of processing and comprehending educational material on television may be greater than those for other media. As a result, although it is important for educational content in any medium to be presented clearly and in an age-appropriate way, this may be particularly important in comprehension of content that is televised.

Conversely, the consequences of failing to understand a portion of an activity on a computer can be more serious than those of failing to understand every moment of a television program. If a viewer fails to understand a particular piece of a television show, the show will continue nevertheless, and there is a fair chance that he or she will still be able to understand and benefit from other parts of the show. (Similarly, readers who encounter a difficult word or section of a text can skip over that section to continue reading the subsequent material.) Yet, because progress through an interactive computer activity is dependent on user input, a failure to understand a portion of an interactive activity can result in users' being unable to advance through the remainder of the activity (Revelle et al., 2001; Schauble, 1990).

Usability. Following from the prior point is the critical role of usability issues in the design and use of interactive materials. As Shneiderman (1998) observed, the earliest pieces of computer software were designed by technically oriented programmers for use by their peers. Today's users, however, tend not to be as technically fluent or as dedicated to the technology. As a result, for interactive material to be usable by a broad audience, interfaces must be designed to be as simple, transparent, and intuitively obvious as possible.

Because of the ubiquity of print and television, usability issues do not generally pose obstacles to the use of these media. From an early age, children typically know how to operate a television or turn pages in a book even if they cannot read the text themselves. By contrast, usability issues emerge in numerous aspects of interactive activities. Navigation icons must be clear, consistent, and intuitive (Hanna, Risden, Czerwinski, & Alexander, 1999; Strommen & Revelle, 1990; Wilson & Talley, 1990). "Hot spots" (i.e., clickable parts of the screen) must be large enough and set far enough apart for users to click easily on the options they desire, and they must be signaled in some way (e.g., via rollover animation or audio that is activated as the cursor passes over the hot spot) so that users know where to click (Hanna et al., 1999; Strommen & Revelle, 1990). Even the control devices that are used to operate the computers on which these activities run (e.g., a mouse or track ball) pose usability issues, particularly in the case of materials designed for young children who may not yet have the eye-hand coordination necessary for using some of these devices (Strommen & Revelle, 1990; Wilson & Talley, 1990). Such issues pose a host of concerns for designers of interactive materials that need not be considered by designers of educational materials in other media. If these issues are not resolved adequately, they can also impair the effectiveness of the materials for their users.

Authoring. Much of the previous discussion about interactive materials is framed primarily in terms of software that presents children with relatively closed-ended or goal-directed activities, such as educational games that set clear-cut goals and challenges for users. Apart from these types of activities, some interactive software for children is intended to serve less as directed experiences than as open-ended authoring tools—that is, tools children can use to create their own multimedia presentations and interactive experiences, using elements such as text, sound, animation, and video. For example, software packages such as *Kid Pix Studio* or the *Elmo's World* CD-ROM are designed for use by young children and include not only drawing tools, but also the ability for children to animate the drawings they have created. Authoring tools provide the opportunity for learning by designing—an example of what Papert (e.g., 1996) termed *constructionist learning*.

Of course, the notion of authoring is not unique to interactive media; it is as old as handing a child a pencil and a blank sheet of paper. However, although media such as broadcast television can encourage viewer participation during a program (e.g., Anderson et al., 2000; Fisch & McCann, 1993), this is a far cry from giving children the ability to create enduring multimedia projects of their own. Print-based media such as magazines can encourage analogous authoring behavior (e.g., by inviting readers to submit drawings or make up stories of their own), yet interactive authoring tools provide children with the opportunity to incorporate a broader range of media in their creations. These multimedia capabilities have the potential to accommodate a wider range of learning styles because they allow greater latitude for children to create in media that suit their individual inclinations, be it text, pictures, music, video, or something else. In addition, children's ability to "bring their creations to life" through sound, animation, and/or video can provide powerful motivation toward engaging in the process of authoring and an equally powerful reward for its completion.

Like other interactive software, authoring tools pose issues of usability, literacy, and need for adult involvement. After all, if it is too difficult for children to use the tools, they will not be successful in translating their ideas into reality.

Beyond these points, however, Druin and Solomon (1996) have argued that, for users to use multimedia authoring tools to their fullest potential, they must also appreciate the full range of what the tools can accomplish. To this end, Druin and Solomon propose that children be presented with models or examples of what is possible for children—and even expert adults—to create with a given authoring tool. Doing so can expand the horizons within which children conceive of ideas to pursue with the tool and lead them to set different goals for their projects. The result may be a richer project than the child would have produced otherwise, and one that might fit more naturally with his or her preferred mode of expression.

Indeed, to the degree that adult involvement is necessary for children to use a particular authoring tool, similar support is likely to be needed for the adults as well. Adults who were not raised with such technology may fail to realize its potential themselves, and may guide children toward employing an authoring tool in only limited ways. By helping parents or teachers understand the true parameters of what can be done, these adults can then encourage children to use it more fully.

COMMONALITIES ACROSS MEDIA: CONTENT ISSUES

Although the issues involved in educational media certainly differ in the ways discussed earlier, these media share many common issues as well. To find them, we must look beyond the surface-level format issues stemming from children's interaction with each individual medium to issues concerning the content that can be carried in all of them. In this respect, many of the characteristics that contribute to the effectiveness of informal educational media apply equally well across a variety of media.

Appeal

Because children's use of informal educational media is frequently voluntary (e.g., choosing to watch an educational television program or read a magazine), appeal becomes a critical issue in determining educational effectiveness across media. After all, if children do not find such activities appealing, they will simply choose not to engage in them, thus eliminating any potential educational benefit of the activities. Appeal is crucial in attracting children's attention to the material and in sustaining attention throughout use.

The appeal of a successful media product is often the result of an idiosyncratic blend of elements that unite to become greater than the sum of their parts; the chemistry that comes together to result in a highly appealing product is difficult to define. Nevertheless, research on children's interaction with television (and, to a lesser extent, other media) has pointed to several broad factors that can play a role in determining appeal. Let us consider each of these factors in turn.

Humor. Humor has been shown repeatedly to contribute to the appeal of educational (and noneducational) television programs, magazines, and interactive products among preschool and school-age children (e.g., Bryant, Zillmann, & Brown, 1983; CTW Program Research Online Team, 1998; Druin & Solomon, 1996; Fisch, Cohen, McCann, & Hoffman, 1993; Lesser, 1972, 1974; Link & Cherow-O'Leary, 1990; McGhee, 1980; Valkenburg & Janssen, 1999; Zillmann, Williams, Bryant, Boynton, & Wolf, 1980). Yet, for humor to be successful in promoting appeal, children in the target audience must find the intended humor to be funny, rather than over their heads, "babyish," or "corny."

Children's appreciation of various types of humor is affected by their age and developmental level. Early formative research conducted in support of the *Sesame Street* television series, for example, found that preschool children consistently enjoyed certain types of humor (e.g., incongruity and surprise, slapstick, adult errors, silly wordplay), but not more sophisticated forms of humor, such as puns that required viewers to appreciate the double meanings of words (Lesser, 1974). These results were subsequently replicated in a different medium through research on *Sesame Street Magazine* and extended to an older population through research on the school-age magazines published by Sesame Workshop (formerly known as the "Children's Television Workshop"). Data from older children showed that: second-grade children were able to appreciate simple puns, fourth graders enjoyed humor that incorporated things that were familiar to them and understood the social context of humor (e.g., "put-downs"), and sixth graders were the most sophisticated and concerned about not appearing "silly" in front of their peers (Link & Cherow-O'Leary, 1990). Thus, designers of effective educational media must not only consider whether to include humor in their products, but also align the type of humor employed with the preferences and developmental level of the target age group they wish to reach.

Once the decision has been made to include humor in an educational product, designers must also consider the ways in which humor is interwoven with educational content. Specifically, the humor must be integrated in a way that draws users' attention toward the educational content and not away from it. This point is discussed in greater detail in the "Salience of Educational Content" section that follows.

Visual Action Versus Dialogue.   A second factor that has been seen repeatedly to contribute to the appeal of television programs is the inclusion of visual action, such as speeded-up motion, slapstick, or simply prominent activity or movement on the screen. Numerous studies have shown that both preschool and school-age children prefer television programs that feature visual action over lengthy "talking heads" scenes (i.e., static scenes centered around dialogue spoken among characters or directly to the camera; e.g., Lesser, 1974; National Institute of Mental Health, 1982; Valkenburg & Janssen, 1999).

Although less research has addressed this issue outside the realm of television, parallel effects have been found in other media as well. Wilsdon (1989) found that school-age children were attracted to magazine covers whose illustrations portrayed action. Similarly, Strommen and Revelle (1990) and Kafai (1999) have written of the importance of keeping written instructions and verbal dialogue brief (even briefer than in television) in interactive products for preschool and school-age children. Across media, then, it appears that the appeal of educational media products is likely to be greater if they avoid the use of lengthy dialogue or blocks of text. This point may be especially true for interactive software because children engaging in such activities usually want to act rather than watch as the dialogue unfolds (Strommen & Revelle, 1990).

Characters and Identification.   A third factor that can contribute to the appeal of a media product is its use of appealing characters. In numerous formative research studies, some children have pointed to appealing characters as reasons for liking television programs (e.g., Fisch et al., 1993; Valkenburg & Janssen, 1999; Williams et al., 1997), magazines (e.g., CTW Program Research School-Age Team, 1998), and interactive products (e.g., CTW Program Research, 1999a; Lieberman, 1999).

Among the traits that make characters appealing are viewers' perceptions of them as smart and/or helpful (e.g., CTW Program Research, 1999b; *The New Ghostwriter Mysteries* Research, 1997a, 1997b). In addition, children often enjoy seeing other children as characters on screen, particularly child characters who are a bit older than themselves. Appeal is also often greater when a character's gender or ethnicity matches that of the individual viewer (Fisch, Wilder, Yotive, & McCann, 1994).[1] Other key similarities between users and characters can be im-

---

[1]Apart from its contribution to appeal, Fisch and Truglio (2001) argued that the presence of same-sex or same-ethnicity characters holds value on other levels as well. For example, when a young, African-American TV viewer sees an African-American character using scientific experimentation to discover something new, the message conveyed to the child is not only the science lesson itself, but also the idea that African Americans can be confident and successful in pursuing scientific activities.

portant as well, as in the case of an asthma education video game in which children with asthma controlled a dinosaur character who also had asthma (Lieberman, 1999).

Music and Sound Effects.   Lesser (1974) catalogued a lengthy list of functions that music can serve in television programs, such as conveying a range of emotions (e.g., joy, sadness), action (e.g., chases, thinking), and situations (e.g., danger, magical occurrence). Apart from conveying meaning and promoting comprehension, music and sound effects have been found repeatedly to capture children's attention and to contribute to the appeal of both television programs (e.g., Bryant, Zillmann, & Brown, 1983; Lesser, 1972, 1974; Levin & Anderson, 1976) and interactive software (Wilson & Talley, 1990).

Music and sound effects can be particularly effective in promoting attention and appeal when they signal the arrival of a familiar character or program element (Lesser, 1972, 1974) or when music is lively and has a fast tempo (Bryant et al., 1983). However, to be effective in sustaining children's attention to television, music and sound effects must also be carefully integrated with visual movement. As Lesser (1974) observed, consistent with the data on visual action discussed earlier, music may capture attention, but probably will not sustain it if the visual that accompanies it is static (e.g., a seated orchestra or stationary folk singer playing their instruments).

Clarity, Explicitness, and Age Appropriateness

In many ways, the same factors serve to make educational content clear and comprehensible to children across a variety of media. Research on magazines has shown comprehension of articles to be stronger when the subject matter is simple, direct, focused, and concrete rather than abstract (CTW Program Research School-Age Team, 1998). Studies on television, too, have shown comprehension of televised narrative to be stronger when it is explicit, as opposed to inferred (e.g., Collins, 1983), and when it is temporally ordered (Collins, Wellman, Keniston, & Westby, 1978). Similarly, Hanna et al. (1999) pointed to the importance of age-appropriate language in instructions, and Strommen and Revelle (1990) recommended keeping dialogue and instruction short and to the point in CD-ROMs (no more than 20 seconds for instructions and 10 seconds for error messages). Indeed Strommen and Revelle noted that children sometimes ignore or miss important content when it is embedded in long streams of dialogue.

"Distance."   The latter point raised by Strommen and Revelle also touches on an additional consideration that can contribute to the effectiveness of educational media. Apart from the importance of the clarity and explicitness of the con-

tent itself, designers of educational media must also be aware of the way in which narrative and educational content interact within a media product. Elsewhere I have argued that comprehension of an educational television program will be greater when there is only a small psychological distance between the narrative of the program and its educational content—that is, when the educational content is integral, rather than tangential, to the narrative (see Fisch, 2000). When the two are closely intertwined, the narrative serves to draw viewers' attention toward the educational content, but when they are only tangentially related to each other, the narrative can pull their attention away from the content instead.

As one might expect, this same point applies across other media as well. Attractive features such as humor and engaging dialogue must support the educational content through judicious decisions about the amount that is included and the timing of its inclusion, to ensure that it works with and not against the educational content. For example, Hanna et al. (1999) noted that characters in interactive materials should not animate or talk constantly or they will distract children from important content or their own accomplishments. Similarly, a 1975 issue of *Sesame Street Magazine* included an eight-sentence story that contained 18 rhyming words; formative research found that the heavy concentration of rhymes pulled children's attention toward the rhymes and away from the story (Kirk & Bernstein, 1975).

Legibility of Text

In attempting to make print attractive to children, producers often employ bright colors, creative layouts with text set at unusual angles, and (in the realms of television and interactive media) animation to "liven up" the text. Yet these conventions must be employed with caution or they may actually make the text more difficult for children to read.

No matter what the medium, for text to be effective in engaging children and conveying information, the physical print must first be legible. Apart from the issues that legibility obviously poses for traditional print media such as magazines, it is also important in creating text for use on computer screens and even on-screen print in television programs. Such issues are particularly critical for materials aimed at poor or reluctant readers, who may not expend the additional effort to decipher text that is not optimally readable.

These complementary considerations are readily evident in the formative research that informed the creation of *Ghostwriter*, a multimedia project intended to encourage literacy among school-age children. Parallel lines of research informed choices of fonts, colors, and treatments of text for *Ghostwriter Magazine* and the print that appeared on-screen in the *Ghostwriter* television series (Williams et al., 1997). The data from these studies pointed to the importance of large fonts, high contrast between print and backgrounds, and standard orientations in creating print for children (CTW Magazine Research Department, 1992; *Ghostwriter* Research, 1992a, 1992b; cf. CTW Program Research School-Age Team, 1998). When text appears in a television program, it must also remain on screen long enough to be read; if animated, it must stay still long enough for target-age children to read it. Additional care is necessary in dealing with text that will be accessed online because different browser software and monitor settings can result in users seeing very different colors on-screen. Because the changes in color can impair the readability of the text, online producers must test their material by accessing it through a variety of browsers and computers to ensure that the text is legible to most or all of its users.

Formal Features

Researchers such as Huston and Wright (1983) have written of the importance of the *formal features* of television programs (e.g., cuts, fades, montage) in affecting viewers' comprehension of those programs. Once children have learned the meaning represented by these conventions, they can contribute to viewers' comprehension of the material. For example, a close-up or pan in a television program can direct children's attention to a specific, relevant object or part of an object, as when the camera tracks a sequence of steps in a complex machine to show how the machine works.

Similar conventions can also serve as aids to comprehension in interactive media. Parallel to the television example earlier, Wilson and Talley (1990) found conventions such as zooms to aid in users' comprehension of an interactive videodisc. All of these uses are analogous to practices that have been long used in print illustration, such as the selection of a close-up or more panoramic photograph to direct readers' eyes to specific aspects of an image. In television and interactive media, as in print, such conventions can serve to focus attention and heighten the salience of the desired material.

IMPLICATIONS FOR USERS

This chapter opened with the observation that, thanks to the rapidly growing number of educational media products on the market, one of the chief issues facing parents, teachers, and other adults who might want to use such materials with children lies in choosing among the available options. The preceding discussion has primarily taken the perspective of those who design such products. Yet these same points can also be employed by users in assessing the quality of existing products and selecting materials to be used in informal (or even formal) education.

To this end, the considerations presented in this chapter can be operationalized as a series of questions for potential users to judge in selecting educational media products. The first set of questions can be applied across all media:

- Will the materials be appealing to children in the target age group?
  - Will they hold and engage children's attention? Is the educational content set in the context of subject matter that children will find inherently attractive?
  - Are visuals, humor, and visual action used in ways that will help maximize appeal?
- Is the presentation of educational content clear?
  - Is the choice and presentation of content at an age-appropriate level?
  - Are the educational points or messages made sufficiently explicit or must they be inferred?
  - Is the content presented simply and directly?
  - Has the material been made as concrete as possible (through discussion, visuals, etc.), even if the underlying concepts may be relatively abstract?
- Is the educational content at the center of any narrative, humor, games, and so on, so that these aspects of the materials will draw children's attention to the educational content and not away from it?
- If there is print, is it legible and easily readable by children in the target age group, or is it likely to be difficult to read (and perhaps even discourage reading by early or poor readers)?
  - Is the font an appropriate size?
  - Is there sufficient contrast between the print and background?
  - Does the layout of print lend itself to easy reading?
- Are formal features, such as close-up views, used to support and enhance comprehension?

In addition, the following questions are more applicable to some forms of media than others:

- Does the presentation require reading by the user? If so, is it written at an appropriate reading level for the target audience?
- Does use of the materials require involvement by an adult? If so, will adults be available to use the materials together with the children?
- Is the presentation of material self-paced and does it allow for review? If not, is the presentation sufficiently clear to be understood by target-age children without the benefit of slowing down or reviewing?

- What are the consequences of failing to understand a piece of the material? Can children continue to advance to another piece that is easier to comprehend, or will they get stuck and be unable to proceed?
- For interactive materials, will these materials be usable by target-age children?
  - Are children physically able to manipulate the required control device?
  - Are navigation icons clear, consistent, and intuitive?
  - Does the size and placement of "hot spots" provide for easy use, and are they signaled in a way that children recognize?
  - Do authoring tools provide examples of what *can* be done with the tools to help children set appropriately broad expectations? If adult participation is called for, do the tools provide similar support for adults?

Together, the answers to these questions can provide insight into the strengths and weaknesses of a particular educational media product, and a means by which to gauge its quality. Although it is unlikely that any one product will emerge as ideal on all of these dimensions, a consideration and prioritization of these issues can aid in selecting products that are well suited to the particular children and settings with which they will be used.

CONCLUSION

From the standpoint of designers, producers, and users, the creation and use of materials for informal education present a host of complex and multifaceted issues. One must consider not only the treatment of the educational content itself (although that is certainly a critical piece), but also issues ranging from the appeal of characters to the availability of adults to support use of the materials.

In many cases, of course, educational media may not be needed at all. Some topics may lend themselves better to one-on-one interaction or hands-on investigation. Some settings may not permit the use of media products. Some children may be most responsive to face-to-face interaction with another person.

In other cases, however, educational media can help introduce children to subjects in ways that would be impossible in verbal instruction (e.g., as in the case of lessons about foreign lands or submicroscopic particles). They can help motivate otherwise disinterested children by embedding educational content in contexts that children find inherently fun and appealing. They can serve as springboards for further activities that continue long after a magazine is closed or a machine is turned off.

To a large degree, however, these benefits depend on the effectiveness of the materials, and this requires a partnership between the creators and users of the materials. It falls to the creators of educational media to produce materials that are educationally rich and well suited to the needs of their audience. It falls to adult users to choose among the materials that are available, to select high-quality materials, and to fit them to the needs of the individual children in their care.

ACKNOWLEDGMENTS

This chapter owes a tremendous debt of gratitude to the many researchers whose work served as the basis for the principles outlined here and, even more important, played vital roles in the creation of numerous educational media products that have benefited children.

REFERENCES

Anderson, D. R., Bryant, J., Wilder, A., Santomero, A., Williams, M., & Crawley, A. M. (2000). Researching *Blue's Clues*: Viewing behavior and impact. *Media Psychology, 2*, 179–194.

Bryant, J., Zillmann, D., & Brown, D. (1983). Entertainment features in children's educational television: Effects on attention and information acquisition. In J. Bryant & D. R. Anderson (Eds.), *Children's understanding of television: Research on attention and comprehension* (pp. 221–240). New York: Academic Press.

Cherow-O'Leary, R. (2001). Carrying *Sesame Street* into print: *Sesame Street* Magazine, *Sesame Street Parents*, and *Sesame Street* books. In S. M. Fisch & R. T. Truglio (Eds.), *"G" is for growing: Thirty years of research on children and Sesame Street* (pp. 197–214). Mahwah, NJ: Lawrence Erlbaum Associates.

Collins, W. A. (1983). Interpretation and inference in children's television viewing. In J. Bryant & D. R. Anderson (Eds.), *Children's understanding of television: Research on attention and comprehension* (pp. 125–150). New York: Academic Press.

Collins, W. A., Wellman, H., Keniston, A. H., & Westby, S. D. (1978). Age-related aspects of comprehension and inference from a televised dramatic narrative. *Child Development, 49*, 389–399.

CTW Magazine Research Department. (1992). Definition of *Ghostwriter Magazine* (Unpublished research report). New York: Children's Television Workshop.

CTW Magazine Research Department. (1993). 1993 *Sesame Street* readership survey (Unpublished research report). New York: Children's Television Workshop.

CTW Program Research. (1999a). Make-a-story parent-child interaction study (Unpublished research report). New York: Children's Television Workshop.

CTW Program Research. (1999b). *One Tree Hill* comic study (Unpublished research report). New York: Children's Television Workshop.

CTW Program Research Online Team. (1998). *Sticker World:* Look and feel, prototype, and other people's Web sites (Unpublished research report). New York: Children's Television Workshop.

CTW Program Research School-Age Team. (1998). Magazine research: What we've learned (Unpublished research report). New York: Children's Television Workshop.

Druin, A. (Ed.). (1999). *The design of children's technology*. San Francisco, CA: Morgan Kaufman Publishers.

Druin, A., & Solomon, C. (1996). *Designing multimedia environments for children.* New York: Wiley.

Eckhardt, B. B., Wood, M. R., & Jacobvitz, R. S. (1991). Verbal ability and prior knowledge: Contributions to adults' comprehension of television. *Communication Research, 18,* 636–649.

Fisch, S. M. (2000). A capacity model of children's comprehension of educational content on television. *Media Psychology, 2,* 63–91.

Fisch, S. M., Cohen, D. I., McCann, S. K., & Hoffman, L. (1993). *Square One TV research history and bibliography.* New York: Children's Television Workshop.

Fisch, S. M., & McCann, S. K. (1993). Making broadcast television participative: Eliciting mathematical behavior through *Square One TV. Educational Technology Research and Development, 41*(3), 103–109.

Fisch, S. M., & Truglio, R. T. (2001). Why children learn from *Sesame Street.* In S. M. Fisch & R. T. Truglio (Eds.), *"G" is for growing: Thirty years of research on children and Sesame Street* (pp. 233–244). Mahwah, NJ: Lawrence Erlbaum Associates.

Fisch, S. M., Wilder, G., Yotive, W. M., & McCann, S. K. (1994, July). How different is "different?": Diversity in the context of overall trends regarding *Ghostwriter* and *Square One TV.* In B. J. Wilson (Chair), *Reaching specific audiences through the mass media: Lessons from the Children's Television Workshop.* Invited symposium presented at the annual meeting of the International Communication Association, Sydney, Australia.

Flagg, B. N. (1990). *Formative evaluation for educational technology.* Hillsdale, NJ: Lawrence Erlbaum Associates.

Ghostwriter Research. (1992a). *Ghostwriter* font study, part 1 (Unpublished research report). New York: Children's Television Workshop.

Ghostwriter Research. (1992b). *Ghostwriter* font study, part 2 (Unpublished research report). New York: Children's Television Workshop.

Hanna, L., Risden, K., Czerwinski, M., & Alexander, K. J. (1999). The role of usability research in designing children's computer products. In A. Druin (Ed.), *The design of children's technology* (pp. 3–26). San Francisco, CA: Morgan Kaufman.

Huston, A. C., & Wright, J. C. (1983). Children's processing of television: The informative functions of formal features. In J. Bryant & D. R. Anderson (Eds.), *Children's understanding of television: Research on attention and comprehension* (pp. 35–68). New York: Academic Press.

Kafai, Y. B. (1999). Children as designers, testers, and evaluators of educational software. In A. Druin (Ed.), *The design of children's technology* (pp. 123–145). San Francisco, CA: Morgan Kaufman.

Kirk, G., & Bernstein, L. (1975). March, 1975 *Sesame Street Magazine* research report (Unpublished research report). New York: Children's Television Workshop.

Lesser, G. S. (1972). Assumptions behind the writing and production methods in *Sesame Street.* In W. Schramm (Ed.), *Quality in instructional television* (pp. 108–164). Honolulu: University Press of Hawaii.

Lesser, G. S. (1974). *Children and television: Lessons from* Sesame Street. New York: Vintage Books/ Random House.

Levin, S. R., & Anderson, D. R. (1976). The development of attention. *Journal of Communication, 26*(2), 126–135.

Lieberman, D. (1999). The researcher's role in the design of children's media and technology. In A. Druin (Ed.), *The design of children's technology* (pp. 73–97). San Francisco, CA: Morgan Kaufman.

Link, N., & Cherow-O'Leary, R. (1990). Research and development of print materials at the Children's Television Workshop. *Educational Technology Research and Development, 38*(4), 34–44.

McGhee, P. E. (1980). Toward the integration of entertainment and educational functions of television: The role of humor. In P. Tannenbaum (Ed.), *The entertainment functions of television* (pp. 183–208). Hillsdale, NJ: Lawrence Erlbaum Associates.

National Institute of Mental Health. (1982). *Television and behavior: Ten years of scientific progress and implications for the Eighties: Vol. 1. Summary report.* Rockville, MD: U.S. Department of Health and Human Services.

Pace, A. J. (1980). *The ability of young children to correct comprehension errors: An aspect of comprehension monitoring.* Paper presented at the annual meeting of the American Educational Research Association, Boston, MA.

Pace, A. J. (1981). *Comprehension monitoring by elementary students: When does it occur?* Paper presented at the annual meeting of the American Educational Research Association, Los Angeles, CA.

Papert, S. (1996). *The connected family: Bridging the generation gap.* Atlanta, GA: Longstreet Press.

Reiser, R. A., Tessmer, M. A., & Phelps, P. C. (1984). Adult–child interaction in children's learning from *Sesame Street. Educational Communication and Technology Journal, 32,* 217–223.

Reiser, R. A., Williamson, N., & Suzuki, K. (1988). Using *Sesame Street* to facilitate children's recognition of letters and numbers. *Educational Communication and Technology Journal, 36,* 15–21.

Revelle, G. L., Strommen, E. F., & Medoff, L. (2001). Interactive technologies research at the Children's Television Workshop. In S. M. Fisch & R. T. Truglio (Eds.), *"G" is for growing: Thirty years of research on children and Sesame Street* (pp. 215–230). Mahwah, NJ: Lawrence Erlbaum Associates.

Salomon, G. (1977). Effects of encouraging Israeli mothers to co-observe *Sesame Street* with their five-year-olds. *Child Development, 48,* 1146–1151.

Schauble, L. (1990). Formative evaluation in the design of educational software at the Children's Television Workshop. In B. N. Flagg (Ed.), *Formative evaluation for educational technology* (pp. 51–66). Hillsdale, NJ: Lawrence Erlbaum Associates.

Schmitt, K. (1999). *The three-hour rule: Is it living up to expectations?* (Annenberg Public Policy Rep. No. 30). Philadelphia, PA: University of Pennsylvania.

Shneiderman, B. (1998). *Designing the user interface: Strategies for effective human-computer interaction.* Reading, MA: Addison-Wesley.

Strommen, E. F., & Revelle, G. L. (1990). Research in interactive technologies at the Children's Television Workshop. *Educational Technology Research and Development, 38*(4), 65–80.

The New Ghostwriter Mysteries Research. (1997a). "The Bad Rap" fine cut study (Unpublished research report). New York: Children's Television Workshop.

The New Ghostwriter Mysteries Research. (1997b). Shows 102, 103, and 104 study (Unpublished research report). New York: Children's Television Workshop.

Valkenburg, P. M., & Janssen, S. C. (1999). What do children value in entertainment programs? A cross-cultural investigation. *Journal of Communication, 49*(2), 3–21.

Williams, M. E., Hall, E., Cunningham, H., Albright, M., Schiro, K., & Fisch, S. (1997). *Ghostwriter research history and bibliography.* New York: Children's Television Workshop.

Wilsdon, A. (1989). *3-2-1 Contact* redesign test (Unpublished research report). New York: Children's Television Workshop.

Wilson, K. S., & Talley, W. J. (1990). The "Palenque" project: Formative evaluation in the development and design of an optical disc prototype. In B. N. Flagg (Ed.), *Formative evaluation for educational technology* (pp. 83–98). Hillsdale, NJ: Lawrence Erlbaum Associates.

Zillmann, D., Williams, B. R., Bryant, J., Boynton, K. R., & Wolf, M. A. (1980). Acquisition of information from educational television programs as a function of differently paced humorous inserts. *Journal of Educational Psychology, 72,* 170–180.

2

Media Forms for Children's Learning

Sandra L. Calvert
Georgetown University

Children in the 21st century are developing in a world of electronic media. These representational media present information to children in visual, verbal, and musical forms. These forms must be decoded for children to make sense of the stream of information being presented to them. This grammar of the information technologies, referred to as *formal features*, provides visual and auditory codes that can help children select, represent, and think about educational content. Sound effects and loud music, for example, can call attention to important contiguous information, thereby improving children's retention of that material. Actions in TV and computer programs can provide a visual way to think about content that children can then use to represent and remember that information, particularly when visual content is paired with language. Singing, by contrast, seems to foster superficial rote learning. Children who master these representational media will have access to, and control of, the information highway—the place where knowledge increasingly will be stored in the 21st century.

MEDIA FORMS FOR CHILDREN'S LEARNING

Media pervade children's daily lives. From the time children get up in the morning until the time they go to sleep, TV, videogames, and computers are a backdrop for everyday interaction (Calvert, 1999).

We think that education is in trouble in the United States. Our children are falling behind other nations in educational attainment, particularly in science and math. Media are often blamed for poor scores, short attention spans, and misplaced priorities. Yet what if children's favorite pastimes were also part of the solution? That topic is the focus of this chapter. We begin with a look at how children extract educational messages from media, and then we discuss social policy initiatives such as the Children's Television Act (CTA), which was implemented to increase children's access to educational TV programs.

What Are Media?

Media are technologically based systems of information delivery. Media include radio and TV, which deliver a broadcast message to an audience; videocassette recorders, which allow us to tape and replay information at our convenience, thereby permitting more user control; and computer-based devices such as video games, computer software, and virtual reality, some of which can be accessed over the Internet. Television as we know it today will eventually merge with the interactive computer technologies—a phenomenon known as convergence (Calvert, 1999).

Media are composed of content, the information and messages presented on a medium, and form, the symbol system by which content is transmitted to users (Huston & Wright, 1998a). Both content and form must be comprehensible for children to learn from media experiences.

What Is Form?

Form (or formal features) refers to audiovisual production features that structure, mark, and represent content (Calvert, 1999). At a macrolevel, form includes action (the amount of physical movement on the screen) and pace (the rate at which scenes and characters change). At a microlevel, there are visual and auditory techniques. Visual techniques include camera devices such as cuts, pans, fades, dissolves, and visual special effects. Auditory techniques include foreground and background music, singing, sound effects, and character vocalizations as well as informative techniques such as adult dialogue, child dialogue, nonhuman dialogue (e.g., dogs can speak in children's TV), and narration. The thesis that I have explored for many years is that form has the potential to enhance or interfere with children's extraction of educational media messages.

What Is Content?

The content of media is as diverse as the experiences of our lives. Violent content, prosocial content, academic content, gender stereotypes, ethnic stereotypes, and advertisements are all part of the viewing experiences of children and adults in this culture. Educational content, the focus of this chapter, historically referred to academic content that was related to school subjects, such as history, math, English, and science (Calvert & Kotler, 2003). With the passage of the CTA, educational content took on a more expansive meaning (Calvert & Kotler, 2003). Specifically, educational and informational content referred to any content that would further the development of the child in any way, thereby including academic as well as social and emotional content in the definition (Federal Communication Commission, 1991). According to the CTA definition, prosocial content, which refers to social lessons such as helping, sharing, and cooperating, also came to be defined as educational content. Therefore, academic and prosocial content are both educational by law.

Content can also be defined as essential or nonessential in understanding media messages. In stories, TV content is both central (i.e., essential, plot-relevant content) or incidental (i.e., nonessential content irrelevant to the plot). A very abstract type of central content, called *inferential content*, is mastered by children as they go beyond the information given and figure out how people feel, what their motivations are, and how the events of the program fit together to make a coherent story (Collins, 1983).

HOW DO CHILDREN LEARN EDUCATIONAL CONTENT FROM MEDIA?

To understand how children learn from media, it is important to understand how children think at different points in their development. There is an evolution in thought as it moves from enactive to iconic to symbolic modes of representation (Bruner, Olver, & Greenfield, 1968). Enactive representation is a representation made through the body, such as pointing to give directions. Iconic representation is often a visual or an echoic image, such as a picture or a sound like boom! Symbolic representation is the most abstract level of reasoning and is typically accomplished via words. As children move across the early years of life, their representations shift from enactive to iconic to symbolic modes of thought (Bruner et al., 1968).

Media rely on visual and verbal symbol systems to get messages across to children and, for that matter, to all users (Huston & Wright, 1998a). Young children are particularly dependent on concrete visual emphasis to help them understand media messages, making TV a powerful medium for commanding attention and teaching lessons to them (Calvert, 1999). Similarly, the reliance of new technologies on these same visual and verbal symbol systems makes form an important ally for the goal of educational development.

I consider three ways that media forms can influence children's learning: (a) as a way to get children to look at certain messages, thereby increasing the chances that they will process certain content; this is called the signal or marker function of formal features; (b) as a mode that children can use to represent content; and (c) as a way to foster active learning.

Signaling or Marking Function of Formal Features

Television is thought of as a visual medium, yet it is the audio qualities that get viewers to look when they are inattentive (Anderson & Lorch, 1983). Certain formal features are considered to be perceptually salient. Perceptually salient features embody characteristics such as movement, contrast, incongruity, surprise, and novelty, which are likely to elicit attention and interest (Berlyne, 1960). Perceptually salient auditory techniques, such as sound effects and character vocalizations, have been particularly effective in getting children to attend to certain content.

Perceptually salient formal features initially elicit a primitive attentional orienting response from viewers. In several studies (e.g., Calvert & Gersh, 1987; Calvert, Huston, Watkins, & Wright, 1982), a well-placed "zip," "bang," or "boom" reliably gets an inattentive viewer to look and an attentive viewer to keep looking. Over time children learn that certain sounds, such as a crescendo in music, reliably signal or mark important story events.

Once attention is elicited, the probability increases that a child will process and understand the contiguously presented content. Enhanced processing occurs for the incidental irrelevant details of a program (Calvert et. al, 1982) as well as for the central, plot-relevant content (Calvert & Gersh, 1987; Calvert & Scott, 1989).

In a study by Calvert and Scott (1989), we examined children's skills at temporally integrating the plot line in programs that varied in pace (i.e., the rate of scene and character change). Children who heard experimentally inserted sound effects were more likely to see the key story transitions, but only in the rapidly paced programs. Selective attention, which involves selecting certain content for processing at the expense of other content, then mediated children's skills at temporally integrating key program content.

In a study by Calvert and Gersh (1987), we studied kindergarten versus fifth graders' comprehension of the central, inferential, and incidental content in an episode of *Spanky and Our Gang*. Kindergartners who viewed the program with sound effects (i.e., a slide whistle blowing) marking three key scenes understood the abstract, inferential program content better than their peers. Older children, by contrast, did not need the features to mark content for them to get the message.

Sound effects are also important in getting young children to understand academic content as well as story messages. For example, *Sesame Street* has long reserved electronic embellishments such as sound effects for parts of the program when the important content was being presented (Bryant, Zillmann, &

Brown, 1983). Taken together, the body of research reveals that highlighting important content can benefit young children's comprehension of visually and verbally presented content. Therefore, marking key content with salient audio formal features, such as sound effects and character vocalizations, can improve children's learning of educational content. Sound effects are also cost-effective. Producers can easily insert sound effects into a new production or even go back to existing productions and insert sound effects at key program points, as we did in our experimental studies.

Features as Modes to Represent Content

The second area to consider involves how features can be used to represent content. Special attention is paid to the ways that action and singing, respectively, impact children's comprehension of content, particularly verbally presented content.

Action as a Developmentally Appropriate Aid to Language. The striking visual and auditory features that are used to present content are not just attention-getting (Calvert et al., 1982). In some cases, they serve as ways that we represent content. Consider action. A well-thrown "bomb" in a football game or a perfectly executed overhead smash in a tennis match may well be remembered in a visual form. This moving icon provides a direct analogue for how many people think. We can view actions, encode that information, and then later recall it, not unlike a replay of an event. Television provides millions of these images to viewers over the course of their lives, allowing people to think visually about the content that they saw earlier.

This opportunity to see and encode visual images may be particularly important for young viewers, who often need visual emphasis to help them understand content. However, there are those who argue that striking visual images may distract children from processing the most important visual images—a phenomenon known as the *visual superiority hypothesis*.

Hayes and Birnbaum (1980), who initially proposed the visual superiority hypothesis, found that preschoolers remembered visually presented content at the expense of auditorially presented content, particularly when the visual and audio tracks were mismatched. Moreover, young children rarely understood that there was any problem with the mismatched visual and audio tracks. Based on this study, the researchers concluded that visual presentation distracts children from remembering important story information.

We (Calvert et al., 1982) became interested in whether visual images are distracting or whether they are simply more perceptually salient and, therefore, more likely to be processed than dialogue on its own. Action is the component of visual presentation that makes it perceptually salient. Initially, this question was examined via an episode of *Fat Albert and the Cosby Kids*, a prosocial cartoon that was broadcast by CBS featuring a group of African-American boys. Kindergartners were compared to third and fourth graders. We expected the action presentations to help the kindergartners remember important verbal story content, but not the third and fourth graders. This developmental prediction was incorrect. Both kindergartners and third and fourth graders understood the central, plot-relevant content best when it was presented with both action and dialogue.

In later studies, my colleagues and I began to examine this issue with computer presentational features, in which movement could be tightly controlled. We (Calvert, Watson, Brinkley, & Bordeaux, 1989) initially created a computer microworld called Parkworld in which small programmable objects, known as *sprites*, appeared with movement or no movement and with sound effects or no sound effects. Kindergartners interacted with this program for 4 days; on Day 5, they told us the names of all the objects they could remember from Parkworld. The results revealed that kindergartners selected and recalled more moving than stationary visual objects, thereby suggesting an important lesson: Visual superiority is really action superiority. That is, the movement of objects made them memorable. The work of Anderson and his colleagues revealed similar beneficial effects of action for memory of TV content (Gibbons, Anderson, Smith, Field, & Fischer, 1986).

Subsequent studies about Parkworld, which became Talkworld when a voice synthesizer was added, revealed the following findings: (a) action presentations benefit, rather than interfere with, children's recall of verbal content (e.g., Calvert, 1991, 1994); (b) action presentations can be particularly beneficial for the verbal recall of second graders who are poor readers (Calvert, Watson, Brinkley, & Penny, 1990); (c) action presentation works, be it on a computer screen or a felt board, the former costing more than $2,000 and the latter costing about $6.86 (Calvert, 1991).

Monique Moore built on this early research and created a computer program for children who have autism. The software utilized a perceptually salient presentation in which words and actions together were used to teach vocabulary. The computer presentation was compared to the Lovaas method—an effective behavioral therapy where children who have autism are taught to pay attention to and focus on what adults are teaching them. We found that young children who had autism were more attentive, more motivated, and remembered more nouns when exposed to the computer presentation than to the Lovaas method alone (Moore & Calvert, 2000).

Taken together, the results of these studies suggest that action is a developmentally appropriate way for children to think about, represent, and remember content, making it an important form to get information across to children. Moderate action that is about the speed of a walk is the most effective level to portray information. Although benefits occur for children as old as ages 9 and 10, action is particularly useful for the youngest children and for those who are developmentally behind their peers (e.g., those with reading difficulties or autism).

Is Singing Overrated as an Educational Technique?   If there is a feature that is overrated as an effective educational technique, my candidate is singing. Educators have long assumed that singing helps children remember information, and therefore it is extensively used in preschool classrooms. Our research indicates that the memorability of songs clearly depends on what you want children to learn. More specifically, song presentations produce superficial, not deep, processing of the verbal content. Let me give you some background and evidence to support this claim.

One day when I was teaching students about the effectiveness of educational TV programs such as *Sesame Street* and *Mr. Rogers' Neighborhood*, a student asked me, "How about *School House Rock?*" I said, "What about it?" That question led me to study how singing impacts children's and adults' memories of educational content.

School House Rock is a series of vignettes, lasting about 3 minutes each, that teach grade-school children about English, science, math, and history. I initially asked undergraduate college students who had viewed this series as children to write the words to the Preamble to the Constitution. Those who reported frequent viewing of this series had better verbatim memory of the words than those who saw it infrequently. In an experimental follow-up, undergraduates' long-term memory was superior when they heard a track in which the words were repeatedly sung than when they heard one in which the words were repeatedly spoken (Calvert & Tart, 1993).

However, in two related studies, grade-school children and college students who viewed other history vignettes from *School House Rock* did not necessarily have better comprehension of the material (Calvert, 2001). In fact the reverse pattern was the case. In one study, a history vignette about the Revolutionary War was better understood after second-grade children were exposed to a spoken version rather than to the original sung soundtrack. In the second study, in which children viewed a history vignette called "I'm Just a Bill," comprehension of the sung material was again relatively poor. For example, a third-grade boy described a bill as something you pay rather than a document that is created to make a law.

Additional documentation for children's relatively poor comprehension of songs comes from a study I conducted with Rebecca Billingsley. We created a song about a child's phone number to compare singing versus prose as an educational technique. The TV presentation was removed entirely, making this a live encounter between a teacher and child. Here we found that spoken presentations were even better recited than sung ones (Calvert & Billingsley, 1998). Taken together, the findings support a levels of processing hypothesis (Craik & Lockhart, 1972) in which sung information is initially processed at a superficial level, not necessarily becoming deeply integrated into one's knowledge base.

We began to wonder about what the specific beneficial effects of song were for children's memory. Surely all those preschool teachers who use songs in the classrooms knew something that we were missing. Tiffany Goodman and I

(Calvert & Goodman, 1999) then taught 2- and 3-year-olds songs under two rehearsal conditions: enactive and singing or singing only. All children sang the targeted songs. In enactive rehearsal conditions, children made motions that emphasized the song meaning, such as being a little teapot that was tipped over and
poured out. Children who enacted story motions while singing the lyrics understood the abstract, inferential content better than those who only sang. Thus, it
seems that some preschool practices, such as using motion with the words, are
what make the sung content comprehensible for the youngest children.

Even with the limitations of songs as an initial way to improve comprehension,
remember that the verbatim memory findings are still quite useful for current educational practice. Specifically, there are many passages that children memorize
verbatim, and songs ensure a rather good reconstruction of content even years after it was initially learned. Thus, the content can be preserved and later processed
more deeply even if it is initially only processed superficially. Repetition also fos-
ters verbatim memory (Calvert & Billingsley, 1998). The key question is how to
get children to process songs at a deeper level in the first place. Perhaps that can
be done by speaking the most important information and having children enact the
most important lyrics.

Active Processing of Media Content

There are those who do not share my enthusiasm for using TV or other media as
educational tools. One criticism leveled against TV in particular is that it creates a
passive learning environment that is not conducive to learning (e.g., Singer,
1980).

Huston and Wright (1998b) responded to the criticisms associated with learning from TV. These include (a) passivity (a lack of physical activity), yet those
reading a book are equally passive when it comes to physical activity, and they are
not considered to be passive; (b) passivity (a lack of interactivity), meaning that
TV is a one-way medium with little ability to elicit individual responses from
viewers, yet young children will often answer the TV when questions are raised;
Blue's Clues, *Sesame Street*, and *Dora the Explorer* are quite successful in eliciting this type of interaction; (c) a lack of user control, meaning the viewer has little
control of program pacing; however, videocassette recorders and DVD players
now make it possible for children to review a program or parts of a program as
much as desired; (d) issues concerning cumulative learning because children who
have seen past episodes of a series differ from those who have not, making it difficult to create programming for everyone in the audience; layering messages in a
program has been one solution to this problem; (e) visual emphasis of content,
which was discussed earlier as the visual superiority effect; (f) suppressing imagination and creativity, which heavy viewing does seem to do, but certain programs
such as *Mr. Rogers' Neighborhood* may also enhance imagination and creativity

(Anderson, Huston, Schmitt, Linebarger, & Wright, 2001); thus, it depends on what you watch; (g) reduced attention span because TV is so rapidly paced, but there is no evidence that it does reduce children's attention span (Anderson, 1998); (h) viewing for entertainment, not learning; but as Bill Cosby, the creator of the cartoon *Fat Albert and the Cosby Kids*, once said, "If you're not careful, you may learn something before we're done"; and (i) displacement of more valuable educational activities, although the bulk of evidence suggests that displacement occurs for activities that fulfill similar needs for viewers, such as TV displacing movies and radio in an earlier era. Given the numerous biases about the detrimental effects of TV viewing, it is amazing that 99% of American homes have at least one, and more often multiple, TV sets.

The evidence suggests that children are actively attempting to understand TV content. Dr. Daniel Anderson's research has been seminal in this regard. His work demonstrates that children monitor the comprehensibility of the verbal track of TV and allocate their visual attention accordingly (Anderson & Lorch, 1983). Moreover, children who grew up watching more educational programs such as *Sesame Street* and *Mr. Rogers' Neighborhood* had better grades and were more creative when they were in high school (Anderson et al., 2001; Schmitt et al., 1997).

Changes in the new media environment will further enhance children's options to interact with the content, control the pacing of material, and decide the level of difficulty so that lessons can build on each other. Increasingly, broadcasters create Internet sites that parallel the TV programs that children view, affording opportunities for youngsters to practice and rehearse what they see. Even video games provide an informal learning environment in which visual-spatial mental skills are cultivated for those who play for their entertainment, not for their education (Greenfield, 1993). Ultimately, convergence allows children to interact with TV content on their TV screen and to view TV content as they interact on their computer. What kind of educational content is there for children to view in this increasingly seamless environment?

HOW EDUCATIONAL ARE "EDUCATIONAL" TV PROGRAMS?

The Children's Television Act (CTA) of 1990 requires broadcasters to provide educational and informational (E & I) TV programs to child audiences as a condition for license renewal. In the beginning, there was serious controversy about what broadcasters classified as educational when programs like *The Jetsons*, an older entertainment cartoon about what life will be like for a typical family when we fly to work in spaceships and have robots for maids, was classified as educational because it taught children about the future.

Because of this controversy, tighter rules by the Federal Communications Commission (FCC), the government agency charged with regulating TV content, came into being. The FCC implemented the 3-hour rule, requiring broadcasters to provide a minimum of 3 hours of educational and informational (E/I) content for the child audience each week (Federal Communications Commission, 1996). This rule went into effect in the fall season of 1997.

Dr. Amy Jordan and her colleagues, from the Annenberg Public Policy Center, have tracked the quantity and quality of children's programs through content analyses. She and her colleagues rate the programs that broadcasters claim to be E/I on several dimensions of educational strength including: lesson clarity, lesson salience, lesson involvement, and lesson applicability. Over several years, Jordan and her colleagues found that most programs qualify as E/I programs. Nonetheless, a persistent 20% of programs remained minimally educational (Jordan & Woodard, 1998; Schmitt, 1999). Moreover, most broadcaster programs focused on social and emotional content rather than academic content (Jordan & Woodard, 1998).

Creating high-quality TV programs is the first step in ensuring a better media environment for teaching children. In addition, we need to know what children are taking away from such experiences. Put another way, what are children learning after viewing these educational and informational TV programs?

To answer this question, we created an Internet site, the Georgetown Hoya TV Reporters, where second- through sixth-grade children came online and told us: (a) what they viewed the preceding week; (b) what their favorite program was; and (c) what they learned from their favorite program. We included E/I programs from the four major networks and compared them to PBS and Nickelodeon programs, the broadcasters who have a history of creating quality TV programs for children. For the 1998 to 1999 season, we (Calvert et al., 2002) learned that children were viewing about 4 of our 30 targeted educational programs each week. Younger children tended to view more E/I programs than did older children, but boys and girls viewed about the same number of programs. Nickelodeon and PBS programs were viewed more often than were programs from the four major broadcasters. The most frequently viewed programs were *Doug* (Nickelodeon and ABC), *Hey Arnold* (Nickelodeon), *Saved by the Bell* (NBC), *Recess* (ABC), *Cousin Skeeter* (Nickelodeon), and *Wishbone* (PBS).

So what do children learn from these educational programs? Lessons about social and emotional skills and about knowledge and information skills were far more prevalent than were lessons about cognitive skills or physical well-being skills, partly reflecting the kinds of programs available for children to view. Consider the social-emotional theme about honesty and resisting peer pressure in the following story about *Wishbone*, a PBS program. The author is a sixth-grade girl.

> In the episode of *Wishbone* I watched, a new kid named Max became friends with Joe. Although Max was nice he had a mean friend who stole things, and tried to talk

Max into helping him. Fortunately Max did the right thing and wouldn't help. I learned from this show that you should do what you think is right, don't be influenced by others.

The quality or educational strength of reports was comparable for commercial broadcaster versus Nickelodeon/PBS programs. Girls' reports were stronger than were boys' reports, particularly in writing clear lessons and generalizing those lessons to their lives. The findings reveal that children are deriving measurable benefits from E/I-mandated programs, making the CTA an effective law for this country's youth.

CONCLUSION

In conclusion, children learn significant social and informational lessons from educational media that are designed to teach and inform them, either implicitly or explicitly. Lessons are learned as children go about the business of entertaining themselves, as when they cultivate visual-spatial skills while playing video games.

We know that certain forms assist children's information-processing activities. Educational benefits can occur by using perceptually salient audio techniques to guide children's selective attention to and comprehension of plot-relevant content, by using action as a mode to reinforce significant verbal messages, and by avoiding singing unless the goal is an exact verbatim rendition of a lesson. These same techniques are effective in the new media that offer additional benefits such as increased interactivity, opportunity for review, and control over the rate of presentation. Even so, broadcast TV remains the staple of children's current media experiences. Policy decisions, such as the implementation of the CTA, are improving the quality of children's TV, and children are often taking away lessons of value from viewing these programs.

As future TV programs become interactive and Internet interactions include moving video, it is imperative that we understand how children learn from media and how to optimize their development through entertaining experiences. Children use media primarily for entertainment purposes. Fortunately, the judicious use of form and content allows us to entertain children as we educate them.

REFERENCES

Anderson, D. R. (1998). Educational television is not an oxymoron. *The Annals of the American Academy of Political and Social Science, 557,* 24–38.

Anderson, D. R., Huston, A. C., Schmitt, K. L., Linebarger, D. L., & Wright, J. C. (2001). Early childhood television viewing and adolescent behavior: The recontact study. *Monographs of the Society for Research in Child Development, 66,* vii–156.

Anderson, D. R., & Lorch, E. P. (1983). Looking at television: Action or reaction? In J. Bryant & D. R. Anderson (Eds.), *Children's understanding of television: Research on attention and comprehension* (pp. 1–33). New York: Academic.

Berlyne, D. E. (1960). *Conflict, curiosity, and arousal.* New York: McGraw-Hill.

Bruner, J. S., Olver, R. R., & Greenfield, P. M. (1968). *Studies in cognitive growth: A collaboration at the Center for Cognitive Studies.* New York: Wiley.

Bryant, J., Zillmann, D., & Brown, D. (1983). Entertainment features in children's educational television: Effects on attention and information acquisition. In J. Bryant & D. R. Anderson (Eds.), *Children's understanding of television: Research on attention and comprehension* (pp. 221–240). New York: Academic.

Calvert, S. L. (1991). Presentational features for young children's production and recall of information. *Journal of Applied Developmental Psychology, 12,* 367–378.

Calvert, S. L. (1994). Developmental differences in children's production and recall of information as a function of computer presentational features. *Journal of Educational Computing Research, 10,* 139–151.

Calvert, S. L. (1999). *Children's journeys through the information age.* Boston: McGraw-Hill.

Calvert, S. L. (2001). Impact of televised songs on children's and young adults' memory of educational content. *Media Psychology, 3*(4), 325–342.

Calvert, S. L., & Billingsley, R. L. (1998). Young children's recitation and comprehension of information presented by songs. *Journal of Applied Developmental Psychology, 19,* 97–108.

Calvert, S. L., & Gersh, T. L. (1987). The selective use of sound effects and visual inserts for children's television story comprehension. *Journal of Applied Developmental Psychology, 8,* 363–375.

Calvert, S. L., & Goodman, T. (1999, April). *Enactive rehearsal for young children's comprehension of songs.* Poster presented at the biennial meeting of the Society for Research in Child Development, Albuquerque, NM.

Calvert, S. L., Huston, A. C., Watkins, B. A., & Wright, J. C. (1982). The relation between selective attention to television forms and children's comprehension of content. *Child Development, 53,* 601–610.

Calvert, S. L., & Kotler, J. A. (2003). Lessons from children's television: Impact of the Children's Television Act on children's learning. *Journal of Applied Developmental Psychology, 24*(3), 275–335.

Calvert, S. L., Kotler, J. A., Murray, W. F., Gonzales, E., Savoye, K., Hammack, P., Weigert, S., Shockey, E., Paces, C., Friedman, M., & Hammar, M. (2002). Children's online reports about educational and informational television programs. In S. L. Calvert, A. B. Jordan, & R. R. Cocking (Eds.), *Children in the digital age: Influences of electronic media on development* (pp. 165–182). Westport, CT: Praeger.

Calvert, S. L., & Scott, M. C. (1989). Sound effects for children's temporal integration of fast-paced television content. *Journal of Broadcasting and Electronic Media, 33,* 233–246.

Calvert, S. L., & Tart, M. (1993). Song versus prose forms for students' very long-term, long-term, and short-term verbatim recall. *Journal of Applied Developmental Psychology, 14,* 245–260.

Calvert, S. L., Watson, J. A., Brinkley, V., & Bordeaux, B. (1989). Computer presentational features for young children's preferential selection and recall of information. *Journal of Educational Computing Research, 5,* 35–49.

Calvert, S. L., Watson, J. A., Brinkley, V., & Penny, J. (1990). Computer presentational features for poor readers' recall of information. *Journal of Educational Computing Research, 6*(3), 287–298.

Collins, W. A. (1983). Interpretation and inference in children's television viewing. In J. Bryant & D. R. Anderson (Eds.), *Children's understanding of television: Research on attention and comprehension* (pp. 125–150). New York: Academic.

Craik, F., & Lockhart, R. (1972). Levels of processing: A framework for memory research. *Journal of Verbal Learning and Verbal Behavior, 11,* 521–533.

Federal Communications Commission. (1991). Policies and rules concerning children's television programming. *Federal Communications Commission Record, 6*, 2111–2127.

Federal Communications Commission. (1996, August 8). *FCC adopts new children's TV rules.* Retrieved January 28, 2004, from http://ftp.fcc.gov/Bureaus/Mass_Media/News_Releases/1996/nrmm6021.html.

Gibbons, J., Anderson, D. R., Smith, R., Field, D. E., & Fischer, C. (1986). Young children's recall and reconstruction of audio and audiovisual material. *Child Development, 57*(4), 1014–1023.

Greenfield, P. M. (1993). Representational competence in shared symbol systems: Electronic media from radio to television. In R. R. Cocking & K. A. Renninger (Eds.), *The development and meaning of psychological distance* (pp. 161–183). Hillsdale, NJ: Lawrence Erlbaum Associates.

Hayes, D., & Birnbaum, D. (1980). Preschoolers' retention of televised events: Is a picture worth a thousand words? *Developmental Psychology, 16*(5), 410–416.

Huston, A. C., & Wright, J. C. (1998a). Mass media and children's development. In W. Damon (Series Ed.), I. Sigel & K. A. Renninger (Vol. Eds.), *Handbook of child psychology: Vol. 4. Child psychology in practice* (5th ed., pp. 999–1058). New York: Wiley.

Huston, A. C., & Wright, J. C. (1998b). Television and the informational and educational needs of children. *The Annals of the American Academy of Political and Social Science, 557*, 9–23.

Jordan, A. B., & Woodard, E. H. (1998). Growing pains: Children's television in the new regulatory environment. *The Annals of the American Academy of Political and Social Science, 557*, 83–95.

Moore, M., & Calvert, S. L. (2000). Vocabulary acquisition for children with autism: Teacher or computer instruction. *Journal of Autism and Developmental Disorders, 30*, 359–362.

Schmitt, K. L. (1999, June). *The three-hour rule: Is it living up to expectations?* Paper presented at the 4th annual conference on the State of Children's Television, Washington, DC.

Schmitt, K. L., Linebarger, D. L., Collins, P. A., Wright, J. C., Anderson, D. R., Huston, A. C., & McElroy, E. (1997, April). *Effects of preschool television viewing on adolescent creative thinking and behavior.* Poster session presented at the biennial meeting of the Society for Research in Child Development, Washington, DC.

Singer, J. (1980). The power and limitations of television: A cognitive affective analysis. In P. H. Tannenbaum (Ed.), *The entertainment functions of television* (pp. 31–65). Hillsdale, NJ: Lawrence Erlbaum Associates.

3

Designing Multimedia Technology That Supports Human Learning

Richard E. Mayer
University of California, Santa Barbara

The purpose of this chapter is to explore ways to help students understand scientific explanations. For example, scientific explanations include giving an account of how a bicycle tire pump works, how a car's braking system works, how the human respiratory system works, how lightning storms develop, or how airplanes achieve lift (Mayer, 1997, 2001, 2002). In particular, I explore instructional techniques that go beyond explaining in words alone.

From its inception, education has been dominated by verbal modes of presentation. In short, words are the stuff that education is made of. For example, if I wanted to explain to you how lightning works, I might ask you to read (or listen to) the following passage.

Cool moist air moves over a warmer surface and becomes heated. Warmed moist air near the earth's surface rises rapidly. As the air in this updraft cools, water vapor condenses into water droplets and forms a cloud. The cloud's top extends above the freezing level, so the upper portion of the cloud is composed of tiny ice crystals. Eventually, the water droplets and ice crystals become too large to be suspended by the updrafts. As raindrops and ice crystals fall through the cloud, they drag some of the air in the cloud downward, producing downdrafts. When downdrafts strike the ground, they spread out in all directions, producing the gusts of cool wind people feel just before the start of the rain. Within the cloud, the rising and falling air currents cause electrical charges to build. The charge results from the collision of the cloud's rising water droplets against heavier, falling pieces of ice. The negatively charged particles fall to the bottom of the cloud, and most of the positively charged particles rise to the top. A stepped leader of negative charges moves downward in a series of steps. It nears the ground. A positively charged leader travels up from such objects as trees and buildings. The two leaders generally meet about 165 feet above the ground. Negatively charged particles then rush from the cloud to the ground along the path created by the leaders. It is not very bright. As the leader stroke nears the ground, it induces an opposite charge, so positively charged particles from the ground rush upward along the same path. This upward motion of the current is the return stroke. It produces the bright light that people notice as a flash of lightning.

What is wrong with giving explanations by using printed or spoken words? Our research seems to show that verbal explanations sometimes are not very effective (Mayer, 1997, 2001, 2002). If you are like most people, you do not retain much of the information in the lightning passage. When we ask students to read this passage and then write down an explanation of how lightning works, they miss more than half of the important steps in the process. In addition, if you are like most people, you do not understand the causal explanation presented in this passage. We can ask students to solve transfer problems such as, "What could you do to decrease the intensity of a lightning storm?" or "Suppose you see clouds in the sky but no lightning. Why not?" When we ask students to solve transfer problems like these based on the passage they have just read, they are unable to generate many useful answers. Failure to be able to apply what you have learned is a classic indication of lack of meaningful learning—that is, an indication that the learner did not understand the presented material.

What can be done to overcome this problem of good verbal explanations leading to a lack of understanding by learners? A potentially useful solution is to add visual modes of explanation to verbal ones, creating what can be called *multimedia explanations*. In our research, we define a multimedia explanation as one that uses both words (such as spoken or printed text) and pictures (such as illustrations, photos, animations, or videos). In this chapter, we focus on one kind of multimedia explanation—the narrated animation. For example, we can create a narrated animation using the words in the lightning passage along with a simple animation depicting the steps in lightning formation. Selected frames (along with corresponding narration) are shown in Fig. 3.1.

Do students learn more deeply from multimedia presentations than from purely verbal ones? Which kinds of multimedia presentations are most likely to lead to student understanding. These are the kinds of questions I explore in this chapter.

Multimedia technology is currently available that allows for instructional presentations involving animation and narration. Stand-alone multimedia CDs and Web-based multimedia presentations are becoming common in instruction. Does this technology offer potential for improving education or will it eventually become just another overhyped and underused educational technology such as motion pictures, radio, and educational TV (Cuban, 1986)?

"Cool moist air moves over a warmer surface and becomes heated."

"Warmed moist air near the earth's surface rises rapidly."

"As the air in this updraft cools, water vapor condenses into water droplets and forms a cloud."

"The cloud's top extends above the freezing level, so the upper portion of the cloud is composed of tiny ice crystals."

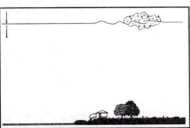

"Eventually, the water droplets and ice crystals become too large to be suspended by the updrafts."

"As raindrops and ice crystals fall through the cloud, they drag some of the air in the cloud downward, producing downdrafts."

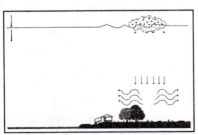

"When downdrafts strike the ground, they spread out in all directions, producing the gusts of cool wind people feel just before the start of the rain."

"Within the cloud, the rising and falling air currents cause electrical charges to build."

FIG. 3.1. *(Continued)*

"The charge results from the collision of the cloud's rising water droplets against heavier, falling pieces of ice."

"The negatively charged particles fall to the bottom of the cloud, and most of the positively charged particles rise to the top."

"A stepped leader of negative charges moves downward in a series of steps. It nears the ground."

"A positively charged leader travels up from such objects as trees and buildings."

"The two leaders generally meet about 165-feet above the ground."

"Negatively charged particles then rush from the cloud to the ground along the path created by the leaders. It is not very bright."

"As the leader stroke nears the ground, it induces an opposite charge, so positively charged particles from the ground rush upward along the same path."

"This upward motion of the current is the return stroke. It produces the bright light that people notice as a flash of lightning."

FIG. 3.1. Selected frames from a multimedia presentation on lightning.

The answer to this questions depends partly on whether educators take a technology-centered approach or a learner-centered approach (Mayer, 1999a; Norman, 1993). In a technology-centered approach, the design of multimedia is based on the capabilities of cutting-edge technology. The goal is for people to adapt how they learn to advances in technology. In a learner-centered approach, the design of multimedia is based on an understanding of how people learn. The goal is to adapt technology so that it can be used to enhance human learning. In this chapter, I take a learner-centered approach.

Multimedia technology may offer the potential to improve human learning, but if the history of educational technology is any indication, much remains to be done for that potential to be met. Taking a learner-centered approach is an important starting point. Fortunately, research in cognitive science has begun to uncover an educationally relevant theory of how people learn (Bransford, Brown, & Cocking, 1999; Bruer, 1993; Lambert & McCombs, 1998; Mayer, 1999b, 2003).

In this chapter, I summarize a cognitive theory of how people learn, I summarize six principles for designing multimedia explanations, and I discuss some implications of advances in our understanding of how to foster multimedia learning.

Cognitive Theory of Multimedia Learning

My theme in this chapter is simple: When the goal is to design multimedia presentations that foster understanding in learners, it is useful for the designer to understand how people learn from multimedia presentations. In short, multimedia design should be based on a theory of how people learn. In this section, I present a cognitive theory of multimedia learning that is based on 12 years of research by my colleagues and I at the University of California, Santa Barbara.

Figure 3.2 summarizes the cognitive theory of multimedia learning (Mayer, 1999c, 2001, 2002). It is based on three well-established concepts in cognitive science: (a) the dual-channel assumption, (b) the limited capacity assumption, and (c) the active learning assumption. The dual-channel assumption is that humans have separate channels for processing visual and auditory information (Baddeley, 1992, 1998; Clark & Paivio, 1991; Paivio, 1986). As shown in Fig. 3.2, the top row involves processing of verbal material that is presented as sounds, whereas the bottom row involves processing of visual material that is presented as pictures. The limited capacity assumption is that the amount of processing in each channel is extremely limited (Baddeley, 1992, 1998; Chandler & Sweller, 1991; Paas, Renkl, & Sweller, 2003; Sweller, 1999). For example, only a few words can be held in auditory working memory at one time (indicated by the box labeled *sounds*), and only a few features of a pictorial presentation can be held in visual working memory at one time (indicated by the box labeled *images*). The active learning assumption is that meaningful learning occurs when learners engage in active processing of the presented material (Mayer, 1996, 2001; Wittrock, 1990).

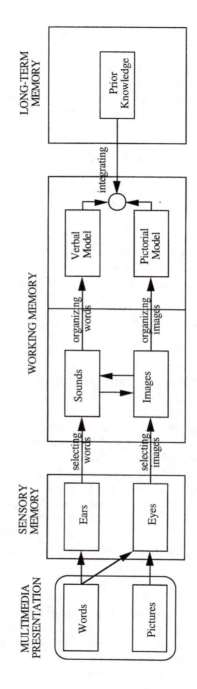

FIG. 3.2.   A cognitive theory of multimedia learning.

These cognitive processes include selecting relevant material (indicated by the arrows labeled *selecting words* and *selecting images*), organizing it into a coherent mental representation (indicated by the arrows labeled *organizing words* and *organizing images*), and integrating it with related material (indicated by the arrow labeled *integrating*).

For example, consider what happens when a person who is seated at a computer clicks on an icon and receives a short narrated animation. The presented narration corresponds to the box labeled *words*, and the presented animation corresponds to the box labeled *pictures*. For example, the narrated animation about lightning in Fig. 3.1 begins with the sounds "Cool, most air moves over a warmer surface" and the corresponding animation of blue wavy arrows moving rightward from above the water to above the land with houses and trees on the land. The words impinge on the ears (indicated by the box labeled *ears*), and the pictures impinge on the eyes (indicated by the box labeled *eyes*).

By paying attention to the incoming sounds and images (indicated by the "selecting sounds" and "selecting images" arrows, respectively), the learner is able to hold some of the material in working memory (indicated by the boxes labeled *sounds* and *images*). For example, the learner may focus on the words *air moves* and on the image of wavy blue lines moving rightward.

By mentally organizing the sounds (indicated by the "organizing words" arrow) the learner can build a coherent mental representation (labeled *verbal model*), and by mentally organizing the images (indicated by the "organizing images" arrow) the learner can build a coherent mental representation (labeled *pictorial model*). For example, on hearing the two statements, "Cool, moist air moves over a warmer surface and becomes heated" and "Warmed moist air near the earth's surface rises rapidly," the learner may mentally build a causal connection between air moving and air rising.

Finally, by mentally integrating the verbal and pictorial models and prior knowledge from long-term memory (indicated by the arrow labeled *integrating*), the learner is able to construct an integrated mental representation. For example, the learner may build a causal chain with words along with corresponding images, and with knowledge from long-term memory to justify each step—such as knowing the principle by which heated air rises.

Design Principles for Multimedia Presentations

Recently, researchers have become increasingly interested in developing research-based principles of multimedia design (Jonassen & Reeves, 1996; Najjar, 1998; Park & Hannafin, 1993). The cognitive theory of multimedia learning allows us to generate testable design principles for multimedia presentations. We begin with the epitome of a multimedia message: a concise narrated animation

(CNA), which explains how something works such as the lightning presentation summarized in Fig. 3.1. A concise narrated animation consists of a short animation that depicts each step along with concurrent narration that describes each step in words. Our research has shown that CNAs foster student understanding as assessed by tests of problem-solving transfer (Mayer, 1997, 2001, 2002). To assess transfer, we ask students to answer open-ended questions such as described earlier (with a 2.5-minute limit for each question), and we count the total number of acceptable answers the student generates across all questions.

Multimedia Principle. A preliminary research question concerns whether a multimedia presentation—such as the CNA—results in deeper understanding than a traditional verbal explanation—such as narration alone. According to the cognitive theory of multimedia learning, students should learn more deeply from animation and narration than from narration alone because they are more likely to engage in all five basic cognitive processes that lead to building an integrated mental representation. In the narration-only condition, students may not be able to form a visual model (i.e., organize images) or connect it with a verbal model (i.e., integrate). Thus, the cognitive theory of multimedia learning predicts that the CNA group will perform better on problem-solving transfer than the narration-only group.

In contrast, the information-delivery theory is based on the idea that media are delivery systems for information. According to this theory, the animation and narration are redundant because they each explain the same thing at the same time—that is, the information is delivered via two routes simultaneously. Thus, students should acquire the same information from narration alone as from narration and animation because the animation adds no new information. The information-delivery theory predicts no difference in the problem-solving transfer performance of the two groups.

In a series of three tests involving explanations of pumps and brakes (Mayer & Anderson, 1991, Exp. 2a; Mayer & Anderson, 1992, Exp. 1 and Exp. 2), we compared the learning outcomes of students who learned from a concise narrated animation (CNA group) and those who learned from the narration only (narration-only group). The CNA group generated a median of 97% more solutions on the problem-solving transfer test than the narration-only group, with a median effect size of 1.90. These results show that students learn deeply when they receive both animation and narration than when they receive narration alone. Similar results were obtained in comparing illustrations and text with text alone (Mayer, 1989; Mayer & Gallini, 1990; Mayer et al., 1996). These results are consistent with the cognitive theory of multimedia learning and inconsistent with the information-delivery theory.

These results lead to the first design principle listed in Table 3.1: the *multimedia principle*. The multimedia principle states that students learn more deeply from narration and animation than from narration alone.

TABLE 3.1
Research-Based Principles for the Design of Multimedia Explanations

1. *Multimedia principle:* Students learn more deeply from narration and animation than from narration alone.
2. *Temporal contiguity principle:* Students learn more deeply when corresponding portions of animation and narration are presented simultaneously rather than successively.
3. *Coherence principle:* Students learn more deeply when extraneous words, pictures, and sounds are excluded rather than included.
4. *Modality principle:* Students learn more deeply from animation and narration than from animation and on-screen text.
5. *Redundancy principle:* Students learn more deeply from animation and narration than from animation, narration, and on-screen text.
6. *Personalization principle:* Students learn more deeply from animation and personalized narration than from animation and nonpersonalized narration.

Temporal Contiguity Principle.   Although words and pictures may lead to deeper learning than words alone in some circumstances, not all multimedia presentations are equally effective in promoting meaningful learning. What are the features of an effective multimedia explanation? In a concise narrated animation, corresponding words and pictures are presented at the same time. For example, when the narration says, "The negatively-charged particles fall to the bottom of the cloud, and most of the positively charged particles rise to the top," the animation shows negatives moving to the bottom of the cloud and positives moving to the top. In this section, I explore how well the animation and narration are coordinated by comparing multimedia messages in which corresponding words and pictures are presented at the same time (i.e., simultaneous presentation, as in the CNA) and multimedia messages in which the entire narration is presented before or after the entire animation (i.e., successive presentation).

According to the cognitive theory of multimedia learning, students must hold corresponding words and pictures in working memory at the same time to build connections between them. This is more likely to occur when corresponding words and pictures are presented at the same time than when they are presented successively. Thus, the cognitive theory of multimedia learning predicts that simultaneous presentation will lead to deeper learning than successive presentation.

In contrast, the information-delivery theory is based on the idea that students learn more when the same information is repeated than when it is just presented once. In successive presentation, the information is presented in one form and then the same information is presented in another form, effectively creating twice as much time with the material. In the simultaneous presentation, the same information is presented in words and pictures at one time, effectively creating just one presentation. Thus, the information-delivery theory predicts that successive presentation will lead to better learning than simultaneous presentation.

To test these predictions, we conducted a series of eight tests in which we compared simultaneous and successive presentations of explanations of pumps, brakes, lungs, and lightning (Mayer & Anderson, 1991, Exp. 1 and Exp. 2a; Mayer & Anderson, 1992, Exp. 1 and Exp. 2; Mayer & Sims, 1994, Exp. 1 and Exp. 2; Mayer, Moreno, Boire, & Vagge, 1999; Exp. 1 and Exp. 2). Overall, the simultaneous group (i.e., who received the CNA) generated a median of 60% more solutions on the problem-solving test than the successive group, and the median effect size favoring the simultaneous group was 1.30. Analogous results were obtained using text and illustrations in which students learned more deeply when corresponding words and illustrations were physically near each other on page rather than far from one another (Mayer, 1989; Mayer, Steinhoff, Bower, & Mars, 1995; Moreno & Mayer, 1999). These results are most consistent with the cognitive theory of multimedia learning and inconsistent with the information-delivery theory.

It is worthwhile to note that students in the successive group received identical material as students in the successive group and had twice as much time to study it. Yet they did not learn it as well presumably because they had more difficulty constructing connections between words and pictures. The results suggest that a critical process in meaningful learning is for learners to connect corresponding words and pictures—a process that is promoted with concise narrated animations.

As shown in Table 3.2, we refer to this finding as the *temporal contiguity principle*: Students learn more deeply from multimedia messages when corresponding portions of animation and narration are presented simultaneously rather than successively.

Coherence Principle.   Suppose we create a concise narrated animation, such as described in the previous section. How can we improve on it? One possibility is to make it more interesting or entertaining. This can be accomplished by adding interesting but irrelevant words and pictures to a concise narrated animation, or by adding background music and environmental sounds that are intended to entertain the learner. For example, we could insert short videos of various lightning storms or narration about interesting lightning facts in a concise narrated animation about lightning formation, or we could add a mellow sound track and weather sounds to a concise narrated animation about lightning formation.

According to the cognitive theory of multimedia learning, adding these interesting adjuncts can result in less understanding. The inserted video and narration can prime inappropriate prior knowledge so the learner tries to organize the material in ways that are not based on the underlying cause-and-effect chain. The inserted music and sounds can overload the auditory channel, making it less likely that the appropriate words will be selected, organized, and integrated with corresponding images. Thus, students who receive interesting adjuncts (CNA with seductive details group) are expected to perform more poorly on transfer tests than students who do not (CNA group).

In contrast, the information-delivery theory predicts that adding the adjuncts will not hurt learning because the same basic information is presented. If the adjuncts serve to increase the learner's motivation to learn, then the adjuncts could even increase the amount learned. Thus, students who receive interesting adjuncts (CNA with seductive details group) are expected to perform as well or better than students who do not (CNA group) on transfer tests.

In three tests, we compared the learning outcomes of students who received a concise narrated animation about lightning or brakes with students who received the same presentation with inserted interesting adjuncts (Mayer & Heiser, 1999, Exp. 1; Moreno & Mayer, 2000; Exp. 1 and Exp. 2). Students receiving the concise narrated animation generated a median of 61% more solutions on the transfer test as compared with students who learned with the same presentation with interesting adjuncts; the median effect size favoring the CNA presentation was .90. Harp and Mayer (1997, 1998) provided similar results involving illustrations and text. Overall, these results are consistent with the cognitive theory of multimedia learning and inconsistent with the information-delivery theory.

These results allow us to add the *coherence principle* to our list of design principles in Table 3.1: Students learn more deeply from a multimedia presentation when extraneous words, pictures, and sounds are excluded rather than included.

Modality Principle.   In our attempts to improve on the narrated animation, we have found that separating the words and pictures is harmful—although it effectively doubles the study time—and inserting entertaining adjuncts is harmful—although they are intended to make the material more interesting. How about converting the narration into on-screen text so the student can reread portions of the text? In multimedia presentations with on-screen text, the words in the narration are presented instead as on-screen text at the bottom of the screen for the same time period as the narration. In this way, corresponding words and pictures are presented at the same time, but the words seem to be presented in a more flexible form.

This suggestion conflicts with the cognitive theory of multimedia learning because it ignores the idea that people possess two separate information-processing channels—one for the eyes and one for the ears. When information is presented as animation and on-screen text, the visual channel can become overloaded, resulting in less material being processed by the learner. This situation creates *split attention* (Sweller, 1999), in which learners must split their visual attention between two different sources—the animation and on-screen text. In contrast, when words are presented as narration, the words can be processed in the auditory channel, effectively increasing the capacity of the visual channel to process the animation. The cognitive theory of multimedia learning predicts that the concise narrated animation will lead to deeper learning and thus better transfer performance than presenting the animation with on-screen text.

In contrast, the information-delivery theory predicts no difference in transfer performance because students receive identical information in both treatments. In short, the words deliver the same information whether they are spoken or printed.

In a series of four tests, we compared students who learned about lightning or brakes from a concise narrated animation or from an equivalent animation with on-screen text (Mayer & Moreno, 1998, Exp. 1 and Exp. 2; Moreno & Mayer, 1999, Exp. 1 and Exp. 2). The CNA group generated a median of 104% more solutions on the transfer test as compared with the animation with on-screen text group, and the median effect size favoring the CNA group was 1.17. Similar results were obtained by Mousavi, Low, and Sweller (1995). These results are consistent with the cognitive theory of multimedia learning and inconsistent with the information-delivery theory.

These results form the basis for the *modality principle* listed in Table 3.1: Students learn more deeply from multimedia presentations when words are presented as narration rather than on-screen text.

Redundancy Principle.   So far we have not been able to improve on the concise narrated animation, but we have been able to generate several important design principles. Let us try another straightforward suggestion for improving CNAs: make them more accommodating by including both narration and on-screen text. The newly created multimedia program would present narration along with animation, but also include on-screen text at the bottom of the screen presented sentence by sentence in a way that mimics the narration.

Unfortunately, this seemingly helpful suggestion conflicts with the cognitive theory of multimedia learning. The problem is that the on-screen text and animation both must be processed in the visual channel, creating a situation that is likely to lead to overloading the processing capacity of the channel. The result is that the learner may not be able to attend to all of the relevant portions of the animation or have capacity left over to organize and integrate the pictorial mental model. As with the modality effect, the learner may experience split attention, in which visual processing must be split between two sources. In contrast, when the on-screen text is eliminated, learners can process the animation in the visual channel and process the narration in the auditory channel. This situation minimizes cognitive load in each channel. Thus, the cognitive theory of multimedia learning predicts superior transfer performance for students who receive animation and narration (i.e., the CNA) rather than animation, narration, and on-screen text.

In contrast, the information-delivery theory supports the recommended addition of on-screen text. The commonsense rationale for this improvement is that it enables students to choose the mode of presentation that best matches their learning preference—processing words by eye or by ear. If students have two ways to receive the words, they can choose the delivery system they are best able to use. If a student is better able to receive words by reading, he or she can pay attention to on-screen text; if the student is better able to receive words by listening, then he or she can pay attention to the narration. Thus, the information-delivery theory predicts that students will perform better on transfer tests when they receive animation, narration, and on-screen text rather than animation and narration.

Mayer, Heiser, and Lonn (2001, Exp. 1 and Exp. 2) tested these predictions in two tests with multimedia programs aimed at teaching students about lightning formation. Overall, students who learned from a multimedia program consisting of animation and narration (i.e., a CNA) produced a median of 28% more solutions on the transfer test than did students who learned from animation, narration, and on-screen text; the median effect size favoring the animation and narration group was .77. Similar results were obtained by Kalyuga, Chandler, and Sweller (1999). These results favor the cognitive theory of multimedia learning over the information-delivery theory.

In light of these results, we are able to add the *redundancy principle* to our list of design recommendations in Table 3.1: Students learn more deeply from animation and narration than from animation, narration, and on-screen text.

Personalization Principle.   As you can see, each of our attempts to improve on the concise narrated animation have resulted in failure—both at the theoretical level by conflicting with the cognitive theory of multimedia learning and at the empirical level by producing decrements in problem-solving transfer. It looks like the most effective way to promote understanding of multimedia explanations is to create a concise narrated animation: a multimedia presentation that describes the main steps of the causal chain in spoken words and depicts the main steps of the causal chain in a simple animation, with corresponding words and pictures being presented at the same time. Just when we were about to give up all hope, however, we tried one last idea for improving on the concise narrated animation that worked so well in dozens of experiments. That idea is to personalize the text to make it more like a conversation and less like a one-way monologue.

Personalization of the text can be accomplished by adding a few direct comments to the learner such as, "As you watch, you tilt your head skyward" or "Brr! I'm feeling cold just thinking about it," and by substituting first- and second-person words rather than third-person words, such as changing "The cloud's top extends above the freezing level . . ." to "Your cloud's top extends above the freezing level." The content of the verbal explanation of lightning formation, however, remains the same, and the animation is unaltered.

According to the cognitive theory of multimedia learning, the added material could be distracting in the same way that adding interesting but irrelevant stories is distracting. If we extended the coherence principle, we could make the case against personalizing the text. However, our research has shown that the main problem with adding irrelevant words and pictures is that they prime an inappropriate schema, which the learner uses for organizing the incoming information (Harp & Mayer, 1997, 1998). In contrast, personalizing the text may prime a schema that includes the learner, creating a cognitive process in the learner that can be called *self-reference* (Rogers, Kuiper, & Kirker, 1977). In short, personalized text may encourage the learner to organize the explanation into an appropriate causal chain that includes the learner as a component. This interpretation is consistent with research on self-reference that suggests self-referential language can promote deeper learning (Symons & Johnson, 1997). Based on this analysis, cognitive theory predicts that students who receive a personal CNA will perform better on a subsequent transfer test than students who receive a standard CNA.

The information-delivery theory predicts that adding self-referential language will have no effect on learning because the same explanation is presented in the standard CNA and the personalized CNA. Thus, the information-delivery theory predicts that both groups will perform the same on the transfer test.

Does personalization affect how deeply students learn from a concise narrated animation? Moreno and Mayer (2000, Exp. 1 and Exp. 2) conducted two tests comparing a traditional CNA about lightning formation with a personalized CNA. The personalized group generated a median of 126% more solutions on the transfer test as compared with the standard group, yielding a median effect size of 1.30 favoring the personalized over the standard CNA. These results are consistent with a version of the cognitive theory of multimedia learning in which self-referential language promotes deeper processing; it is inconsistent with the predictions of the information-delivery theory.

These results suggest that concise narrated animations can be improved by creating personalized concise narrated animations. The final design principle in Table 3.1 is the *personalization principle*: Students learn more deeply when words are presented in conversational style rather than monologue style.

Conclusion

How can we help students understand multimedia explanations? This question has driven our research for the past 12 years. As I summarized in this chapter, the result has been: (a) a research-based framework for describing how people learn from words and pictures, which we call a cognitive theory of multimedia learning (shown in Fig. 3.2); and (b) a research-based set of design principles for multimedia presentations that are intended to explain how something works (shown in Table 3.1).

In terms of a theoretical framework, the single most salient aspect of the cognitive theory of multimedia learning is that learners must be able to hold corresponding visual and verbal representations in working memory at the same time. In short, students learn more deeply from multimedia presentations that are consistent rather than inconsistent with the way that humans process visual and verbal information. According to the cognitive theory of multimedia learning, understanding occurs when students can select relevant portions of the presented words and pictures, organize them into coherent verbal and pictorial mental models, and integrate the models with one another and prior knowledge. Multimedia presentations that foster these processes are more likely to lead to meaningful learning than those that inhibit these processes.

In terms of multimedia design principles, the single most salient product of our research program is the concise narrated animation (CNA). A CNA is a multimedia explanation that depicts the main steps in a cause–effect process using a simple animation, describes the same steps using a simple narration, and presents corresponding portions of the animation and narration at the same time. A CNA is concise because it presents only essential aspects of the causal chain rather than extraneous material. A CNA is a multimedia presentation because it involves both words (i.e., narration) and pictures (i.e., animation). A CNA is coordinated because it presents corresponding words and pictures at the same time. More important, our preliminary results suggest that CNAs can be improved by making the text more personal—that is, by using words that are more in conversational style and less in monologue style.

It is important to note that the principles are not intended as rules to be rigidly applied to all multimedia learning situations. Rather, decisions about the design of multimedia messages should be based on an understanding of how people learn from words and pictures, as summarized in the cognitive theory of multimedia learning. As our search for design principles continues, we are guided by the cognitive theory of multimedia learning that is emerging.

Finally, our focus has been on how to foster deep understanding rather than solely on how to increase the amount of learning. Thus, my primary focus in this chapter was on how design changes affect problem-solving transfer. Transfer tests are a useful way to measure understanding because they attempt to tap the degree to which learners can use what they have learned in new situations. However, in many of studies, we also asked students to write down the explanation they had just learned about (i.e., we gave them a retention test). In general, patterns of performance on this kind of retention test paralleled the transfer tests (Mayer, 1997, 1999c, 2001, 2002).

Our research is limited by virtue of its focus on one kind of instructional goal (i.e., to help students understand explanations of how a scientific system works) and on one kind of learners (i.e., college students who are inexperienced with the topic). In addition, we focused on multimedia learning in a short-term, nonclassroom environment. Further research is needed to examine the ecological validity of our principles in a variety of educational venues.

ACKNOWLEDGMENTS

The research summarized in this chapter was conducted in collaboration with Richard B. Anderson, Joan Gallini, Shannon Harp, Valerie Sims, and Roxana Moreno.

REFERENCES

Baddeley, A. (1992). Working memory. *Science, 255*, 566–559.

Baddeley, A. (1998). *Human memory.* Boston: Allyn & Bacon.

Bransford, J. D., Brown, A. L., & Cocking, R. R. (Eds.). (1999). *How people learn.* Washington, DC: National Academy Press.

Bruer, J. T. (1993). *Schools for thought.* Cambridge, MA: MIT Press.

Chandler, P., & Sweller, J. (1991). Cognitive load theory and the format of instruction. *Cognition and Instruction, 8*, 293–332.

Clark, J. M., & Paivio, A. (1991). Dual coding theory and education. *Educational Psychology Review, 3*, 149–210.

Cuban, L. (1986). *Teachers and machines: The use of classroom technology since 1920.* New York: Teachers College Press.

Harp, S., & Mayer, R. E. (1997). Role of interest in learning from scientific text and illustrations: On the distinction between emotional interest and cognitive interest. *Journal of Educational Psychology, 89*, 92–102.

Harp, S., & Mayer, R. E. (1998). How seductive details do their damage: A theory of cognitive interest in science learning. *Journal of Educational Psychology, 90*, 414–434.

Jonassen, D. H., & Reeves, T. C. (1996). Learning with technology: Using computers as cognitive tools. In D. H. Jonassen (Ed.), *Handbook of research for educational communication and technology* (pp. 693–719). New York: Macmillan.

Kalyuga, S., Chandler, P., & Sweller, P. (1999). Managing split-attention and redundancy in multimedia instruction. *Applied Cognitive Psychology, 13*, 351–372.

Lambert, N. M., & McCombs, B. L. (1998). *How students learn.* Washington, DC: American Psychological Association.

Mayer, R. E. (1989). Systematic thinking fostered by illustrations in scientific text. *Journal of Educational Psychology, 81*, 240–246.

Mayer, R. E. (1996). Learning strategies for making sense out of expository text: The SOI model for guiding three cognitive processes in knowledge construction. *Educational Psychology Review, 8*, 357–371.

Mayer, R. E. (1997). Multimedia learning: Are we asking the right questions? *Educational Psychologist, 32*, 1–19.

Mayer, R. E. (1999a). Instructional technology. In F. Durso (Ed.), *Handbook of applied cognition* (pp. 551–570). Chichester, England: Wiley.

Mayer, R. E. (1999b). *The promise of educational psychology.* Upper Saddle River, NJ: Prentice-Hall.

Mayer, R. E. (1999c). Multimedia aids to problem-solving transfer. *International Journal of Educational Research, 31*, 611–623.

Mayer, R. E. (2001). *Multimedia learning.* New York: Cambridge University Press.

Mayer, R. E. (2002). Multimedia learning. In B. H. Ross (Ed.), *The psychology of learning and motivation* (Vol. 41, pp. 85–139). San Diego, CA: Academic Press.

Mayer, R. E. (2003). *Learning and instruction.* Upper Saddle River, NJ: Prentice-Hall.

Mayer, R. E., & Anderson, R. B. (1991). Animations need narrations: An experimental test of a dual-coding hypothesis. *Journal of Educational Psychology, 83*, 484–490.

Mayer, R. E., & Anderson, R. B. (1992). The instructive animation: Helping students build connections between words and pictures in multimedia learning. *Journal of Educational Psychology, 84*, 444–452.

Mayer, R. E., Bove, W., Bryman, A., Mars, R., & Tapangco, L. (1996). When less is more: Meaningful learning from visual and verbal summaries of science textbook lessons. *Journal of Educational Psychology, 88*, 64–73.

Mayer, R. E., & Gallini, J. K. (1990). When is an illustration worth ten thousand words? *Journal of Educational Psychology, 82*, 715–726.

Mayer, R. E., Heiser, J., & Lonn, S. (2001). Cognitive constraints on multimedia learning: When more material results in less understanding. *Journal of Educational Psychology, 93*, 187–198.

Mayer, R. E., & Moreno, R. (1998). A split-attention effect in multimedia learning: Evidence for dual information processing systems in working memory. *Journal of Educational Psychology, 90*, 312–320.

Mayer, R. E., Moreno, R., Boire, M., & Vagge, S. (1999). Maximizing constructivist learning from multimedia communications by minimizing cognitive load. *Journal of Educational Psychology, 91*, 638–643.

Mayer, R. E., & Sims, V. V. K. (1994). For whom is a picture worth a thousand words? Extensions of a dual-coding theory of multimedia learning. *Journal of Educational Psychology, 86*, 389–401.

Mayer, R. E., Steinhoff, K., Bower, G., & Mars, R. (1995). A generative theory of textbook design: Using annotated illustrations to foster meaningful learning of science text. *Educational Technology Research and Development, 43*, 31–44.

Moreno, R., & Mayer, R. E. (1999). Cognitive principles of multimedia learning: The role of modality and contiguity. *Journal of Educational Psychology, 91*, 358–368.

Moreno, R., & Mayer, R. E. (2000). A coherence effect in multimedia learning: The case for minimizing irrelevant sounds in the design of multimedia messages. *Journal of Educational Psychology, 92*, 117–125.

Moreno, R., & Mayer, R. E. (2000). Engaging students in active learning: The case for personalized multimedia messages. *Journal of Educational Psychology, 93*, 724–733.

Mousavi, S., Low, R., & Sweller, J. (1995). Reducing cognitive load by mixing auditory and visual presentation modes. *Journal of Educational Psychology, 87*, 319–334.

Najjar, L. J. (1998). Principles of educational multimedia user interface design. *Human Factors, 40*, 311–323.

Norman, D. A. (1993). *Things that make us smart*. Reading, MA: Addison-Wesley.

Paivio, A. (1986). *Mental representations: A dual coding approach*. Oxford, England: Oxford University Press.

Park, I., & Hannafin, M. J. (1993). Empirically-based guidelines for the design of interactive multimedia. *Educational Technology Research and Development, 41*, 63–85.

Paas, F., Renkl, A., & Sweller, J. (2003). Cognitive load theory and instructional design: Recent developments. *Educational Psychologist, 8*, 1–5.

Rogers, T. B., Kuiper, N., & Kirker, W. S. (1977). Self reference and the encoding of personal information. *Journal of Personality and Social Psychology, 35*, 677–688.

Sweller, J. (1999). *Instructional design in technical areas*. Camberwell, Australia: ACER Press.

Symons, C. S., & Johnson, B. T. (1997). The self-reference effect in memory: A meta-analysis. *Psychological Bulletin, 121*, 371–394.

Wittrock, M. C. (1990). Generative processes in reading comprehension. *Educational Psychologist, 24*, 345–376.

II

Affordances
of Technology

GOVERNORS STATE UNIVERSITY
UNIVERSITY PARK
IL 60466

4

Opportunities for Learning and Development in an After-School Computer Club

Mary Gauvain
Sharon Borthwick-Duffy
University of California

Despite the tendency to shut ourselves away and sit in Rodinesque isolation when we have to learn, learning is a remarkably social process. Social groups provide the resources for their members to learn.
—Brown and Duguid (2000, p. 137)

Developing skill with computers is considered critical to children's present success in school as well as to their future success when they assume more independent roles in society. Unfortunately, the equipment, support systems, and instructors needed to help children develop this skill are in short supply, especially in low-income communities. Furthermore, when computers are available in classrooms with poorer children, there is evidence that teachers tend to use them for drill and practice rather than cognitive enrichment (Archer, 1998; Laboratory of Comparative Human Cognition, 1985; Rochelle et al., 2000). This gap in computer opportunities for children (and adults) in poorer versus more affluent communities is known as the *digital divide* (National Telecommunications and Information Administration, 1999). Presently, a number of public and private efforts are directed at remedying the digital divide in schools (see Becker, 2000; Bransford, Brown, & Cocking, 1999). However, due to the limited availability of technology in classrooms, the lack of teachers trained to integrate technology effectively into the curriculum, and the fact that children's school days are already chock full of curricular and noncurricular demands, it is clear that efforts outside of school are also needed to "bridge the divide" and attain some sort of parity in this regard.

53

To address this issue, after-school computer programs, especially for low-income children, have sprung up across the nation. These programs are housed in a variety of settings, including Boys and Girls Clubs, public libraries, community centers, and elementary and middle schools. The primary objective of these programs is to enhance the understanding and use of computers among low-income children so they are not "left behind" in a society that is increasingly defined by the rapid processing and exchange of information. A second, equally important objective is to provide children with constructive and safe options for how they spend their time when they are not in school (Belle, 1999; Eccles & Gootman, 2002; The Future of Children, 2000; Gauvain & Perez, in press; Miller, 2001).

Although after-school programs that involve technology share the goal of teaching children computer skills, the social context in which this learning occurs can differ dramatically across settings. In many of these programs, the emphasis is on children's opportunity to work on computers on their own by having them use software designed to guide and support individual learning. In other programs, it is assumed that children prefer to work alone rather than with others at computers. In settings in which children typically work alone, the primary reason that more than one child may be placed at a computer is to provide access to more children when resources are not sufficient to have one computer per child. Regardless of the reasoning behind solitary computer activity, programs that emphasize individual work assume that computer-guided instruction and ample individual practice are the keys to developing competence in this domain. In several ways, this approach to after-school computer learning mimics the traditional classroom setting, especially in its emphasis on repeated practice, solitary seat work, and the positioning of the teacher and curriculum (in this case, the software) as the repositories of knowledge.

Several questions can be asked about the effectiveness of the solitary, one-child-per-computer approach to teaching children computer skills outside of school. The most obvious question is whether this approach actually teaches children computer skills. Little evidence exists to answer this question directly because this type of after-school setting has not been the focus of systematic research. Extrapolating from classroom research, it seems that the answer would depend on what children do at the computer (Cuban, 2001). When technology is used in inappropriate ways, at least inappropriate in terms of promoting learning, such as when children spend their time following explicit and limited sets of instructions, playing with font styles and colors, or surfing the Internet, little learning results (Bransford et al., 1999). In addition, practice that emphasizes drill does not appear to teach children skills, but instead builds the fluency of the skills that children already possess (Trotter, 1998). In contrast, more interactive use of technology that has children learn by doing, receive feedback on their work, and refine and build new knowledge can promote learning (Bransford et al., 1999; Rochelle et al., 2000). However, even when more interactive ingredients are built into the children's experience with technology in after-school settings, problems arise if the activities at the setting too closely resemble the types of activities that are typically part of the school experience. If children perceive the after-school program as merely a lengthening of the school day, behaviors or attitudes that interfere with children's learning and motivation in the classroom may emerge in the after-school setting. Additionally, after-school programs that resemble school are not likely to attract older children and adolescents who have many choices as to how to spend their time after school and typically attend such programs voluntarily (Belle, 1999; Hofferth & Jankuniene, 2001; Quinn, 1999).

In this chapter, we make the point that purposeful planning in an after-school computer program for collaboration involving dyads or small groups of peers and adults around a single computer, even when resources would make it possible to provide each child with his or her own computer, leads to benefits in a wide range of child outcomes. Research has shown that computers can enhance children's understanding when they are used to create learning environments that are interactive in two distinct ways (Bransford et al., 1999; Rochelle et al., 2000). Specifically, learning may be enhanced through interactive computing experiences, as well as through the social interactions generated in a computer-based setting. These benefits reflect current theory and research in child development, which emphasize the importance of contexts of interaction that support learning (Gauvain, 2001; Rogoff, 2003). In our view, social interactions in computer-based programs may be especially important for learning because they involve children in active and directive roles with more experienced partners who may offer support for or scaffold this learning (Rogoff, 1998; Vygotsky, 1978). Thus, solitary learning situations in which children are expected to learn computer skills essentially on their own are at odds with this contemporary approach to intellectual development, whereas programs that consider children's learning about computers as a dialogic process guided by more experienced participants are consistent with this view (Sandholtz, Ringstaff, & Dwyer, 1997).

Recognition of the important role that social interaction can play in the development of computer skills is not entirely absent in after-school computer programs for children. In fact some programs have been deliberately designed so that children can learn about computers and computing from collaboration with others (Cole, 1996). The premise underlying these programs is that, over time, as participants communicate about and negotiate their understanding of computers with each other and learn to coordinate their computer use to meet shared goals, a community of learners will emerge (Brown & Campione, 1994, 1996; Rogoff, Turkanis, & Bartlett, 2001). The idea of a community of learners is based on the view that learning and development result from participation in the sociocultural activities of a community (Vygotsky, 1978). In contrast to an adult-centered view that considers learning a process in which knowledge is transmitted from an adult to a child or a child-centered view that casts learning as the process in which children discover knowledge on their own, a sociocultural view sees learning and development as a process of transformation in the roles and responsibilities that individuals assume in the activities in which they participate (Rogoff, 1998, 2003). Both children and adults are active participants in this process. As children's roles and responsibilities change, so do the roles and responsibilities of the adults who are involved.

Classroom research has shown that computer-based learning environments based on the idea of a community of learners can promote children's learning in several academic domains (Brown, 1997; Sandholtz et al., 1997). Therefore, extending this idea to after-school settings designed to teach children about computers has both theoretical and empirical support. In addition, it provides yet another alternative, and a potentially valuable one, to the myriad of programs designed to enrich children's experiences outside of school (Eccles & Gootman, 2002; The Future of Children, 1999). Finally, building social interaction in systematic ways into computer-based programs outside of school is consistent with how adults use computers in the workplace. Adults often rely on the knowledge and skills of others when they use computers in their own work (Brown & Duguid, 2000; Pea, 1993a). Thus, having children learn to use computers entirely on their own is contrary to the way in which computers are used in most adult work settings and, as a result, may interfere with the transfer of learning beyond this setting (Pea, 1993b). Transfer, or the ability to extend what one has learned in one context to new contexts, is influenced by many factors, including the degree to which tasks across settings share cognitive elements (Singley & Anderson, 1989). If one feature of cognitive activity in the workplace is social interaction, this same type of experience in earlier computer-related learning may help bootstrap children's transfer of these early computer experiences to later computer use.

To explore the contribution of social practices in an after-school setting to children's learning about and use of computers, this chapter discusses a program in which social interaction among children and between children and adults is integral to the program and to learning about computers. The chapter examines how this type of after-school program supports the development of children's understanding and use of computer technology. It also examines other social and intellectual opportunities that arise as children and others work together to accomplish mutual goals in a computer-based environment for learning. We are interested in a broad range of learning opportunities that may emerge in this setting. In addition to computer competence, we examine how participation in this type of program may contribute to the development of social and intellectual confidence in children. Social and intellectual confidence are aspects of the child's developing self-concept that may be especially likely to benefit from participation in an after-school program in which the type of competence that is the focus of the program—namely, computer skills—is both recognized and valued by others. Self-development in relation to socially valued skills may be especially critical for children during middle childhood, the age period that is the focus of the program described later. Research has shown that children's self-concept about their own abilities and expectations for success in academic realms and other challenging

tasks tends to decline over the elementary years (Eccles, 1999). This decline is associated with a decrease in motivation to learn, which shows a steady drop from late childhood through adolescence. Therefore, programs designed to contribute in positive ways to a child's self-concept during these critical growth years are important to study to determine whether and what program characteristics may support positive youth development during this period (Larson, 2000).

To summarize, the program described next emphasizes the social context of computer learning and activity. The setting and activities that children do in this setting are designed to enrich and broaden their interactions with computers and with other people. Following a description of the program, evidence regarding how participation in this program may support children's learning and development is discussed. The chapter concludes with an examination of the theoretical and practical implications of programs of this sort.

THE RIVERSIDE TROLLEY: AN AFTER-SCHOOL COMPUTER PROGRAM FOR SIXTH GRADERS

An after-school computer program for children based on the Fifth Dimension Program (see Cole, 1996; Nicolopoulou & Cole, 1993) was established in the fall of 1996 at the University of California at Riverside. This program involves the collaboration of the university and an elementary school near the campus. The elementary school, which is located in a lower to lower middle-income neighborhood, has a diverse student body. Data collected each year of the program indicate that, on average, approximately 70% of the students are entitled to a free or reduced lunch, 68% are from minority groups, and 20% have limited English proficiency.

The after-school program was designed to serve sixth-grade children (recently some fifth graders have been included to provide some continuity in child participation across the academic years). Sixth-grade students were identified as the target group for several reasons. These students would soon be moving to middle school, where they would be confronted with increased expectations related to technology. Students who are skilled in research methods involving technology, report writing, and multimedia presentations are at a distinct advantage in middle school. Because the majority of the children in the school where our program is located do not have access to computers at home, development of these skills seemed essential and appropriate for the after-school program. Moreover, we expected that the acquisition of these skills would have a positive influence on the self-confidence the students have about their own learning abilities. This confidence would be beneficial to them as they enter a new phase of academic life in which class-related work based on these skills is both expected and valued. Thus, like many after-school programs, this program has educational goals. However, the philosophy of the program is less aligned with interventions that emphasize remedial or compensatory instruction and more similar to youth development programs in which children are seen as resources to be developed rather than as problems to be solved (Miller, 2001).

The program is called *The Riverside Trolley*, and it is located in the elementary school library where there are 30 personal computers. Computers were introduced to this setting when the after-school program was established. The University of California Office of the President as part of the president's K–12 outreach efforts supplied the first nine computers. Following the initial investment by the university, the elementary school's leadership immediately saw the overall benefit of providing technology access to their students. Since that time, the elementary school has more than matched the ongoing contributions of the university and has integrated technology training into the routine of the school. In fact the original nine computers were upgraded and, most recently, were replaced by the elementary school when 30 computers were purchased for the library setting in which the Trolley takes place. (Incidentally, the presence of the Trolley program in the school has contributed to the transformation of the school and neighboring community in several ways, including its use during the school day by teachers and administrators for group activities, after school when the computer program is not in session for workshops and meetings of school personnel, and on weekends for parent classes [Gauvain et al., 1998].)

Although the library space where the program is located is used by teachers and school staff during the school day, it is clearly associated with the after-school program. The walls are painted with a large mural of the Trolley map (which looks like a subway map with stops identified, and blue, red, yellow, and green "lines" to travel between stops). A three-dimensional depiction of the map is on one wall. The program has an office in the library where all software and program records (including the children's activity journals) are stored and the printer is located. Thus, it appears as if the school is borrowing the space from the Trolley program rather than the other way around. This appearance is reinforced by the after-school program staff, which includes UCR faculty and graduate students and at least 10 to 12 undergraduates at each of the two weekday afternoons the program operates.

The Riverside Trolley is part of a statewide network of university–community–school partnerships involved in computer-based after-school educational activities for K to 12 children throughout California. This initiative reflects recent efforts to merge the expertise housed at universities with those of the community so as to meet goals valued by both settings (Lerner, 1999). Programs established under this initiative are consistent with current emphases in education on service learning. These programs accomplish the goals of service learning by providing K to 12 youth access to new instructional technologies after school while affording both academic and community service opportunities to university faculty and students (Underwood, Welsh, Gauvain, & Duffy, 2000). Thus, through informal and structured interactions with undergraduates who function as the staff at the computer club, K to 12 youth receive intensive learning experiences in computer-based math, science, and basic literacy activities. The undergraduates, in turn, develop research skills as ethnographers of children's computer and learning practices. Through their observations and interactions, university students have opportunities to examine the principles of learning and development that are the academic focus of their practicum course. University faculty provides feedback, and student reflection reinforces the learning process in the practicum course. Participating faculty also pursue research on children's learning through instructional technology and carry out applied evaluative research on the expected benefits from participation by the various individuals and groups involved in the program.

A fundamental feature of *The Riverside Trolley*, derived from the Fifth Dimension model (Cole, 1996; Nicolopoulou & Cole, 1993), is the creation of an organized, after-school activity setting that provides opportunities for children to learn as they interact with others and with computer technology. The design of the program draws on principles of human learning and developmental psychology. It rests on the assumption that learning and development are largely social processes in which less experienced individuals are guided and supported by more experienced partners and by the tools and material resources from their culture (Rogoff, 1998). In keeping with this view, the setting includes a group of participants, rules and a structure that guide the behavior of the participants, resources and tools to carry out their activities, and learning goals for those involved. Participants are a heterogeneous group in a number of ways. They include school-age children, university undergraduates and graduate students, site staff, and school and university faculty and administrators. They represent a range of social and ethnic backgrounds and language skills. They are of different ages and expertise and occupy different roles in the setting. Rules and structure are defined by the practices of the activity setting instantiated in the ways in which information is presented and operated on by the participants. Resources and tools are primarily technological, but they also include other material and social components of the setting, such as software manuals, activity journals, and the language and cognitive skills of the participants. Learning goals are set for each type of participant.

The primary goals of the program are: the acquisition by children of basic computer literacy across several important domains of computer usage; the creation of a bidirectional exchange of knowledge and support regarding computers and computing in a heterogeneous social setting; and the provision of a safe and fun learning environment for children in the after-school hours. These are addressed in the following specific objectives:

- to provide opportunities for children to work with computers and gain experience installing and using programs, troubleshooting hardware and software problems, and keyboarding;

- to expose children in the course of practical activity to a wide range of computer skills using a variety of types of computer programs, including word processing, spread sheets, and presentation software, to prepare children for their transition to the demands of middle school where such skills are often expected of students;
- to provide opportunities for children to socialize and work with peers in problem-solving situations;
- to provide opportunities for children to work with young adults (primarily university undergraduates) in a relaxed and familiar atmosphere that allows time for them to converse and develop relationships with older individuals who are neither family members nor teachers;
- to develop information literacy through the use of semistructured activities, described on task cards, that guide the children's use of the software programs available on site (there are presently over 100 software programs available);
- to impact the children's future aspirations through collaboration with university students and faculty; and
- to positively impact children's attitudes toward school.

The program is in operation throughout the traditional academic year. In September, all sixth-grade children in the school are recruited for the program. Children who volunteer choose one of two program days to attend. Children who do not sign up initially are welcome to join later if their availability or interests change. Participation has ranged somewhat over the 4 years of operation, but it averages around 60 children a year, which is approximately half of the sixth-grade population at the school. Attendance is excellent.

Children come to the library to participate in the program directly from their classes at the end of the day. After having a snack provided by the program, they go to the computers and practice keyboarding using commercial software for approximately 10 minutes. After this practice, children pair up at computers and approximately 30 minutes are spent on an activity, described in a task card (discussed later), followed by about 20 minutes using a software program of their choice without task card guidelines. Closing activities involve recording the computer activities for the session in the children's journals, putting away software, and shutting down the computers. Undergraduates are involved in all aspects of program activities; in addition to working with children on the computers and helping them with their journal entries, the undergraduates are assigned responsibilities related to attendance, walking children to buses and off campus, and so forth. The ratio of undergraduates to children at the site is approximately 4:1 per session. Some Trolley alumni—that is, children who participated in the program in previous years—come back to help with the program. These students, now in middle and high school, return to the program as Conductor's Assistants, adding yet another age group and developmental perspective to the mix.

The main activity in the program is the completion of task cards designed by the program directors and undergraduate students. Each task card describes in a procedural fashion a specific learning activity involving the computer. Children are expected to work on task cards in self-selected pairs. Undergraduates spend time with two different pairs during the course of an afternoon session. Task cards place the children in a hypothetical setting and guide them through the software as they respond to instructions, make choices, and experience the theme of the software. Thus, even software that would not be considered entertaining is used in playful ways as children participate in hypothetical situations that teach the software and promote creativity. The situations described on the task cards are based on the computer software available at the site (and most recently includes Internet sites), but are tailored to the local community and rooted in the children's personal interests and experiences. Providing a familiar context to the tasks is in keeping with Dewey's (1938) emphasis on the importance of meaningful experience in children's learning.

The Riverside Trolley is thematically organized around a trolley line similar to the transportation system that ran through Riverside at the turn of the century. Today the children are familiar with a bus route, with buses decorated like the historic trolley cars, that connects downtown Riverside to the university and other city locations. Thus, the trolley metaphor seemed ideal for a program designed to link the university, elementary school site, and community at large. The specific computer activities that children do at the program actively foster their understanding of and connection with the community. Each trolley "station" represents an important place in Riverside, such as the local newspaper office, the university's botanical gardens, the downtown library and museums, and the sports complex. Computer activities, using commercially available software, promote exploration of these sites. For instance, at the newspaper office, students may use various methods of computer-based research to learn the practices of gathering news and use word processing programs to write articles of interest for the Trolley newsletter published by the children. Task cards are designed to teach computer skills, including expertise using Microsoft Office software, multimedia reference programs, graphic and data display, and a wide range of topics that include science, history, foreign cultures and languages, problem solving, and so on. Once children have traveled to 10 stops along the Trolley line (i.e., completed 10 task cards), they are given the title of Young Conductor's Assistant (YCA). YCAs have responsibilities and privileges that allow them greater freedom to use software and assist with program development. The incentive to become a YCA motivates the children to stay focused and, in some sense, to become a "winner" in the Trolley game.

The activities in which the children engage are interesting, challenging, and motivating. Through these activities, children are able to broaden their understanding of how technology can be integrated in various ways inside and outside of school. For instance, by using programs such as Microsoft's Power Point, students become aware of different methods and options for creating and presenting projects spanning the curriculum. Children also become aware of the different types of research that can be achieved via computer technology. They also use the computers for personal and recreational activities, such as creating greeting cards for relatives and designing games to play with other children at the site. The intrinsic curiosity and motivation that children bring to new situations are built on in this setting. It is significant that this program is centered on computer knowledge as well as situated at the school. It is reasonable to expect that this experience may help foster intrinsic motivation rather than anxiety in the context of technology and education that may then follow these children to middle and high school.

By having collaboration as a core ingredient of the program, the potential benefits of this computer-based after-school program on cognitive, affective, and social development are enhanced. Collaboration has been shown to benefit children's learning in many ways, including increases in domain-specific knowledge (Healy, Pozzi, & Hoyles, 1995; Howe, Tolmie, Greer, & Mackenzie, 1995; Hughes & Greenhough, 1995), development and use of logic and strategies (Ellis, 1997; Nunes, Light, & Mason, 1995), and affective support for learning (Ellis & Gauvain, 1992). One way in which collaboration aids learning is that children become privy to other people's thoughts and actions as they work alongside them on a task. In this way, thinking and decision making may be made "visible," thereby providing access to another's ideas that can support learning (Damon & Phelps, 1989). The benefit of collaboration in technology-rich classrooms was a key finding of the Apple Classrooms of Tomorrow (ACOT) study (Sandholtz et al., 1997). ACOT researchers concluded that increased peer interaction and student collaboration, combined with opportunities for students to assume the role of an expert in relation to technology, resulted in a variety of positive changes in students, including enhanced self-efficacy and academic performance. In other research, observations of children collaborating at computers indicate that children routinely correct each other's mistakes and cooperate in defining a task and completing their work (Hawkins, Sheingold, Gearhart, & Berger, 1982; Levin, Riel, Boruta, & Rowe, 1985). Several investigators report that collaboration at a computer helps reduce children's low-level errors, offers them support for higher level cognitive activities (Levin & Souviney, 1983), and can improve student attitudes and academic performance in the classroom (Nastasi & Clements, 1991).

The undergraduate practicum course that sends students to the after-school program is offered fall, winter, and spring quarters. Students can repeat the course up to three times for credit, which is one way to ensure continuity in the program. Each quarter has a different focal theme, although the basic format and requirements are the same. In addition to their practicum experience, undergraduates participate in a variety of site-related activities during the course. They write, critique, and modify task cards, which we consider an instrumental exercise in helping them develop understanding of the idea of the zone of proximal development (Vygotsky, 1978) and many of the other concepts taught in the course. For example, the concept of the zone of proximal development is the idea that children benefit from participating in cognitive activities with more experienced partners before they are able to do these activities on their own. Hence, for task cards to be effective learning tools, they need to be calibrated to fit with the current and prospective learning needs of the children at the after-school program. To accomplish this learning goal, all new and revised task cards are field tested at the site, thus providing the undergraduates with first-hand experience in adjusting the activities to meet the developmental needs of the children who use them.

To create a community of practice among the undergraduates—that is, a setting with its own norms and social behaviors (Lave & Wenger, 1993), students post comments on electronic bulletin boards. Here students can extend classroom discussions and bridge theory covered in class with their experiences at the site, as well as share their successes and failures in the program. These discussions increase student participation along with their understanding of course material, and they frequently give rise to "online discussion leaders" who are typically not the same students who lead the classroom discussions. These electronic bulletin boards also increase communication between students and site leadership, which is especially helpful for explaining and sometimes revising practices and policies at the site. Finally, participation in the bulletin board discussions helps strengthen the group as people jointly evaluate and plan further development of the program.

The next section of this chapter concentrates on the various ways that this program supports the development of children's computer competence and contributes to children's social and intellectual confidence. Although children's social and intellectual confidence is rarely considered in assessing the impact of computer-based programs for children, we consider this feature to be critical to children's learning in this context and throughout life. The ACOT researchers found that opportunities for students to share their technological expertise with peers or teachers resulted in unanticipated benefits in the affective domain. For instance, students who were best able to develop and share their expertise with others were often not those with the highest grade point averages in their classes (Gearhart, Herman, Baker, & Novak, 1990). Teachers saw low-achieving students blossom, unpopular students gain peer approval, and unmotivated students stay inside the class to work during recess (Sandholtz et al., 1997). This type of social learning experience may play a particularly important role during periods of major developmental change, such as that which occurs when children leave elementary school and move into middle school and early adolescence. As Eccles (1999) pointed out, children's development during the period of middle childhood and early adolescence is ". . . driven by psychological needs to achieve competence, autonomy, and relatedness. They seek opportunities to master and demonstrate new skills, to make independent decisions and control their own behavior, and to form good social relationships with peers and adults outside the family" (p. 31). The observations described next suggest that the Trolley program provides opportunities for child development along these very lines.

OPPORTUNITIES FOR LEARNING
AND DEVELOPMENT THROUGH
PARTICIPATION IN THE
AFTER-SCHOOL PROGRAM

Over the years that the program has been in operation, we have observed that during the time that children participate in the program, their involvement with one another, with computers, and with individuals from outside the school have all changed in a positive direction. Recall that the goals of the program are to foster children's development in several domains, including computer competence, specifically to help the children become information literate and develop basic computer skills. We are also interested in the development of social behaviors instrumental to learning about computers, primarily the ability and willingness to engage others in computer-related discourse and practice. In fact this seems to be the keystone for establishing a community of learners (Brown, 1997) in this setting, in which knowledge and expertise are distributed across people rather than held by one individual (Pea, 1993b). Finally, we are interested in other outcomes that might result from this experience, including changes in children's attitudes toward school and their educational aspirations, and the nature of the relationships children form with the undergraduates.

For some of these dimensions, we examined comparisons with same-age peers who did not participate in the after-school program. For others we analyzed the field notes written by the undergraduates and the children's own records of their experiences at the site. Other indexes of the children's behaviors at the setting, such as rate of task card completion and attendance, were also examined. All data reported next are from the third year of operation. We chose this year to report because it was the first year for which we had the full set of measures discussed later. Thus, the information presented not only describes varying processes observed in this setting, but these processes can be considered as a whole in that they pertain to a single cohort of children.

Computer Competence

One way to assess changes in computer competence is by examining the rate of task card completion over the year. The most dramatic change in this rate occurred in the first third of the year; in fact, there was little change beyond that. Over the first 9 weeks in the program, children's skill at completing task cards improved substantially $[F(1,35) = 70.01, p < .001]$. Early on, children completed, on average, around 2 task cards per session, with substantial variation in completion among the children $(SD = .87)$. By Week 9, children were completing an average of 3.5 task cards per session, with much less variation within the group $(SD = .48)$.

Furthermore, as time went on, children were tackling more difficult task cards, which is another index of increasing skill with the technology. Gender differences and their interaction with time were not significant. This pattern suggests an overall increase in children's ability to use the computers to carry out the activities described on the task cards. These changes not only reflect increased computer skill, but also suggest changes in the children's ability to interact with others in ways that support their understanding of and use of computers (discussed more later). Such interaction was essential for children to navigate successfully through the computer activities in the early weeks in the program.

Growth in children's self-confidence in interacting with others about the computers was especially evident among the low-achieving children in the program. This pattern suggests to us that experience in the program builds computer confidence in two ways. First, children gain confidence and pride by being successful at something they and others value. We have particularly observed attitudinal shifts among low-achieving students and special education students when they are successful at computer tasks and even able to help adults or other children accomplish tasks on the computer. Children for whom reading is a struggle, for example, are likely to find the task cards and some software programs difficult to use. Yet perseverance (documented in undergraduate ratings described later) and successful completion of task cards, even if the children require assistance from an undergraduate, make these children no different than their high-achieving peers. At the end of the session, all children who have completed a task card can have their achievement recognized by having their Trolley Pass punched by a Conductor's Assistant. A second contribution to children's self-confidence results from the fact that the children are able to work with software programs that can help them develop proficiency in their weak academic areas. This type of activity helps set the stage for further improvement and a sense of accomplishment in these domains.

Another change along these lines was evident early in winter quarter, and it is a consequence of the fact that the same children participate in the program throughout the entire school year, whereas the undergraduate students usually participate for one quarter only. This different pattern of participation has led to an interesting growth point for the children. Some children begin the program in the fall, feeling very unsure of themselves at the computers and at the activities involved. Not surprisingly, the children perceive the undergraduates as very knowledgeable relative to themselves. However, come second quarter, when a mostly new group of undergraduates enters the scene, the children transform, literally overnight, into experts relative to these new, albeit older, participants. By this time, the children are used to installing software, troubleshooting hardware and software problems, negotiating task card instructions that require computer skills, and understanding the goals and rules of the Trolley game that guides their choice of activities. Many of the new undergraduates, however, have fewer computer skills than the children have. Even those with advanced computer skills know little about the Trolley system.

This naturally occurring reversal of roles prompted us to study the help-seeking behavior of children during the last two academic quarters (i.e., the quarters in which seasoned children met new groups of undergraduates). Undergraduates completed a rating form after each weekly session that asked about the behavior of the children with whom they had spent the most time during the session. Overall, children's help seeking from peers declined from January to June [$t(53) = 2.30, p < .03$]. During this same period, children's reliance on help from the undergraduate students did not change. Given that these ratings were based on children with whom the undergraduates had spent the most time that day, they may have been influenced by a selection factor. That is, children who did not have ratings completed on them would have been less likely to spend extended time with an undergraduate and those who asked for help were those who were having difficulties. Nevertheless, field note data suggest that, although the children continued to seek help from undergraduates, their questions or problems became more technical and reflected a more sophisticated level of computer-related discourse, which is one goal of the program.

School-Related Attitudes

The impact of the program on children's attitudes toward school is tangible and immediately recognizable. The most obvious indication is in the children's attendance at this voluntary school-based program. Remember that this program competes with many attractive alternatives, like organized sports, informal play, and socializing with friends. Some alternatives are even available at the school in the after-school hours, such as Americorp, an open well-equipped playground, and an academic tutorial program. Despite these competing activities, absences in the after-school program were rare. Over 80% of the children attended every session for which they were registered, and 40% of the children regularly came to the program on another day in addition to their regular day.

We asked parents of all fifth- and sixth-grade children at the school to provide consent for their child to complete a six-item survey at the beginning and end of the school year. The survey tapped school-related attitudes, defined in terms of both attitudes (levels of importance assigned) and self-reported behavior related to getting good grades, preparing for class, and studying for tests. Twenty-six children who participated in the after-school program completed the survey, and 27 children who did not participate in the program also completed the survey. These surveys were completed in the children's classrooms during school time and asked the following questions: (a) How important is it for you to receive good grades in school? (b) How likely is it that you will receive good grades in school? (c) How important is it for you to be well prepared for class in the morning? (d) How likely is it for you to be well prepared for class in the morning? (e) How important is it to you that you study hard before a test? and (f) How likely is it that you study hard before a test? All questions were answered using a 4-point Likert scale, with the scale for the questions about importance (Questions 1, 3, and 5) having 1 = *not important* and 4 = *very important* and the questions about likelihood (Questions 2, 4, and 6) having 1 = *not likely* and 4 = *very likely*.

When we compared the responses of children who did and did not participate in the after-school program, we found no differences in their ratings at the beginning of the school year. However, at the end of the school year, there were significant differences between the two groups of children on two of these items and a trend for a third item. All showed higher ratings for the children who participated in the program. Specifically, at the end of the year, children who participated in the after-school program had a higher rating for the likelihood that they would be well prepared for school in the morning [$M = 3.65$, $SD = .56$, $F(1, 51) = 4.37$, $p < .04$], and that studying hard before a test was important [$M = 3.65$, $SD = .48$, $F(1, 51) = 4.37$, $p < .04$] than children who did not participate in the program (for whom the Ms and SDs were 3.33 [.62] and 3.18 [1.00], respectively). A trend that favored participants appeared for the item that asked how important it was for the child to be well prepared for school in the morning [$M = 3.69$ ($SD = .55$) for participants and $M = 3.41$ ($SD = .04$) for nonparticipants, $F(1,51) = 3.04$, $p < .09$]. No differences appeared on the other three items. These data suggest that participation in this after-school program may contribute to the development of positive attitudes and behaviors associated with school success.

Educational Aspirations

One hundred and seven fifth- and sixth-grade children at the elementary school were asked about their educational aspirations at the beginning and end of the school year. Thirty-three (31%) of the children participated in the after-school program on a weekly basis, and the remaining 74 (69%) children did not participate in the program. Children were asked about the level of schooling they hoped to achieve as well as the level of schooling they actually expected to achieve. The distinction between the two questions is particularly meaningful among children who may dream of future success, but do not really believe that they have the ability or resources to break out of family and neighborhood patterns of poverty and lack of higher education.

Comparisons indicate that at the beginning of the school year, before the Trolley program had started, the two groups did not differ in the highest level of schooling they would like to achieve [$t(105) = 1.63$, n.s.]. Both groups reported that they would like to graduate from a 4-year college. However, at the end of the school year, the children who participated in the Trolley program differed from those who did not in this response [$t(105) = 2.98$, $p < .004$]. Whereas the children who did not participate in the program continued to aspire to graduate from a 4-year college, the children who participated reported that they hoped to achieve a master's degree or equivalent.

The second question asked the children about the educational level they actually expected to achieve. At the beginning of the school year, the two groups of children did not differ on this question, with both groups reporting that they expected to graduate from a 2-year community college. However, at the end of the year, the groups differed in their responses [$t(105) = 2.68, p < .009$]. Children who participated in the after-school program had a higher level of educational expectation, reporting that they expected to graduate from a 4-year college. Nonparticipants did not change from their earlier expectation of graduating from a 2-year college. Although all the children had many different experiences over the year that could explain these patterns, these results suggest that involvement in this organized after-school program may have enhanced children's educational aspirations and their perception of whether they would actually achieve them.

Child–Adult Interactions in the Program

The interactions of children and the university undergraduates who staffed the after-school program are reported in the field notes written by the undergraduates over the year. We analyzed the field notes from 90 undergraduates (approximately 30 undergraduates in each academic quarter) to determine the nature of their conversations with the sixth graders. The field notes were used to help understand the connections that these two groups of participants created in this setting. To conduct this analysis, we examined all the field notes from the entire year ($N = 625$) using ATLAS/ti software for visual qualitative data analysis (Muhr, 1993). The categories of conversational topics that were developed for field note analysis ranged from activity-specific discussions, such as task card instructions and software manipulations, to more personal topics, such as family and future aspirations.

A conceptual framework based on preliminary readings of the data was developed to help with the systematic analysis of field notes (see Fig. 4.1). Four higher level conceptual dimensions were defined to categorize the range of topics that occurred in these interactions, including (a) task engagement, (b) help seeking and receiving, (c) enforcing or negotiating activity policies and practices, and (d) personal identity-related topics. Figure 4.1 shows these four categories and representative behaviors that were reported often in each category. This framework has been used to systematically investigate research hypotheses related to developmental change during the year, the influence of child gender, the role of technology in adult–child interactions, and so on.

Our analysis of field note data using this scheme suggests that although the bulk of the adult–child interactions in the program pertained to task engagement and program activities, a substantial portion of the children were also willing to discuss their family experiences and other personal topics with the undergraduates. In fact about 17% of the discussions were unrelated to the tasks at hand and

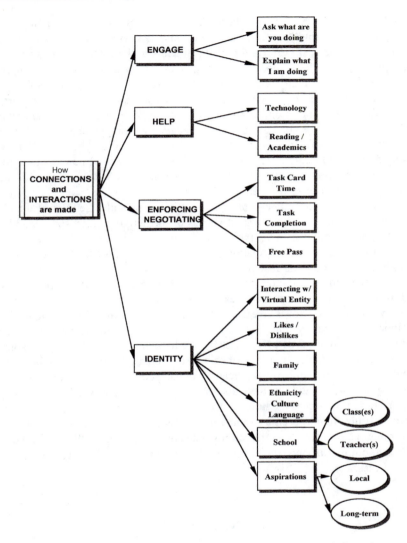

FIG. 4.1. Conceptual dimensions used to categorize the topics of discussion among children and university undergraduates.

addressed more personal issues. This pattern was somewhat unexpected given that the sixth graders had known the undergraduates only a short time (1–10 weeks) and typically spent less than 1 hour with them in any given session. It suggests that the young adults in this setting are functioning as mentors for the children. Bronfenbrenner (1986) defined *mentoring* as a one-to-one relationship between a pair of unrelated individuals usually of different ages that is developmental in nature. Mentoring has been shown to benefit children in many ways (Freedman, 1993), ranging from academic guidance to emotional support. The discussions between children and college students in the informal, yet structured atmosphere of the after-school program appear to provide guidance and support from a source other than their family and teachers regarding matters of importance to the children. This type of contact may be especially helpful in the years of middle to late childhood and early adolescence when children are establishing their own identity, yet the development of academic competence and social and intellectual self-confidence is at risk (Eccles, 1999). Positive youth development during these years is supported by opportunities to interact with adults on a relatively equal footing (Quinn, 1999)—an experience that occurred in the after-school program discussed here.

The unique social arrangement of this setting, especially the ages of the children and adults involved, the attractiveness of the activities they shared, and the knowledge and enthusiasm the participants brought to the setting set the stage for the emergence of complex relationships between the children and adults. Although the most obvious resource one would identify on entering the program would be the computers, it only takes a moment to register evidence of the other, and in our view more important, feature of the setting—the participants. This is most apparent in the noise level, which at its lowest is loud. The computers are equipped with speakers that play the sounds from the various software programs. Yet most of the noise is actually made by live human voices. These are the sounds of learning through play and relationship formation as children engage in interactions with interested and knowledgeable others. These are the sounds that we believe support the changes we have discussed here. In many ways, the computers in this program function as the lure (M. Cole, personal communication, 1997). They serve to bring the children and undergraduates forward into active, supportive, and sometimes contentious interactions. The computers may be the medium of the program, but in our view social interaction and the relationships that are formed are the message.

CONCLUSIONS

According to Bransford et al. (1999), the use of computer technology to support children's learning is not just a technical matter. Computers are used in social environments, and the interactions that children have with each other and with more experienced individuals in these settings are an important part of what occurs and, therefore, what is learned in these settings. Our observations of children's participation in an after-school program designed to teach them about computers by having them share activities with others reflect this view. From our perspective, learning basic computer skills is just one part of what children take away from this type of experience. In our program, understanding and using computers is an on-going process that relies in integral ways on social interaction. For instance, as new hardware and software are introduced, which happens regularly as systems fail and software is added, children experience first hand the rapid pace of change in this technology. For the children to continue to engage in the activities of inter-est using this technology, they need to interact with others. Children appear to learn rather quickly that much of what they need to know to use an unfamiliar sys-tem or software is not written down anywhere; if it is written down, it may not be accessible to them because of insufficient detail or because it surpasses their liter-acy skills. Children may also discover that no single person knows all the needed information. They may even find out that, in some instances, a child is the most knowledgeable person about a topic. Thus, through practical experience solving computer-related problems in a social setting, children have the opportunity to learn that the knowledge they need to use a computer to meet their goals is distrib-uted across individuals (Pea, 1993b). They also learn that interacting with others is essential to learning about and using this technology to meet the activity goals in this setting. In other words, children learn about the social life of information and information systems (Brown & Duguid, 2000).

According to Vygotsky (1981), the introduction of a new cultural tool trans-forms human activity, and in so doing it changes the social community. It does this by altering "the entire flow and structure of mental functions" (Vygotsky, 1981, p. 137) as it determines the shape and direction of new instrumental acts. In other words, activities—what Vygotsky called *mediational means*—transform how people understand and interact with the world. In the program described in this chapter, the social world includes the technology and the other people pres-ent, as well as more remote social partners, especially those who designed the hardware and software that is used (Pea, 1993b). In this type of setting, children are able to participate in interactions that may provide them with opportunities to develop many types of skills. Moreover, the social processes fostered in this set-ting appear particularly well suited for this age group of children.

During middle childhood, children need to achieve competence, autonomy, and relatedness (Eccles, 1999). Programs that offer children the chance to master and demonstrate new and valued skills in collaboration with peers and adults can be fertile settings for emerging competence. Overtures at autonomy may be sup-ported through opportunities to share and negotiate actions and decisions with others. Finally, the relationships that children form with adults other than family members and teachers are important. In middle childhood and early adolescence, children have a great need for guidance and support from nonfamilial adults. Op-portunities for this assistance may be limited at school because of large class and school size and because during these years children are beginning to have several teachers who teach in their specialized areas rather than one teacher throughout the day. Even in elementary school, such as the school where the Trolley is lo-cated, teacher–student ratios are often more than 30:1. These structural features can interfere with children's opportunity to form relationships that foster the type of communicative exchange that supports learning. Our observations suggest that children were able to form relationships of this sort with the undergraduates involved in the after-school program, and these relationships emerged in rather short order.

The fact that this program relies heavily on verbal communication is important to discuss. This emphasis may make the program particularly suitable for children in the later years of middle childhood and early adolescence who are capable of participating in and managing many of the social and verbal requirements of collaborative learning (Gauvain, 2001; Teasley, 1995). Whether this type of program would benefit younger children in the same way is not clear. We know that younger children have difficulty establishing and maintaining peer and adult–child collaborations (Crook, 1995). Therefore, a different type of setting may be a better fit for children in preschool and early school years. Our experience in another after-school program for second graders suggests that peer collaboration at computers for this younger age group is not as effective as it is with the sixth graders.

IMPLICATIONS

Many features of this after-school program and the local setting are important to consider in evaluating its contribution to children and their development. We were fortunate to have been able to adopt a successful model based on the idea that learning and development are inherently social processes (Cole, 1996). Furthermore, this model was structured enough to provide guidance in critical areas of program development, yet sufficiently flexible to allow for unique formulations. We also benefited from the outset by a dedicated team that brought a range of expertise and interests to the program, as well as the support and enthusiasm of administrators at both the elementary school and university. Finally, many poor children cannot participate in after-school enrichment programs because they cannot afford them, they do not have transportation to and from the program, and such programs may not exist in their neighborhoods (Belle, 1999). The program described here is free for children to attend, transportation is provided, and it is located in the neighborhood school. The support of the university and the elementary school allowed us to bypass these usual roadblocks to less advantaged children's participation in technology-based after-school programs.

One goal of a sociocultural approach to human development is to describe the relations between mental functioning and the sociocultural settings in which this thinking takes place. A second, equally important, goal is to make the human sciences "more capable of addressing today's major social issues" (Wertsch, del Rio, & Alvarez, 1995, p. 3). Although our observations suggest several aspects of an after-school computer program that may be important to assess to determine the effectiveness of a program, they also point to the difficulty of defining and measuring the effectiveness of any such intervention. The usual method of evaluating educationally related interventions for children—namely, changes in scores on standardized tests or class grades—would not be useful here (Gearhart et al., 1990). Methods for evaluating the children's increased ability at understanding and using the technology and the role technology plays in children's experiences outside the program would be useful. Perhaps changes in understanding and use would be evident in children's behaviors, like their increased ability or willingness to explore or implement new software or help others with the computer in the classroom or at home. Such behaviors were an important finding of the ACOT study, as students who had developed technical abilities were found to be sharing them at home, in other parts of the school, and in the community (Sandholtz et al., 1997). Benefits may also be evident in longer range outcomes, such as the child's sense of computer competence or confidence when he or she moves onto middle school. As anecdotal evidence in this regard, we have been told by the computer instructor at the middle school that the Trolley alumni attend that these children have been instrumental in his classroom by helping less experienced children with the computers.

In the main, many of the contributions to learning and development that result from children's participation in programs like ours are difficult to evaluate. In addition, we do not have (nor do we know how to reliably design) the control study that includes as a comparison group children in programs organized largely around solitary work at computers. Furthermore, we assert that a certain type of social arrangement benefits children's learning about computers—namely, a social arrangement based on the processes of scaffolding (Wood & Middleton, 1975) and guided participation (Rogoff, 1990), although this assertion was not tested in this setting. Based on classroom research (Brown, 1997), the claim that an interactive process in which a learner and a more knowledgeable person work together to share understanding, negotiate the meaning of the information they exchange, and regulate the discourse to fit with the children's developing needs and constraints does have empirical support. Finally, we suggest that opportunities for children to have their accomplishments on the computer recognized and valued by others, and especially put to practical use in the setting, are critical to children's learning and engagement in this type of setting. Such experiences may be especially helpful to children during the years of middle childhood—a time when children undergo dramatic changes in their social, educational, and emotional lives.

ACKNOWLEDGMENTS

This work was supported by the University of California Office of the President, the University of California at Riverside, and Highland Elementary School in Riverside, California. We are appreciative of the support given by Michael Cole,

David Hubbard, Regina Hazlinger, David McDowell, Tena Peterson-Petix, Yvette Pinson, Russ Plewe, Sandi Simpkins, Guy Trainin, Charles Underwood, and Mara Welsh.

REFERENCES

Archer, J. (1998). The link to higher scores. *Education Week, XVIII*, 10–12.

Becker, H. J. (2000). Who's wired and who's not: Children's access to and use of computer technology. *The Future of Children: Children and Computer Technology, 10*(2), 44–75.

Belle, D. (1999). *The after-school lives of children: Alone and with others while parents work.* Mahwah, NJ: Lawrence Erlbaum Associates.

Bransford, J. D., Brown, A. L., & Cocking, R. R. (1999). *How people learn: Brain, mind, experience, and school.* Washington, DC: National Academy Press.

Bronfenbrenner, U. (1986, February). Alienation and the four worlds of childhood. *Phi Delta Kappan, 67*, 430–436.

Brown, A. L. (1997). Transforming schools into communities of thinking and learning about serious matters. *American Psychologist, 52*, 399–413.

Brown, A. L., & Campione, J. C. (1994). Guided discovery in a community of learners. In K. McGilly (Ed.), *Classroom lessons: Integrating cognitive theory and classroom practice* (pp. 229–270). Cambridge, MA: MIT Press/Bradford Books.

Brown, A. L., & Campione, J. C. (1996). Psychological learning theory and the design of innovative learning environments: On procedures, principles, and systems. In L. Schauble & R. Glaser (Eds.), *Contributions of instructional innovation to understanding learning* (pp. 289–325). Hillsdale, NJ: Lawrence Erlbaum Associates.

Brown, J. S., & Duguid, P. (2000). *The social life of information.* Boston: Harvard Business School Press.

Cole, M. (1996). *Cultural psychology.* Cambridge, MA: Harvard University Press.

Crook, C. (1995). On resourcing a concern with collaboration within peer interaction. *Learning and Instruction, 13*, 541–547.

Cuban, L. (2001). *Oversold and underused: Computers in the classroom.* Cambridge, MA: Harvard University Press.

Damon, W., & Phelps, E. (1989). Strategic uses of peer learning in children's education. In T. Berndt & G. Ladd (Eds.), *Peer relationships in child development* (pp. 135–157). New York: Wiley.

Dewey, J. (1938). *Experience and education.* New York: Collier Books.

Eccles, J. (1999). The development of children ages 6 to 14. *The Future of Children, 9*(2), 30–44.

Eccles, J., & Gootman, J. A. (2002). *Community programs to promote youth development.* Washington, DC: National Academy Press.

Ellis, S. (1997). Strategy choice in sociocultural context. *Developmental Review, 17*, 490–524.

Ellis, S., & Gauvain, M. (1992). Social and cultural influences on children's collaborative interactions. In L. T. Winegar & J. Valsiner (Eds.), *Children's development within social context: Vol. 2. Research and methodology* (pp. 155–180). Hillsdale, NJ: Lawrence Erlbaum Associates.

Freedman, M. (1993). *The kindness of strangers: Adult mentors, urban youth, and the new volunteerism.* Cambridge, England: Cambridge University Press.

The Future of Children. (1999). *When school is out, 9*(2). Los Altos, CA: The David and Lucille Packard Foundation.

The Future of Children. (2000). *Children and computer technology, 10*(2). Los Altos, CA: The David and Lucille Packard Foundation.

Gauvain, M. (2001). *The social context of cognitive development.* New York: Guilford.

Gauvain, M., Borthwick-Duffy, S., Welsh, M., Plewe, R., Hubbard, D., Newman, R., & Peterson-Petix, T. (1998). *UC Links at UC Riverside: A tool for individual and community transformation.* Unpublished manuscript, Department of Psychology, UC Riverside.

Gauvain, M., & Perez, S. M. (in press). Not all hurried children are the same: Children's participation in planning their after-school activities. In J. E. Jacobs & P. Klaczynski (Eds.), *The development of judgment and decision-making in children and adolescents.* Mahwah, NJ: Lawrence Erlbaum Associates.

Gearhart, M., Herman, J., Baker, E., & Novak, J. (1990). *A new mirror for the classroom: The effects of technology in instruction.* Paper presented at the annual meeting of the American Educational Research Association, Boston.

Hawkins, J., Sheingold, K., Gearhart, M., & Berger, C. (1982). Microcomputers in classrooms: Impact on the social life of elementary classrooms. *Journal of Applied Developmental Psychology, 3,* 361–373.

Healy, L., Pozzi, S., & Hoyles, C. (1995). Making sense of groups, computers, and mathematics. *Cognition and Instruction, 13,* 483–503.

Hofferth, S. L., & Jankuniene, Z. (2001). Life after school. *Educational Leadership, 58,* 19–23.

Howe, C., Tolmie, A., Greer, K., & Mackenzie, M. (1995). Peer collaboration and conceptual growth in physics: Task influences on children's understanding of heating and cooling. *Cognition and Instruction, 13,* 483–503.

Hughes, M., & Greenhough, P. (1995). Feedback, adult intervention, and peer collaboration in initial Logo learning. *Cognition and Instruction, 13,* 483–503.

Laboratory of Comparative Human Cognition. (1985). Kids and computers: A positive vision of the future. *Harvard Educational Review, 59,* 73–86.

Larson, R. W. (2000). Toward a psychology of positive youth development. *American Psychologist, 55,* 170–183.

Lave, J., & Wenger, E. (1993). *Situated learning: Legitimate peripheral participation.* New York: Cambridge University Press.

Lerner, R. M. (1999). Policy perspectives about university–community collaborations: A view of the issues. *Applied Developmental Science, 3,* 194–196.

Levin, J. A., Riel, M., Boruta, M., & Rowe, R. (1985). Muktuk meets Jacuzzi: Electronic networks and elementary schools. In S. Freedman (Ed.), *The acquisition of written language* (pp. 160–171). New York: Ablex.

Levin, J. A., & Souviney, R. (Eds.). (1983). Computers and literacy: A time for tools (Special Issue). *The Quarterly Newsletter of the Laboratory of Comparative Human Cognition, 5,* 45–46.

Miller, B. M. (2001). The promise of after-school programs. *Educational Leadership, 58,* 6–12.

Muhr, T. (1993). *ATLAS/ti: Computer aided text interpretation and theory building* (Computer software). Berlin: Author.

Nastasi, B. K., & Clements, D. H. (1991). Research on cooperative learning: Implications for practice. *School Psychology, 20,* 110–131.

National Telecommunications and Information Administration, U.S. Department of Commerce. (1999). Falling through the net: Defining the digital divide. http://ntia.doc.gov/ntiahome/fttn99//.

Nicolopoulou, A., & Cole, M. (1993). Generation and transmission of shared knowledge in the culture of collaborative learning: The Fifth Dimension, its play-world, and its institutional contexts. In E. A. Forman, N. Minick, & C. A. Stone (Eds.), *Contexts for learning: Sociocultural dynamics in children's development* (pp. 283–314). New York: Oxford University Press.

Nunes, T., Light, P., & Mason, J. (1995). Measurement as a social process. *Cognition and Instruction, 13,* 483–503.

Pea, R. D. (1993a). Learning scientific concepts through material and social activities: Conversational analysis meets conceptual change. *Educational Psychologist, 28,* 265–277.

Pea, R. D. (1993b). Practices of distributed intelligence and designs for education. In G. Solomon (Ed.), *Distributed cognitions* (pp. 47–87). Cambridge, England: Cambridge University Press.

Quinn, J. (1999). Where need meets opportunity: Youth development programs for early teens. In *The Future of Children, 9(2): When school gets out* (pp. 96–116). Los Altos, CA: The David and Lucille Packard Foundation.

Rochelle, J. M., Pea, R. D., Hoadley, C. M., Gordin, D. N., & Means, B. M. (2000). Changing how and what children learn in school with computer-based technologies. In *The Future of Children, 10(2): Children and Computer Technology* (pp. 76–101). Los Altos, CA: The David and Lucille Packard Foundation.

Rogoff, B. (1990). *Apprenticeship in thinking: Cognitive development in social context.* New York: Oxford University Press.

Rogoff, B. (1994). Developing understanding of the idea of a community of learners. *Mind, Culture, and Activity, 1,* 209–229.

Rogoff, B. (1998). Cognition as a collaborative process. In W. Damon (Ed.), D. Kuhn & R. S. Siegler (Vol. Eds.), *Handbook of child psychology: Vol. 2. Cognition, perception, & language* (pp. 679–744). New York: Wiley.

Rogoff, B. (2003). *The cultural nature of human development.* Oxford: Oxford University Press.

Rogoff, B., Turkanis, C. G., & Bartlett, L. (2001). *Learning together: Children and adults in a school community.* Oxford: Oxford University Press.

Sandholtz, J. H., Ringstaff, C., & Dwyer, D. C. (1997). *Teaching with technology: Creating student-centered classrooms.* New York: Teachers College Press.

Singley, K., & Anderson, J. R. (1989). *The transfer of cognitive skill.* Cambridge, MA: Harvard University Press.

Teasley, S. D. (1995). The role of talk in children's peer collaboration. *Developmental Psychology, 31,* 207–220.

Trotter, A. (1998). Beyond drill and practice. *Education Week, XVII,* 25–27.

Underwood, C., Welsh, M., Gauvain, M., & Duffy, S. (2000). Learning at the edges: Challenges to the sustainability of service learning in higher education. *Journal of Language and Learning Across the Disciplines, 4,* 7–26.

Vygotsky, L. S. (1978). *Mind in society.* Cambridge, MA: Harvard University Press.

Vygotsky, L. S. (1981). The instrumental method in psychology. In J. V. Wertsch (Ed.), *The concept of activity in Soviet psychology* (pp. 134–143). Armonk, NY: Sharpe.

Wertsch, J. V., del Rio, P., & Alvarez, A. (1995). Sociocultural studies: History, action, and mediation. In J. V. Wertsch, P. del Rio, & A. Alvarez (Eds.), *Sociocultural studies of mind* (pp. 1–34). Cambridge: Cambridge University Press.

Wood, D. J., & Middleton, D. (1975). A study of assisted problem solving. *British Journal of Psychology, 66,* 181–191.

5

Learning Affordances of Collaborative Software Design

Yasmin B. Kafai
University of California–Los Angeles

Cynthia Carter Ching
University of Illinois–Champaign-Urbana

Sue Marshall
University of California–Irvine

In the past decade, many curricular efforts have been developed under the label of *project-based learning* that provide students with "long-term, problem-focused, integrative and meaningful units of instructions" (Blumenfeld, Soloway, Marx, Krajcik, Guzdial, & Palincsar, 1991, p. 370). Project-based learning approaches have been developed for a variety of subject matters such as mathematics (e.g., Harel, 1991; Kafai, 1995; Shaffer, 2002), sciences (Brown, 1992; Colella, 2002; Davis, 2003; Kafai & Ching, 2001; Linn, Bell, & Hsi, 1998; Penner, Lehrer, & Schauble, 1998; Sandoval, 2003), engineering (Hmelo, Holton, & Kolodner, 2000; Roth, 1998), and social sciences (Erickson & Lehrer, 1998). In all of these projects, collaborative interactions among students, teachers, and computational tools are seen as instrumental. Students are often asked to work in teams and create collaborative products. Most, but not all, of these projects integrate computer use in various forms: In some instances, students use computers to create collaborative research reports and presentations, in others, students use computers to design and implement their own software.

A central issue is whether all students benefit equally in project-based interventions given the often uneven nature of collaborative interactions, the diverse background experiences in using computational tools, and the difficulty of assessing individual learning contributions in collaborative projects. In the case of collaborative multimedia designs, we may wonder what difference it makes whether students contribute to all or only particular aspects of the final design. In the case of shared computer use, we may wonder whether all students have equal access to the computer tool throughout the project. In the case of collaborative design and research, we may wonder about the individual learning benefits. Although project-based learning activities afford opportunities for collaboration, it is not clear how students take advantage of these opportunities.

This chapter reports on a project-based learning intervention called the *software design project*, in which a class of 26 fourth and fifth graders was asked to create instructional software to teach astronomy to younger students in their school. The students were organized in mixed-gender teams with three to four members each; they worked for 10 weeks designing, implementing, and testing their software while daily science lessons and activities were integrated. The analyses reported in this chapter focus on the issues raised earlier and expand on previous published reports (Ching, Kafai, & Marshall, 2000; Kafai, Ching, & Marshall, 1998). We examine a set of complex relationships between students' individual contributions to the collaborative multimedia software and their individual learning of science, programming, and planning skills. Furthermore, we place these results in perspective by examining gender differences in access to computational resources and their development over the course of the project. In our discussion, we also address how the differential participation in software design and computer access impacted students' learning outcomes.

RESEARCH REVIEW

Learning within project-based contexts provides students with rich learning experiences. Rather than separating out the learning of science and design skills into different curriculum units, many approaches to project-based learning integrate them within one context. A particular form of project-based learning is software design (Harel & Papert, 1990). Software design requires more than the mere production of programming code: Students have to consider interface design issues, deal with content aspects, and create, debug, and maintain their programs (see also Palumbo, 1990). Learning programming is consequently situated within a larger learning context and integrated with the learning of science. Several studies have used this approach to study the thinking and learning of young software designers. One series of projects focused on children designing instructional software for mathematics (e.g., Harel, 1991) and instructional games in science and mathematics (e.g., Kafai, 1995). Although these studies made special use of programming as a vehicle to foster children's learning of content, other studies used platforms such as hypermedia or graphical authoring and design environments (e.g., Erickson & Lehrer, 1998; Shaffer, 2002; Spoehr, 1995). In all of these studies, the researchers reported significant learning results. Students not only increased their understanding of the targeted subject matter, but they also developed substantial programming skills.

One explanation for these learning benefits has been that, in the process of software design activities, students engage in knowledge reformulation and personal expression: Students reformulate their knowledge by creating and implementing external representations in their software. In our particular study, we chose the domain of astronomy because it is part of the regular elementary curriculum. Furthermore, research documented students' extensive problems with understanding interstellar processes such as the rotation of planets and the life cycle of stars (Finegold & Pundak, 1991; Vosniadou, 1994). We postulated that the design of multimedia resources would facilitate students' knowledge reformulation because it allows them to express and combine their astronomy understanding in multiple formats—from writing texts to creating graphics and animations, with a focus on explaining processes rather than facts.

Although knowledge reformulation is an important aspect of learning through software design, personal expression of one's ideas is another. The use of multimedia is situated within a larger cultural context, that of interactive media, which has become a significant part of children's culture (Kaiser Family Foundation, 1999). With the increasing proliferation of commercial education and entertainment software, students have become accustomed to a software production level that makes extensive use of multimedia features. Although students might have a wealth of experience in using multimedia applications, they have little experience in expressing their ideas in making multimedia software.

Creating multimedia software is a complex, collaborative enterprise. In research and commercial contexts, groups of professional designers, programmers, and content specialists work together for several months (Lammers, 1986). Therefore, multimedia software design appears to be a good context for students to learn about collaborative project management. Much of the research related to project management has treated it as goal-directed behavior comprised of several distinct components, including construction of a mental representation, goal selection, plan formation and execution, and plan review and revision (for an extensive overview, see Friedman & Scholnick, 1997). Research evidence points to young children's deficiencies in several of these areas. The inefficient execution of plans by children has been blamed on an inability to effectively self-monitor their steps and deficiencies in plan detail, flexibility, or scope of the plans (Friedman, Scholnick, & Cocking, 1987). In this study, we ascribe to planning a broader meaning that encompasses the various components of project management. Students need to negotiate which kind of tasks one takes over in a team of designers, when one has access to scarce resources such as computers, and how one coordinates all these activities, and many others. We were particularly interested in students' own conceptions of plan formation, execution, and monitoring and how these changed as part of their collaborative software design experience.

Learning through designing software then stresses the importance of students' knowledge reformulation, personal expression, and collaborative management—

all within the context of a project (Blumenfeld et al., 1991). These learning experiences are also impacted by other factors such as observed gender differences in team collaborations and access to computational resources. Studies have found that when computers are used during classtime, boys are more likely to dominate available computer resources (American Association of University Women, 2000), initiate and maintain control of school computers during nonclassroom hours such as lunchtime and before or after school (Canada & Brusca, 1991; Kinnear, 1995), and engage in social behaviors online that can effectively "silence" female voices in computer-mediated conversation (Fey, 2001). These factors, which relate to amount of experience with computers, have a significant effect on students' attitudes and perceptions with boys showing higher ratings than girls on: perceived competence with computers, positive attitudes toward computers, and perceived utility value of computers (Shashaani, 1994). Although recent evidence suggests that the technological gender gap may be closing in terms of home access and everyday use, the different ways that girls are using computers are not always valued in school contexts (American Association of University Women, 2000; Cone, 2001).

Even when computers are not involved, putting students in mixed-gender teams for collaborative work in academic subjects can result in different experiences for boys and girls. Research shows that gender is often a strong predictor of status in heterogeneous groups. Thus, girls' contributions to group work are being less valued than boys' (see review by Cohen, 1994). These interaction patterns sometimes have consequences for girls' ability to make the most out of collaborative work, as evidenced by subsequent knowledge assessments. Even when these differences in interaction do not affect academic achievement in question, girls' self-esteem and interest in the subjects may suffer (Webb & Palincsar, 1996).

In the context of the software design projects, we were particularly concerned about how to measure and track changes in students' levels of participation and access to software design in their collaborative groups. The task of creating an instructional multimedia resource is comprised of several interrelated activities: programming, planning, content research, collaborative team management, and graphical design. Ideally, all students would participate in all activities equally. However, the fact that some of these activities are computer based (programming, graphic design), whereas others are not, led us to consider that gender might be a factor in students' opportunities to participate in all design components. Furthermore, as the nature of the design task changes over the course of the project (from initial planning and paper designs to computer implementation), we were also interested to see how students' participation in design would likewise change. Similar patterns of participation change have been documented in out-of-school communities (Lave & Wenger, 1991) and classrooms (M. Roth, 1995; W. Roth, 1998). These studies, however, have not focused on the important component of computer technology in the classroom—important particularly for issues of gender equity.

The affordances of software design covered in this study are students' learning of science, programming, and planning with special attention to gender differences in access and participation. We used the final computational artifacts as a starting point for investigating what kind of learning opportunities the design of an interactive multimedia astronomy resource offered to students and how this was related to individual students' contribution to the multimedia product over time. Our research questions addressed whether all learners benefited equally from collaborative multimedia design in terms of learning science, programming, and planning and whether gender differences in access and participation had an impact on this learning.

RESEARCH METHODS

Research Site

The project took place in an urban elementary school that functions as the laboratory school site for UCLA. The participating classroom was equipped with seven computers; one of each was set up as a workstation for the seven table clusters. An additional seven computers were in an adjacent room and were mostly used for related Internet searches.

Research Participants

An integrated class of 26 fourth- and fifth-grade students participated in this project. There were 10 girls and 16 boys (19 White; two Hispanic; three African American; two Asian) ranging between 10 and 12 years of age. With the exception of 10 students—8 who had participated in another design project the previous year and 2 who knew programming from home—none of the other students had any programming experience before the start of the project. All the students had used computers in school and were familiar with word-processing software, spreadsheets, Grolier's™ multimedia encyclopedia, and searches on the World Wide Web.

Students were grouped by the teacher in seven teams according to the following criteria: one "experienced" designer (who had participated in the previous design project) mixed gender, and different academic achievement levels. Our primary goal, in addition to creating mixed-gender teams, was to balance the levels of existing technological knowledge across the groups so that each collaborative team would contain at least one student who had done some programming previously.

Classroom Activities

One week before the start of the project, students were given an introduction to the main features of the Microworlds™ Logo programming environment. The project assignment was to build an interactive multimedia resource about astronomy for younger students—third graders—in their school. Over the course of 10 weeks, students created their own research questions about astronomy, researched these questions using various sources, and represented their findings in a group software product. Students worked 3 to 4 hours per week on the project for 10 weeks. Students spent 46 hours on the project, of which 23 hours were dedicated to independent work researching and creating screens in Microworlds representing the astronomy information they had learned. The other 23 hours were spent in whole-class activities: science instruction, class discussions about science issues and project logistics, and group presentations.

Research Instruments and Procedures

We collected data from a variety of sources: field notes and videotaping of students' interactions, students' notebook entries about work assignments and distribution, daily log files from the software, interviews with team members, and pre- and posttests assessing students' science and programming knowledge, and their views on collaboration and project management.

The subject matter pre- and posttests that students received were designed to assess multiple factors in their developing understandings of Logo programming (see Palumbo, 1990) and astronomy content. Students took the Logo test just after they completed the brief introduction to Microworlds™. The Logo test assessed the following components: amount of Logo commands known by the student, correct code syntax, ability to explain the function of known commands, and ability to classify commands by function, animation, and perspective taking. Quantitative scores on the Logo test were produced by combining student results on the command knowledge, code generation, syntax, and explanation sections.

The astronomy test was administered before and after students received instruction on astronomy. The test was designed to assess students' astronomy vocabulary, descriptive and systemic knowledge of interstellar processes such as the rotation of planets and the life cycle of stars, and common student conceptions about astronomy as informed by existing research (Finegold & Pundak, 1991; Vosniadou, 1994). Again on the astronomy assessments, the same items were used to create both pre- and posttest scores.

The planning questionnaire asked students to mark all the planning strategies they considered important in conducting a software design project. Among the proposed 25 planning strategies were items such as "Decide on your goals for the project," "Start with the biggest part of the project and then work on the smaller parts," "Decide on the order for doing different parts of the project as you go," and "Do work on different ideas, then pick the best one." These items were generated from individual interviews and surveys about planning, which we had conducted with students after a previous software design project. Questionnaire analyses included a count for the number of strategies selected by each student for both a pre- and postproject questionnaire, a strategy count change score (from pre- to postperiod), and scores for the number of strategies each student added, eliminated, or kept from one questionnaire to the next. Additionally, we looked at the total number of marks given to different types of strategies and the change from pre- to postquestionnaires.

Final software team products were analyzed to examine the nature of their program functions and the contributions of individual team members. At the end of the project, each team was given a package of screen printouts of the multimedia encyclopedia and instructed to write down all the names of people who contributed to each screen and what their contribution was (e.g., text, graphics, and animations). We classified the screens into different categories: content screens that represented some piece of knowledge about the field of astronomy; content animation screens that exemplified animations or simulations of dynamic aspects; information/navigation screens that provided information about the designers and guided the user through the software; and quiz/feedback screens that asked questions about the content, but also linked answers to feedback screens.

We not only counted how many screens were created by each team, but also assigned points for each student's individual contribution to a screen (i.e., a student who designed and implemented one screen completely independently received one point; three students who contributed equally to designing and programming one screen each received .33 points; two students sharing credit for one screen each received .5 points). Each student's raw score was then created by summing all his or her points for the whole team product. Thus, out of a group product containing 30 screens, one student might have a raw score of 8.5 points.

We also examined the ways in which individual contributions to each group's final product had different affordances for product appearance, individual credit taking, and learning benefits. We created a "design differentiated score" by looking at the types of screens created by individuals in the context of their total contribution. For that purpose, we used the four types of screens defined earlier, content screens, animation screens, quiz/feedback screens, and information/navigational screens. Student-differentiated scores for each type of screen were created using the same values as the raw scores. To create screen type scores for each student, we added all their points for each category of screen. Scores for each category were then normalized so comparisons could be made across screen types: Low > 1 SD below mean, Med = within 1 SD, High > 1 SD above mean. A more detailed description of the screen type classification and development of design-differentiated scoring can be found in Kafai, Ching, and Marshall (1998).

Student participation and access were documented through videotaping and field note taking. We classified all the activities we saw students doing on a daily basis. We recognized that although various activities in the classroom environment were all necessary for astronomy research and working on the multimedia encyclopedia, these activities afforded different levels of access to technological fluency, which is the acquisition of software design expertise. We were interested in what affordances these project activities had for the following technological fluency goals among students: (a) access to actually designing and implementing screens in multimedia design, not just thinking about how to implement them; (b) experience using computers not only as consumers of software, but also as producers; and (c) use of computational media in conjunction with traditional media such as paper and pencil.

We classified all the activities into three categories. Activities that used only traditional paper-and-pencil (traditional) activities were viewed as having little affordance for developing or enriching students' fluency with new technology (see Table 5.1). A second category (constancy activities) was comprised of activities, which used computer technology, but only that with which students were already familiar. Thus, participation in those activities was viewed as having affordances for maintaining a constant level of students' technological fluency, but not for challenging them to develop new skills. Finally, the activities in the third category (enriching activities) involved students working with computers in ways many had not encountered before, thus enriching their development of greater technological fluency. A detailed description and application of the coding scheme can be found in Ching, Kafai, and Marshall (2000).

To document changes in access over time, we selected two time points in the project: the third full week of project work and the eighth week of project work. To integrate the various forms of data that were collected during those 2 weeks, we looked at all field notes and videotapes for each day during those times and created a "Week 3" and "Week 8" case file for each group. The case files included each student's name and the activities he or she was observed doing. A group member received an activity code when he or she was engaged in a particular task for most of a given class period. Sporadic activity, such as watching someone program for only a few minutes, was not counted. In this way, the most codes one person could get on a given day would be two, spending roughly half the period on one task and half on

TABLE 5.1
Classification of Design Activities

Enriching Activities	Constancy Activities	Traditional Activities
Microworlds programming	Grolier's Encyclopedia research	Book corner research
Internet research	Isaac Asimov CDs research	Drawing screens on paper
Leading group demos	Word processing	Team progress reports
Teaching others to program	Watching others program	

another. For example, during the whole eighth week, Joey (a sixth-grade boy) was documented creating screens in Microworlds three times, researching with the Isaac Asimov CD set once, researching comets in a book once, and watching another group member program twice. Tallies were created for how many times each student was observed participating in all three categories of design activities at each of the two time points. These scores were then used for further analysis of change in students' access to the practice of software design.

RESULTS

This section presents the analysis of the final collaborative software design products (i.e., the astronomy multimedia resources created by each team). Here the collaborative as well as individual contributions to the software are evaluated in terms of quantity and quality. These results are then used to assess what kind of benefits they afforded for students' individual learning of science, programming, and planning skills. In addition, we examine the kind of access students had to various production resources, computer-based or not, at the two time points during the project.

Final Software Product Analyses

Each interactive multimedia resource consisted of a set of interrelated screen pages that were linked together with the help of buttons or objects that could be activated with a mouse click. Some of the screens had combined media elements such as text and graphics, whereas others worked in only one medium—text or graphics. The number of created screen pages differed considerably for each design team, but this was not a good measure of production value because screens differed in their functionality. We defined three categories of screens: content, quiz/feedback, and information/navigational. Table 5.2 provides an overview of the distribution of the different screen functions.

TABLE 5.2
Distribution of Screen Page Functions

Team	Content Screens	Animations	Info/Navigation	Quiz/Feedback
1	17	2	4	6
2	15	3	3	11
3	9	2	3	—
4	12	1	6	13
5	14	2	2	12
6	23	1	6	18
7	11	0	2	31

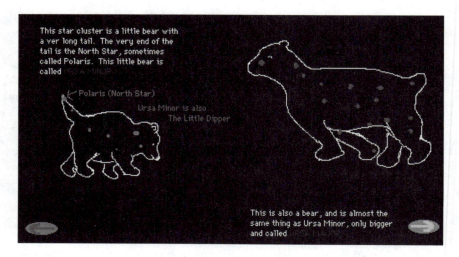

FIG. 5.1.   Content screens.

Content screens represent some piece of knowledge about the field of astronomy (see Fig. 5.1). They can take the form of text, pasted pictures, drawings, or any combination of these three design elements. The larger category of content screens was also broken down further to specify content animation (CA) screens. CA screens contained animations or simulations that exemplified dynamic aspects of the solar system such as the lunar eclipse (see Fig. 5.2), the life cycle of a

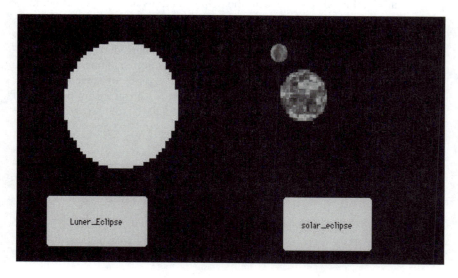

FIG. 5.2.   Animation screen.

star, or the effects of gravity. Only in one instance was the player given the possibility to set the parameters for a gamelike animation (Team 3).

Many groups in the project decided to include *Quiz/feedback* screens to complement their multimedia resource (see Fig. 5.3). Quizzes usually asked questions about the content displayed elsewhere in the product, but occasionally introduced new material. Most quiz screens contained one or two multiple-choice questions with buttons linking the user to feedback on his or her response. Feedback screens consisted primarily of simple pages exclaiming "right!" or "wrong!" in a large font. Only in a few instances were users provided with additional information, as in the question, "Can Martians Dance: Yes or No?" The answer page in either case replied, "There is no right or wrong answer to this question, because we don't know if there are Martians on other planets" (Team 6).

Another type of screen common to group products was *Information/navigational screens*, which provided information about the designers or displayed the title of the software and subtitles of topic areas such as, "This is the Planets Section!" Other screens contained buttons or turtles that linked to different topic areas and provided information to the user about how to navigate the software, such as a table of contents (see Fig. 5.4). The graphical arrangements on these pages differed considerably. Although in a few instances students took advantage of a graphical representation of the solar systems as an entrance to different planets, many others just placed a variety of buttons on the page.

Our examination of team design efforts also revealed an extensive use of multimedia features that emulated commercial software models such as MathBlaster™ or Where in the World is Carmen San Diego™. A comprehensive analysis of all seven final versions of the educational multimedia resources showed that all of them used "Point&Click" as their main mode of advancing through the program.

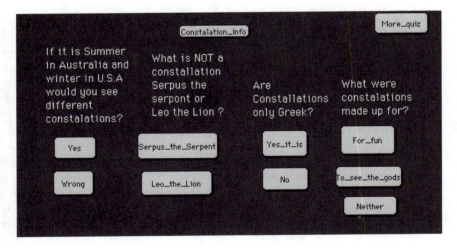

FIG. 5.3. Quiz screen.

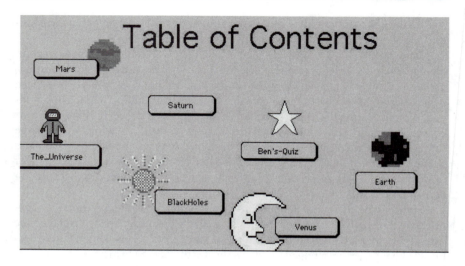

FIG. 5.4.   Navigation screen.

They provided menu options, had navigational features such as title screens, introductions, content overviews, and final screen and credit messages. In the instructional component, students (with the exception of one team) provided limited positive and negative feedback and sometimes explanations. However, students' software did not provide the player with a "Quit" option—a feature that either many designers did not have time to implement or did not consider important. Furthermore, "Help" options were absent as well. As beginning interface designers, the students were able, in a limited way, to foresee their users' needs.

Although all students contributed to the final versions of their software, the levels of individual effort among the students in any group needed further examination. In a first effort to analyze individuals' total contribution to their group products, students were assigned points based on how many screens they worked on. The overall results show that students had an average of 8.3 screens (SD = 5.91). A closer examination of these data revealed some unexpected patterns. In several cases, those students with the highest raw scores for their groups, indicating that they created the most screens, were not the same students who spent the most time at the computer, as reflected in field notes and researcher recollections. Those students who had created many screens were often not the ones captured in video and field notes as displaying the most group leadership and the most astronomy knowledge during class presentations.

Looking at screen types rather than raw scores seemed to be a more viable measure of participation than total screens. Thus, we created design-differentiated scores for the final analysis of individual contributions to the collaborative software product (see Table 5.3). Students who created the most content screens and content animations were the same as those who displayed the most leadership,

TABLE 5.3
Distribution of "Design Differentiated Scores"

Team	Content Screens	Animations	Info/Navigation	Quiz/Feedback
1	10	1	.75	2
	2.5	—	.25	—
	2.5	—	2.25	4
	2	1	.75	—
2	1.25	1.5	1	5.5
	6.75	.5	—	1.5
	4.25	1	—	0
	2.75	0	2	4
3	3	—	2	—
	1	1.5	1	—
	5	.5	—	—
4	3	1	6	—
	4	—	—	—
	3	—	—	—
	2	—	—	13
5	3.33	1	.25	—
	3	1	.25	2
	4.83	—	1.25	10
	2.83	—	.25	—
6	4.5	1	2.5	0
	13.5	—	1	10
	2.5	—	1.5	8
	2.5	—	1	0
7	2	—	1.5	5
	8	—	.5	14
	2	—	—	12

spent the most time at the computer, and showed the most developing astronomy knowledge. In the group products, where the student with the most total screens was not the same as the most dominant and knowledgeable student, we saw that the one with the highest raw score created mostly quiz/feedback and information/ navigational screens. This finding is interesting because it lends support for measuring individual performance and contribution by some other means than merely counting the number of pages created.

DEVELOPMENT OF SCIENCE UNDERSTANDING

In terms of the effectiveness of the overall intervention, we found that the design project was a successful vehicle for astronomy science learning. To assess students' improvement in their knowledge of science content, we administered pre- and posttests in astronomy. Our analysis showed significant differences for the pre- and posttests in students' understanding of astronomy (pretest: $M = 31.5$, posttest: $M = 37.2$, $t(25) = 5.65$, $p < .05$). Navigation screens were the only significant predictors for science change scores ($R^2 = .32$, $F = .002$): Students who created fewer navigation screens scored higher. No other screen types were significant predictors. No significant gender differences were found in the astronomy knowledge scores.

DEVELOPMENT OF SOFTWARE DESIGN SKILLS

Students' development of general software design skills was another area of interest. We found that students' understanding of Logo improved as assessed by the tests (pretest: $M = 13.3$, posttest: $M = 18.6$, $t(24) = 4.38$, $p < .05$). All students (with the exceptions noted) started out at ground zero, knowing no Logo at all, and yet they showed significant gains. Not surprisingly, we found that students who created more screens scored higher on the Logo tests: The total number of screens was significant in predicting Logo change scores ($R^2 = .15$, $F = .05$). Those students who created a large number of quiz screens also created a large number of screens in general ($r = .89$, $p = .00$). This result is not surprising considering that quiz screens were easy to create and, thus, a good way to increase one's total number of pages. Navigation screens were the only other screen type significant in predicting Logo change scores ($R = .19$, $F = .025$). Students who created more navigation screens scored higher. No significant gender differences were found in the Logo change scores.

Development of Project Management

In a comparison of pre- and postproject questionnaires about important strategies for planning a software design project, our analyses indicate that those students' conceptions of project planning were expanding with the inclusion of some iterative and more flexible strategies that were better suited for design problems. A look at student strategy response scores (number of strategies marked as important) sheds more light on what we mean by expanding conceptions. Of 25 items, students selected a mean of 11.0 and 12.35 strategies on the pre- and postquestionnaires, respectively. The mean number of strategies that remained stable (i.e., the number of strategies that students selected in both the pre- and postquestionnaire) was 7.4. From pre- to postproject, students selected a mean of 4.9 additional strategies. The mean number of strategies that students selected preproject but not again in the postquestionnaire was 3.6. These numbers reflect that, although students did not abandon the prior conceptions they held about what it takes to plan a software design project, they did both eliminate and add some strategies as a result of their experience with this multimedia design project.

A closer look at particular types of strategies that were marked more or less frequently from the pre- to postquestionnaire reveals the students' increased awareness of the iterative nature of design problems, which demand opportunistic changes in plans and consideration of multiple alternatives. We looked at strategies for three general components of planning: plan formation, plan execution, and plan monitoring. Greater flexibility in forming plans was evidenced by an increase in the number of students who reported brainstorming strategies as important. (Two different questionnaire items had increases from 12–16 and from 11–18, respectively.) This included brainstorming of ideas for what their multimedia products should look like and include, both before starting to work on the project and during the course of project work. Although they got started with a particular idea or concept, they entertained alternative ideas at different stages of project development. Additionally, there was a decrease (from 14–8) in the number of students who reported writing down plans as important. Having observed students' reluctance to write down plans during the project, we speculate that this may reflect students' recognition that software design plans might be more easily and efficiently represented and changed in the software artifacts. Responses to other items on the questionnaire indicate that this decrease does not necessarily reflect a belief that making plans was not useful or needed.

There was evidence of students' expanded conceptions of the dynamic nature of design projects when executing plans. We found an increase in the number of students who marked strategies involving plan changes. This was true for making changes in designs when students recognized problems in their plans (increase from 13–18 responses), as well as making changes in response to feedback students received about their designs from others (increase from 8–15 responses). Another example of increased flexibility in plan execution conceptions was illustrated by student responses to sequencing strategies. We found a decrease (from 11–6) in the number of students who indicated that it was important to decide on an order for doing things before you start. However, because less than half of the students thought that planning a sequence as you go was important, it may be that more of them believed planning a work sequence in general was not useful in a changing design environment. From other questionnaire selections, it was evident that many students continued to emphasize the importance of "planning ahead," although they recognized instances where it was useful to employ more iterative plan execution strategies. One can speculate whether parents' and teachers' frequent admonitions "to plan ahead" are responsible for these deeply engrained conceptions.

The research literature has reported students' lack of plan monitoring experience (e.g., Björklund, 1991). Although this was evident for the students in this project, some of them gained an awareness of the strategy of looking ahead. Thirteen students (up from 6 in the prequestionnaire) indicated that it was important to think ahead about possible problems or difficulties when making a planning decision. This may be a reflection of the students' awareness of the amount of troubleshooting required of a programmer or designer in the course of developing software over a long time period. Although our analysis of the pre- and post-questionnaires indicated a general increase in flexible planning strategies, a regression analysis revealed that only content screens were significant in predicting planning strategy change scores ($R^2 = .20$, $F = .022$): Students who created more content screens increased their repertoire of flexible planning strategies.

Access to Computational Resources Over Time

If we examine the mean number of times boys and girls were engaged in the different categories of software design activities at Weeks 3 and 8, we can see interesting trends (see Fig. 5.5). At the first time point, girls' average participation in traditional activities was twice as frequent as boys', and they were performing less fluency-enriching activities than boys were. However, boys' and girls' participation in technological constancy activities was fairly equitable. By the eighth week, the differences between boys and girls on traditional and enriching activities appeared to even out. Additionally, the frequency of participation in constancy activities decreases across the board for boys and girls. These results seem to suggest that constancy activities somehow became obsolete or less popular for all students as the project progressed. If we consider that three of the constancy activities—word processing, Grolier's research, and Asimov CD research—all have to do with obtaining information about research questions and writing up that information in students' own words to design their simulations, these results make sense. Most students conducted their research during the first half of the project and spent the remaining time planning and implementing their designs and/or helping others. The change in participation we see in constancy activities, then, was most likely affected by the order of events in the project progression and not gender or other collaborative dynamics.

As displayed in the differences in mean levels of activity in the prior table, girls appeared to move from more traditional activities at Week 3 to activities affording more technological fluency at Week 8. The sort of changes that took place across the classroom as a whole suggest that gender played an important role in students' initial activity participation, but that these gender differences did not remain constant throughout the 10 weeks. What we found is that participation in enriching, computer-intense activities at the first time point predicted significantly the Logo change scores (R^2: .32, $F = 3.30$; $p = .04$). It also correlated significantly with the extent to which students engaged in creating animations (r: .39, $p = .04$, $n = 26$). In other words, the higher level of access to category three activities, the more animations produced. We also found that participation in programming at

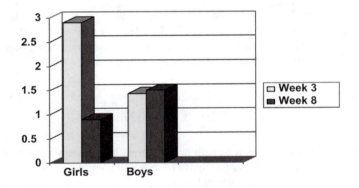

FIG. 5.5a.   Traditional activities at Weeks 3 and 8.

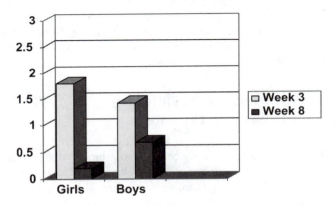

FIG. 5.5b.   Constancy activities at Weeks 3 and 8.

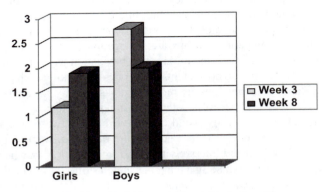

FIG. 5.5c.   Enriching activities at Weeks 3 and 8.

Week 3 was a predictor of change in flexible planning strategies for making iterative design decisions ($R^2 = .24$, $F = .017$). This finding goes along with our other results providing support for the argument that early involvement in programming is essential to reap the benefits of software design.

DISCUSSION

These results present a complex picture of collaborative software design. We found that not all students contributed equally to the collaborative products and not all contributions had equally significant effects on students' learning of science and programming. Furthermore, we found that access to computational resources differed for boys and girls in the course of the project. Although it leveled out at the end, it still had a significant impact on the production and development of programming skills. We discuss these findings in regard to learning affordances of different multimedia screen types, learning outcomes with attention to observed gender differences, and development of project management skills.

Learning Affordances of Different Multimedia Resource Functions

It is clear from our results that merely counting the number of screen pages is not a good indicator for learning affordances. As stated previously, working on different screen types served different ends for the designers, in both science content and programming learning. Although informational/navigational screens presenting tables of contents, title pages, or personal information about the designers may not necessarily contain science content, they have definite value in terms of technological fluency. Making tables of contents, main title pages, and topic area title pages requires taking the perspective of the user and considering what he or she would find most helpful in navigating the software. Navigational screens are not by nature devoid of content, but many of the information/navigation pages designed by students in this study had little to no content. The process of making such pages is relatively easy because no animations are required, no astronomy research is required, and little programming is necessary other than linking buttons.

Quiz/feedback pages afford several benefits from a software design perspective. For one, the type of drill-and-practice quiz designed by most groups is a "quick and dirty" way to add interactivity to the software. In fact when asked by researchers why they were making a quiz, the students often responded that it was because the users would want more interactive features. Making a quiz takes relatively little time when all that is required is a series of questions with buttons leading to pages that say "right" or "wrong." Another benefit is that students who felt that their contribution was too small were able to increase the number of pages they created by adding a quiz on some topic at the last minute. From a science learning perspective, making quizzes does not allow the designer to experience the maximum benefits of the software creation process. Most quizzes in this project were a disjointed set of questions with little or no relation to one another, followed by feedback pages, which gave no explanations of the correct answer. The process of designing a quiz such as the ones we saw may not help the designer develop systemic understanding in science because a quiz only requires that he or she know the right answers to a series of unconnected science facts.

Content/animation screens are the most difficult to create, but they also afford the most learning benefits in terms of technological fluency, systemic understanding, and project management strategies. Even the most basic kind of content page, one with only text and/or pictures, requires more sophisticated levels of thinking about astronomy than the disjointed kind of knowledge represented by a quiz. Because students had to think about their users, they had to write all the text sections in their own words and explain astronomy phenomena in language that younger students would understand. This consideration discouraged practices such as cutting and pasting of text from the Internet or copying word-for-word from books. Opportunities for even more sophisticated thinking about users, programming, and the subject matter are afforded by more elaborate content pages, which use animation to depict some astronomy phenomenon. Creating animations requires the designers to learn Logo beyond relying on the basic point-and-click controls of the Microworlds system because they have to direct the turtle in complex patterns and series. Most important, animations afford remarkable growth in systemic understanding. They require the designer to comprehend something well enough to create a model of the whole phenomenon, as opposed to merely possessing a descriptive understanding of "what happens."

Engagement in content screen design, which required a complex negotiation of collaborative programming, research, and screen design, also afforded the development of more flexible and iterative project management strategies. Students' ideas and implementations for content screens in particular continually evolved as they gained more information and experience over a long time frame. This offered a unique opportunity for consideration of additional strategies that are better suited for design projects than for the short-term, well-defined projects in which students more typically engage.

After looking at the affordances of the different screen types made by the students, it is not surprising that those who made mostly content screens did not have the highest raw scores. Our measure of "design-differentiated scores" was more sensitive to the fact that content screens are difficult and require more time, energy, and background research than other types. One student could be working on a single animation for a week while during the same time another student could complete a five-item quiz and a title page. Although content screens and animations may eat up time that could be spent increasing the sheer number of one's pages, the rewards for the creator in terms of understanding and skill make them the most beneficial for learning. This is not to say that students should only be creating content pages. A true multimedia encyclopedia would not be complete without some kind of title page, navigation aids, interactivity, and instructive aspects like a quiz. Children's fascination with these other elements of computational products, however, is just one more example of how classroom software creation can be problematic; inexperience and lack of foresight can get in the way of reaping the full benefits of the design experience.

Learning Outcomes and Issues of Access and Participation

Additionally, when we look at the access data for boys and girls, the absence of gender differences in astronomy learning could also be attributed to the fact that there were no gender differences in fluency-enriching activities at Week 3 or Week 8. In addition to watching and word processing, fluency-enriching activities included some of the most information-rich sources students had available to them in astronomy—the Grolier's Multimedia Encyclopedia and the Isaac Asimov's Universe CD-ROMs. Our results show that boys and girls were able to manage these resources equitably. Although girls did not have initial access to the medium for representing their growing knowledge of astronomy, they may have learned a great deal about that topic through research. Furthermore, our data collection did not examine the degree to which students were creating pages in Microworlds that might facilitate deep understanding of astronomy. Many students spent a significant amount of time modifying music and special effects for user feedback during the quiz part of their software—a task with relatively low affordance for scientific understanding. Thus, more time working with programming does not guarantee an increase in astronomy knowledge.

It is reasonable to expect that Logo learning would have been impacted by the amount of access boys or girls had to the actual programming software. More experience working in Microworlds should lead to more learning of Logo or so one would think. Careful reflection on the nature of the Microworlds environment and the kinds of programming with which students were engaged, however, leads to the conclusion that the relationship between access and learning is more complex. Students created many different types of multimedia pages: quiz pages, animation pages, textual information pages, navigational pages, and graphics pages. The amount and sophistication of programming required for these different page types varied widely. Considering these findings, it is possible that a student who programmed for a shorter amount of time in Microworlds on a more challenging task would have learned more about Logo than another student who sat at the computer for a long time but programmed many simplistic pages. Information about what kinds of programming students are doing when engaged in Microworlds on a daily basis, which was not included in our data collection, might account for differences in Logo learning better than gender alone.

Affordances for Developing Project Management

Although there is evidence that support structures implemented within the science design project facilitated girls' transformation from low- to high-status activities, there is a potential for girls to pay a price in their struggle for greater computer access. An investigation of boys' and girls' beliefs about what is needed to successfully plan and manage a design project indicated that, as a result of participation in this project, boys were more likely than girls to expand their beliefs in a way that demonstrated greater flexibility and adaptation to the planning requirements of an ill-defined design problem. Girls, in contrast, were more likely to report the use of less flexible planning strategies that were better suited to the types of well-defined project tasks with which they had past experience.

These results were based on case study data from seven students (three girls and four boys) who participated in the science design project twice over a 2-year period. In the first year, these students worked on their projects independently. During the second-year project, which provided the data for this study of gender differences in negotiating computer access, these students faced a new challenge of planning and managing a team project. Both prior to and at the conclusion of the second project, the students were asked in questionnaires and interviews to explain what is "planning" when one has to plan a project. Responses were classified into one of two categories: (a) top–down beliefs and strategies suited to well-defined problems (examples include doing things ahead of time, such as setting goals, deciding what to do, and deciding an order for doing things); and (b) bottom–up beliefs and strategies that lend themselves to ill-defined design problems (examples include doing things in a more iterative manner, such as brainstorming different ideas for what the artifact should be, reviewing and/or changing one's plans in response to new information, and recognizing the need to get more information about a topic while working on a project). Responses from three of the four boys demonstrated that, although they had not abandoned beliefs about the usefulness of top–down strategies, their planning repertoire included an increased percentage of bottom–up strategies at the end of the science design project. This was not the case for the girls, who at the end of the project had not expanded their planning repertoire to include more bottom–up strategies. Although girls' focus on conflict resolution led to increased status and computer access, it appears that boys benefited from greater initial computer access and from their focus on project work, rather than on solving collaborative problems; they developed a more flexible view than the girls of what it takes to plan and manage a project.

OUTLOOK

In this chapter, we investigated the learning benefits of collaborative interactions and software production. Furthermore, we addressed the issue of differential participation in content production and access to computational resources. What these results and the preceding discussion suggest is that learning affordances of collaborative interactions and productions were not the same for all participants, and measures need to be undertaken to create a more equitable playing field for all participants. We have addressed some of these issues, in particular those of the gender differences in access to computational resources, in a previous paper (see Ching, Kafai, & Marshall, 2000).

Our current attention is directed toward understanding the impact of more experienced designers in the software teams. In this project, one student (i.e., oldtimer) in each team had participated in a previous software design project. We are studying now more systematically how these old-timers compare to the newcomers in terms of their learning benefits and group contributions. In future studies, we examine whether there are specific contributions of old-timers in student team discussions and how these impact the newcomers' introduction into project skills and practices.

One of our recent studies examined the quantity and quality of science discussions in software design teams (Kafai & Ching, 2001) and found that old-timers orchestrated in significant number the directions and extent of science conversations. Marshall (2000) analyzed the development of collaborative project management in the context of a software design project. She looked not only at the quantity and quality of students' contributions, but also whether those changed at different time points in the project and whether old-timers in teams offered particular assistance to the planning conversations. Ching (2000) compared a class composed of fourth-grade newcomers and fifth-grade old-timers with a class composed of fourth- and fifth-grade newcomers to the software design project experience and found that differences in programming knowledge, collaboration patterns, and breadth of students' reflections on the design experience could all be attributed to previous design project experience.

ACKNOWLEDGMENTS

The research and analyses reported in this chapter have been supported by a grant from the Urban Education Studies Center at the University of California, Los Angeles, and a grant from the National Science Foundation (REC-9632695) to the first author. The opinions expressed do not necessarily reflect the position or policy of the funding agencies. The results were first presented with Cynthia C. Ching and Sue Marshall at the annual meeting of the American Educational Research Association in 1998 in Chicago, IL. Portions of this chapter and results have appeared in previous publications. We thank the teacher and students of the upper elementary grade at the Corinne Seeds University Elementary School for their participation.

REFERENCES

American Association of University Women. (2000). *Tech-savvy: Educating girls in the new computer age.* Washington, DC: AAUW Educational Foundation.

Björklund, D. F. (1991). *Children's strategies: Contemporary views of cognitive development.* Hillsdale, NJ: Lawrence Erlbaum Associates.

Blumenfeld, P. C., Soloway, E., Marx, R. W., Krajcik, J. S., Guzdial, M., & Palincsar, A. (1991). Motivating project-based learning: Sustaining the doing, supporting the learning. *Educational Psychologist, 26*(3 & 4), 369–398.

Brown, A. (1992). "Design experiments:" Theoretical and methodological issues. *The Journal of the Learning Sciences, 2*(2), 1–37.

Canada, K., & Brusca, F. (1991). The technological gender gap: Evidence and recommendations for educators and computer-based instruction designers. *Educational Technology Research & Development, 39*(2), 43–51.

Ching, C. C. (2000). *Apprenticeship, learning and technology: Children as oldtimers and newcomers in a culture of learning through design.* Unpublished doctoral dissertation, University of California, Los Angeles.

Ching, C. C., Kafai, Y. B., & Marshall, S. (2000). Spaces for change: Gender and technology access. *Journal of Science Education and Technology, 9*, 67–78.

Cohen, E. (1994). Restructuring the classroom: Conditions for productive small groups. *Review of Educational Research, 64*, 1–35.

Colella, V. (2002). Participatory simulations: Building collaborative understanding through immersive dynamic modeling. In T. Koschman, R. Hall, & N. Miyake (Eds.), *CSCL 2: Carrying forward the conversation* (pp. 357–391). Mahwah, NJ: Lawrence Erlbaum Associates.

Cone, C. (2001). Technically speaking: Girls and computers. In P. O'Reilly, E. Penn, & K. Mareis (Eds.), *Educating young adolescent girls* (pp. 171–187). Mahwah, NJ: Lawrence Erlbaum Associates.

Davis, E. (2003). Prompting middle school science students for productive reflection: Generic and directed prompts. *The Journal of the Learning Sciences, 12*, 91–141.

Erickson, J., & Lehrer, R. (1998). The evolution of critical standards as students design hypermedia documents. *The Journal of the Learning Sciences, 7*(3 & 4), 351–386.

Fey, M. H. (2001). Gender and technology: A question of empowerment. *Reading and Writing Quarterly, 17*, 357–361.

Finegold, M., & Pundak, D. (1991). A study of change in students' conceptual frameworks in astronomy. *Studies in Educational Evaluation, 17*, 151–166.

Friedman, S. L., & Scholnick, E. K. (Eds.). (1997). *The developmental psychology of planning: Why, how and when do we plan?* Mahwah, NJ: Lawrence Erlbaum Associates.

Friedman, S. L., Scholnick, E. K., & Cocking R. R. (Eds.). (1987). *Blueprints for thinking.* Cambridge, MA: Cambridge University Press.

Harel, I. (1991). *Children designers.* Norwood, NJ: Ablex.

Harel, I., & Papert, S. (1990). Software design as a learning environment. *Interactive Learning Environments, 1*(1), 1–32.

Hmelo, C. E., Holton, D. L., & Kolodner, J. L. (2000). Designing to learn about complex systems. *The Journal of the Learning Sciences, 9*(3), 247–298.

Kafai, Y. B. (1995). *Minds in play: computer game design as a context for children's learning.* Hillsdale, NJ: Lawrence Erlbaum Associates.

Kafai, Y. B. (1998). Children as designers, testers and evaluators of educational software. In A. Druin (Ed.), *The design of children's technology* (pp. 123–146). San Francisco: Morgan Kaufman.

Kafai, Y. B., & Ching, C. C. (2001). Affordances of collaborative software design planning for elementary students' science talk. *The Journal of the Learning Sciences, 10*(3), 323–363.

Kafai, Y. B., Ching, C. C., & Marshall, S. (1998). Children as designers of educational multimedia software. *Computers and Education, 29,* 117–126.

Kaiser Family Foundation. (1999). *Kids, media and the millennium.* Sacramento, CA: Author.

Kinnear, A. (1995). Introduction of microcomputers: A case study of patterns of use and children's perceptions. *Journal of Educational Computing Research, 13,* 27–40.

Lammers, S. (1986). *Programmers at work.* Redmond, WA: Tempus Books.

Lave, J., & Wenger, E. (1991). *Situated learning: Legitimate peripheral participation.* New York: Cambridge University Press.

Linn, M. C., Bell, P., & Hsi, S. (1998). Using the Internet to enhance student understanding of science: The Knowledge Integration Environment. *Interactive Learning Environments, 6*(1–2), 4–38.

Marshall, S. (2000). *Planning in context.* Unpublished doctoral dissertation, Graduate School of Education & Information Studies, University of California, Los Angeles.

Palumbo, D. B. (1990). Programming language/problem-solving research: A review of relevant issues. *Review of Educational Research, 60*(1), 65–89.

Penner, D. E., Lehrer, R., & Schauble, L. (1998). From physical models to biomechanics: A design-based modeling approach. *The Journal of the Learning Sciences, 7*(3&4), 429–450.

Roth, M. (1995). Inventors, copycats, and everyone else: The emergence of shared resources and practices as defining aspects of classroom communities. *Science Education, 79*(5), 475–502.

Roth, W.-M. (1998). *Designing communities.* New York: Kluwer Academic Publishers.

Sandoval, W. (2003). Conceptual and epistemic aspects of students' scientific explanations. *Journal of the Learning Sciences, 12,* 5–52.

Shaffer, D. (2002). Design, collaboration, and computation: The design studio as a model for computer-supported collaboration in mathematics. In T. Koschman, R. Hall, & N. Miyake (Eds.), *CSCL 2: Carrying forward the conversation* (pp. 197–222). Mahwah, NJ: Lawrence Erlbaum Associates.

Shashaani, L. (1994). Gender differences in computer experience and its influence on computer attitudes. *Journal of Educational Computing Research, 11,* 347–367.

Spoehr, K. (1995). Enhancing the acquisition of conceptual structures through hypermedia. In K. McGilly (Ed.), *Classroom lessons: Integrating cognitive theory and classroom practice* (pp. 75–101). Cambridge, MA: MIT Press.

Vosniadou, S. (1994). Capturing and modeling the process of conceptual change. *Learning and Instruction, 4,* 45–69.

Webb, N., & Palincsar, A. (1996). Collaborative learning. In D. Berliner (Ed.), *Handbook of educational psychology* (pp. 345–413). New York: Macmillan.

6

How the Internet Will Help Large-Scale Assessment Reinvent Itself

Randy Elliot Bennett
Educational Testing Service

Whether for educational admissions, school and student accountability, or public policy, large-scale assessment in the United States is undergoing enormous pressure to change. This pressure is most evident with respect to high-stakes tests, like those used for grade promotion or college entrance. However, it is becoming apparent for lower stakes survey instruments too, like the National Assessment of Educational Progress (NAEP; e.g., Pellegrino, Jones, & Mitchell, 1999).

Several factors underlie the pressure to change. First, whereas our tests have incorporated many psychometric advances, they have remained separated from equally important advances in cognitive science, in essence measuring the same things in ever more technically sophisticated ways. Although decades of research have documented the importance of such cognitive constructs as knowledge organization, problem representation, mental models, and automaticity (Glaser, 1991), our tests typically do not account for them explicitly. As a result, our tests probably owe more to the behavioral psychology of the early 20th century than to the cognitive science of today (Shepard, 2000).

A second factor is the mismatch with the content and format of curriculum—a criticism more true of the developed ability tests commonly used in post-secondary admissions than of school achievement measures, but relevant to the latter as well. The mismatch arises in part from the fact that the elemental, forced-choice problems dominating many tests are effective *indicators* of skills and abilities, and thus provide an efficient means to estimate student standing on those constructs. However, the mismatch becomes problematic because of the increasing attention being paid to test preparation. Although persistent direct training on these indicator tasks may increase test performance, it certainly is *not* the best way to improve the underlying skill the test is intended to measure. Further, it distracts attention from other, arguably more critical, learning activities (Frederiksen, 1984).

A third factor encouraging change is the lower performance of some minority groups and of women. Because of the curricular mismatch, it is easy to blame group differences on purported bias in the test and more difficult to create a convincing defense than it would be if the tests were strongly linked to learning goals. In a high-stakes decision setting like admissions, tests become a lightning rod for the failure of schools and society to educate all groups effectively. With the potential weakening of affirmative action in university admissions, there is no politically acceptable choice but to reduce the role of such tests. This outcome is evident in recent proposals to eliminate the SAT I Reasoning Test from University of California admissions and replace it with a test more closely aligned with state curricular standards ("Atkinson Calls for Dropping," 2001). At the same time, accountability tests tied to curricular standards are being put into place in the states to encourage schools to teach all students valued skills. Although in Texas one such test was challenged in court on the basis of differential performance, that challenge was rejected (Schmidt, 2000). This rejection suggests that when well-constructed tests closely reflect the curriculum, group differences should become more an issue of instructional inadequacy than test inaccuracy (Bennett, 1998).

As attention shifts to the adequacy of instruction, the ability to derive meaningful information from test performance becomes more critical. A weak connection between test and curriculum ensures that the value of feedback for the examinee will be limited. Even for tests where the connection is stronger, feedback is still too often of marginal value, in part, because of the additional cost and processing time that would be incurred. For achievement surveys like NAEP, which offer *no* information to individuals, schools, or districts, motivation to participate is undoubtedly diminished.

Finally, there is efficiency. Testing programs are expensive to operate. That expense gets passed on to taxpayers for a state or federal test like NAEP or directly to examinees in the case of admissions measures. Further, to be maximally useful, test results are needed quickly. Rapid information delivery is certainly a requirement in the education policy arena, where the results of national surveys may sometimes take years to produce. It is also increasingly true in the admissions context, where more rapid feedback is needed not only for early decisions, financial aid, and the rolling acceptances that are beginning to characterize some distance learning programs, but also for guidance and placement.

Will reinvention solve all of these problems? Of course not. Yet I do believe it will allow us to make significant progress on each of them. Does reinvention mean abandoning educational testing as it now exists? No. It only means combining the best of the old with the most promising of the new to engineer radical improvements.

THE PROMISE OF NEW TECHNOLOGY

Radical improvements in assessment will derive from advances in three areas: technology, measurement, and cognitive science (Bennett, 1999). Of the three, new technology will be the most influential in the short term; thus, I focus on it in this chapter. New technology will have the greatest influence because it—not measurement and not cognitive science—is pervading our society. Billions of dollars are being invested annually to create and make commonplace powerful, general technologies for commerce, communications, entertainment, and education. Due to their generality, these technologies can also be used to improve assessment.

These technological advancements revolve primarily around the Internet. The Internet is (or will be) interactive, broadband, switched, networked, and standards-based. What does that mean?

Interactive means that we can present a task to a student and quickly respond to that student's actions. *Switched* means that we can engage in different interactions with different students simultaneously. In combination, these two characteristics (interactive and switched) make for individualized assessments. *Broadband* means that those interactions can contain lots of information. For assessment tasks, that information could include audio, video, and animation. Those features might make tasks more authentic and engaging, as well as allow us to assess skills that cannot be measured in paper and pencil (Bennett et al., 1999). We might also use audio and video to capture answers, for example, giving examinees choice in their response modalities (typing, speaking, or, for a deaf student, American Sign Language). *Networked* indicates that everything is linked. This linkage means that testing agencies, schools, parents, government officials, item writers, test reviewers, human scorers, and students are tied together electronically. That electronic connection can allow for enormous efficiencies. Finally, *standards-based* means that the network runs according to a set of conventional rules that all participants follow. That fact permits both the easy interchange of data and access from a wide variety of computing platforms, as long as the software running on those platforms (e.g., Internet browsers) adheres to those rules too.[1]

As an embodiment of these characteristics, what does the Internet afford? It affords the *potential* to deliver efficiently on a mass scale individualized, highly en-

---

[1]The Internet takes advantage of many such standards, including Internet Protocol (IP) for transmitting packets of information; Transmission Control Protocol (TCP/IP) for verifying the contents of those packets; HyperText Transfer Protocol (HTTP) for transferring Web pages; and HyperText Markup Language (HTML) and Extensible Markup Language (XML) for representing structured documents and data on the Web. XML provides a significant advance over HTML in that it allows for the representation of unlimited classes of documents. Leadership in developing and implementing the many standards used by the Internet is provided by the World Wide Web Consortium (www.w3.org). For more on Internet standards, see their Web site or see Green (1996), who gives a more basic introduction.

gaging content to almost any desktop; get data back immediately; process it; and make information available anywhere in the world, anytime, day or night. Paper delivery cannot compete with this potential.

The Internet is, of course, not being built to service the needs of large-scale assessment. It is, instead, being built for e-commerce: to sell products and services over the Web to consumers and businesses directly. Coincidentally, the capabilities needed for e-commerce are essentially those needed for e-assessment:

- interactive (so that products can be offered and orders transacted),
- switched (so different business transactions can be conducted with different customers simultaneously),
- broadband (so that those offers can be as engaging and enticing as possible),
- networked (so that product offers, orders, shipping, inventory, and accounting can be integrated), and
- standards-based (so that everyone can get to it regardless of computing platform).

Will we be able to count on continued investment in the Internet to support its use as a delivery medium? By any measure, the Internet and use of it has grown dramatically to say the least. As a communications medium, in 1998, the Internet surpassed the telephone, with 3 billion e-mail messages sent each day (Church, 1999). The number of host computers, a good indicator of the network's size, went from about 30 million to 180 million between January 1998 and January 2003 ("Internet Domain Survey Host Count," 2003). In terms of use, the percentage of U.S. homes with Internet access increased from 26% in December 1998 to 51% in September 2001 (U.S. Department of Commerce, 2002). Worldwide, the number of users has grown from somewhere between 117 and 142 million in 1998 to about 600 million in 2002 ("Big Fish," 1999; Global Reach, 2002; "How Many Online?", 2003). This phenomenal growth may slow as investment subsides from the speculative rates of the past few years. However, the vast size of the Internet and its user base constitutes a critical mass that should continue to attract substantial capital.

For commerce, the promise of the Internet is all about being faster, cheaper, *and* better. Two "laws" of the digital era illustrate this promise. Moore's Law predicts the doubling of computational capability (specifically, at the level of the microchip) every 18 months. As Negroponte (1995) explained, what filled a room yesterday is on your desk today and will be on your wrist tomorrow. Metcalfe's Law says that the value of a network increases by the square of the number of people on it. The true value of a network is, thus, less about information and more about community (Negroponte, 1995). One can see this effect clearly in eBay, the online auction broker (Cohen, 1999). Each new user potentially benefits every other existing user because every eBay member can be both buyer and seller.[2] Metcalfe's law is playing out well beyond eBay. Online business-to-business auction brokers are appearing in a variety of industries, including metals, electricity, and bandwidth (Friedman, 2000; Gibney, 2000).

Another illustration of this cheaper-faster-better result is the effect of the Internet on the traditional relationship between *richness* and *reach*, where *richness* is the depth of the interaction that a business can have with a customer and *reach* is the number of customers that a business can contact through a given channel. Traditionally, one limited the other. That is, a business could attain maximal reach, but only limited richness. For example, through direct mail, broadcast, or newspaper ads, a company could communicate with many people, but have a meaningful interaction with none of them. Similarly, a business could attain maximal richness, but limited reach. Via personal contact (e.g., door-to-door sales), very deep interactions can occur, but with only a relatively small number of people. What has the Internet done? It has transformed the relationship between richness and reach by allowing businesses to touch many people in a personalized but inexpensive way (Evans & Wurster, 2000). What does richness *with* reach make for? It makes for *mass customization*.

We can already see the effects in Dell Computer Corporation's business model. Customers can log onto Dell's Internet site (www.dell.com), choose from a menu of basic machine designs, and then configure a particular design to meet their needs. A second example is Customatix (www.customatix.com/customatix/common/homepage/HomepageGeneral.po), which allows the customer to design shoes using up to *three billion trillion* combinations of colors, graphics, logos, and materials per shoe. You design them. They build them. *Nobody else* is likely to have exactly the same ones.

REINVENTING ASSESSMENT

Reinventing the Business

There are two major dimensions to reinventing assessment. One is the business of assessment. This dimension centers on the core processes that define an enterprise. In many cases, those core processes can become many times more efficient because moving bits is faster and easier than moving atoms (Negroponte, 1995);

---

[2]It works. eBay is reported to be the most successful company in cyberspace (Cohen, 2001). Why? It has none of the costs of retailing: no buying, no warehousing, no shipping, no returns, no overstock.

that is, electronically processing information is far more cost-effective than physically manipulating things.

For large-scale testing programs, some examples of the potential for electronic processing are in:

- developing tests, making the items easier to review, revise, and automatically morph into still more items (e.g., Singley & Bennett, 2002) because the items are digitally represented;
- delivering tests, eliminating the costs of printing, warehousing, and shipping tons of paper;
- presenting dynamic stimuli like audio, video, and animation, making the need for specialized testing equipment (e.g., audio cassette recorders, VCRs) obsolete (Bennett et al., 1999);
- transmitting some types of complex constructed responses to human graders, removing the need to transport, house, and feed the graders (Odendahl, 1999; Whalen & Bejar, 1998);
- scoring other complex constructed responses automatically, reducing the need for human reading (Burstein et al., 1998; Clauser et al., 1997); and
- distributing test results, cutting the costs of printing and mailing reports.

To get a sense of how reinventing the business of assessment might affect testing organizations, take a look at reference book publishing, in particular the case of *Encyclopaedia Britannica* (Evans & Wurster, 2000; Landler, 1995; Melcher, 1997). *Encyclopaedia Britannica* was established in Scotland in 1768. It is the oldest and most famous encyclopedia in the English-speaking world. By 1990, its sales had reached $650 million per annum. Then suddenly, *Britannica's* fortunes drastically changed. In 1996, the company was sold for less than *half* its net worth (i.e., the value of its assets, including its encyclopedia inventory, minus its liabilities). That same year, it eliminated its *entire* door-to-door North American sales force. By 1998, sales had fallen *80%*. What happened?

What happened was that the reference book business was reinvented because of the emergence of new technology. At its peak, *Britannica* was a 32-volume set of books costing well over $1,000. In 1993, Microsoft introduced *Encarta* on CD-ROM for under $100; although *Britannica* was much more comprehensive, the difference for most people was not worth an extra $900+. Initially, *Britannica* did not respond because it did not take the threat from *Encarta* seriously. When it did respond, it did so ineffectively because *Britannica* would not fit on a single CD-ROM and because the company's large sales force was not suited to selling software. Ultimately, *Britannica* was not ready to cannibalize its existing paper business to enter this new electronic one.

Why is this story important? Because similar (although less extreme) scenarios are playing themselves out now in individual investing, book selling, travel planning, music distribution, newspapers, long-distance telephony, photography, and even business-to-business transactions. (As to the last, Cisco Systems makes 90% of its revenue from business-to-business transactions done over the Internet [Cisco Systems, Inc., 2000]). These reinvention scenarios are forcing organizations—including some in educational assessment—to come quickly to grips with where new technology *will* and *will not* help core business processes.

As should be obvious, technology-driven changes in business processes can occur quickly, and their consequences can be significant for the organizations that service a particular market. In fact, if radical and pervasive enough, process changes can force shifts in the substance of the business. Although reinventing the business of assessment by incorporating technology into specific assessment processes is about trying to achieve the efficiencies needed to remain competitive today, reinventing the substance of assessment—most fundamentally, the reason we do it—is not about today. It is about tomorrow.

Reinventing the Substance

The populations seeking education are changing and so are their purposes for learning. At the college level, a minority of students fits the traditional profile: 18 to 22 years old, full-time, on-campus resident (Levine, 2000a). This is not because fewer 18- to 22-year-olds are going to college. It is because more adults are. Working adults over age 24 constitute some 44% of college students ("Education Prognosis 1999," 1999).

Why are so many adults returning to college? Over the past 25 years, employer demand in the United States has shifted toward higher educational qualifications, as indicated by an increasing premium paid for those with a college degree (Barton, 1999). In addition to this rise in entry qualifications, the knowledge required to maintain a job in many occupations is changing so fast that 50% of all employees' skills are estimated to become outdated within 3 to 5 years (Moe & Blodget, 2000). Witness any job that requires interaction with information technology (IT), which is a growing proportion of jobs. In fact by 2006, almost half of all workers will be employed by industries that are either major producers or intensive users of IT products and services (Henry et al., 1999).

Hence, more people want postsecondary education because they need to have it if they want to become—and stay—employed. More of these individuals are nontraditional students who may work, travel in their jobs, or have families. For these people, physically attending classes is not always feasible, let alone convenient.[3]

---

[3]A recent, but potentially significant, addition to this population is the U.S. Army. In July, 2000, Secretary of the Army, Louis Caldera, announced a $600 million program to allow any interested soldier to take college courses over the Internet at little or no cost (Carr, 2000).

This population's unmet educational need is increasingly becoming the target of distance learning. Although the proportion of students taking distance courses is still relatively small—about 8% of undergraduates and 10% of graduate students took at least one distance-learning course in 1999 to 2000—that proportion has been growing so fast that by 2002 most 4-year institutions offered such courses (Ashby, 2002; National Center for Education Statistics, 2003). Further, the course-delivery method used by the majority of students is the Internet. Finally, as one might expect, those taking such courses are more likely to be older, married, employed full time, and attending school part time (Ashby, 2002).

At the same time, Internet-based distance learning is finding its way into high schools. Home-schooled students, districts without a full complement of qualified teachers, and the children of migrant workers generate the need. So-called "virtual high schools" have emerged in at least 16 states (Ansell & Park, 2003). These programs can cross state lines, with offerings open to students regardless of residence and with course grades earned through accredited online institutions applicable toward high school graduation.

The growth of Internet-based distance learning will have a significant impact on traditional education. For one, it may threaten the existence of established institutions (Dunn, 2000; Levine, 2000b). Many in the private sector see education as a huge industry that produces mediocre results for a high cost. If the private sector can leverage new technologies, like distance learning, to deliver greater value, the institutions that dominate education today may not be the leaders tomorrow.

A second reason that the growth of Internet-based distance learning will influence traditional education is that, regardless of its impact on nonprofit institutions, the distance learning industry will produce sophisticated software that everyone can use, in school and out. Both Dunn (2000) and Tulloch (2000) suggested that this occurrence will blur the distinctions between distance learning and local education. APEX offers an example (http://apex.netu.com/). This company markets online Advanced Placement (AP) courses, targeting districts that want to offer AP, but that do not have qualified teachers. Thus, districts can use APEX offerings on site.[4]

The considerable potential of online learning—local or distance—is reflected in a report to the president and congress of the bipartisan Web-Based Education Commission (Kerrey & Isakson, 2000). The Commission reached the following conclusion:

> The question is no longer *if* the Internet can be used to transform learning in new and powerful ways. The Commission has found that it can. Nor is the question *should* we invest the time, the energy, and the money necessary to fulfill its promise in de-

---

[4]A second, perhaps more interesting, example is Florida's Daniel Jenkins Academy, where students physically attend but take all academic courses *online* from *off-site* teachers (Thomas, 2000).

fining and shaping new learning opportunity. The Commission believes that we should. (p. 134; italics original)

If acted on, the consequences of this statement for assessment are profound. As online learning becomes more widespread, the substance and format of assessment will need to keep pace. Another quote from the Commission's report read:

Perhaps the greatest barrier to innovative teaching is assessment that measures yesterday's learning goals. . . . Too often today's tests measure yesterday's skills with yesterday's testing technologies—paper and pencil. (p. 59)

Thus, as students do more and more of their learning using technology tools, asking them to express that learning in a medium different from the one they typically work in will become increasingly untenable, especially where working with the medium is part of the skill being tested (or otherwise impacts it in important ways). Searching for information using the World Wide Web or writing on computer are examples.[5]

These changes in learning methodology offer exciting possibilities for assessment innovation. On site or off, an obvious result of delivering courses via the Internet is the potential for embedding assessment, perhaps almost seamlessly, in instruction (Bennett, 1998). Because students respond to instructional exercises electronically, their responses can be recorded, leaving a continuous learning trace. Depending on how the course and assessment are designed, this information could conceivably support a sophisticated model of student proficiencies (Gitomer, Mislevy, & Steinberg, 1995). That model might be useful both for dynamically deciding what instruction to present next *and* for making more global judgments about what the student knows and can do at any given point.

In addition to assessment embedded in Internet-delivered courses, one can imagine Internet-delivered assessment embedded in traditional classroom activity. Such assessment might take the form of periodically delivered exercises that both teach and test. In this scenario, the exercises would be standardized and performance might serve, depending on the level of aggregation, to indicate individual, classroom, school, district, state, or national achievement. Thus, these exercises could serve summative as well as formative purposes and be useful to individuals as well as institutions. If the exercises were of high enough quality, such a model might improve the motivation to participate in voluntary surveys like NAEP.

To be sure, there are many difficult issues:

---

[5]Russell conducted several studies on the mismatch between learning and testing methods in writing (e.g., Russell & Plati, 2001). The repeated result is that the writing proficiencies of students who routinely use word processors are underestimated by paper-and-pencil tests.

- How can we generate comparable inferences across students and institutions when variation in school equipment may cause items to display differently from one student to the next, potentially affecting performance?
- How can we deliver assessment dependably given the unreliable nature of computers and the Internet, and the limited technical support available in most schools?
- How might we make sense of the huge corpus of data that the electronic recording of student actions might provide?
- How would student learning be affected by knowing that one's actions are being recorded?
- How can we prevent assessments that serve both instructional and accountability purposes from being corrupted by unscrupulous students or school staff?
- How can we manage the costs of online assessment?
- How can we ensure that all parties can participate?

Let us, for the moment, turn to this last issue.

ARE THE SCHOOLS READY?

A continuing concern with such reinvention visions is whether schools (and students) are ready technologically and, in particular, what to do about technology differences across social groups. The National Center for Education Statistics (NCES) reports that, as of fall 2001, 99% of schools were connected to the Internet—up from 35% in 1994 (Tabs, 2002). Schools in *all* categories (i.e., by grade level, school size, poverty concentration, and metropolitan status) were equally likely to have Internet access. Further, most schools had dedicated lines: Only 5% were using dial-up modem, a slower and less reliable access method.

Clearly, many of these schools could have only a single connected machine, and that machine could be the one sitting on the principal's desk. How many classrooms were actually wired? According to NCES (Tabs, 2002), as of fall 2001, 87% of all instructional rooms had Internet access (up from 3% in 1994). The ratio of students to Internet-connected computers was 5:1—down from 12:1 only 3 years earlier. These are staggering numbers—they imply that classrooms are connecting to the Internet at a very rapid rate.

This success is in no small part due to federal efforts. The government's *e-rate* program has been giving public schools and libraries discounts of up to 90% on phone service, Internet hook-ups, and wiring for several years ("FCC: E-rate subsidy funded," 2000). In 1998 and 1999 alone, the program committed $3.65 billion to over 50,000 institutions, helping connect more than 1 million public school classrooms (Kennard, 2000). In addition, the majority of the program's funding has typically gone to schools in low-income areas.

However, even with these significant efforts, equity issues continue. As of fall 2001, in high-poverty schools, the ratio of students to Internet computers was 7:1. In low-poverty schools, it was closer to 5:1 (Tabs, 2002). Still this difference has been dramatically reduced from only 2 years earlier (1999), when the respective ratios were 17:1 versus 8:1.

What should we conclude? Certainly, with few exceptions, it would be impossible to electronically deliver assessment to each child's desktop today. Yet the trend is clear: The infrastructure is quickly falling into place for Internet delivery of assessment to schools. As evidence, in the 2002 to 2003 school year, 12 states were administering on a pilot or operational basis some type of online state examination (Olson, 2003).

Assuming that every classroom is wired, will all students then have the technology skills needed to take tests online? Clearly, more students are becoming computer familiar every day, and developing such skills is a stated goal of the federal "No Child Left Behind" legislation (U.S. Department of Education, 2002). Yet as Negroponte (1995) suggested, computer familiarity is really the wrong issue. The secret to good interface design is to make it *go away*. Thus, advances in technology will eventually eliminate the need to be computer familiar (Dertouzos, 2001). After *nomadic* computing, which we are now entering with the proliferation of wireless Internet devices and personal digital assistants, comes *ubiquitous* computing (Olsen, 2000)—the embedding of new technology into everyday items. Inventions like "radio" paper (Gershenfeld, 1999, p. 18; Maney, 2000; "NCS Secures Rights," 2000) may allow students to interact with computers in the same way that they interact with paper today. Smart desks are another likelihood, in which case a test may be electronically delivered, quite literally, to every desktop.

In the United States, then, we may see a future in which every classroom is wired and every student can easily take tests online. What of the rest of the world? To be sure, the Internet is an American phenomenon. It derives from research sponsored by the Defense Department in the 1960s (Cerf, 1993). As a result of this history, the overwhelming majority of users were, until very recently, from our shores. At this writing, some 70% of Net users reside *outside* of the United States, and the foreign growth rate now exceeds the domestic one ("How Many Online?", 2003; "U.S. Dominance Seen Slipping," 2001).

The largest numbers of foreign Internet users are, of course, in developed nations. These nations have the telecommunications infrastructure and citizens with enough disposable income to afford the trappings of Internet use. Yet what about developing nations? Will they be left irretrievably behind? The challenges for these nations are undoubtedly great. Over time, however, we should see significant progress in building the infrastructure and user base here too (Cairncross, 1997; Fernandez, 2000). This progress will occur for at least two reasons. First, the cost of technology has been dropping precipitously and, by Moore's law, will continue to decline. Further, because the future of computing is undoubtedly in wireless devices (Grice, 2000), a telecommunications infrastructure will be much cheaper to acquire than the land lines of old. Second, as Metcalfe's law suggests, markets will become all the more valuable as they are interconnected. (Witness the global economy and economic benefits resulting to nations from integration with it.) That developing nations join the e-commerce network means greater opportunity for all. It means more vendor choice for the people of developing nations, more opportunity for developed nations to serve these markets, and a new opportunity for Third World businesses to compete globally.[6]

The same holds true for assessment. The Internet will make it easier for developing nations to get access to assessment services from elsewhere and for those nations to distribute their own assessment services regionally or around the world. This ease of access and distribution should make it possible to form international consortia. Such consortia will be able to assemble technical resources that a single nation might not be able to acquire. In addition, those consortia may be able to purchase services from others more efficiently than nations could obtain individually. Finally, an electronic network should make it easier to participate in international studies, bringing the benefits of benchmarking to nations throughout the world.

BUT IS TECHNOLOGY-BASED ASSESSMENT REALLY WORTH THE INVESTMENT?

One of the largest instantiations of technology-based assessment to date is computer-based testing (CBT) in postsecondary admissions. As programs like the Graduate Record Examinations, the Graduate Management Admission Test, and the Test of English as a Foreign Language have found, CBT can be enormously costly. Being among the first large-scale programs to move to computer, they bore the brunt of creating the infrastructure for what was essentially a new business. The building of that infrastructure was initiated in the early 1990s *before* test developers had tools for efficiently creating electronic tests, *before* computers were widely available for individuals to take tests on, and *before* the Internet was ready to bring those tests to students. In essence, these programs needed to build *both* a factory to stamp out a new product *and* a new distribution mechanism. A first-generation infrastructure now exists, but it is not yet optimized to produce and deliver tests as efficiently as possible. Right now, there is no question about it: For these programs, assessment by computer costs *far* more than assessment by paper.

---

[6]Developing a technology infrastructure and integrating into the e-commerce network may, in fact, help jump-start the growth required to deal with the serious problems of public health, education, and welfare that these countries typically face (Friedman, 2000).

If we have learned anything from the history of innovation, it is that new technologies are often initially far too expensive for mass use. That was true of the automobile, telephone service, commercial aviation, and the personal computer, among many other innovations. For example, in 1930, the cost of a 3-minute telephone call from New York to London was $250 (in 1990 dollars). By 1995, the cost had dropped to under $1 (World Bank, 1995; cited in Cairncross, 1997, p. 28). As a second instance, when the IBM Personal Computer was introduced in 1981, it cost around $5,000. At the time, the median family income in the United States was on the order of $25,000, so that a computer cost about 20% of the average family's earnings—not very affordable. At this writing, the cost of a computer with *many* times greater capability is a little more than $500, and the median income is closer to $63,000.[7] A computer now costs about 1% of average income.[8]

When a promising new technology appears, individuals and institutions invest, allowing the technology to evolve and a supporting infrastructure to develop. Over the course of that development, failures inevitably occur. Eventually, the technology either dies or becomes commercially viable—that is, efficient enough.

So who is investing in CBT? At this point, it is an impressive list including nonprofit testing agencies, for-profit testing companies, school districts, state education departments, government agencies, and companies with no history in testing at all. The list includes ACT; the Bloomington (MN) Public Schools; CITO (the Netherlands); the College Board; CTB/McGraw-Hill; Edison Schools; ETS; Excelsior College (formerly Regents College); Harcourt Educational Measurement; Heriot-Watt University (Scotland); Houghton-Mifflin; Microsoft; the National Board of Medical Examiners; the National Institute for Testing and Evaluation (Israel); NCS Pearson; the Northwest Evaluation Association; a dozen U.S. states; the Qualifications and Curriculum Authority (Great Britain); Thomson Corporation; the University of Cambridge Local Examinations Syndicate (UCLES); the U.S. Armed Forces; Vantage Technologies; and the Victoria (Australia) Board of Studies. These organizations are producing tests for postsecondary admissions, college course placement, course credit, school accountability, instructional assessment, and professional certification and licensure. In concert, they already administer *millions* of computerized tests each year.[9]

---

[7]The median income for a family of four in calendar year 1981 was $26,274 (U.S. Census Bureau, 2002). For 2001, it was $63,278.

[8]Price and quality-adjusted data tell a similar story. In 1983, the quality-adjusted cost of a personal computer (PC) in constant 1996 dollars was $1,098 (D. Wasshausen, personal communication, April 13, 2000). By 1996, the cost of a PC, holding quality constant, was $100, less than a tenth of the 1983 cost. By 1999, that quality-adjusted PC had further deflated to $29.

[9]I based this statement on unduplicated volumes claimed by Thomson Prometric (http://www.prometric.com/PressRoom/PressKit/Metrics/default.htm), Vantage Technologies (http://www.vantage.com/), and the U.S. Armed Forces (A. Nicewander, personal communication, November 2, 2000). These three organizations *alone* claim some 20 million tests annually. These tests include both high- and low-stakes assessments.

Why are these organizations investing? I think it is because they believe that technology-based assessment will eventually achieve important economies over paper and that, fundamentally, assessment will benefit. I also think it is because they do not want to become *Britannica*. That is, they see improvements in the business and substance of assessment, which, if they fail to embrace, will lead them to the same fate as that encyclopedia publisher.

CBT as a Disruptive Technology

As the case of admissions testing suggests, the road to improvement may be a difficult one because CBT might not be a typical innovation. Christensen (1997) distinguished two types of innovation—*sustaining* and *disruptive* technologies. Sustaining technologies enhance the performance of established products in ways that mainstream customers have traditionally valued. Historically, most technological advances in any given industry have been sustaining ones (e.g., in the personal computer industry, faster chips and bigger, higher resolution monitors). Occasionally, disruptive technologies emerge. Companies introduce these technologies hoping their features will provide competitive edge. However, these features characteristically overshoot the market, giving customers more than they need or are willing to pay for. Thus, disruptive technologies result in *worse* product performance, at least in the near term, on key dimensions in a company's established markets.

Interestingly, a few fringe customers typically find the features for a given disruptive technology attractive. In these niche markets, the technology may thrive. If and when it advances to the level and nature of performance demanded in the mainstream market, the new technology can invade it, rapidly knocking out the traditional technology and its dependent practitioners. Remember *Britannica*.

CBT has many of the characteristics of a *disruptive* technology. Established testing organizations are applying it in their mainstream markets, most notably postsecondary admissions. This innovation was introduced, in good part, to provide competitive edge through features like the ability to take a test at one's convenience and get score reports immediately. As it turned out, these features overshot the market. At least initially, registrations for continuously offered computer-based admissions tests mirrored those for fixed-date paper administrations, suggesting that scheduling convenience was not a highly valued feature in the market of the time. Moreover, examinees were dissatisfied with losing some of the features of paper exams, including the ability to proceed through the test nonlinearly, the option to review the scoring of items actually taken, and the low cost (Perry, 2000).

Although CBT encountered difficulty in the mainstream admissions testing market, fringe players found greater success with it in niche markets. One example is information technology (IT) certification, which individuals pursue to document their competence in some computer-related proficiency. In 1999, over 3 *million* examinations in 25 languages were administered in this market (Adelman, 2000). Most of these tests were delivered on computer, and most were offered on a continuous basis. Three delivery vendors provided the bulk of examinations: Prometric (a subsidiary of Thomson Corporation), Vue (a subsidiary of NCS Pearson), and CAT, Inc. (now Promissor, a subsidiary of Houghton-Mifflin). Together these vendors operated some 5,000 testing centers in 140 countries. As of June 2000, over 1.9 million credentials had been awarded, most for Microsoft or Novell technologies.

Why is the CBT of today so well suited to this market niche? Let us start by asking what features a testing product must have to succeed in this niche. First, it must be continuously offered because these test candidates build technology skill on their own schedules—at home or on the job, very often through books or on-line learning. These individuals want to test when *they* are ready, not when the testing companies are. Second, such a test must generally be offered on computer because technology use is the essence of the certification.

What are the financial considerations associated with serving this market? One consideration is whether the test fee can cover the cost of assessment. As it turns out, this market is less price-sensitive than postsecondary admissions. Why? With IT testing, employers pay the fee for over half the candidates (Adelman, 2000). In addition, certified employees command a substantial salary premium (4%–14%), which makes examinees more willing to absorb the higher fees that CBT currently requires. A second consideration is that security is not as critical as in admissions testing, so large item pools are not needed, reducing production cost. Lower security is tolerable because if an individual appears on the job with a dishonestly obtained credential, but without the required skill, he or she will not last. Finally, test volume is self-replicating: There are many repeat test takers because IT changes rapidly, so skills must be updated constantly. From an innovation perspective, then, IT certification may be one context in which the CBT of today can flourish and develop to better meet the needs of other assessment markets.

So why do industry leaders tend to fail with disruptive technology while fringe players succeed? Industry leaders often fail precisely because they attempt to introduce disruptive technologies into major markets before it is time (Christensen, 1997). Because niche markets are often too small to be of interest, leaders do not pursue those opportunities to refine the technology. Instead they give up, having run out of resources or credibility. Making a disruptive technology work requires iteration, and iteration means failure. Because they risk neither large resources nor reputations in the mainstream market, it is the fringe players who can fail early, often, and inexpensively enough to eventually challenge and overtake the industry leaders.

Toward the Technology-Based Assessment of Tomorrow

Are there other niche markets in which CBT might evolve? One such niche may be online learning. If we believe the Web-Based Education Commission (Kerrey & Isakson, 2000), online learning will become a major enterprise, especially for the lifelong updating of skills. In this market, institutions will be less concerned with questions of who gets *in* and more with who gets *out*, and what it is they have to do to get out (Messick, 1999). Why? Because once hired, businesses are becoming more concerned with what employees know and can do and less with where they went to school. Similarly, individuals are becoming more concerned with finding course offerings that meet their skill development goals and less with whether those offerings come from one institution or a half dozen.

What is the assessment need? First, it is for *knowledge facilitation*, and, second, it is for *knowledge certification*; that is, to help people develop their skills and then document that they have developed them. What is the assessment challenge? The challenge is to figure out how to design and deliver embedded assessment that provides instructional support *and* that globally summarizes learning accomplishment. In other words, the challenge is to combine richness with reach to achieve mass customization—use the Internet's ability to deliver the richness of customized assessment to reach a mass audience.

Can assessment be customized? In rudimentary ways, it already is. Certainly, we can dynamically adapt along a global dimension, as is done in many of today's computerized tests. Yet as we move assessment closer to instruction, we should eventually be able to adapt to the interests of the learner and the particular strengths and weaknesses evident at any particular juncture, as intelligent tutors now do (e.g., Schulze, Shelby, Treacy, & Wintersgill, 2000). Likewise, we should be able to customize feedback to describe the specific proficiencies the learner evidenced in an instructional sequence.

Perhaps the most far-reaching customization of assessment will come through modular online courses, whereby an instructor—or even a sophisticated learner—assembles a series of components into a unique offering. The Department of Defense (DOD) has taken a significant step through the Sharable Courseware Object Reference Model (SCORM) (www.adlnet.org). SCORM embodies specifications and guidelines providing the foundation for how DOD will use technology to build and operate the learning environment of the future. SCORM should allow mixing and matching of learning segments to create lower cost, reusable training resources.[10] If embedded assessment can be built into course modules following a

---

[10]SCORM is being built on the work of the IMS Global Learning Consortium (IMS) (www.imsproject.org/aboutims.html). IMS is developing open specifications for facilitating distributed learning activities, such as locating and using educational content, tracking learner progress, reporting learner performance, and exchanging student records between administrative systems. Both IMS and SCORM incorporate XML (see Footnote 1).

similar set of conventional specifications, the assessment too will be customized by default.

CONCLUSION

Whether for postsecondary admissions, school and student accountability, or national policy, large-scale educational assessment must be reinvented. Reinvention is not an option. If we do not reinvent it, much of today's paper-based testing will become an anachronism—"yesterday's testing technology," in the words of the Web-Based Education Commission (Kerrey & Isakson, 2000)—because it will be inconsistent with what and how students learn.

This reinvention must occur along *both* business and substantive lines. As educators, we often behave as if business considerations are unimportant, even distasteful. However, the business and substance of assessment are intertwined. Even for nonprofit educational institutions—state education departments, federal agencies, schools, research organizations—providing quality assessment for a low cost matters. Using new technology to do assessment faster and cheaper can free up the resources to do assessment better.

We *will* be able to do assessment better because advances in technology, cognitive science, and measurement are laying the groundwork to make reinvention a reality. Whereas the contributions of cognitive and measurement science are in many ways more fundamental than those of new technology, it is new technology that is pervading our society. Therefore, my thesis is that new technology will be the primary facilitating factor precisely because of its widespread societal acceptance.[11] In the same way that the Internet is already helping to revolutionize commerce, education, and even social interaction, this technological advance will help revolutionize the business and substance of large-scale assessment. It will do so by allowing richness with reach—that is, mass customization on a global scale—as never before. However, as the history of innovation suggests, this reinvention will not come immediately, without significant investment, or without setback. We are not yet ready for universal assessment via the Internet (at least in our schools). However, as suggested earlier, this story is not so much about today. It really is about *tomorrow*.

ACKNOWLEDGMENTS

This chapter is based on a paper presented at the annual conference of the International Association for Educational Assessment (IAEA), Jerusalem, May 2000. An earlier version of this article appeared under the same title in the *Educational Pol-*

---

[11]That the largest *facilitating* factor will be technological is not to say that we should necessarily let technology drive the substance of assessment. We should not.

icy Analysis Archives, 9(5), February 14, 2001. I appreciate the helpful comments of Isaac Bejar, Henry Braun, Howard Everson, and Drew Gitomer on an earlier draft of this manuscript.

REFERENCES

Adelman, C. (2000). *A parallel postsecondary universe: The certification system in information technology.* Washington, DC: Office of Educational Research and Improvement, U.S. Department of Education. Available: www.ed.gov/pubs/ParallelUniverse/

Ansell, S. E., & Park, J. (2003). Tracking tech trends: Student computer use grows, but teachers need training. *Education Week, 12*(35), 43–48.

Ashby, C. M. (2002). *Distance education: Growth in distance education programs and implications for federal education policy* (GAO-02-1125T). Washington, DC: General Accounting Office. Available: http://www.gao.gov/new.items/d021125t.pdf.

Atkinson calls for dropping SAT from UC admission requirements. (2001). *Higher Education and National Affairs, 50*(4) [On-line]. Available: www.acenet.edu/hena/issues/2001/03-05-01/sat.html.

Barton, P. E. (1999). *What jobs require: Literacy, education, and training, 1940–2006.* Princeton, NJ: Policy Information Center, Educational Testing Service. Available: www.ets.org/research/pic.

Bennett, R. E. (1998). *Reinventing assessment: Speculations on the future of large-scale educational testing.* Princeton, NJ: Policy Information Center, Educational Testing Service. Available: ftp://ftp.ets.org/pub/res/reinvent.pdf.

Bennett, R. E. (1999). Using new technology to improve assessment. *Educational Measurement: Issues and Practice, 18*(3), 5–12.

Bennett, R. E., Goodman, M., Hessinger, J., Ligget, J., Marshall, G., Kahn, H., & Zack, J. (1999). Using multimedia in large-scale computer-based testing programs. *Computers in Human Behavior, 15*, 283–294.

Big fish in a big pool. (1999, December 2). *TIME Digital.*

Burstein, J., Braden-Harder, L., Chodorow, M., Hua, S., Kaplan, B., Kukich, K., Lu, C., Nolan, J., Rock, D., & Wolff, S. (1998). *Computer analysis of essay content for automated score prediction* (RR-98-15). Princeton, NJ: Educational Testing Service.

Cairncross, F. (1997). *The death of distance: How the communications revolution will change our lives.* Boston, MA: Harvard Business School Press.

Carr, S. (2000, August 18). Army bombshell rocks distance education. *The Chronicle of Higher Education,* p. A35.

Cerf, V. (1993). How the Internet came to be. In B. Aboba (Ed.), *The online user's encyclopedia.* New York: Addison-Wesley. Available: http://www.bell-labs.com/user/zhwang/vcerf.html.

Christensen, C. M. (1997). *The innovator's dilemma: When new technologies cause great firms to fail.* Boston, MA: Harvard University Press.

Church, G. J. (1999). The economy of the future? *TIME, 154*(14). Available: http://www.time.com/time/magazine/article/0,9171,31522,00.html.

Cisco Systems, Inc. (2000). *Discover all that's possible on the Internet: 2000 annual report.* San Jose, CA: Cisco Systems, Inc. Available: www.cisco.com/warp/public/749/ar2000.

Clauser, B. E., Margolis, M. J., Clyman, S. G., & Ross, L. P. (1997). Development of automated scoring algorithms for complex performance assessments: A comparison of two approaches. *Journal of Educational Measurement, 34*, 141–161.

Cohen, A. (1999). The attic of e. *TIME, 154*(26). Available: http://www.time.com/time/magazine/article/0,9171,36306-1,00.html.

Cohen, A. (2001). eBay's bid to conquer all. *TIME, 157*(5), 48–51.

Dertouzos, M. L. (2001). *The unfinished revolution: Human-centered computers and what they can do for us*. New York: HarperCollins.

Dunn, S. L. (2000). The virtualizing of education. *The Futurist, 34*(2), 34–38.

Education prognosis 1999. (1999, January 11). *Business Week*, pp. 132–133.

Evans, P., & Wurster, T. S. (2000). *Blown to bits: How the economics of information transforms strategy*. Boston, MA: Harvard Business School Press.

FCC: E-rate subsidy funded at $2.25 billion cap. (2000). *What Works in Teaching and Learning, 32*(8), 8.

Fernandez, S. M. (2000). Latin America logs on. *TIME, 155*(19), B2–B4.

Frederiksen, N. (1984). The real test bias: Influences of testing on teaching and learning. *American Psychologist, 39*, 193–202.

Friedman, T. L. (2000). *The Lexus and the olive tree: Understanding globalization*. New York: Anchor Books.

Gershenfeld, N. (1999). *When things start to think*. New York: Holt.

Gibney, Jr., F. (2000). Enron plays the pipes. *TIME, 156*(9), 38–39.

Gitomer, D. H., Mislevy, R. J., & Steinberg, L. S. (1995). Diagnostic assessment of troubleshooting skill in an intelligent tutoring system. In P. D. Nichols, S. F. Chipman, & R. L. Brennan (Eds.), *Cognitively diagnostic assessment* (pp. 72–101). Hillsdale, NJ: Lawrence Erlbaum Associates.

Glaser, R. (1991). Expertise and assessment. In M. C. Wittrock & E. L. Baker (Eds.), *Testing and cognition* (pp. 17–30). Englewood Cliffs, NJ: Prentice-Hall.

Global Reach. (2002). *Global Internet statistics* (by language). Available: www.glreach.com/globstats/index.php3.

Green, C. (1996). *An introduction to Internet protocols for newbies*. Available: www.halcyon.com/cliffg/uwteach/shared_info/internet_protocols.html.

Grice, C. (2000). Wireless handhelds will rule the day, PC execs predict. *CNET News.com* [On-line]. Available: http://news.cnet.com/news/0-1004-200-1560446.html.

Henry, D., Buckley, P., Gill, G., Cooke, S., Dumagan, J., Pastore, D., & LaPorte, S. (1999). *The emerging digital economy II*. Washington, DC: U.S. Department of Commerce. Available: www.ecommerce.gov/ede/ede2.pdf.

How many online? (2003). Nua Internet Surveys. Available: www.nua.ie/surveys/how_many_online/index.html.

Internet domain survey host count. (2003). Internet Software Consortium. Available: www.isc.org/ds/hosts.html.

Kennard, W. E. (2000, January). *E-rate: A success story*. Presentation at the Educational Technology Leadership Conference—2000, Washington, DC.

Kerrey, B., & Isakson, J. (2000). *The power of the Internet for learning: Moving from promise to practice* (Report of the Web-based Education Commission). Washington, DC: Web-Based Education Commission. Available: http://interact.hpcnet.org/webcommission/index.htm.

Landler, M. (1995, May 16). Slow-to-adapt *Encyclopaedia Britannica* is for sale. *New York Times*, pp. D1, D22.

Levine, A. (2000a, March). *The remaking of the American university*. Paper presented at the Blackboard Summit, Washington, DC.

Levine, A. (2000b, March 13). The soul of a new university. *New York Times*, p. 21.

Maney, K. (2000). E-novel approach promises new chapter for book lovers. *USA Today, 18*(169), 8A–9A.

Melcher, R. A. (1997). Dusting off the *Britannica*: A new order has digital dreams for the august encyclopedia. *Business Week Online*. Available: www.businessweek.com/1997/42/b3549124.htm.

Messick, S. (1999). Technology and the future of higher education assessment. In S. Messick (Ed.), *Assessment in higher education: Issues of access, student development, and public policy* (pp. 245–254). Hillsdale, NJ: Lawrence Erlbaum Associates.

Moe, M. T., & Blodget, H. (2000). *The knowledge web: People power—Fuel for the new economy*. San Francisco: Merrill Lynch.

National Center for Education Statistics. (2003). A profile of participation in distance education: 1999–2000 (NCES 2003-154). Washington, DC: US Department of Education, Office of Educational Research and Improvement. Available: http://nces.ed.gov/pubs2003/2003154.pdf.

NCS secures rights to iPaper electronic technology in testing and education market. (2000, July 11). Minneapolis, MN: National Computer Systems (NCS). Available: www.ncs.com/ncscorp/top/news/000711.htm.

Negroponte, N. (1995). *Being digital*. New York: Vintage.

Odendahl, N. (1999, April). *Online delivery and scoring of constructed-response assessments*. Paper presented at the annual meeting of the American Educational Research Association, Montreal.

Olsen, F. (2000, February 18). A UCLA professor and net pioneer paves the way for the next big thing. *The Chronicle of Higher Education, 46*.

Olson, L. (2003). Legal twists, digital turns: Computerized testing feels the impact of "No Child Left Behind." *Education Week, 12*(35), 11–14, 16.

Pellegrino, J. W., Jones, L. R., & Mitchell, K. J. (1999). *Grading the nation's report card*. Washington, DC: National Academy Press.

Perry, J. (2000). Digital tests spark controversy: Critics say revamped exams limit the options to challenge a score. *Online US News* [On-line]. Available: www.usnews.com/usnews/edu/beyond/grad/gbgre.htm.

Russell, M., & Plati, T. (2001). Effects of computer versus paper administration of a state-mandated writing assessment. *Teachers College Record*. Available: www.tcrecord.org/Content.asp?ContentID=10709.

Schmidt, P. (2000, January 21). Judge sees no bias in Texas test for high-school graduation. *Chronicle of Higher Education*, p. A27.

Schulze, K. G., Shelby, R. N., Treacy, D. J., & Wintersgill, M. C. (2000, April). Andes: A coached learning environment for classical Newtonian physics. In *Proceedings of the 11th International Conference on College Teaching and Learning*, Jacksonville, FL. Available: www.pitt.edu/~vanlehn/icctl.pdf.

Shepard, L. A. (2000). The role of assessment in a learning culture. *Educational Researcher, 29*(7), 4–14.

Singley, M. K., & Bennett, R. E. (2002). Item generation and beyond: Applications of schema theory to mathematics assessment. In S. Irvine & P. Kyllonen (Eds.), *Item generation for test development* (pp. 361–384). Hillsdale, NJ: Lawrence Erlbaum Associates.

Tabs, E. D. (2002). *Internet access in US public schools and classrooms: 1994–2001 (NCES 2002-018)*. Washington, DC: US Department of Education, Office of Research and Improvement, National Center for Education Statistics.

Thomas, K. (2000, April 6). One school's quantum leap. *USA Today*, p. 1A. Available: www.usatoday.com/usatonline/20000406/2117463s.htm.

Tulloch, J. B. (2000). Sophisticated technology offers higher education options. *T.H.E. Journal* [On-line]. Available: www.thejournal.com/magazine/vault/A3165.cfm.

U.S. Census Bureau. (2002). Median income for 4-person families, by state. Available: www.census.gov/ftp/pub/hhes/income/4person.html.

U.S. Department of Commerce. (2002). *A nation online: How Americans are expanding their use of the Internet*. Available: http://www.ntia.doc.gov/ntiahome/dn/nationonline_020502.htm#_Toc250410.

U.S. Department of Education. (2002). *No Child Left Behind*: A desktop reference—Enhancing education through technology (II-D-1&2). Washington, DC: Author. Available: http://www.ed.gov/offices/OESE/reference/2d.html.

U.S. dominance seen slipping in Internet use, commerce. (2001). Cyberatlas: The Big Picture Geographics. Available: http://cyberatlas.internet.com/big_picture/geographics/article/0,,5911_377801,00.html.

Whalen, S. J., & Bejar, I. I. (1998). Relational databases in assessment: An application to online scoring. *Journal of Educational Computing Research, 18*, 1–13.

7

Technology, the Columbus Effect, and the Third Revolution in Learning

J. D. Fletcher
Institute for Defense Analyses

The apocryphal tale goes something like this:

An Enlightened Leadership discovers that relatively minor investments in educational technology can significantly enhance the capabilities—productivity, competitiveness, and competence—of their domain. The next step, of course, is to appoint a "Blue-Ribbon" Committee. The task of the Committee is to design the ideal technology for education. The Committee meets, deliberates, and issues specifications for the new technology.

Physically it must be rugged, lightweight, and easily portable, available anytime, anywhere. It must operate indoors and out, under a wide range of temperature, humidity, and other environmental conditions, and it must require only minimal, if any, external power support. Functionally, it must provide easy, rapid, and random access to high-quality text, black-and-white or full-color graphics, and high-resolution photographs. It must include an interface that is easily understood and usable by all, preferably communicated in natural language. It should allow self-pacing—learners should be able to proceed through instructional content as rapidly or as slowly as needed. It should be suitable for lifelong learning and readily available to a wide range of users in home, school, and workplace settings. Economically, it must be inexpensive or, as the Committee reports "requires only minimal financial investment on the part of potential end users."

The Enlightened Leadership receives the Committee's report with relief. Development of the technology will require no lengthy research and development, no new taxes, no new infrastructure, and no difficult political or administrative decisions or compromises. In fact, all it will require is business as usual. The reason may be as obvious to readers here as it is to the Enlightened Leadership. The recommended technology is, of course, the technology of books—already available and in place.

It seems hard to deny that writing and books effected revolutions in learning—or more precisely how we go about the business of learning. Prior to their appearance, during the earlier 100,000 or so years of human (i.e., *Homo sapiens*) existence, instruction had to take place person to person. It was expensive, slow, and produced uneven results, depending heavily on the knowledge, capabilities, and instructional expertise of the teacher. Matters concerning more than basic subsistence reached few people.

Writing developed about 7,000 years ago and progressed from picture-based ideographs to consonants and vowels represented with alphabet-based phonetization by perhaps 1000 BC. It allowed the content of advanced ideas and teaching to transcend time and place. Because of that capability, it effected a major revolution in learning. People with enough time and resources could study the words of the sages who went before them without having to rely on face-to-face interaction or the vagaries of human memory.

As discussed by Kilgour (1998), books (i.e., something beyond mud and stone tablets) were based first on papyrus and later on parchment rolls until about 300 BC, when the Romans began to sew sheets of parchment together into codices. These resembled books of today and allowed easier and random access to their content. They were also cheaper than papyrus rolls to produce because they were based on locally available parchment made from animal skin and allowed content to be placed on both sides of the sheets. Use of paper prepared from linen and cotton in about 100 AD (China) and 1200 AD (Europe) made books even less expensive. Books were by no means inexpensive, but their lowered costs made them more available to a literate and growing middle-class who, in turn, increased the demand for even more cost reductions and for greater availability of books and the learning they provided.

The full technology called for by the Committee finally became available with the introduction of books printed from moveable type (Kilgour, 1998). These printed books were first produced in China around 1000 AD and in Europe in the mid-1400s. At this point, the content of knowledge and teaching became widely and increasingly inexpensively available. The only item lacking from the Committee's list of specifications was availability of high-resolution photographs, which had to await development of photography in the mid-1800s.

The impact of writing and printed books on learning has been profound. It seems reasonable to view the emergence of writing as (among other things) the first major revolution in learning. Learning, the acquisition of knowledge, was neither inexpensive nor widely available, but it no longer required face-to-face interaction with sages. By making the content of learning, teaching, and educational material widely and inexpensively available—anytime, anywhere—the development of books printed from moveable type effected a second revolution in learning.

THE THIRD REVOLUTION IN LEARNING

At this point, we might consider an argument often advanced, but best articulated, by Clark (1983). In discussing all the means (media) we have for delivering instruction, Clark asserted that: "The best current evidence is that media are mere vehicles that deliver instruction but do not influence student achievement any more than the truck that delivers our groceries causes changes in our nutrition" (p. 445). Of course Clark had in mind more recently developed media than books, but printed books seem fair game for discussion in this context.

Are books "mere vehicles" for delivering instruction? Do they deserve more credit than that for influencing student achievement? Just as trucks are essential components in an infrastructure that has improved the nutrition of nations, so books are essential components in an infrastructure that has improved the learning, performance, and competence of people everywhere. Both trucks and books may be vehicles, but their contributions seem to be more fundamental than "mere."

However, the heart of Clark's argument remains sound. Books do not guarantee learning or student achievement. Ignorance remains plentiful, although books have appreciably diminished its supply. Clark's concern may be summed up by the notion that technology alone does not define an instructional approach—what is done with the technology matters a great deal. This point of view seems both fair and unequivocal. The presence of any technology is no guarantee that effective instructional content, effective ways to present it, or even that the unique strengths of the technology itself will be present or used. However, the absence of a technology is a reasonable guarantee that its functionalities will be missing. Without printed books, we may be back to the 1400s.

How do we improve on books? Do we have anything better? Computer technology arises as a possibility. One of the most important statements in higher order computer languages (based necessarily on what is available in every digital computer's lower order instruction set) is the "if" statement. This statement is of the (very) general form:

If <some condition> is true then do <something> otherwise do <something else>

We can well marvel at the capabilities of computers to perform millions of operations a second with perfect accuracy on the immense amounts of data that they retrieve with equal rapidity and accuracy. But what is central for this discussion is the capability of computers to adapt both the sequence and type of operations they perform based on conditions of the moment. More specifically, they can adapt the content, sequence, type, difficulty, granularity, etc. of presentations to learners and other users based on their assessment of learners' and users' current needs.

For this reason, computer technology may effect a third revolution in learning. While preserving the capabilities of writing and books to present the content of excellent instruction anytime, anywhere, they can further provide the interactions of excellent teachers, instructors, tutors, and mentors as needed by individual learners. This is not something books, movies, television, or videotape technologies can do affordably or to any appreciable degree. This interactivity is a new and significant capability. It is the core of what future commentators may view as the third revolution in learning.

DOES INTERACTIVITY MATTER?

Much of the discussion from here on centers on whether or not the instructional interactivity provided by technology matters. Can we expect a revolution in instruction equivalent to that wrought by writing and books? What can we say about the nature of this revolution and what it implies for instructional practice?

Whether interactivity matters is to some degree addressed by studies in which as much of the instruction as possible is held constant except for the level of interactivity. Two such studies were performed by Fowler (1980) and Verano (1987). Fowler compared branched presentations using computer-controlled, adaptive videodisc instruction with instruction in which the same materials were held to a fixed-content, linear sequence. She reported an effect size of 0.72 (roughly an improvement from 50th to 76th percentile performance) for ability to operate and locate faults in a movie projector, which was the objective of her instruction. Similarly, Verano compared an interactive, adaptive, branching approach for presenting instructional material with a strictly linear approach used to present identical instruction in beginning Spanish. Both of his treatments used videodisc presentations. He reported an effect size of 2.16 (roughly an improvement from 50th to 98th percentile performance) in end-of-course knowledge. These two studies, among others, suggest that interactivity—at least interactivity as defined by these studies—matters perhaps a great deal. But there is, of course, more to the story.

TUTORING AND THE INDIVIDUALIZATION
OF INSTRUCTION

Individualized tutoring (one student working with one instructor) has long been viewed and used as an effective instructional procedure. Evidence of its value is found in its continued use for instruction in highly complex and high-value activities, such as aircraft piloting, advanced scientific research, and specialized medical practice. Comparisons of one-on-one tutoring with one-on-many classroom instruction might be expected to favor individualized tutoring—and they do. What is surprising about these comparisons is not the direction of their findings, but the magnitude of the differences in instructional effectiveness that they find.

Benjamin Bloom's results may be the most widely noted of these. Combining the findings of three empirical studies that compared one-on-one tutoring with classroom instruction, Bloom (1984) reported a general difference in achievement of two standard deviations (roughly an improvement from 50th to 98th percentile performance) favoring tutoring. These and similar studies suggest, on the basis of considerable empirical evidence, that differences between the results of one-on-one tutoring and classroom instruction are not just likely, but very large.

Why, then, do we not provide these manifest benefits to all our students? The answer is straightforward, obvious, and has doubtless already occurred to the reader. We cannot afford it. The issue is not effectiveness, but costs. Unless our policies toward educational funding change dramatically, we cannot afford a single tutor for every student. Bloom (1984) popularized this issue as the Two-Sigma (as in two standard deviations) Problem.

In 1975, Scriven argued that individualized instruction was an instructional imperative and an economic impossibility. Is it? Must instruction remain constrained by this reality?

Enter Moore's (famous) Law. Gordon Moore is a semiconductor pioneer and cofounder of the Intel Corporation. As recounted by Mann (2000), *Electronics* magazine interviewed Moore in 1965 and asked him about the future of the microchip industry. To make a point, Moore noted that engineers were doubling the number of electronic devices (basically transistors) on chips every year. In 1975, Moore revised his prediction to say that the doubling would occur every 2 years. If we split the difference and predict that it will occur every 18 months, our expectations fit reality quite closely. As Mann pointed out, the consequence of Moore's Law is that computers that initially sell for $3,000 will cost about half that in about 18 months.

The implication of Moore's Law for learning applications is that computers are getting exponentially less expensive and the computational capabilities we need to support instruction that is very much like individualized tutoring are becoming progressively affordable—if they are not already. The issue then becomes how we should use this increasingly affordable computational power to support learning.

We have had computer-based instruction that could tailor the content, sequence, and difficulty of instructional content to the needs of individual learners since the 1960s (e.g., Atkinson & Fletcher, 1972; Suppes, 1964), and these approaches were shown to be effective. The Stanford beginning reading programs presented on Model 33 teletypewriters running at 110 baud (about 10 characters per second) with randomly accessible digitized audio achieved effect sizes in excess of 0.80 standard deviations (Fletcher & Atkinson, 1972). Similar results were obtained for elementary school mathematics (Suppes, Fletcher, & Zanotti, 1975).

Instructional approaches used in these early programs required $2 to $3 million computers. They could easily be presented today by computers costing under $1,000.

These approaches did not seek to directly mimic the interactions that occur in human tutorial instruction. Instead they were attempts to apply results emerging from empirical studies of human cognition, memory, and learning as discussed by Suppes (1964) and Atkinson (1972). Efforts to provide tutorial dialogue emerged from approaches that were initially described as intelligent computer-assisted instruction and later as intelligent tutoring systems (Sleeman & Brown, 1982; Woolf & Regian, 2000). These have been found to be effective, occasionally yielding effect sizes in excess of 1.00 (e.g., Gott, Kane, & Lesgold, 1995). These approaches raise the question of what is it in one-on-one tutorials that accounts for their success? Can we do the same with computers?

Intensity of Instruction

This issue was discussed by Graesser and Person (1994), who compared instruction using one-on-one tutoring with classroom practice in two curriculum areas: research methods for college undergraduates and algebra for seventh graders. Tutors for the research methods course were psychology graduate students, and tutors for the algebra course were high school students. Graesser and Person found the following:

- Average number of questions teachers ask a class in a classroom hour: 3
- Average number of questions asked by any one student during a classroom hour: 0.11
- Average number of questions asked by a student and answered by a tutor during a tutorial hour:
    Research methods: 21.1
    Algebra: 32.2
- Average number of questions asked by a tutor and answered by a student during a tutorial hour:
    Research methods: 117.2
    Algebra: 146.4

Hard-core cause-and-effect is not proved by these data, but they show great differences in sheer interactivity between two approaches that also show great differences in instructional effectiveness.

Is this level of interactivity echoed by computer-based instruction? Few studies report the number of questions students using technology answer per unit of time. However, this author (Fletcher) found that K to third-grade students receiving technology-based beginning reading and arithmetic instruction on the earlier mentioned 110-baud teletypewriters were answering 8 to 12 questions a minute—questions that were individually assigned and whose answers were immediately assessed.

This level of interactivity extrapolates to 480 to 720 such questions an hour if children of this (or any) age were able to sustain this level of interaction for 60 minutes. Instead these children generally worked with the computer-based materials in daily 12-minute sessions, which extrapolates to 96 to 144 individually selected and rapidly assessed questions that these children received each day. As mentioned earlier, this computer-assisted instruction was producing effect sizes in excess of 0.80 standard deviations in comparisons with classroom instruction in both mathematics and reading.

The success of these and other computer-assisted instruction programs may have been due as much to the sheer volume of interactivity they provided as to clever instructional design or anything else. Graesser, Person, and Magliano (1995) pointed out that neither the students nor the tutors they observed were particularly sophisticated in their use of questions. Specifically, they found that the tutorial techniques long advanced by researchers and scholars—techniques such as shaping and fading (Skinner, 1968), scaffolding (Ausubel, 1960; Rogoff, 1990), reciprocal instruction (Palincsar & Brown, 1984), error diagnosis and repair (Burton, 1982; van Lehn, 1990), or advanced motivational approaches (Lepper & Woolverton, 2001)—were largely absent. About half of the questions asked by both the students and their tutors required simple yes/no responses. The techniques the tutors used were far from sophisticated, but, as the data tell us, effective. Simple approaches that aim primarily to increase interactivity may, by themselves, fill much of Bloom's two-sigma gap.

However, greater sophistication in one-on-one tutoring also pays off. Semb et al. (2000) reviewed a number of empirical studies of on-the-job training and concluded that greater knowledge and use of tutorial techniques result in greater achievement and more efficient learning. These applications are primarily found in the military and industrial world, but they are effectively one-on-one tutoring. Including advanced tutorial techniques in our computer-based tutors may allow us to exceed Bloom's two-sigma threshold. We may have just begun.

Pace of Instruction

The possibility that simple approaches may by themselves do much to fill Bloom's two-sigma gap is supported by considerations of pace—the speed with which students learn material and reach instructional objectives. Easily adjusted pacing is a capability claimed by even the most rudimentary of computer-based instruction systems.

Many teachers have been struck by the differences in the pace with which their students can learn. Consider, for instance, some findings on the time it takes for different students to reach the same instructional objectives:

- Ratio of time needed by individual kindergarten students to build words from letters: 13:1 (Suppes, 1964)
- Ratio of time needed by individual hearing-impaired and Native American students to reach mathematics objectives: 4:1 (Suppes, Fletcher, & Zanotti, 1975)
- Overall ratio of time needed by individual students to learn in Grades K to 8: 5:1 (Gettinger, 1984)
- Ratio of time needed by undergraduates in a major research university to learn features of the LISP programming language: 7:1 (A. T. Corbett, personal communication, April 30, 1998)

As with the differences between one-on-one tutoring and classroom instruction, we may not be particularly surprised to discover differences among students in the speed with which they are prepared to learn, but the magnitudes of the differences may be much larger than we expect. As we might expect from Gettinger's (1984) review, a typical K to 8 classroom will have students who are prepared to learn in 1 day what it will take other students in the same classroom 5 days to learn. This difference does not seem to be mitigated by more homogeneous grouping of students based on their abilities. The students in Corbett's (1998) university are highly selected, averaging well above 1,300 on their SATs, yet the differences in time they required to learn the fundamentals of a modestly exotic programming language remain large.

As it turns out, the differences in the speed with which different students reach given objectives may be initially due to ability, but this effect is quickly overtaken by prior knowledge as a determinant of pace (Tobias, 1989). Despite our efforts to sustain common levels of prior knowledge in classrooms by bringing every student to some minimal threshold of learning, we instead appear to increase the differences among students by about 1 year for every year they spend in elementary school (Heuston, 1997). For instance, the average spread of academic achievement in Grade 3 is about 3 years. By Grade 6, it increases to about 6 years. We are, then, working hard to make the classroom teacher's job more difficult.

The challenge this diversity presents to classroom teachers is daunting. How can they ensure that every student has enough time to reach given instructional objectives? At the same time, how can they allow students who are ready to do so surge ahead? The answer, of course, despite heroic efforts to the contrary, is that they cannot. Most classrooms contain many students who, at one end of the spectrum, are bored and, at the other end, are overwhelmed and lost.

One-on-one tutoring allows us to alleviate this difficulty by adjusting the pace of instruction to the needs and abilities of individual students. We can proceed as rapidly or as slowly as needed. We can skip what individual students have mastered and concentrate on what they have not.

As with intensity or interactivity, we do not have a direct cause-and-effect case to make for the contributions of individualized pace of instruction. But with pace as with interactivity, we find a large difference in instructional treatment associated with a large difference in instructional outcome. It does not seem unreasonable to conclude that the ability to adjust pace of instruction may also account for some of the large differences favoring individual tutoring over classroom instruction.

Again we might ask if, like one-on-one tutoring, computer-based instruction allows us to individualize the pace of instruction—pace as defined by the amount of time it takes students to reach given instructional objectives. Research findings suggest that it does. If students who could move through instructional material more quickly are prevented from doing so in classrooms, but allowed to do so in computer-based instruction, then overall we should find students reaching instructional objectives more quickly under computer-based instruction than in classrooms.

This finding arises repeatedly in reviews of instructional technology. Orlansky and String (1977) found that reductions in time to reach instructional objectives averaged about 54% across 12 evaluations of computer-based instruction used in military training. Fletcher (2002) found an average time reduction of 31% in six studies of interactive videodisc instruction applied in higher education. Kulik (1994) and his colleagues found time reductions of 34% in 17 studies of CBI used in higher education and 24% in 15 studies of adult education. These reviews are effectively independent in that they reviewed different sets of evaluation studies. From these reviews, it seems reasonable to expect reductions of about 30% in the time it takes students using computer-based instruction to reach a variety of given instructional objectives.

It is not certain that these reductions result from the speed with which students progress through fixed sets of items, from adjustments in content to take advantage of what students already know or have mastered or from some combination of these. But if we simply consider pace to be the rate with which students reach instructional objectives, then it seems reasonable to conclude that computer-based instruction reduces time to learn, as does one-on-one tutoring, primarily by not holding back students who are ready to progress.

There are three points to add to this discussion. First, the self-pacing enabled by technology-based instruction does not simply allow students to skip through content as rapidly as they can. Instead most, perhaps all, technology-based instruction includes an executive agent, which might be called an instructional management system, that allows students to progress through content as rapidly as possible, but only after they demonstrate their readiness to do so. The instructional management system ensures both instructional progress and quality in ways that books, as passive media, cannot.

Second, it turns out that 30% is a fairly conservative target. Commercial enterprises that develop technology-based instruction for the Department of Defense (DoD) regularly base their bids on the expectation that they can reduce instructional time by 50%, while holding instructional objectives constant. Noja (1991) has reported time savings through the use of technology-based instruction as high as 80% in training operators and maintenance technicians for the Italian Air Force.

Third, time saved in learning is not a trivial matter. For instance, the DoD spends about $4 billion a year on specialized skill training, which is the postbasic training needed to qualify people for the many technical jobs (e.g., wheeled vehicle mechanics, radar operators and technicians, medical technicians) needed to perform military operations. If the DoD were to reduce by 30% the time to train 20% of the people undergoing specialized skill training, it would save over $250 million per year. If it were to do so for 60% of the people undergoing specialized skill training, it would save over $700 million per year.

It is harder to assign dollar values to the time that students spend in educational settings, especially our K to 12 classrooms. This difficulty may account for the paucity of results we can find for time savings in K to 12 education. But time so spent or saved is not without cost and value. Aside from the obvious motivational issues of keeping students interested and involved in educational material, using their time well will profit both them and any society that depends on their eventual competency and achievement. The time savings offered by technology-based instruction in K–12 education could be more significant and of greater value than those obtained in posteducation training.

COST-EFFECTIVENESS

The issue for any educational decision maker faced with a unyielding budget, an unpredictable revenue stream, and unending demands for expenditures that are both urgent and imperative is not limited to instructional effectiveness. The core of such decision making is not just effectiveness, but what must be given up to get it. Most often and most specifically, this consideration centers on costs and cost-effectiveness.

Is there evidence that applications of technology in instruction are cost-effective? Despite the uncompromising need of decision makers for such evidence, little of it exists to aid their deliberations. This situation is especially prevalent among innovations, such as technology-based instruction, where researchers often seek to learn if an approach works or works better than existing practice, but very seldom to determine if it works well enough to justify its expense. The latter issue requires consideration of costs, cost models, and similar issues that researchers in instructional procedures and practices prefer to leave to others. Cost-effectiveness of an innovation is rarely considered by anyone other than the decision maker who will be pressured to adopt it.

Of course asking if an approach is cost-effective oversimplifies the issue. Cost-effectiveness is a relative term. We cannot meaningfully label some approach as cost-effective without specifying the alternatives with which it is being compared. Cost-effectiveness studies require that a single experimental paradigm be used to compare the alternatives under consideration using comprehensive models of both costs and effectiveness. Typically, cost-effectiveness investigators either observe different levels of effectiveness achieved while holding costs constant or they observe the different costs required to reach fixed thresholds of effectiveness.

Such comparisons in technology-based instruction are hard to find—even in industrial training where all decisions are a matter of profit and loss and in military training where allocations of resources may literally be a matter of life and death. A limited cost effectiveness argument for technology-based education was reported by Fletcher (2002), who presented empirical data gathered from earlier studies by Jamison et al. (1976), Levin, Glass, and Meister (1987), and Fletcher, Hawley, and Piele (1990) to compare the costs (adjusted for inflation) of different educational interventions to raise fifth-grade mathematics scores on a standard achievement test by one standard deviation. Providing 10-minute daily sessions of computer-based instruction was found to be less expensive (and hence more cost-effective) than peer tutoring, professional tutoring, decreasing class size from 35 to either 30 or 20, or increasing the length of the school day by 30 minutes. More work of this sort is needed, but this finding suggests that a strong cost-effectiveness position for technology-based instruction is likely even at this early (relative to what may be coming) stage of development. Given that we are most likely in the horseless carriage years of the third revolution in learning, these are promising results.

INTELLIGENT TUTORING SYSTEMS

If interactivity and individualization of pace are achievable by standard approaches to computer-based instruction, is there any reason to pursue more exotic approaches? Specifically, is there any reason to develop what are called *intelligent tutoring systems* (e.g., Woolf & Regian, 2000)?

Intelligent tutoring systems may be as intelligently or unintelligently designed as any others. They involve a capability that has been developing since the late 1960s (Carbonell, 1970), but has only recently been expanding into general use. In this approach, an attempt is made to directly mimic the one-on-one dialogue that occurs in tutorial interactions. Carbonell was a computer scientist who focused on the underlying computation capabilities needed to support this approach. He contrasted ad hoc frame-oriented (AFO) approaches with information structure-oriented (ISO) approaches. Today we might be more likely to discuss "knowledge representation" as the requisite capability, but in either case the requirement is for the software to represent human knowledge—knowledge of the subject matter, knowledge of the state of the student, and knowledge of teaching strategies.

More important for those who wish to focus on instructional rather than computational capabilities are the functionalities that distinguish intelligent tutoring systems from those that have gone before. Despite current marketing efforts to describe any instructional system using technology as an intelligent instructional system, there are clear differences between what has long been the objective of these systems and what has long been available in the state of the art.

Two functionalities are critical and discriminating. First, we expect to find in an intelligent instructional system an ability to generate computer presentations and responses in real time, on demand, and as needed or requested by learners. Second, we expect to find an ability to support mixed initiative dialogue in which either the computer or the (human) student can generate, ask, and answer open-ended questions. Notably, instructional designers do not need to anticipate and prestore these interactions. The motivation for funding development of intelligent instructional systems in the early 1970s was not to apply artificial intelligence or ISO techniques to computer-based instruction, nor was it to mimic one-on-one tutorial dialogue. Instead it was to reduce the costs of instructional materials preparation by developing capabilities to generate them online in real time. Generative capabilities were intended to reduce the time and resources needed by other approaches to anticipate and prespecify all possible student–computer interactions.

Currently, intelligent tutoring systems are more sophisticated computationally and functionally than other more typical computer-based instructional systems, but they remain expensive to produce. These systems can of course adjust pace, sequence, interactivity, style, difficulty, etc. of instruction to the needs of individual learners, just as other approaches can. Notably, they can make many of the adjustments to individual learners that human tutors can. Costs to produce these systems will decrease as our techniques to develop them improve, but they may also be justified by increases in learner achievement. For instance, they show an increase in average effect size to 0.84 standard deviations (Fletcher, 2002) over the average 0.42 standard deviations (e.g., Kulik, 1994) found for other computer-based instruction approaches.

However, the main argument in favor of these systems is that they raise the bar for the ultimate effectiveness of technology-based instruction. Their unique generative and mixed initiative capabilities should eventually allow richer, more comprehensive, and more effective interactions to occur between students and the instructional system.

If Kurzweil (1999) is correct, we can expect a $1,000 unit of computing to equal the computational capability of the human brain by the year 2019 and exceed it thereafter. Computers may then become more effective in providing instruction than human tutors even if humans use all the techniques Graesser et al. (1995) found they now neglect. We may not be implanting integrated circuits in our brains as Kurzweil suggested we might by 2029. However, using computers to discover more than any human agent can about the unique potential of every individual, and then devising effective and individualized procedures to reach it, seems both an appealing and realistic prospect.

Whatever the case, the extensive tailoring of instruction to the needs of individual students that can be obtained through the use of generative, intelligent tutoring systems can only be expected to increase. Our current approaches may be reaching their limits. Intelligent tutoring systems may make available far greater instructional effectiveness and efficiencies than we can obtain from the approaches we are using now.

THE COLUMBUS EFFECT IN INSTRUCTIONAL TECHNOLOGY

Prognostications aside, these technological approaches to instruction may provide yet another example of what might be called the Columbus Effect. As readers will recall, Columbus sailed west intending to find India (and a lucrative spice route). Instead he (re)discovered what became a new world for Europeans. Such a result typifies technological progress. Seeking one thing based on familiar, common practice, we inevitably end up with something else, unforeseen and unexpected. Wireless telegraph produced something functionally quite different than the telegraph—namely, radio. Similarly, efforts to make a carriage run without a horse produced automobiles—to say nothing of gas stations, motels, and the Santa Monica Freeway. Seeking affordable one-on-one tutoring through automation, we may end up with something no one now envisions. The metaphor based on current practice gets us started. The result may surprise us all.

As we begin with a vision of one-on-one tutoring made affordable through the use of computing and telecommunications technologies, our work may center on efforts to mimic the interactions that occur between human tutors and their students. We may be pursuing humanless tutoring—just as books, television, and other noninteractive media may be viewed humanless lecturing, but we are likely to end up with something quite different—in function, appearance, and use.

Some hint of what this different result may be is perhaps seen in the vision promulgated by the advanced distributed learning (ADL) initiative currently pursued jointly by the Department of Defense and the White House Office of Science and Technology Policy. This vision is based on the expectation that most, if not all, human knowledge will become available as shareable, interoperable objects in the World Wide Web. The ADL initiative seeks specification and development of these objects, but it does so because it envisions something that might be called a personal learning associate (PLA).

Physically, a PLA will be a computer that is either carried or worn. In keeping with the suggestions of Kurzweil among others, it may even be implanted to provide direct brain–computer interaction, although that possibility seems more remote and subject to more review and consideration than the current discussion requires.

Functionally, a PLA will provide wireless connection to the Web or its successor in the global communication ether. A student of any age will use it for learning or a decision maker, such as an electronics technician, military tactician, or business planner, will use it to help solve practical problems. All will interact with it using spoken natural language. The PLA will provide a full range of display capabilities including text, graphics, and photographs as specified by the apocryphal Committee's specifications. It will also provide animation, digital video of some sort augmented by a full range of high-fidelity sound, and perhaps tactile and haptic feedback as well. Olfaction remains under review.

Most of the physical capabilities of the PLA are in the state of the art. Many of the software capabilities are also available or, like shareable courseware objects, soon will be (Fletcher & Dodds, 2000). Its instructional and decision-aiding functionalities remain longer term and more elusive. These functionalities call for the PLA to develop and then use comprehensive, intimate, and accurate knowledge of the student/user to identify, collect, and integrate shareable instructional objects. This process will be accomplished on demand, in real time, and be precisely tailored to the individual's needs, capabilities, interests, and cognitive style. If the intention is to help solve a problem, information the PLA provides will not just be expert, but delivered in a form that the individual is prepared to understand. If the intention is to establish a more permanent change in the individual's cognitive ability (i.e., to bring about learning), it will do so efficiently and effectively in ways far superior to those we now imagine.

Obviously, we have a way to go to realize this vision. What form it eventually takes, how it is used, what infrastructure it engenders, and what impact it has on our lives all remain to be seen, but its key capabilities may well arise from the intelligent instructional systems we are now learning how to build. The Columbus Effect will kick in sooner or later, but beginning with a guiding metaphor based on individualized, tutorial instruction and mentoring seems as good a way as any to advance. The goal of learning to do something that is within our reach but outside our grasp has long been a stimulus for human progress.

IMPACT ON RESEARCH AND THEORY

Reviews by Krendl and Lieberman (1988) and Schacter and Fagnano (1999) continue to echo earlier recommendations by Suppes (1964) and others to apply advances in cognitive and learning theory to the development of technology-based instruction. Such efforts will improve the quality of instruction delivered. More important, they will provide feedback to theories of cognition and learning about where they are right, where they might use some improvement, and where they have left serious gaps that need to be filled. This is the traditional interplay of theory and empirical research that has served other areas of systematic investigation so well. Technology-based instruction, with its precise control over stimulus inputs and equally precise measurement of response outputs, should play a unique role in completing the feedback loop between theory and empirical research.

Such feedback will produce significant advances not just in instruction, but in related areas as well. Instructional applications using technology test the notions—or theories—of human cognition, learning, and instruction embodied in them in at least two ways. First, the ability to put a proposed notion, model, or theory into a computer algorithm is a significant demonstration by itself. If a notion cannot be captured by an algorithm, it may not be testable; if it is not testable, it is not worth serious consideration.

Second, an instructional application is an instantiation that tests the correctness of a notion, model, or theory. To the extent that an application achieves its goals, the notion(s), model(s), or theory of cognition, learning, and instruction on which it is based may be viewed as correct. However, tests of instructional applications seldom yield simple answers. The fine-grain data that technology-based instruction makes available will increase the richness of feedback we receive. Few theories will be shown to be perfectly and thoroughly correct. The more complete diagnostic information concerning where they are correct, where they are not, and what they lack is critical. Detailed and specific information of this sort produces significant advances in other fields, and we should expect nothing less from our instructional applications.

THE ENGINEERING OF INSTRUCTION

Beyond issues of feedback for theory, our third revolution in learning may effect a shift in instruction from art to engineering. We tend to view teaching as an intensely human activity—something that at best can only be accomplished by human teachers interacting with human students. Master teachers do exist, and many of us have benefited from the attentions of at least one teacher who, if not a master, was at least able to impress on us the value, benefits, and pleasure of scholarship. But such occasions appear to be more the exception than the rule. Our perceptions of teaching as a warmly experienced, human activity are at variance with much that we experience in real classrooms, where each student is one of many waiting for that portion of instruction that addresses his or her individual needs.

To a great extent, successful instruction is a matter of design—the creation of an environment to maximize the probability that learning will occur and that specified instructional objectives will be achieved by every student. Mostly we seek and test for accuracy of knowledge. However, we may also seek other objectives such as speed of response, retention, insight, and transfer of knowledge as well as continued interest in and respect for the subject matter. These goals may be compatible to some extent, but at some point they diverge and require different approaches that compete with each other for classroom resources of human energy, funding, and, especially, time.

The design of such an environment may be viewed as an art—a highly personal, hit-or-miss affair. To be fair to our students and productive in our instruction, we need to establish a science of design that allows these many instructional objectives to be accomplished by many different hands. In short, we need an engineering of instruction in which specific designs reliably yield specific instructional outcomes.

The notion of instruction as engineering may well be unpopular. Fox (1994) noted that, "One of the more difficult problems in dealing with improvement in public education is to replace the notion of teaching as an art form with that of instructional delivery as a systems science" (p. 2). In classroom instruction, sufficiently precise control of instruction environments may be out of the question. Tailoring learning environments to the needs, interests, and capabilities of individual students can be achieved, at substantial expense, by one-on-one tutoring. As suggested earlier, technology can make such engineering of learning environments affordable. However, it may also do it better.

This possibility is suggested by Meehl's studies of decision making. These studies were intended to determine the degree to which human judgment would be needed to augment purely algorithmic (linear regression) predictions of such outcomes as patient responses to treatment and graduate school applicants' academic success. Instead, as described by Dawes (1971), the statistical prediction "floor" turned out to be a ceiling. In all 20 cases reviewed by Meehl, statistical predictions based on straightforward (algorithmic) linear models turned out to be superior to the judgments of humans, even though the linear models were derived solely from human decisions. The same superiority may obtain for decision making by technology-based tutors.

IMPACT ON OUR CURRICULAR GOALS

In 1960, T. F. Gilbert wrote:

> If you don't have a gadget called a 'teaching machine,' don't get one. Don't buy one; don't borrow one; don't steal one. If you have such a gadget, get rid of it. Don't give it away, for someone else might use it. This is the most practical rule, based on empirical facts from considerable observation. *If you begin with a device of any kind, you will try to develop the teaching program to fit that device.* (p. 478; italics original)

Gilbert may be both right and wrong. He is certainly correct in suggesting that instructional designers and developers who adapt a teaching machine will try to fit the teaching program to it. The new functionalities such a device makes available motivate its adaptation in the first place. One can imagine students long ago poring over clay tablets or papyrus rolls once their teachers learned how to design teaching programs to take advantage of written language. The same may be said for printed books, which, simply by being more accessible and less expensive than papyrus rolls or codices, allowed teachers different assumptions in the development of their teaching programs. The same is doubtlessly true for our third instructional revolution, which applies interactive, computer-based technology to the problems and processes of instruction.

It is less certain that such adaptations, fitting the teaching program to the device, is a significant evil to be avoided at all costs. Certainly if technology causes us to remove or de-emphasize essential elements of our teaching programs, it will diminish their effectiveness. It is also true that if properly applied, technology will improve, if not revolutionize, the effectiveness and efficiency of our teaching programs. It is up to researchers, developers, and instructors, not the technology itself, to see that it does.

In either case, the application of technology will change both what and how we teach. Technology will raise the bar for our curricular aspirations. Tutorial simulations will afford our students experiences, access to exotic (i.e., expensive and unavailable) devices, and immersion in collaborative problem solving that we could not provide in any other way. Intelligent tutoring capabilities will permit tutorial interactions or simple conversations with experts and expertise that would otherwise be out of the question. Because these interactions will be geared to each student's level of ability and prior knowledge, they will produce levels of understanding that would otherwise be unattainable. Sooner or later we will be forced by necessity, public pressure, or our own professional integrity to adapt our teaching programs to the new functionalities technology makes available. The most important consequence of the third revolution in instruction may not be that it improves efficiency and effectiveness of what we do now, but that it will change what it is that we choose to do.

SUMMARY

There is more to be discussed about the third revolution in learning wrought by technology, but that must await wiser, better informed commentary. A few statements can be made about this revolution with modest certainty:

- It will make the functionalities of individualized tutoring widely accessible and affordable.
- It will permit interactive, individualized learning to take place anytime, anywhere.

- It will (eventually) bring about profound changes in our educational institutions and the roles and responsibilities of people (teachers, students, and administrators) in them.
- It will help bring into being a nation of lifelong learners who are prepared to meet the challenges of the new century and thrive in the global marketplace.
- Thanks to the Columbus effect, it will lead to capabilities, uses, and functionalities of which we are now only dimly, if at all, aware.
- It will produce radical change in the practice and processes of instruction.

Basically there is just one way that people learn, most likely involving growth or chemical changes in the synapses. The third revolution in learning will not change learning at this level any more than writing or books did. But substantially increasing the probability that such fundamental changes will occur across all manner of humans in all manner of environments, does seem to qualify as a radical change—one that warrants the term *revolution*. Because it will increase the tempo with which learning occurs, it might well be called a revolution in learning—the magnitude of which we have only seen twice before in human history.

REFERENCES

Atkinson, R. C. (1972). Ingredients for a theory of instruction. *American Psychologist, 27*, 921–931.

Atkinson, R. C., & Fletcher, J. D. (1972). Teaching children to read with a computer. *The Reading Teacher, 25*, 319–327.

Ausubel, D. P. (1960). The use of advanced organizers in the learning and retention of meaningful verbal material. *Journal of Educational Psychology, 51*, 267–272.

Bloom, B. S. (1984). The 2 sigma problem: The search for methods of group instruction as effective as one-to-one tutoring. *Educational Researcher, 13*, 4–16.

Burton, R. R. (1982). Diagnosing bugs in a simple procedural skill. In D. Sleeman & J. S. Brown (Eds.), *Intelligent tutoring systems* (pp. 157–183). New York: Academic Press.

Carbonell, J. R. (1970). AI in CAI: An artificial intelligence approach to computer-assisted instruction. *IEEE Transactions on Man-Machine Systems, 11*, 190–202.

Clark, R. E. (1983). Reconsidering research on learning from media. *Review of Educational Research, 53*, 445–459.

Dawes, R. M. (1971). A case study of graduate admissions: Application of three principles of human decision-making. *American Psychologist, 26*, 180–188.

Fletcher, J. D. (2002). Evidence for learning from technology-assisted instruction. In H. F. O'Neil, Jr. & R. Perez (Eds.), *Technology applications in education: A learning view* (pp. 79–99). Hillsdale, NJ: Lawrence Erlbaum Associates.

Fletcher, J. D., & Atkinson, R. C. (1972). An evaluation of the Stanford CAI program in initial reading (Grades K through 3). *Journal of Educational Psychology, 63*, 597–602.

Fletcher, J. D., & Dodds, P. V. W. (2000). All about ADL. *Learning Circuits*. An Internet publication of the American Society for Training & Development: http://www.learningcircuits.org/may2000/.

Fletcher, J. D., Hawley, D. E., & Piele, P. K. (1990). Costs, effects, and utility of microcomputer assisted instruction in the classroom. *American Educational Research Journal, 27*, 783–806.

Fowler, B. T. (1980). *The effectiveness of computer-controlled videodisc-based training.* Unpublished doctoral dissertation, University of Iowa, Iowa City, IA (University Microfilms No. 8114254).

Fox, R. G. (1994). *A systems approach to education.* Warrenton, VA: Learning Technology Institute.

Gettinger, M. (1984). Individual differences in time needed for learning: A review of the literature. *Educational Psychologist, 19,* 15–29.

Gilbert, T. F. (1960). On the relevance of laboratory investigation of learning to self-instructional programming. In A. A. Lumsdaine & R. Glaser (Eds.), *Teaching machines and programmed learning: A source book* (pp. 475–485). Washington, DC: National Education Association of the United States

Gott, S. P., Kane, R. S., & Lesgold, A. (1995). *Tutoring for transfer of technical competence* (AL/HR-TP-1995-0002). Brooks AFB, TX: Armstrong Laboratory, Human Resources Directorate.

Graesser, A. C., & Person, N. K. (1994). Question asking during tutoring. *American Educational Research Journal, 31,* 104–137.

Graesser, A. C., Person, N. K., & Magliano, J. P. (1995). Collaborative dialogue patterns in naturalistic one-to-one tutoring. *Applied Cognitive Psychology, 9,* 1–28.

Heuston, D. H. (1997). *School improvement models: The manual model and the speed of light.* Sandy, UT: Waterford Institute.

Jamison, D. T., Fletcher, J. D., Suppes, P., & Atkinson, R. C. (1976). Cost and performance of computer-assisted instruction for education of disadvantaged children. In J. T. Froomkin, D. T. Jamison, & R. Radner (Eds.), *Education as an industry* (pp. 201–240). Cambridge, MA: Ballinger.

Kilgour, F. G. (1998). *The evolution of the book.* New York: Oxford University Press.

Krendl, K. A., & Lieberman, D. A. (1988). Computers and learning: A review of recent research. *Journal of Educational Computing Research, 4,* 367–389.

Kulik, J. A. (1994). Meta-analytic studies of findings on computer-based instruction. In E. L. Baker & H. F. O'Neil, Jr. (Eds.), *Technology assessment in education and training* (pp. 9–33). Hillsdale, NJ: Lawrence Erlbaum Associates.

Kurzweil, R. (1999). *The age of spiritual machines: When computers exceed human intelligence.* New York: Viking Press.

Lepper, M. R., & Woolverton, M. (2001). The wisdom of practice: Lessons learned from the study of highly effective tutors. In J. Aronson (Ed.), *Improving academic achievement: Contributions of social psychology* (pp. 133–156). Orlando, FL: Academic Press.

Levin, H. M., Glass, G. V., & Meister, G. R. (1987). Cost-effectiveness of computer-assisted instruction. *Evaluation Review, 11,* 50–71.

Mann, C. C. (2000). The end of Moore's Law? *Technology Review.* Available: http://www.techreview.com/articles/may00/mann.htm.

Noja, G. P. (1991). DVI and system integration: A further step in ICAI/IMS technology. In R. J. Seidel & P. R. Chatelier (Eds.), *Advanced technologies applied to training design* (pp. 161–189). New York: Plenum.

Orlansky, J., & String, J. (1977). *Cost effectiveness of computer-based instruction in military training* (IDA Paper P-1375). Arlington, VA: Institute for Defense Analyses.

Palincsar, A. S., & Brown, A. L. (1984). Reciprocal teaching of comprehension-fostering and comprehension-monitoring activities. *Cognition and Instruction, 1,* 117–175.

Rogoff, B. (1990). *Apprenticeship in thinking: Cognitive development in social contexts.* New York: Oxford University Press.

Schacter, J., & Fagnano, C. (1999). Does computer technology improve student learning and achievement? How, when, and under what conditions. *Journal of Educational Computing Research, 20,* 329–343.

Scriven, M. (1975). Problems and prospects for individualization. In H. Talmage (Ed.), *Systems of individualized education* (pp. 199–210). Berkeley, CA: McCutchan.

Semb, G. B., Ellis, J. A., Fitch, M., & Kuti, M. B. (2000). On-the-job training (OJT): Theory, research, and practice. In S. Tobias & J. D. Fletcher (Eds.), *Training & retraining: A handbook for business, industry, government, and the military* (pp. 289–311). New York: Macmillan Reference.

Skinner, B. F. (1968). *The technology of teaching*. New York: Appleton, Century, Crofts.

Sleeman, D., & Brown, J. S. (1982). *Intelligent tutoring systems*. New York: Academic Press.

Suppes, P. (1964). Modern learning theory and the elementary-school curriculum. *American Educational Research Journal, 1*, 79–93.

Suppes, P., Fletcher, J. D., & Zanotti, M. (1975). Performance models of American Indian students on computer-assisted instruction in elementary mathematics. *Instructional Science, 4*, 303–313.

Tobias, S. (1989). Another look at research on the adaptation of instruction to student characteristics. *Educational Psychologist, 24*, 213–227.

van Lehn, K. (1990). *Mind bugs: The origins of procedural misconceptions*. Cambridge, MA: MIT Press.

Verano, M. (1987). *Achievement and retention of Spanish presented via videodisc in linear, segmented, and interactive modes*. Unpublished doctoral dissertation, University of Texas, Austin, TX (DTIC No. ADA 185 893).

Woolf, B. P., & Regian, J. W. (2000). Knowledge-based training systems and the engineering of instruction. In S. Tobias & J. D. Fletcher (Eds.), *Training and retraining: A handbook for business, industry, government, and the military* (pp. 339–356). New York: Macmillan Reference.

III

Affordances
of Software

8

Asynchronous Learning in Graduate School Classes

Fran C. Blumberg
Meira Torenberg
Lori M. Sokol
Fordham University

The use of computer-mediated communication (CMC) to facilitate learning has spawned new research areas and interest in the instructional efficacy of CMC, particularly in situations in which face-to-face interactions may be compromised (Light, Nesbitt, Light, & Burns, 2000; Weller, 2000). In these situations, CMC may be a viable option for providing repeated, albeit brief, interchanges among students and between student and instructor. A frequently investigated CMC instructional application is computer-based conferencing (Santoro, 1995), which has enjoyed frequent use in instructional delivery since the mid-1980s. Computer-based conferencing allows for interpersonal contact, whereby the computer serves as a vehicle for distributing, storing, and retrieving messages in the form of electronic mail, interactive messaging, or group conferencing systems, thus facilitating asynchronous discussions. Within the instructional environment, these discussions are often in the service of collaborative learning and problem solving (Hathorn & Ingram, 2002; Koivusaari, 2002).

Despite the technological strides made in distance learning over the past few years, the use of e-mail as an integral component of asynchronous communication remains a frequently and widely used learning tool within higher education (Smith, Whiteley, & Smith, 1999). Students' evaluations of e-mail as an integral component of classroom learning are generally positive. For example, Wepner (1997) found that e-mail enabled students to communicate information they might not readily share in face-to-face interactions with their classmates or instructor. Smith, Whiteley, and Smith (1999) also reported the successful use of e-mail lectures in college-level psychology courses, although students' satisfaction with this form of pedagogy was moderated by their lack, at the time of the study's implementation, of access to technology needed to print the lectures for viewing.

Internet resources such as newsgroups and listservs have been used to support graduate-level education since the early 1980s (Hathorn & Ingram, 2002; Howe, 2000). For example, Renninger (1996) reported the successful use of an Internet forum in her graduate-level Educational Psychology course. As part of their class assignments, students were asked to correspond with precollege mathematics instructors through a mathematics newsgroup. This exchange was designed to provide students with an opportunity to reflect on the implications of their classroom learning through interaction with classroom practitioners. Kazmer and Haythornthwaite (2001) reported on the intense involvement of master's-level library science students in the maintenance of their online discussions of course content with fellow classmates. Ellsworth (1995) incorporated CMC into her graduate-level research methods course as a vehicle to facilitate collaborative brainstorming and student-to-student interaction. Similarly, Dueber, Duffy, and Sloffer (1999) reported the efficacy of asynchronous discussions in promoting critical thinking among graduate students in an education seminar.

In recent years, computer-based conferencing has been increasingly incorporated in traditional on-campus course offerings (Light et al., 2000). This chapter provides a case study of such an inclusion in a doctoral-level psychology course in which Internet-based discussion groups was the only technology-based instructional tool in an otherwise conventional course. Our goal in sharing our experiences is to illustrate the efficacy of CMC and similar instructional tools in graduate-level courses where intensive student–student and instructor–student interaction is desirable. Because the most efficient and readily available CMC tool at the time of the course were the forums provided by Delphi, a pioneer in World Wide Web forums, the review that follows highlights the first-time use of a Delphi forum to supplement classroom interaction.

INTERNET FORUMS AS AN INSTRUCTIONAL TOOL

Delphi forums are designed as a means to share information concerning particular areas of interest ranging from the academic to the recreational. Once the forum has been constructed, the "host" or moderator of the particular forum has the flexibility to designate the forum as available for public or private use. The latter distinction allows for restriction of membership to individuals invited by the forum host. Without this stipulation, individuals outside the class could access and participate in the forum. As part of the invitation, potential members receive information about the goal of the forum and appropriate login and registration procedures. Once the invitee has registered for the forum, she is given access to messages within the folders established by the forum host. Postings are organized by threads, whereby an original message and its subsequent replies are on view. New and unread messages are flagged. Participants in the forum also have the option to send e-mail messages to one another either privately or for viewing by other participants in the forum.

Within the forum, the screen is divided into a topic organizer and a series of message folders. The forum host can construct as many message folders as necessary.

Internet Forum Usage in the Classroom

During 1999, the first author incorporated an Internet forum into two of her graduate classes: a doctoral-level graduate seminar in Developmental Psychology for students in the Graduate School of Education's (GSE) counseling, educational, and school psychology programs, and a master's-level survey course in Educational Psychology for GSE's students in the Initial Teacher Education program. Since that time, the instructor has used the forum, and similar instructional tools such as Blackboard (which was not available at the time of this study), as part of instruction at the graduate and undergraduate levels. The incorporation of the forum in the Advanced Developmental Psychology course, which reflected the instructor's first usage of the medium, is the focus of this discussion.

The forum was established as an Internet-based supplement to classroom discussions about given lecture topics and readings, and as a venue for class assignments. Students were instructed to use the forum as a basis for informed discussion, thereby emphasizing the desired academic tone of the comments to be posted. Participation in the forum was mandatory; students were asked to log onto the forum at least once per week. All students had prior experience using word processing programs, using Internet search engines, and maintaining e-mail accounts. All but one of the students had home access to a personal computer.

Class Structure.   The Advanced Developmental Psychology class is designed as a doctoral-level seminar that reviews topics within the developmental periods of infancy through middle age. Topics considered in the seminar included children's play behavior during early childhood, attention and memory strategies during middle childhood, identity formation during adolescence, transitions during young adulthood, and women's perception of well-being in middle age. The students enrolled in the course were four doctoral-level students and three master's-level students. The prerequisite for the course was an undergraduate class in developmental psychology.

As part of their course assignments, students were asked to individually prepare a brief review of research pertaining to a topic on the syllabus. This summary was to be posted on the forum. Members of the class were then encouraged to post questions concerning the research and theoretical issues evoked by a classmate's review. Students were also prompted to consider the relationship between information raised in the review and content covered in class. The student who had posted the review also moderated the Internet discussion pertaining to their review for 1 week's time. After this another student was responsible for posting a review to accompany the next topic on the syllabus. Students' assignments also included the preparation of a research proposal addressing a key issue within any of the developmental periods covered in the syllabus. This proposal was then to be presented in class. Part of the assignment involved sharing resources with fellow students by posting the proposal reference lists on the forum.

Forum Organization.   The forum was organized by the instructor into six distinct folders: announcements, article presentations, class readings, comments/questions, conferences, and research opportunities. The organization of folders as seen by the forum visitor is shown in Fig. 8.1.

Four of the folders were dedicated to general information about the course and professional events of potential interest to class members: Announcements included the posting of information and classroom administrative issues, such as pending assignments and scheduling of class presentations; research opportunities included postings about research studies within the educational psychology

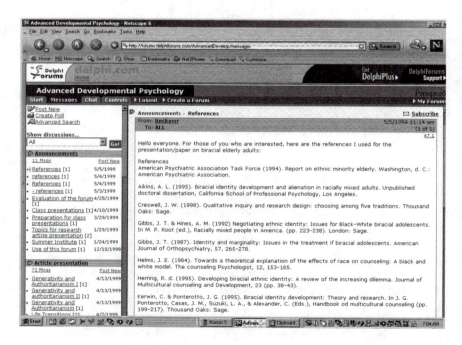

FIG. 8.1.   Sample screen from the forum.

and allied programs that were seeking participants; conference presentations included information about guest lectures and upcoming professional conferences; the comments/questions folder included postings concerning the format of the class (e.g., should class discussion comprise half or two thirds of class time?) and queries about assignments and make-up classes.

The remaining folders were dedicated to class discussion and assignments. One of these folders, class readings, was the most active in the forum. The instructor used this folder to post the class readings for a given lecture (as already indicated on the class syllabus) and questions to guide students' readings. According to student evaluations of the forum at the end of the semester, this pedagogical approach was appreciated. This folder was most inclined to include a mixture of student and instructor comments and would often consider a topic long beyond its treatment on the syllabus.

Students posted their research synopses in the article presentations folder. This assignment, as indicated earlier, entailed a brief summary of a research article pertinent to a topic covered in the syllabus. The instructor participated in the discussion, but made efforts to avoid redirecting the line of student questions unless deemed necessary (e.g., erroneous information was being communicated or clarification of a concept was warranted). Students also used this folder to post reference lists from their proposals. The majority of postings in these folders also originated from the students. The frequency of postings made by the instructor and students by forum folder is shown in Table 8.1.

Characterization of Messages on the Forum

As shown in Table 8.1, over the course of the semester, 196 messages, comprised of 50 threaded discussions, were posted. The students initiated over 60% of the messages and 46% of the threaded discussions; the course instructor initiated the remaining percentage of the messages and threaded discussions. These messages,

TABLE 8.1
Frequency of Messages by Forum Folder

Forum Folder	Frequency of Comments (Percentage of Total Comments)	
Announcements	11	(6%)
Article presentations	71	(36%)
Class readings	92	(47%)
Comments/questions	7	(4%)
Conferences	13	(6%)
Research opportunities	2	(1%)
Total number of comments	196	

TABLE 8.2
Frequency of Messages by Category

Forum Folder	Frequency of Comments (Percentage of Total Comments)
General information	38
Attitudinal	22
Reading-based	7
Discussion-based	125
Total number of comments	196

as agreed on by the first two authors, reflected four categories of postings: general information, attitudinal, reading-based, and discussion-based. The percentage of messages by category is shown in Table 8.2.

The general information postings comprised 19% of messages shared on the forum. These messages generally pertained to the format of the class, such as allocation of time devoted to student discussion and instructor lecture, as reflected in the following postings:

"I enjoyed last week's discussion format during class. It is always interesting to hear the viewpoints of peers. However, I think I would personally be more comfortable with a format that is part lecture and part discussion at this point in the semester."

"I enjoy discussions more than lecture, but I think that some lecture will help tie everything together. Help pin point the main ideas we are all discussing."

Reading-Based. Messages specifically pertaining to content in the course readings comprised the smallest number of postings. Student postings were often made in response to an instructor query, but clearly demonstrated an interest in mastering issues and concepts addressed in the readings as reflected in the following postings:

"I have a question regarding the prosocial behaviors proposed in the articles. Is the idea that with the encouragement of prosocial behaviors with those children who display aggression, that aggression will decrease? This seems like a great idea but somewhat idealistic. Are we aiming for totally prosocial behavior among all children?"

"I really enjoyed Bjorklund's article regarding immaturity as adaptive rather than viewing it only in the maladaptive sense. I thought it was interesting especially coming from the evolutionary perspective used as the basis. It gave new insight to a popular view of immaturity especially in young children."

These postings often became platforms for students to discuss related issues to content presented in their assigned articles. In fact 64% of all postings were characterized as discussion-based. These discussions frequently took the form of students posing a question to the instructor or the instructor correcting misconceptions presented in a given student's posting. However, students often posed questions to one another indicating less of a reliance on the instructor for initiating discussion points and more on fellow classmates. This form of interchange has been referred to as horizontal in nature, whereby student–student communication is intrinsically motivated rather than extrinsically motivated by an authority figure, as would be characterized by vertical interactions (Hatano & Inagaki, 1991). The following exchange exemplifies the types of student–student exchanges that appeared on the forum; in this instance, they are in response to readings about gender-based differences in children's aggressive behavior:

"I am having an issue with this aggression-gender difference thing. From what I am getting from the articles, aggression in boys is physical and aggression in girls is relational. That is fine, but what about the boys that are relationally aggressive and the girls that are physically aggressive. Do they not matter because there are not as many children who fit into that category? AND I think that one of the articles brought this up—but do the two aggressions affect people in the same way?"

"Which form of aggression do you think is more detrimental to the victim of the aggressive behavior (overt physical vs. relational)? I am guessing that relational aggression is more harmful because it involves the threat of being rejected and excluded from a group. I think physical aggression might be less harmful because the aggressor is likely to be unpopular, according to the articles, and being attacked by him would not necessarily result in a loss of status or rejection from a group. Being beat up by someone who is unpopular with a reputation for aggressive behavior could even lead to more acceptance or support from the group rather than rejection. This is pure speculation and I would like to know what the group thinks."

Attitudinal messages comprised a little over 11% of the postings. These messages typically referred to ideas evoked by a given reading or students' comfort with the class. Representative postings are presented next:

"I think that generativity during middle-adulthood is of particular concern because of the fact this has traditionally been the time when energy previously devoted to child rearing is no longer necessary."

"Things are starting to make sense after reading this week's articles and integrating the old info from last week."

Student Evaluations of the Forum

At the end of the semester, students responded anonymously to five open-ended questions that were posted on the forum. These questions concerned aspects of the forum students liked most and least, ways in which the forum enhanced or hindered their understanding of course content, whether the forum should be used for future offerings of the course, and suggestions for making the forum a more effective learning tool. The results of the evaluation are briefly summarized next.

Students' evaluation of the forum as an adjunct to class learning was overwhelmingly positive: All students recommended its continued use in future offerings of the course. The most frequent criticism, in response to that aspect of the forum liked the least, concerned the amount of additional work involved and the status of the forum as an additional class. This type of comment attests to the rigor of the forum as an adjunct to class activity.

Among those aspects liked most was the opportunity to continue classroom discussions beyond class time, and the collegial discourse the forum provided. Students also appreciated a vehicle by which to keep up with and discuss class readings and integrate content from different lectures. Greater access to the instructor was an additional aspect noted.

When asked to consider the benefits and liabilities of the forum for understanding course content, students mentioned their appreciation of exposure to classmates' opinions and the "original" thinking fostered by the forum. Reference to the intellectual support facilitated through the student–student contact is consistent with findings in the literature concerning graduate students' assessment of online discussions (Kazmer & Haythornthwaite, 2001). Students also thought that the forum helped focus their reading of assigned articles. However, students thought that lack of substantiation of student comments hindered their understanding of course content. This comment was echoed in response to suggested improvements for the forum and is certainly not without precedent in documented evaluations of online discussions in graduate (Salmon, 2000) and undergraduate education (Light, Nesbitt, Light, & Burns, 2000). Specifically, students sought greater involvement of the instructor to extend and correct student responses. Other suggested improvements included the posing of reading-based questions and allowing students from the master's developmental class to view the forum's postings. The latter comment reflected students' willingness to extend their academic community beyond that of the class to contribute others' learning. Use of computer forums as a vehicle for tutorial purposes, as implied by the students' sentiments, is increasingly becoming a staple of distance learning (Weller, 2000).

Overall, the students evaluated the forum positively and believed that it had ramifications for facilitating course learning. This sentiment is consistent with other evaluations of asynchronous learning groups used in academic settings.

Implications of Findings for Course Instruction

As intended by the instructor, the forum facilitated thoughtful and informative discussion both in and outside the classroom. As the course progressed, issues raised between class meetings provided a foundation for discussions in future classes. Particular topics, such as the continuity of the parent–child attachment for future romantic relationships and peer relations, fostered forum discussions long after their consideration on the course syllabus. Students' sharing of ideas made for exciting end-of-semester class presentations and for two dissertation proposals, one of which culminated in a dissertation submitted for publication and an independent research project.

The success of the asynchronous discussion component of the class can be attributed as much to the caliber of students and small size of the class as to the virtues of asynchronous discussion—a point recognized by other instructors using CMC (Wepner, 1997). Despite the provocative exchange of messages midway through the course, as students ostensibly became more comfortable with the medium, activity flagged amid the press of final papers and class presentations. This situation may be inevitable as students and instructors tire toward the final push of the semester. However, the availability of an outside-the-class venue by which to share and critique ideas may be beneficial regardless of how many times students use the venue.

In general, the use of the forum in the course described here was successful, and lessons learned through having used the forum were taken into account when developing forums in subsequent courses. A few of these lessons are reviewed next.

Instructors Must Be Vigilant in Their Monitoring of the Discussion

Asynchronous discussions allow for time to elapse between comments. They also allow for lag in the instructor's ability to correct misconceptions reflected in students' comments. The liability of the former situation is that the discussion may suffer from lack of activity. Accordingly, the instructor needs to prompt and promote discussion in an enthusiastic, provocative, and collegial fashion to avoid prolonged online inactivity. The liability of the latter situation is that students may persist in discussing points based on erroneous assumptions or content. Accordingly, the instructor needs to be a frequent presence in forum discussions to address misconceptions as they occur.

The demands of serving as both a discussion facilitator and monitor are frequently cited in evaluations of educational Internet discussions (Peregoy & Kroder, 2000) and need to be considered when adopting online discussions as an instructional tool for use in doctoral-level seminars.

Students Should See the Continuity Between Their Online and In-Class Discussions

One of the more flattering criticisms of the forum, as noted earlier, was that it was labor-intensive and "like another class." That effort involved being fluent enough with concepts and ideas presented in class readings to participate in a discussion with classmates and the instructor.

A contributing factor to the high level of discussion on the forum may be the deliberate efforts to link issues raised by the students online to those made in a successive class—a goal consistent with that recommended by other instructors using CMC (Funaro & Montell, 1999). For example, during the early part of the semester, the instructor started class with a discussion of questions or current debates presented on the forum, such as the continuity of children's sociometric status during middle childhood. Initiating the class in this fashion was intended to create an expectation that comments made in the forum were potential fodder for discussion in class and, more important, that the forum was an integral part of the course experience. Developing this mindset among the members of the class allowed for thought-provoking and informal conversations about course content and consideration of that content long after class hours.

Students and Their Instructors Should Be Comfortable (and Patient) Using Technology

Finally, requiring students to use a technological tool as an integral component of course requirements and class activities requires a comfort level with the technology used on the part of all class members. This point has often been cited as a disadvantage of CMC in instructional settings (Smith, Whiteley, & Smith, 1999). Instructors, in particular, should be willing and able to guide their students in their use of the forum or Web-based learning resources in general. In fact much recent research on technology adoption in education has addressed issues of instructor comfort and facility with technological tools (Sherry, Billig, Tavalin, & Gibson, 2000). Similarly, patience is needed with recurring, inexplicable difficulties connected to the Internet, interruptions in the network, or servers going down (Peregoy & Kroder, 2000). As technology improves and becomes more pervasive, these difficulties, however, may be expected to ameliorate.

CONCLUSION

The use of an asynchronous discussion group to facilitate learning outside the classroom can be highly effective in primarily discussion-based graduate courses. Although the online communication may not take the place of personal interaction so fruitful in upper level academic courses, its efficacy as a powerful adjunct to instruction cannot be overstated. Specifically, online communication may provide a venue in which students experience greater comfort expressing themselves and are able to spend greater time constructing their response to a peer- or instructor-initiated comment than in class discussion. Research dedicated to characterizing the nature of discussion convened online in doctoral-level psychology and social science seminars in general should be undertaken to better understand the basis for that efficacy as online learning becomes an integral component of training future scholars.

ACKNOWLEDGMENTS

Partial support for the preparation of this chapter was provided through a Fordham University School of Education Quality of Teaching award to the first author. The authors wish to thank the students who so thoughtfully contributed to the Internet forum discussion reviewed in this chapter. We also wish to acknowledge the insightful comments and suggestions of John Randall.

REFERENCES

Dueber, B., Duffy, T. M., & Sloffer, S. J. (1999). *Using asynchronous conferencing to promote critical thinking: Two implementations in higher education* (CRLT Technical Report No. 8-99). Bloomington, IN: Center for Research on Learning and Technology, Indiana University.

Ellsworth, J. (1995). Using computer-mediated communication in teaching university courses. In Z. L. Berge & M. P. Collins (Eds.), *Computer mediated communication and the online classroom: Vol. 1. Overview and perspective* (pp. 29–36). Cresskill, NJ: Hampton.

Funaro, G. M., & Montell, F. (1999). Pedagogical roles and implementation guidelines for online communication tools. *ALN Magazine, 3.* Retrieved May 22, 2000 from http://www.aln.org/alnweb/magazine/Vol3_issue2/funaro.htm.

Hatano, G., & Inagaki, K. (1991). Sharing cognition through collective comprehension activity. In L. B. Resnick, J. M. Levine, & S. D. Teasley (Eds.), *Perspectives on socially shared cognition* (pp. 331–348). Washington, DC: American Psychological Association.

Hathorn, L. G., & Ingram, A. L. (2002). Cooperation and collaboration using commuter mediated communication. *Journal of Educational Computing Research, 26*, 325–347.

Howe, W. (2000). A brief history of the internet. Retrieved May 21, 2000 from http://www.delphi.com/navnet/faq/history.html.

Kazmer, M. M., & Haythornthwaite, C. (2001). Juggling multiple social worlds. *American Behavioral Scientist, 45*, 510–529.

Koivusaari, R. (2002). Horizontal and vertical interaction in children's computer-mediated communications. *Educational Psychology, 22*, 235–247.

Light, V., Nesbitt, E., Light, P., & Burns, J. R. (2000). "Let's you and me have a little discussion": Computer mediated communication in support of campus-based university course. *Studies in Higher Education, 25*, 85–96.

Peregoy, R., & Kroder, S. (2000). Developing strategies for networked education. *T.H.E. Journal, 28*, 49–52, 54.

Renninger, K. (1996). Learning as the focus of the educational psychology course. *Educational Psychologist, 31*, 3–76.

Salmon, G. (2000). Computer mediated conferencing for management learning at the Open University. *Management Learning, 31*, 491–502.

Santoro, G. M. (1995). What is computer-mediated communication? In Z. L. Berge & M. P. Collins (Eds.), *Computer mediated communication and the online classroom: Vol. 1. Overview and perspective* (pp. 11–27). Cresskill, NJ: Hampton.

Sherry, L., Billig, S., Tavalin, F., & Gibson, D. (2000). New insights on technology adoption in schools. *T.H.E. Journal, 27*, 43–46.

Smith, C. D., Whiteley, H. E., & Smith, S. (1999). Using email for teaching. *Computers & Education, 33*, 15–25.

Weller, M. (2000). Implementing a CMC tutor group for an existing distance education course. *Journal of Computer Assisted Learning, 16*, 178–183.

Wepner, A. (1997). "You never run out of stamps" electronic communication in field experiences. *Journal of Educational Computing Research, 16*, 251–268.

9

Hints in Human and Computer Tutoring

Rachel E. DiPaolo
Arthur C. Graesser
Holly A. White
University of Memphis

Douglas J. Hacker
University of Utah

The use of hints has long been advocated in pedagogical practice, but we know little about the psychological mechanisms and processes of hinting. Current cognitive models of hint generation are indeed very much at their infancy. Systematic research on hinting has periodically surfaced in the areas of problem solving and computer-assisted learning, but to date no theory has been formulated that can describe hints and explain the facilitative role they presumably play in learning. So two fundamental questions present themselves: How are good hints generated? How is learning affected by hints?

The purpose of this chapter is to offer a deeper understanding of hinting strategies. The goal is to provide a systematic, principled approach to the generation of hints and thereby enhance the learning process. We begin by reviewing the literature and presenting some empirical data from naturalistic tutoring sessions where hints occur. We subsequently discuss the many functions of hints based on available literature and our own research. The available research takes quite different approaches, some focusing on memory recall, some on problem solving, and some on discourse. We then present empirical data on hinting from simulated tutoring sessions. The data analysis unveiled several tactics for improving the hinting strategy. In conclusion, we briefly mention future directions for advancements in hinting mechanisms.

DEFINITION OF A HINT

Hints are widely used in everyday conversation because they play a useful role in communicating ideas. Consider how hints are used in the context of a young man and woman on a date. They use hints to assess the current mental state of their partners in courtship, maintain an air of politeness, and guard themselves against blunt rejections. Consider the following exchange when they say good night at the end of their first date:

Man: I had a really nice time tonight. (Hinting that he would like to she her again)

Woman: Okay, thank you, uh, good night. (Hinting that she does not want to see him again)

The man used a hint to inquire about going out again, but in a fashion that spares him any direct rejection. It is rather obvious from the woman's response that she does not want to see him again, although a dense young man might not detect the rejection. Hints play this dual social and cognitive function in a variety of conversational settings, such as the monologues of politicians, business transactions, and the humor of comedians. The effectiveness of hints is obvious in these situations, but the underlying mechanisms that make them effective are not at all obvious.

Webster's dictionary defines a *hint* as an indirect, covert, or helpful suggestion or clue (Flexner, 1997). This definition, however, is hardly sufficient for describing the complexity and characteristics of hints, particularly in one-on-one tutoring sessions. The Webster's definition does not specify the context in which a hint is used, the purpose of a hint, and the response expected of the recipient. These issues need to be addressed in any serious scientific theory of hint generation.

IMPORTANCE OF THE HINTING STRATEGY IN TUTORING

Empirical studies have documented that one-on-one interaction and instruction during tutoring is superior to traditional classroom instruction (Bloom, 1984; Cohen, Kulik, & Kulik, 1982; Graesser & Person, 1994; Hume, Michael, Rovick, & Evens, 1996; Merrill, Reiser, Ranney, & Trafton, 1992; Mohan, 1972; Trismen, 1981). The effect size of the advantage of tutoring over classroom ranges from .4 to 2.3 standard deviation units (Bloom, 1984; Cohen et al., 1982; Mohan, 1972). Graesser, Person and Magliano (1995) identified some of the possible reasons that tutors are effective in the learning process, although they are usually unskilled in the vast majority of tutoring programs in schools. The reasons include (a) the occurrence of interactive dialogue throughout the learning process, (b) collaborative construction of knowledge, (c) explanations, (d) concrete examples, and (e) questions that promote deep reasoning. As we see, hints help the tutor manage some of these learning processes. Hints are not only extremely useful in everyday dialogue, but are also powerful dialogue moves in tutoring.

One reason that hints are such powerful dialogue moves in tutoring is that they facilitate active construction of knowledge (Graesser et al., 1995; Lepper, Aspinwall, Mumme, & Chabay, 1990; Merrill et al., 1992). Instead of the tutoring giving instructions to the student, the tutor uses hints to get the student to construct the knowledge, as is illustrated later in this chapter. It is well documented that active construction of knowledge and problem solving is effective in promoting learning (Aleven & Koedinger, 2002; Chi et al., 2001; Cognition and Technology Group at Vanderbilt, 1997; VanLehn et al., 2002; Webb, Troper, & Fall, 1995). Constructive activities lead the student to an integrated and prolonged involvement with the material. In Trismen's (1981) study of hinting in mathematics, items with hints increased and extended the students' involvement with mathematical problems—problems that most likely would have otherwise been abandoned because of their difficulty. A related advantage of the hinting strategy can be attributed to increasing student control in the learning process (Milheim & Martin, 1991). Understanding is presumably fostered when students attempt to solve problems for themselves (Merrill et al., 1992). Hinting encourages students to take the helm in the acquisition of knowledge.

A second advantage of hints is that they guide the student in productive directions rather than having the student flounder while actively constructing his or her knowledge (Anderson, Corbett, Koedinger, & Pelletier, 1995). Most hints provide good direction for the student, preventing the student from actively constructing knowledge in the wrong arena. In essence, a hint is a dialogue move that may optimally manage the trade-off between active knowledge construction on the part of the student and effective direction on the part of the tutor. More will be said about this later in the chapter.

The scarcity of psychological research on hinting presents a significant obstacle to constructing intelligent tutoring systems. Zhou, Freedman, Glass, Michael, Rovick, and Evens (1999) identified three aspects of hints that continue to create challenges: (a) intuitiveness of production, (b) flexibility, and (c) context sensitivity. First, hinting is a subtle tactic that is intuitively produced by tutors who generally lack training in generating effective hints. Tutors have a difficult time self-diagnosing the reasons that they generated a hint in a specific manner. Second, the form of hints is very flexible. Hints are delivered as suggestions, questions, examples, counterexamples, analogies, and simple statements. This flexibility causes difficulty in formulating a single model for generating hints. Third, hints are context-sensitive. A tutor creates a hint in a fashion that is adaptive to both the student's knowledge and the material that needs to be covered. These three challenges make it difficult to systematically dissect hints, especially for the development of computer programs that employ this dialogue move to promote learning. These are all obstacles to overcome as we try to apply the hinting strategy to a simulated tutor.

A REVIEW OF HINTING STRATEGIES

When Do Tutors Use Hints?

One important role of the tutor is to monitor for errors, expose misunderstandings, and help the student correct these errors (Anderson, Boyle, Corbett, & Lewis, 1990; Anderson et al., 1995; VanLehn, 1990). Tutors use hints aimed at correcting errors by engaging the student in an interactive dialogue that reveals the underlying misconceptions and lack of knowledge. Hints are also used in response to missed steps, knowledge gaps, and errors of omission (Collins & Stevens, 1982; VanLehn, Jones, & Chi, 1992). However, many hints are used in response to a student's error of commission.

Hinting in Naturalistic Tutoring

We performed a reanalysis of an existing corpus of tutoring sessions that were videotaped and analyzed by Graesser and Person (1994). The details of this corpus are described shortly. Our reanalysis of the transcripts revealed that the frequency of hints vary greatly in open-world versus closed-world domains of knowledge. In a closed-world domain, all the items within an answer set are known. For example, consider the question, "Is Mississippi a state?" It is easy to answer yes or no to this question because all the states are known. In closed-world domains, the tutor expects a specific answer from the student in response to a question. In contrast, all the possible items within a set are not known in the case of open-world domains. It is difficult to answer yes or no to the question "Is Marmaduke a city?" because every city would need to be known and that is unreasonable to expect for most humans. Hints were expected to differ in closed-world versus open-world domains (Collins, Warnock, Aiello, & Miller, 1975; Fox, 1993).

Graesser and Person explored the tutoring strategies that were effective in guiding students through deep reasoning questions (Graesser & Person, 1994; Graesser, Person, & Magliano, 1995; Person, Kreuz, Zwaan, & Graesser, 1995). The tutors were unskilled in the sense that they had no formal training on tutoring strategies and had only moderate expertise on the topic. The sample of tutoring sessions involved cross-age tutoring, where older, more experienced students tutored younger students—a form of tutoring most common in schools. In one corpus, graduate students tutored undergraduate psychology majors on difficulties in research methods. In the other corpus, high school students tutored seventh graders on trouble areas in algebra. The corpora consisted of research methods, which is an open-world domain, and algebra, which is a closed-world domain. To illustrate these differences, consider the following two answers to questions:

Open-world domain of research methods: "It's a powerful effect."

Closed-world domain of algebra: "The answer is nine."

In the first case, the answer was correct, but it was also imprecise and vague. There are several alternative correct answers rather than one decisive answer. The boundaries of what is powerful versus not powerful is vague, fuzzy, and possibly indeterminate. In the second case, no other response other than nine is correct, and the set of alternatives is specifiable. An open-world domain is less discriminating than a closed-world domain. As we see from our reanalysis of the tutoring data, complications arose for tutors when generating hints on the fly for open-world domains.

There were 44 one-hour tutoring sessions in the corpora collected by Graesser and Person. The sessions were videotaped during a 1-month period and transcribed for study. The transcripts include all verbal utterances, notes made on marker board, hand gestures, head nods, and simultaneous speech acts between the student and tutor. Random samples of deep reasoning questions were taken from each corpus. These questions consisted of why, how, and what-if question categories as identified in Table 9.1 (see also Graesser, Person, & Huber, 1993).

To analyze hinting strategies, we identified the instances of error-driven student contributions while the deep reasoning questions were collaboratively answered by student and tutor. As mentioned earlier, hinting sometimes occurs in tutoring situations other than a response to an error. However, these other discourse contexts are more difficult to define and code; it is difficult to spot when a student is missing information or expressing extraneous material. We randomly extracted a sample of 48 errors made by students in the research methods and 47 errors in the algebra sessions. These were the total set of errors that students committed while answering deep reasoning questions posed by tutors.

TABLE 9.1
Deep Reasoning Questions

Questions	Abstract Specification	Example
1. Why	What are the motives or goals behind an agent's action?	Why did you put decision latency on the y-axis?
2. How	What instruments or plans allow an agent to accomplish a goal?	How do you present the stimulus on each trial?
3. What-if	What are the consequences of an event or state?	What happens when this level decreases?

According to Norman (1981), there were three types of errors: slips, bugs, and deep misconceptions. A slip is a form of human error in which the performance of an action is not what was intended. For example, the intended contribution might have been "three times two is six," whereas the actual verbalization is "three times two is five." Most students know their mathematics and know what was intended, but the words did not come out that way. Bugs occur when a procedure employed by the student is correct, but contains one or more small perturbations (Brown & Burton, 1978; Burton, 1982; VanLehn, 1990). For example, in VanLehn's (1990) study, a student discovered that her rule for subtraction was wrong when she began to work a problem by applying her rule for borrowing from the units column, left-most and left-adjacent. The bug was her ill-conceived rule. Both bugs and slips can be corrected rather easily in tutoring. Deep misconceptions occur when the student has errors in underlying conceptual knowledge. These misconceptions are revealed in errors made by the student in response to deeper questions such as, "Why did an expected state or event not occur?" and "What if X occurred?"

Table 9.2 lists the error categories and tutor's treatment of the errors. The distribution of errors was approximately the same for the research methods corpus and the algebra corpus. Deep misconceptions were more frequent than were bugs and slips. However, the tutors' treatment of the errors were rather different for the open-world versus closed-world domains. It should be noted that more than one response could be produced by the tutor when a student error occurred, so the proportions total more than 1.00 in the case of tutor responses.

TABLE 9.2
Probabilities of Responses to Student Errors Manifested
in the Sample of Tutor Questions

	Corpus	
	Research Methods	Algebra
Number of Errors in Sample	48	47
Type of error		
1. Slip	.16	.13
2. Bug	.25	.23
3. Deep misconception	.59	.63
Tutor's treatment of error		
1. Error is acknowledged in short or long feedback	.12	.36
2. Tutor splices in correct answer	.40	.36
3. Tutor supplies a hint	.10	.45
4. Tutor reasons to expose derivation of correct answer	.17	.34
5. Tutor asks student question to extract correct answer	.17	.21
6. Tutor issues directive to extract correct answer	.04	.06
Likelihood of student catching his/her own error	.00	.04

Note. The proportions represent the occurrence of the error or response over all of the sessions in each corpus.

The similar incidence of splices (algebra = .36, research methods = .40) suggested that the tutors detected errors with the same likelihood across the two domains. A splice occurs when the tutor quickly and directly corrects a student's error-ridden contribution. Similarly the incidence of tutor questions and directives were no different in the research methods and algebra corpora. However, differences between the two corpora emerged for the other categories of tutor responses. The tutors used the following correction methods significantly less often in research methods than in algebra: (a) hints, (b) short or long feedback, and (c) reasons to expose derivation of correct answer. Approximately four to five times as many hints were given by tutors in the algebra corpus than the research methods corpus.

The difference in the domains—open versus closed world—influenced the tutors' abilities to generate a variety of responses: hints, error acknowledgment, and error reasoning. All of these responses were apparently used more often when there was a precise, clear-cut answer to a question as in the closed-world domain of algebra. The well-defined nature of the concepts in algebra made it cognitively less taxing for the unskilled tutor to generate a well-defined discriminating response to a student's error.

It appears that the process of generating hints on the fly for open-world domains is a profound challenge for tutors. Nevertheless, there are important benefits for hinting even in open-world domains. Having a systematic model for the tutor to follow, instead of relying on intuition, should enable the tutor to effectively use the hinting strategies in both open and closed worlds.

FUNCTIONS OF HINTS

Hints perform various functions, often simultaneously, to foster an integrated understanding in the student. Twelve functions of hints were identified from the literature or deduced from our research: (a) directing thought processes; (b) redirecting current thought (Perrent & Groen, 1993; Trismen, 1981; Weisberg & Alba, 1982); (c) drawing on the effectiveness of indirect speech acts (Gibbs, 1999); (d) engaging the student in interactive dialogue (Collins & Stevens, 1982); (e) handling mixed initiatives or multiple intentions (Hume et al., 1996); (f) prompting the student to access information (Hume et al., 1996); (g) isolating relevant information from the rest of the domain (Hume et al., 1996); (h) conveying information; (i) increasing learner control; (j) providing a response to an error or request (Hume et al., 1996; Merrill, Reiser, Merrill, & Lands, 1995); (k) activating thinking (Hume et al., 1996); and (l) increasing the speed in the problem-solving processes (Abu-Mostafa, 1990; Bowden, 1997; Trismen, 1981). When gathering this extensive list of functions, there emerged a natural division that clustered around three comprehensive categories: memory retrieval, problem solving, and discourse.

Memory Retrieval

Hints can serve as memory cues that activate the appropriate knowledge. For a hint cue to be used, the following sequence of events take place: (a) at some point in the past, the student learns a piece of information, M; (b) the tutor believes that the student has M stored in memory; (c) the tutor wants the student to be able to retrieve M instead of the tutor retrieving it for the student; (d) the tutor believes that the cue, C, is strongly associated with M; (e) the tutor also believes the student knows this association between C and M; (f) the tutor presents C as a hint; and ideally (g) the student supplies M. Therefore, the tutor presents hints as cues with the purpose of helping a student who is having difficulty retrieving knowledge from memory storage.

In the following example, the tutor engages the student in correcting the student's error by giving the student a hint (green). This cue helps the student retrieve the desired piece of knowledge from memory (Ireland).

T1: What European country had a major potato famine?
S1: England.
T2: Well, consider the color green.
S2: Oh, I remember. Ireland.
T3: Yes!

Hints that trigger memory storage supply the student with a piece of information that will stimulate the student's recall of the facts needed to answer a question. In this sense, the hint redirects the thoughts of the student (Trismen, 1981). Consequently, these hints can have the following cognitive functions: direct thought processes, prompt the student to access information, provide a response to an error, activate thinking, and increase learner control by putting the cognitive work on the student.

We examined several classic studies in the memory literature that used cue hints as an effective method for handling retrieval failures. In the classic tip-of-the-tongue phenomenon called TOT (Brown & McNeill, 1966), a person temporarily experiences an inability to recall a piece of information. The person, however, usually does have access to partial information related to the nonretrievable word. The hint is the trigger that activates that bit of knowledge in memory and alleviates the TOT state. The cue has the power to clarify a connection between stored information and the current stimulus that originally produced the TOT state. A cue that directly conveys the desired information (i.e., a copy cue) enables the student to retrieve the correct answer immediately. There are no additional cognitive processes required to answer this type of hint.

In a classical study by Tulving and Pearlstone (1966), free recall was contrasted with cued recall. Students recalled much more with the help of a cue.

Tulving and Pearlstone also demonstrated that people often have the information they learned in memory storage, but need the help of a cue to access that information. Similarly, a tutor gives a hint that acts as a cue to elicit the correct memory item. Consider the previous example about Ireland for conceptualizing the range in which a tutor can aid the student's memory in retrieving a concept.

Tutor's question: What European country had a potato famine?

Ranges of tutor response:
- Recognition: The answer is given in a question—"Is it Ireland?"
- Cued recall: The hint of an associated concept is given—"Consider the color green."
- Free recall: The question is repeated or no help is given—"What country had the potato famine?"

At one end of an underlying continuum is a recognition test, where the answer is given to the student as a copy cue. In the middle case, cued recall, an association or cue to the answer, is given to trigger the correct answer. In the free recall situation, the student is offered no help in the recall process.

The phenomenon of cue retrieval cannot be fully conceptualized without the notion of "encoding specificity" that was explained by Tulving and Thompson (1973). This principle states that information is not recorded in the memory in isolation. Instead each item of information is connected to an elaborate, context-specific, memory representation with details about the setting in which the information was originally learned. Hints can be viewed as context information that was encoded at the time of the initial learning stage.

In the following example, the tutor draws on previous information in a hypothetical computer tutoring session. The cue is derived from information surrounding a misconception to help the student retrieve the knowledge.

T1: What happens to the contents of RAM when the computer is turned off?
S1: Nothing.
T2: Okay, think back to what type of memory RAM is. Can you tell me?
S2: Short term.
T3: So . . .
S3: It disappears and is lost unless you save it.

In this example, the student was able to answer the tutor only after the tutor reintroduced information from an earlier discussion by means of the hint in T2. The student then applied the previous information to construct an answer in S3.

Unlike these memory retrieval studies, which are comparatively simplistic, a hint can involve more complex cognitive processes as in problem solving. Hints fall on a continuum. At one end, a hint is a simple cue such as, "the country begins with an 's.' " At the other end, it is a clue that results in the "aha" experience. This experience occurs when the entire solution to a complex problem is immediately recovered after receiving a clue. Hints as clues to problem solving are discussed next.

PROBLEM SOLVING

Hints can help the student retrieve a piece of information and then use this information to make an inference and solve the problem (Hume et al., 1996). The clue can be the key insight that the student needs to reason through the problem and come to the solution. This type of hint has the following cognitive functions: pointing to information that is new (Hume et al., 1996; Trismen, 1981), stopping the train of thought and redirecting it, stimulating inferences (Hume et al., 1996), increasing the speed of problem solving (Abu-Mostafa, 1990; Bowden, 1997; Trismen, 1981), and connecting information by filling in the gaps (Abu-Mostafa, 1993).

As in the case of the cue hint used in memory retrieval, conditions need to be fulfilled that enable the tutor to use a clue hint for problem solving. The following conditions are needed: (a) the tutor believes that the student can find the solution, S; (b) the tutor wants the student to be able to infer S, as opposed to telling the direct path to the student; (c) the tutor believes that the student can find the solution path if given clue CL; (d) the tutor believes that the student will not find solution path S without the clue CL; (e) the tutor presents clue CL as a hint; and (f) ideally the student discovers S.

In the following example from a hypothetical computer tutoring session, the tutor gives a hint with all the criteria previously listed assumed. The tutor wants to know how the student would design an operating system that would free up the computer's memory so that the operating system could perform multiple jobs.

T1: How would you free up the computer's memory?

S1: Umm . . .

T2: Could you shift the memory? (Clue hint)

S2: Yeah, you could move information to external memory devices.

T3: Right.

The student in S1 was unsure about what direction to take in considering the tutor's question in T1. The tutor supplied a clue hint in T2, which gave the student the key idea of information to the solution in S2—namely, moving information to external storage devices.

The tutor who uses a hint to help the student through the problem-solving process has the intention to help the student without actually providing the answer, as was the case in memory retrieval (Hume et al., 1996). When using hints in problem solving, it is not simply a question of the student forgetting previously learned information, as in a memory retrieval situation, but instead the student requires guidance in making a mental path to the solution. The student should therefore take the information from the hint and make an inference that will lead to the solution. In Trismen's (1982) study, some of his participants commented, "I know that," after receiving a clue. Interestingly, this comment was followed by the "aha" reaction, with a solution to the problem. Although the hint did not offer new information per se, it clearly indicated to the student a path not yet considered to the solution. This "aha" experience has been documented in the literature as a common feeling in response to clue hints in problem solving (Ghiselin, 1952; Hadamard, 1949; Haefele, 1962).

Problem solving involves a sequence of actions that dictate the steps in a solution and when these steps should occur. Hints provide an excellent means for the tutor to guide the student through these actions but not reveal the complete process. It is the ability to work through this process that is pertinent to deep understanding in learning.

There are several aspects of problem solving that have been defined by Anderson et al. (1990) and often play a role in a tutoring session. These include (a) maintenance of the main goal, (b) decomposition of subgoals, (c) sequence of operations, and (d) cognitive processes taking place. The first aspect involves maintaining the main goal of the problem to be solved. The tutor has local and global learning objectives that are carried out by the use of hints (Hume et al., 1996). Hints unravel the contents along the path to the larger goal, which is an important function for correctly encoding the problem-solving experience. According to Merrill et al. (1995), errors include students' goals that were not required in the problem in addition to the goals that were forgotten. Hints redirect thoughts and thereby remind students of the main goal that is often lost in the problem-solving process. This main goal is then broken down into subgoals, which may also be introduced by the tutor.

One way that the subgoals are exposed to the student is by hints, as in the case of main goals. The subgoals are deduced from a curriculum script (Putnam, 1987) and slightly adjusted in a fashion that adapts to the contributions of the student. Collins and Stevens (1982) documented how subgoals and steps in causal chains are revealed through hints. For example, one student was asked about the causal factors leading to heavy rainfall in Oregon. The student's response lacked three basic steps in the tutor's first-order theory of the process leading to rainfall. The tutor gave clues regarding the first missed step in the sequence, "Why is the air so

moist?", followed by questions leading to the other two missed steps. The subgoals that the tutor had about the factors that lead to rainfall directed the agenda of
the tutor's actions (Putnam, 1987). The subgoals of the problem and the steps in
the causal chain drove the content of the hints.

The subgoals form a sequence of actions that are preferably delivered in a logical and rational way. One of the benefits of staying on course within the sequence
of operations is the time saved in the learning process. The Anderson et al. (1990)
study of the LISP tutor found that students without a tutor took more than twice as
long on several problems. By keeping the student on the path led by the curriculum script, the tutor generates hints that can eliminate the number of options in the
student's mind, thus reducing the time to progress to the next step to the solution
(Abu-Mostafa, 1990).

Careful timing must be considered when giving hints during problem solving.
Timely hints have the potential to redirect or guide the student to the solution in
profitable ways. Hints given immediately encourage the student to independently
continue the problem-solving process, but also time gets saved. A delayed hint
can lead to a misunderstanding by the student as to the initial cause of the error.
The tutor presumably should initiate a hint before moving on to the next step to
maintain the logical and temporal systematicity of the knowledge. This requires a
fine-tuned representation of the goal hierarchy, causal network, logical argument,
or other type of representational structure that is relevant to the domain knowledge. However, there are conditions in which a delayed hint is effective, after the
student has had the opportunity to reflect on the problem. The timing of hints is
clearly one important direction for future research.

So far we have illustrated that hints direct thoughts toward the correct information. Hints can also disengage retrieval processes from irrelevant information, and thereby redirect the student to the relevant information. If the student
effectively uses the hint, the student fills in the missing link, corrects the error of
omission, or draws a required inference to progress to the next step of the problem-solving process.

Discourse Features

Hints are tailored to satisfy a variety of discourse functions. An understanding of
these functions is needed to appreciate the role of hints in tutoring. The discourse
functions of speech acts in tutoring have been examined in some detail by researchers who study tutorial dialogue (Fox, 1993; Graesser et al., 1995; Hume et
al., 1996; Person et al., 1995; Shah, Evens, Michael, & Rovick, 2002).

(1) Indirect Speech Acts.   Hints are indirect speech acts that fulfill social and
pedagogical goals of the tutor. Hints maintain a social politeness while upholding
pedagogical standards (Person et al., 1995). The tutor wants to be as encouraging

as possible while engaging the student in an interactive dialogue and correcting misconceptions. Indeed the tutor needs to provide negative and corrective feedback, but to avoid criticisms and "face-threatening" acts (Brown & Levinson, 1987). Hume et al. (1996) proposed that hints often carry a dual purpose as indirect speech acts: (a) a negative acknowledgment, and (b) a function of pointing to or conveying information. Using hints to handle student errors and provide direction comes across as more of a polite response than a negative response.

Maintaining the balance in the interaction of correction and politeness is not a simple endeavor. Indirect requests expedite this mixed agenda. The following are examples of indirect requests in a hypothetical tutoring session on computer hardware:

T1: Could you tell me how you connect to the Internet?
S1: Through a telephone line.
T2: Good. Can you tell me what is required?
S2: A network card.
T3: Okay. Would you have to hook your phone up to something?
S3: Umm, a modem.
T4: Correct!

The tutor phrases the request in each move, T1 to T3, in ways that have been shown to be more polite than more direct methods, such as saying "no, you are wrong" in T3 (Fox, 1993; Gibbs, 1999; Person et al., 1995). The tutor wants the student to consider other options, but worries that negative feedback alone will traumatize the student or reduce his or her willingness to supply information. Using phrases such as "could you" or "would you" present options to students in how they can respond to a tutor's request. The experience is less face threatening when options are available. Tutoring potentially consists of many face-threatening acts, such as requests, criticisms, and demands.

Not only are the indirect speech acts more polite, but they also put more of the cognitive load on the student. The following examples illustrate the range from direct to indirect remarks. All of the tutor remarks in T1 to T4 are correcting a student who had the misconception that ROM is the only primary memory. The range from T2 to T4 exemplifies the options a tutor has in ways to deliver a hint.

Direct   T1: The other primary memory is RAM.

          T2: What about the other primary memory besides ROM?
          T3: What about the other primary memory?
Indirect T4: ROM is not the ONLY primary memory.

The first and most direct response is to simply state the correct answer, as in T1. The next level, going from direct to indirect, is to give a specific hint (T2) or a less specific hint (T3). Finally, the tutor gives an indirect hint by using intonation to signal the error of the student, hinting that the student should consider another answer. We discuss the role of intonation shortly.

The benefit of the indirect speech acts, besides being more polite, is that they are delivered in such a way that forces the student to think, and thereby maintains the pedagogical quality of the interaction. Fox's (1993) view is that tutors avoid telling students directly that they are wrong. Instead they help students to discover errors through leading questions, cues, clues, and other indirect methods. The tutor's indirect speech act encourages a more intricate thought process by students, challenging their knowledge integration.

Surface features of conversation can promote indirect forms, which serve to fulfill this dual purpose of social politeness and pedagogy. Intonation contrasts (including stress) are surface features that discriminate new information from old information; they help bridge the information known by the student and the information the tutor wants the student to consider. This is illustrated in the following example.

T1: What is primary memory?
S1: ROM.
T2: ROM is not the ONLY primary memory. (Indirect)
    OR
    Another primary memory is RAM. (Direct)

In the indirect case (T2), the tutor corrects the student with a statement that suggests the answer in S1 is incomplete. The tutor emphasizes "ONLY" to point out the incomplete expression of knowledge by the student. By emphasizing the word "ONLY," the tutor is relying on the student to focus on what is missing—namely, the other common primary memory. Intonation and emphasis are used to obtain the desired pedagogical effect while maintaining politeness by not expressing that the student's answer is incomplete. Compare this with the direct response in T2 ("Another primary memory is RAM"), in which the answer is given with no effort required on the part of the student.

As we have seen, hints as indirect requests can contribute to solving the mixed agenda of tutoring. Yet being too indirect or too direct can sometimes hinder effective tutoring (Person et al., 1995). Person et al. (1995) proposed that there is often a trade-off between pedagogy and politeness in tutoring. An inexperienced tutor simply follows the politeness conventions of normal conversation, but this politeness sometimes occurs at the expense of the tutor failing to repair a faulty mental model in the mind of the student.

There can be unfortunate consequences for the student if the indirect speech act is too direct or too indirect. If a hint is too indirect, the student can be misled or end up missing the problem, so the misconception is never corrected. If a hint is too direct, then the student is not challenged and does not actively construct knowledge. Presumably, an ideal hint is in between these two extremes. A hint that is too direct may even result in poorer learning than if there were no feedback at all given by the hints (Merrill et al., 1992). Consider the following example of a tutor giving a hint that is too direct and gives too much information.

T1: What type of scale would that be?

S1: Oh, let me think, which one, I don't know.

T2: Try to think. Nominal or . . . ?

S2: Ordinal, yeah.

T3: It would be. Why would it be an ordinal scale?

The hint does not challenge the student because there is only one other scale the student and tutor have been discussing (ordinal). So in S2, the student is not required to do much cognitive work.

(2) *Engaging the Student.* Hints can take the form of instructions, suggestions, examples, counterexamples, questions, and other categories of speech acts (Perrent & Groen, 1993). Out of all these strategies, a hint in the form of a question has a number of pedagogical advantages. Consider the following example in which hints are questions that engage the student:

T1: Would you tell me how the CPU processes information?

S1: All at once.

T2: Well, what can you tell me about the function of RAM?

S2: It is short-term memory.

T3: So, why would you need that short-term memory?

S3: To hold information the CPU is not using.

T4: So do you still believe that the CPU handles all information at once?

S4: Well, no, RAM stores some.

Presenting hints in a question format engages the student in an interactive dialogue by enabling a transfer of control from tutor to student (Lepper et al., 1990; Lepper & Chabay, 1988), directing thoughts effectively (Trismen, 1981), establishing an interactive dialogue (Collins, 1988), and teaching self-monitoring skills to students (Collins, 1988). Lepper et al. (1990) and Lepper and Chabay (1988) reported that tutors who asked leading questions helped students identify and repair errors, and thus placed the learning responsibility on the student. Hints in the form of questions and counterexamples helped students uncover the faults in their own reasoning (Collins & Stevens, 1982; Collins, Warnock, & Passafume, 1975).

A question virtually always requires a response by listener, and therefore is a subtle imposition on the student. In this sense, questions facilitate an interactive dialogue. The number of available options of responding is removed when questions are posed. Consider the following example of two types of hinting formats:

Tutor 1:   You can move from Web page to Web page somehow.

Tutor 2:   How do you move from Web page to Web page?

The tutor's first response leaves many options of how the student could respond to the tutor. The student could ignore the statement, remain silent, ask a question, request a clarification, assert a fact, give a nonverbal response, perform an action, and so on. In contrast, the tutor's second move is much more likely to get a verbal response from the student—namely, an answer to the question. Questions remove any ambiguity about whose turn it is. Removing options directs the students to what exactly is expected in a turn, in addition to revealing to the tutor what the level of student understanding is. If the guidance from the tutor does not require a response, the level of student understanding remains vague. Posing hints as questions may appear to clash with the virtue of the importance of providing students options, rather than taking them away. However, there needs to be some way to elicit student contributions and hints as questions appear to strike a perfect balance in juggling multiple discourse goals.

Another advantage of hints as questions is that effective tutors can provide a model of the inquiry to teach students self-monitoring skills (Collins, 1988). The tutor essentially models good question-asking skills by asking the questions through hints. This inquiry method is similar to the Socratic method. Questions are the only dialogue move of the tutor in the *bona fide* Socratic method. By careful selection of questions, students end up discovering and correcting their own misconceptions during the process of answering the questions. It takes sophisticated tutorial skills to effectively scaffold a student in this fashion.

SIMULATED TUTORING

Computers are currently being used to simulate the tutoring strategies of humans and implement ideal pedagogical methods. The intelligent tutoring systems enterprise has made impressive breakthroughs that yield substantial gains in learning (Aleven & Koedinger, 2002; Anderson et al., 1995; Graesser et al., 2003; Graesser, VanLehn, Rose, Jordan, & Harter, 2001; Lesgold, Lajoie, Bunzo, & Eggan, 1992; VanLehn et al., 2002). These systems, as well as those in computer-assisted instruction, integrate theories of learning and cognition in the their design (Clancey & Soloway, 1990; Eberts & Brock, 1987).

The Tutoring Research Group at The University of Memphis is currently developing an intelligent tutoring system called AutoTutor (Graesser, Wiemer-Hastings, Wiemer-Hastings, Kreuz, & the Tutoring Research Group, 1999; Graesser, Person, Harter, & the Tutoring Research Group, 2001; Person, Graesser, Kreuz, & Pomeroy, 2001). AutoTutor simulates the dialogue moves of an unskilled human tutor. Instead of an information delivery system that unloads an unmanageable amount of information on the student, this system is a discourse prosthesis. That is, AutoTutor uses naturalistic discourse strategies to engage the student in exploring the material, get the student communicating, and promote an active constructive of knowledge. The goal is to encourage students to produce more elaborate answers that manifest deep reasoning, as opposed to reciting pieces of shallow knowledge. Along with a variety of other kinds of discourse moves to accomplish this goal, AutoTutor produces hints that are intended to encourage students to talk and thereby assist in their construction of coherent knowledge about the domain. AutoTutor is the only intelligent tutoring system that presents hints in naturalistic tutorial dialogue.

Several other computer tutor programs have developed alternate hinting strategies. Gertner, Conati, and VanLehn (1998) developed a tutoring system named ANDES. Their system has an interface, ANDES' Procedural Helper, which uses templates to generate hints from nodes in the solution graph. The LISP tutor of Anderson et al. (1995) generates hints from production rules and templates. CIRCSIM-Tutor uses heuristics to choose a hinting strategy that is sensitive to the type of student's answer, a tutorial plan, and the tutoring history (Shah et al., 2002; Zhou et al., 1999). In all of these systems, hints are presented with graduated specificity, starting with minimal clues and clues and ending with direct assertions.

Language and discourse pose barriers in efforts to build tutoring systems. As a result, the systems are limited in discourse interactions with the student. Recent developments have minimized some of these barriers and have increased the feasibility of a naturalistic dialogue. AutoTutor incorporates many of these recent developments in natural language processing and discourse processing. It is the only system that has an extensive language dialogue component that is also supported by psychological research and naturalistic tutoring corpora.

MECHANISMS OF AUTOTUTOR

AutoTutor's design incorporates discourse patterns and pedagogical strategies of unskilled tutors. Most tutors lack training in tutoring techniques and lack extensive expertise on the tutoring topic. However, despite this fact, they are effective in promoting learning gains. AutoTutor assists college students in learning the basics of an introductory computer literacy course taught at the University of Memphis. AutoTutor also has been developed for teaching students conceptual physics. AutoTutor introduces problems and questions from a curriculum script, strives to comprehend student keyboard contributions, formulates dialogue moves through production rules tailored to the student's contributions (such as feedback, pumps, prompts, and hints), and holds a conversation with the student through a talking head.

The ensemble of components in AutoTutor distinguishes the system from comparable systems. We briefly explain some of the components that are crucial to AutoTutor's hinting mechanism. One of the significant underlying components in AutoTutor is Latent Semantic Analysis (LSA). LSA is a statistical representation of world knowledge that capitalizes on the fact that particular words co-occur in particular packages of world knowledge (Foltz, 1996; Landauer, Foltz, & Laham, 1998). For example, RAM and CPU frequently co-occur in articles on computers, whereas ketchup and french fries co-occur in articles on fast foods. However, RAM and ketchup rarely co-occur in documents that describe various domains of world knowledge. Research by Foltz and Landauer have used LSA as a backbone for grading essays of students (Foltz, Gilliam, & Kendall, 2000; Landauer et al., 1998). Their LSA-based essay grader can assign grades to essays with the same reliability as experts in composition. This indeed is no small achievement in the field of discourse processing! AutoTutor uses LSA for evaluating whether the quality of student contributions matches expected answers to deep reasoning questions and expected solutions to problems. As student contributions are typed into the keyboard, their input is compared with the good answers. An LSA match between the student input and a good answer (or a piece of a good answer) can vary between 0 and 1. We have found that the AutoTutor's evaluations of students' answers are comparable to intermediate experts of conceptual physics (Olde, Franceschetti, Karnavat, Graesser, & the Tutoring Research Group, 2002) and computer literacy (Wiemer-Hastings, Wiemer-Hastings, Graesser, & the Tutoring Research Group, 1999). Moreover, LSA is capable of discriminating among levels of student ability, such as good, vague, mute, and erroneous students (Graesser, Wiemer-Hastings, Wiemer-Hastings, Harter, Person, & the Tutoring Research Group, 2000).

A production system is a set of "if–then" production rules that directs when and how the computer tutor produces different classes of speech acts. Examples of such speech acts are feedback (positive, negative vs. neutral), pumps ("yeah," "tell me more"), prompts for specific information, assertions, corrections, summaries, and (of course) hints. These rules are related to (a) the quality of the student's contributions as computed by Latent Semantic Analysis (LSA); (b) global parameters that measure the ability, verbosity, and initiative of the student; and (c) the extent to which the content has been covered. The two production rules for a hint are presented next:

IF [student ability = MEDIUM or HIGH & good answer = LOW]

   THEN [select HINT]

IF [student ability = LOW & student verbosity = HIGH & good answer = LOW]

   THEN [select HINT]

According to the first production rule, hints are used when a high-ability student is pursuing the wrong track and needs a hint to get the student in the appropriate conceptual arena. The second production rule for hints handles low-ability students (low in knowledge about computers) who are high verbal. The production rules in AutoTutor are fuzzy, so they accommodate ill-defined boundaries among categories of student ability, verbosity, initiative, and so forth.

The curriculum script organizes the topics, questions, and problems covered in the tutorial dialogue. The content of the script covers three macrotopics in computer literacy: hardware, operating system, and Internet. The script includes questions/problems posed by the tutor, ideal responses to them, anticipated bugs and misconceptions, and figures and diagrams. The topics within the script are scaled on three levels of difficulty (easy, medium, and difficult). AutoTutor selects topics for the student by matching the difficulty level to the student's ability as computed by LSA. In essence, AutoTutor follows the zone of proximal development (ZPD), in the sense that topics are selected that move students on the frontiers of their knowledge (i.e., not too difficult, but not too easy).

The ZPD was originally introduced by Vygotsky (1978). It was defined as the distance between the (a) actual developmental level when a person works independently, and (b) level of potential development when a person has adult guidance or acts in collaboration with more capable peers. The hints in AutoTutor help students to a level of knowledge that could not be obtained on their own. The delicate balance between providing information to the students and allowing them to discover it on their own is a crucial task for tutors to accomplish to gain significant learning outcomes.

AUTOTUTOR'S HINTING STRATEGIES

We implemented hinting strategies into the mechanisms of AutoTutor in light of its proven effectiveness in tutoring. If the student has trouble answering a question or solving a problem, AutoTutor selects a hint via its production rules that operate on the curriculum script and the current LSA values that assess the coverage of answers. Hints present facts, ask leading questions, or reframe the problem. AutoTutor uses the hints to redirect the student back to the topic that was addressed in the question by stimulating the recall of specific information or facilitating the student's inferential processing. The two explicit functions of a hint that have been integrated in the tutoring program are to (a) redirect students to the relevant topic, and (b) direct students to a specific aspect of the answer to a question. The following example illustrates the function of redirecting the student:

T1: What is the process of putting digital photos on the Internet?
S1: Well, there is software that can manipulate the photos.
T2: Okay, could you tell me about the ways to hook-up to the Internet?
S2: By a telephone line.
T3: Yes!

In this example, the student in S1 started to discuss an aspect of digital photography that was not directly related to the tutor's subgoals for answering this question. So the tutor responded with a hint in T2 to get the student focused on the relevant information. As a consequence, the student gets on the right track in S2. The next example illustrates the second function of hinting that directs the student to a specific aspect of a good answer; an aspect is approximately one sentence in length, with 10 to 25 words.

T1: How would you free up the computer's memory?
S1: Umm.
T2: Could you shift the memory?
S2: Yeah, you could move information to external memory devices.
T3: Right.

The student in S1 had trouble getting started, so the tutor gave a hint in T2 to help lead the student's thought process to converge on a particular aspect (i.e., moving information to an external storage device).

Table 9.3 is an example of 1 of the 36 topics scripted for AutoTutor. The focal question is the main question to be answered by the student under the guidance from the computer tutor. The ideal answer is segmented into a set of critical "aspects" to be covered by the tutor and student by the end of the exchange for the topic. Currently one hint corresponds to each of these critical aspects. Discourse markers are added to the hints to help signal the student to the type of dialogue move. For example, a hint may follow the markers: "and remember," "don't forget," "well, this might help," or even "here's a hint."

FIRST EVALUATION
OF AUTOTUTOR'S HINTS

The dialogue moves of AutoTutor have been evaluated with respect to pedagogical quality and conservational smoothness (Person et al., 2001). Undergraduate students enrolled in a computer literacy course at the University of Memphis were

TABLE 9.3
Topic Question for Computer Hardware

Focal Question

What Are the Features of RAM?

Ideal Answer Aspects
1. RAM is the most common type of primary storage.
2. RAM is used by the central processing unit (CPU) as short-term memory storage in the CPU's execution of programs.
3. The CPU can read from RAM.
4. The CPU can write from RAM.
5. The contents of RAM disappear when the computer is turned off.
6. RAM is considered to be volatile memory, which is memory that can be changed.

Hints corresponding to each of the ideal answer aspects
1. What kind of storage is RAM?
2. The CPU uses something as a temporary memory store.
3. How does the CPU get information into RAM?
4. How does the CPU get information into RAM?
5. What happens to RAM when you turn off your computer?
6. RAM can be changed.

asked to provide hand-written answers to 12 questions on computer literacy that were randomly selected from a pool of 36 questions. After the data were collected from the students, the answers were divided into two categories: (a) a diverse group that included all types of student contributions (vague, correct, bad), and (b) a group consisting of contributions from only the very good coherent students.

We generated the contributions of virtual students by divided responses in each answer category into small sets that resemble a student's contributions in spoken dialogue. The responses for each category (good, erroneous, vague) were entered in a random order into AutoTutor to form a mixed-dialogue between AutoTutor and the virtual student. The tutor and student alternated taking turns in a simulated conversation. There was no guarantee that the dialogue would have coherence when AutoTutor interacted with different types of virtual students. The idea was to test the computer tutor's handling of the various types of contributions. We then evaluated each category on how well AutoTutor handled the students' contributions based on the two criteria previously mentioned: pedagogical quality and conversational smoothness.

AutoTutor's hints were rated on pedagogical quality by two professors who were experts in human tutoring. The pedagogical quality rating was determined by holistically evaluating the overall pedagogical effectiveness and appropriateness of each hint in the simulated conversations between AutoTutor and the virtual students. In making their ratings of pedagogical quality, the two raters considered their knowledge from extensive observations of what unskilled human tutors would do in similar situations. They determined whether the move was the best choice given the current interaction between tutor and student. They also considered the content that had been covered by the student and tutor during the evolution of the conversation for a topic. For example, they determined whether AutoTutor made the best move in choosing a hint (vs. a prompt or some other dialogue move category). The scale ranged from 1 (*very poor*) to 6 (*very good*), with values of 3 and 4 being "undecided but guess poor" and "undecided but guess good." Mean ratings of 3.5 or greater would be considered good for pedagogical quality if a discrete good/bad contrast were adopted.

Two graduate students who worked on the tutoring project rated the dialogue moves of AutoTutor on conversational smoothness. The conversational smoothness rating took into account each tutor move in terms of (a) overall coherence of the move within the dialogue, (b) relevance of the move to the particular situation, (c) consideration of the Gricean maxim of quantity (e.g., saying too much or not enough), and (d) overall awkwardness of the contribution. Ratings of conversational smoothness were based on a 6-point scale that was analogous to the scale on pedagogical quality. Again ratings with 3.5 or higher were considered good for conversational smoothness.

Table 9.4 presents mean ratings of pedagogical quality and conversational smoothness. We segregated virtual students who randomly selected contributions of different categories of quality from the virtual students who provided good coherent answers. The ratings for conversational smoothness were quite high for both groups of virtual students. This suggests that AutoTutor maintained an appropriate flow of conversation throughout the session, functioning as a good conversational partner. The mean ratings on the pedagogical quality of AutoTutor were modest, and perhaps acceptable, but not outstanding. Apparently AutoTutor should have responded with some other dialogue move that would be more helpful to the student.

SECOND EVALUATION
OF AUTOTUTOR'S HINTS

The second evaluation of AutoTutor used nine undergraduate students at the University of Memphis in a "think-aloud" study. Some of the students in the study had been previously enrolled in the computer literacy class, but most had not yet taken the course. They were given class credit for participating in the study.

TABLE 9.4
Performance Scores of AutoTutor's Hints

Virtual Student Group	Pedagogical Quality	Conversational Smoothness
Random selection	4.18	5.32
Very good and coherent	3.67	5.00

TABLE 9.5
Questions in the Think-Aloud Study on AutoTutor

	Question
Seed Question	What are the parts and uses of the computer?
Question 1	What are the features of RAM?
Question 2	How does the operating system interact with the word processing program when you create a document?
Question 3	Why is the World Wide Web so popular?

The nine students spoke aloud their thoughts as they worked with AutoTutor. Each student's session was videotaped and took approximately 25 to 30 minutes to complete for four of the topics. The students first answered a basic (seed) question that was given to help the students adjust to the computer-tutoring program. This question was followed by three questions on computer literacy, one from each of three topics: hardware, operating system, and Internet. The focal questions the students received in the study are presented in Table 9.5.

The tutoring sessions were transcribed and analyzed. Three main issues arose from this second evaluation regarding the hinting strategy: (a) use of inappropriate discourse markers that introduced the hint dialogue move, thus causing confusion; (b) ambiguity between the use of hints versus elaborations; and (c) lack of sufficient intonation. The first issue regarding discourse markers is an easier problem to resolve than (b) or (c). Currently, the discourse markers that precede a hint are selected at random from a word list of possible options. The results of this evaluation provide some guidance in eliminating discourse markers that were semantically awkward and would mislead the student.

The second issue involved the many occasions in which the student was not able to discriminate whether AutoTutor was giving a hint or merely stating an assertion. In the following example, the student had difficulty understanding what to do in response to the hint given by the tutor in T1. The discourse marker "Well this might help" is followed by the hint.

T1: Well this might help. You can jump from Web page to Web page somehow.

S1 (spoken out loud): I don't understand if that's a question or he's just stating that.

This ambiguity and confusion of not knowing how to respond is a serious concern for the current hinting strategy. If hints are not understood as hints, then all the functions become void. Overall, hints were discernible only about half the time, clearly indicating that we needed to improve the wording of the hints.

The third problem addressed the intonation contours in the computerized voice of AutoTutor. Intonation helps the listener understand the intent of the statement or question. In the case of hints, intonation informs the student what to focus on and that a response is desired after the tutor's statement, which was intended to be a hint. A good hint presumably needs a rising intonation in the final words of the hint, whereas an assertion has a falling intonation at the end. Such a generalization is perhaps overly simplistic. There is also the question of whether the synthesized speech of AutoTutor (Microsoft Agent) has inherent limitations in expressing the appropriate intonations for particular speech act categories.

IMPROVEMENTS FOR HINTS

We are currently attempting to correct the problems that were manifested in the second evaluation. We believe that these solutions should be incorporated in any intelligent tutoring system that has conversational tutorial dialogue. We are correcting the manifested problems by implementing the following features: (a) relevant dialogue markers, (b) question form, and (c) appropriate intonation.

The appropriate dialogue marker sets the stage for the next dialogue move—in this case, hints. They can unambiguously signal that a hint is being delivered to the student. Two examples of good dialogue markers are, "Consider the following hint" or "Now, remember." The dialogue markers help students to know what is coming next and clue them on how they should respond.

Posing hints as questions also resolves the problem of ambiguity, in addition to having the benefits discussed earlier in this chapter. These benefits include the transfer of learner control to the student, the fact that questions require a response, the engagement of the student in articulating theories and principles, and the modeling of good question asking.

An intonation pattern that is appropriate for hints will help distinguish a hint from an information-seeking question. In the following example, the first question is a sincere information-seeking question, whereas the second question is a hint. The difference is captured in the intonation, which is illustrated by all capital letters.

Information seeking: What about OUTPUT?

Hint: What ABOUT output?

The use of intonation in the previous example enabled the listener to understand the intended meaning of the question. The emphasis on certain words was the mechanism that revealed this information to the listener. Currently, AutoTutor's computerized voice lacks the significant change in the intonation, so the participants had a difficult time assessing the intent of the statements given. Table 9.6 lists several rules that we are currently implementing to improve the intonation. These rules mark up the text with symbols that the computer will understand

TABLE 9.6
Mark-Up Rules for Naturalistic Conversation

Discourse Move	Rule
Question	Rising intonation at the end.
Hints	Said at a slower speed and rising intonation at the end if in question form.
Prompts	Said at a slower speed and rising intonation at the end, with last word drawn out.
Assertion	Said at normal conversational speed with falling intonation at the end.

to alter the voice, thus enhancing intonation. In the future, we hope to evaluate these intonation mark-up rules.

CLOSING COMMENTS

In this chapter, we set out to dissect the functions of hints in tutoring and speculate on the potential impact of hints on learning gains. Hopefully we have presented a convincing argument that hints have a special role in tutoring. They encourage active learning, provide effective scaffolding for advancing pedagogical goals, and help manage polite conversation. They are unique dialogue moves because they satisfy multiple goals of discourse and pedagogy. Nevertheless, it is still unclear whether they in fact provide learning gains. Thus, we leave our readers with a hint on what we regard as a goldmine for future research.

ACKNOWLEDGMENT

The Tutoring Research Group (TRG) is an interdisciplinary research team comprised of approximately 35 researchers from psychology, computer science, physics, and education (visit http://www.autotutor.org). This research was supported by the National Science Foundation (SBR 9720314, REC 0106965, REC 0126265, ITR 0325428) and the Department of Defense Multidisciplinary University Research Initiative (MURI) administered by the Office of Naval Research under grant N00014-00-1-0600. Any opinions, findings, conclusions, or recommendations expressed in this material are those of the authors and do not necessarily reflect the views of NSF or ONR.

REFERENCES

Abu-Mostafa, Y. S. (1990). Learning from hints in neural networks. *Journal of Complexity, 6*, 192–198.
Abu-Mostafa, Y. S. (1993). Hints and the VC dimension. *Neural Computation, 5*, 278–288.

Aleven, V., & Koedinger, K. R. (2002). An effective metacognitive strategy: Learning by doing and explaining with a computer-based Cognitive Tutor. *Cognitive Science, 26*, 147–179.

Anderson, J. R., Boyle, C. F., Corbett, A. T., & Lewis, M. W. (1990). Cognitive modeling and intelligent tutoring. *Artificial Intelligence, 42*, 7–49.

Anderson, J. R., Corbett, A., Koedinger, K., & Pelletier, R. (1995). Cognitive tutors: Lessons learned. *Journal of the Learning Sciences, 4*, 167–207.

Bloom, B. S. (1984). The 2-sigma problem: The search for methods of group instruction as effective as one-to-one tutoring. *Educational Researcher, 13*, 4–16.

Bowden, E. M. (1997). The effect of reportable and unreportable hints on anagram solution and the aha! experience. *Consciousness and Cognition, 6*, 545–573.

Brown, J. S., & Burton, R. B. (1978). Diagnostic models for procedural bugs in basic mathematical skills. *Cognitive Science, 2*, 155–192.

Brown, P., & Levinson, S. C. (1987). *Politeness: Some universals in language use.* Cambridge: Cambridge University Press.

Brown, R., & McNeill, D. (1966). The "tip-of–the-tongue" phenomenon. *Journal of Verbal Learning and Verbal Behavior, 5*, 325–337.

Burton, R. B. (1982). Diagnosing bugs in a simple procedural skill. In D. H. Sleeman & J. S. Brown (Eds.), *Intelligent tutoring systems* (pp. 157–183). New York: Academic Press.

Chi, M. T. H., Siler, S., Jeong, H., Yamauchi, T., & Hausmann, R. G. (2001). Learning from human tutoring. *Cognitive Science, 25*, 471–533.

Clancey, W. J., & Soloway, E. (1990). Artificial intelligence and learning environments: Preface. *Artificial Intelligence, 42*, 1–6.

Cognition and Technology Group at Vanderbilt. (1997). *The Jasper project: Lessons in curriculum, instruction, assessment, and professional development.* Mahwah, NJ: Lawrence Erlbaum Associates.

Cohen, P. A., Kulik, J. A., & Kulik, C. C. (1982). Educational outcomes of tutoring: A meta-analysis of findings. *American Educational Research Journal, 19*, 237–248.

Collins, A. (1988). Different goals of inquiry teaching. *Questioning Exchange, 2*, 39–46.

Collins, A., & Stevens, A. L. (1982). Goals and strategies of inquiry teachers. In R. Glaser (Ed.), *Advances in instructional psychology* (Vol. 2). Hillsdale, NJ: Lawrence Erlbaum Associates.

Collins, A., Warnock, E. H., Aiello, N., & Miller, M. L. (1975). Reasoning from incomplete knowledge. In D. G. Bobrow & A. Collins (Eds.), *Representation and understanding* (pp. 453–494). New York: Academic.

Collins, A., Warnock, E. H., & Passafume, J. J. (1975). Analysis and synthesis of tutorial dialogues. In G. H. Bower (Ed.), *The psychology of learning and motivation* (pp. 49–87). New York: Academic.

Eberts, R. E., & Brock, J. F. (1987). Computer-assisted and computer-managed instruction. In G. Salvendy (Ed.), *Handbook of human factors* (pp. 976–1011). New York: Wiley.

Flexner, S. B. (Ed.). (1997). *Random House Webster's Unabridged Dictionary* (2nd ed.). New York: Random House.

Foltz, P. W. (1996). Latent semantic analysis for text-based research. *Behavior Research Methods, Instruments, and Computers, 28*, 197–202.

Foltz, P. W., Gilliam, S., & Kendall, S. (2000). Supporting content-based feedback in on-line writing evaluation with LSA. *Interactive Learning Environments, 8*, 111–127.

Fox, B. A. (1993). *The human tutorial dialogue project: issues in design of instructional systems.* Hillsdale, NJ: Lawrence Erlbaum Associates.

Gertner, A. S., Conati, C., & VanLehn, K. (1998). Procedural help in ANDES: Generating hints using a Bayesian network student model. In *Proceedings of the 15th National Conference in Artificial Intelligence* (pp. 106–111). Menlo Park, CA: American Association for Artificial Intelligence.

Ghiselin, B. (1952). *The creative process.* Berkeley, CA: University of California Press.

Gibbs, R. W. (1999). *Intentions in the experience of meaning.* Cambridge: Cambridge University Press.

Graesser, A. C., Jackson, G. T., Mathews, E. C., Mitchell, H. H., Olney, A., Ventura, M., Chipman, P., Franceschetti, D., Hu, X., Louwerse, M. M., Person, N. K., & the Tutoring Research Group. (2003). Why/AutoTutor: A test of learning gains from a physics tutor with natural language dialog. *Proceedings of the 25th Annual Conference of the Cognitive Science Society* (pp. xx). Mahwah, NJ: Lawrence Erlbaum Associates.

Graesser, A. C., & Person, N. K. (1994). Question asking during tutoring. *American Educational Research Journal, 31*, 104–137.

Graesser, A. C., Person, N. K., Harter, D., & the Tutoring Research Group. (2001). Teaching tactics and dialog in AutoTutor. *International Journal of Artificial Intelligence in Education, 12*, 257–279.

Graesser, A. C., Person, N. K., & Huber, J. (1993). Question asking during tutoring and in the design of educational software. In M. Rabinowitz (Ed.), *Cognitive science foundations of instruction* (pp. 149–172). Hillsdale, NJ: Lawrence Erlbaum Associates.

Graesser, A. C., Person, N. K., & Magliano, J. P. (1995). Collaborative dialogue patterns in naturalistic one-to-one tutoring. *Applied Cognitive Psychology, 9*, 459–522.

Graesser, A. C., VanLehn, K., Rose, C., Jordan, P., & Harter, D. (2001). Intelligent tutoring systems with conversational dialogue. *AI Magazine, 22*, 39–51.

Graesser, A. C., Wiemer-Hastings, K., Wiemer-Hastings, P., Kreuz, R. J., and the Tutoring Research Group. (1999). AutoTutor: A simulation of a human tutor. *Journal of Cognitive Systems Research, 1*, 35–51.

Graesser, A. C., Wiemer-Hastings, P., Wiemer-Hastings, K., Harter, D., Person, N., & the Tutoring Research Group. (2000). Using latent semantic analysis to evaluate the contributions of students in AutoTutor. *Interactive Learning Environments, 8*, 129–148.

Hadamard, J. (1949). *The psychology of invention in the mathematical field.* Princeton, NJ: Princeton University Press.

Haefele, J. W. (1962). *Creativity and innovation.* New York: Reinhold.

Hume, G. D., Michael, J. A., Rovick, A. A., & Evens, M. W. (1996). Hinting as A tactic in one-on-one tutoring. *The Journal of the Learning Sciences, 5*, 23–47.

Landauer, T. K., Foltz, P. W., & Laham, D. (1998). An introduction to latent semantic analysis. *Discourse Processes, 25*, 259–284.

Lepper, M. R., Aspinwall, L., Mumme, D., & Chabay, R. W. (1990). Self-perception and social perception processes in tutoring: Subtle social control strategies of expert tutors. In J. M. Olson & M. P. Zanna (Eds.), *Self-inference processes: The sixth Ontario symposium in Social Psychology* (pp. 217–237). Hillsdale, NJ: Lawrence Erlbaum Associates.

Lepper, M. R., & Chabay, R. W. (1988). Socializing the intelligent tutor: Bringing empathy to computer tutors. In H. Mandl & A. Lesgold (Eds.), *Learning issues for intelligent tutoring systems* (pp. 242–257). New York: Springer-Verlag.

Lesgold, A., Lajoie, S., Bunzo, M., & Eggan, G. (1992). SHERLOCK: A coached practice environment for an electronics troubleshooting job. In J. H. Larkin & R. W. Chabay (Eds.), *Computer-assisted instruction and intelligent tutoring systems* (pp. 210–238). Hillsdale, NJ: Lawrence Erlbaum Associates.

Merrill, D. C., Reiser, B. J., Merrill, S. K., & Lands, S. (1995). Tutoring: Guided learning by doing. *Cognition and Instruction, 13*, 315–372.

Merrill, D. C., Reiser, B. J., Ranney, M., & Trafton, J. G. (1992). Effective tutoring techniques: A comparison of human tutors and intelligent tutoring systems. *The Journal of the Learning Sciences, 5*, 277–305.

Milheim, W. D., & Martin, B. L. (1991). Theoretical bases for the use of learner control: Three different perspectives. *Journal of Computer Based Instruction, 18*, 99–105.

Mohan, M. (1972). *Peer tutoring as a technique for teaching the unmotivated.* New York: State University of New York, Teacher Education Research Center (ERIC Document Reproduction service No. ED 061 154).

Norman, D. A. (1981). Categorization of action slips. *Psychological Review, 88*(1), 1–15.

Olde, B. A., Franceschetti, D. R., Karnavat, A., Graesser, A. C., & the Tutoring Research Group. (2002). The right stuff: Do you need to sanitize your corpus when using latent semantic analysis? In W. G. Gray & C. D. Schunn (Eds.), *Proceedings of the 24th Annual Conference of the Cognitive Science Society* (pp. 708–713). Mahwah, NJ: Lawrence Erlbaum Associates.

Perrent, J., & Groen, W. (1993). A hint is not always a help. *Educational Studies in Mathematics, 25*, 307–329.

Person, N. K., Graesser, A. C., Kreuz, R. J., Pomeroy, V., & the Tutoring Research Group. (2001). Simulating human tutor dialog moves in AutoTutor. *International Journal of Artificial Intelligence in Education, 12*, 23–39.

Person, N. K., Kreuz, R. J., Zwaan, R. A., & Graesser, A. C. (1995). Pragmatics and pedagogy: Conversational rules and politeness strategies may inhibit effective tutoring. *Cognition and Instruction, 13*, 161–188.

Putnam, R. T. (1987). Structuring and adjusting content for students: A study of live and simulated tutoring of addition. *American Educational Research Journal, 24*, 13–48.

Shah, F., Evens, M., Michael, J., & Rovick, A. (2002). Classifying student initiatives and tutor responses in human keyboard-to-keyboard tutoring sessions. *Discourse Processes, 33*, 23–52.

Trismen, D. A. (1981). *Mathematics items with hints*. Princeton, NJ: Educational Testing Service.

Trismen, D. A. (1982). *Development and administration of a set of mathematics items with hints*. Princeton, NJ: Educational Testing Service.

Tulving, E., & Pearlstone, Z. (1966). Availability versus accessibility of information in memory for words. *Journal of Verbal Learning and Verbal Behavior, 5*, 381–391.

Tulving, E., & Thompson, D. M. (1973). Encoding specificity and retrieval processes in episodic memory. *Psychological Review, 80*, 352–373.

VanLehn, K. (1990). *Mind bugs: The origins of procedural misconceptions*. Cambridge, MA: MIT Press.

VanLehn, K., Jones, R. M., & Chi, M. T. H. (1992). A model of the self-explanation effect. *Journal of the Learning Sciences, 2*, 1–60.

VanLehn, K., Lynch, C., Taylor, L., Weinstein, A., Shelby, R., Schulze, K., Treacy, D., & Wintersgill, M. (2002). Minimally invasive tutoring of complex physics problem solving. In S. A. Cerri, G. Gouarderes, & F. Paraguacu (Eds.), *Intelligent tutoring systems 2002* (pp. 367–376). Berlin, Germany: Springer.

Vygotsky, L. S. (1978). *Mind in society: The development of higher psychological processes*. Cambridge, MA: Harvard University Press.

Webb, N. M., Troper, J. D., & Fall, R. (1995). Constructive activity and learning in collaborative small groups. *Journal of Educational Psychology, 87*, 406–423.

Weisberg, R. W., & Alba, J. W. (1982). Problem solving is not like perception: More on Gestalt Theory. *Journal of Experimental Psychology: General, 111*, 326–330.

Wiemer-Hastings, P., Wiemer-Hastings, K., & Graesser, A. (1999). Improving an intelligent tutor's comprehension of students with Latent Semantic Analysis. In S. P. Lajoie & M. Vivet (Eds.), *Artificial intelligence in education* (pp. 535–542). Amsterdam: IOS Press.

Zhou, Y., Freedman, R., Glass, M., Michael, J. A., Rovick, A. A., & Evens, M. W. (1999). What should the tutor do when the student cannot answer a question? In A. Kumar & I. Russell (Eds.), *Proceedings of the 12th Florida Artificial Intelligence Research Symposium* (pp. 187–191). Menlo Park, CA: American Association for Artificial Intelligence Press.

10

Intelligent Tutors Need Intelligent Measurement, or the Other Way 'Round

Howard T. Everson
The College Board

When commenting on advances in artificial intelligence (AI) and its implications for education, the late Herbert Simon (1987) remarked that "a *good* tutor plays the role of a knowledgeable friend, who only suggests and advises, leaving the control of the learning situation essentially in the hands of the student" (p. 115). When it comes to using AI to create a computer-based tutor, the nature of the information this "knowledgeable friend" draws on is elusive. Surely, it includes a working knowledge of the subject matter (e.g., mathematics, history, or biology). After all, a friend could hardly be considered a helpful tutor if she knew little or nothing about the subject at hand. A good tutor, as Simon implies, knows more than simply the relevant facts or theories of a particular field or discipline. A good tutor, no doubt, has a strong sense of what the student understands. He or she possesses an understanding of what the student knows about the subject and how he reasons using that knowledge. This often includes an assessment of how much the student has learned, as well as an estimate of the amount and rate of learning taking place. The tutor integrates this information, often in real time, with a dynamic, strategic plan that sequences instructional materials and orders and reorders the presentation of those materials to facilitate learning.

Clearly, a good tutor has a working model of the learner, revising and updating it throughout the tutoring process. Revisions of the working model require continuous assessments of the evidence of learning and adjustments to the subsequent instruction. When tutoring is most effective, instruction and assessment are often seamless.

The rapidly growing literature on intelligent tutoring systems (ITS) contains many references to the challenge of creating and simulating mental models of the tutor (see e.g., Anderson, 1993; VanLehn, 1988). This challenge is simply referred to as the *student modeling problem* (Sleeman & Brown, 1982). Just as mental models play a role when humans do the tutoring, student models provide the ITS with a reasonable estimate—based on an array of prior information and response vectors—of the student's current understanding of a given content domain. In turn, the ITS uses this estimate, this model of the student, to adapt instruction to the learner's changing knowledge state (Diognon & Falmagne, 1985). Simulating a good tutor, the student model component informs the ITS and the system suggests, advises, and adapts instruction to meet the needs of the learner. In this way, a network of inferences derived by the student modeling component serves to guide the presentation, sequencing, and pacing of the instruction. Viewed broadly, the student model comprises two distinct components: the data structure (i.e., information structures representing the knowledge, skills, and abilities of the student as learner) and the inference engine that permits a diagnosis or suggests a prescription (VanLehn, 1988).

This chapter offers a perspective on the student modeling problem informed by cognitive science, psychology, and educational measurement. In doing so, we draw on the tools of mathematical probability and characterize the student model problem as one of making reasonable inferences about students' knowledge states when evidence is incomplete and certainty is low. Hence, the need for intelligence measurement is apparent (Bunderson, Inouye, & Olsen, 1984). This orientation contrasts with earlier ITS designs, which relied on detecting misconceptions or "bugs" (see e.g., Johnson & Soloway, 1984) and employed production rules and (or) model tracing methods (Anderson, 1993) or other diagnostic techniques (see e.g., VanLehn, 1988). In many ways, the probability-based measurement approaches reviewed in this chapter advance the interactive diagnostic techniques of student modeling described by VanLehn (1988) and Burton (1982). Thus, by highlighting recent developments in the larger fields of cognitive psychology and educational measurement, intelligent measurement approaches that promise improvements in ITS design are reviewed.

For the most part, the measurements models presented in this chapter emphasize the changing nature of educational assessment and underscore the growing influence of the cognitive sciences on learning theory, instructional design, and assessment (National Research Council, 2001). It is argued that advances in cognitive science and psychology are informing test theory, and these scientific advances in turn allow us to recast its design problem in terms of the forms of evidence required to support the inferences of the system. This shift in perspective may move the student modeling problem in its design beyond the heuristic solutions and production rule methods found in earlier exemplars, such as DEBUGGY (VanLehn, 1990), IDEBUGGY (Burton, 1982), and ACT-R (Anderson, 1993). By characterizing the design challenge as a problem of evidence and inference, the solutions may be found in new models of intelligence measurement (Mislevy, 2000).

We begin by identifying the coordinates of where the student model fits in the larger framework of ITSs. This is followed by a sampling of a number of relatively new approaches to model-based educational measurement, and a discussion of their potential to drive cognitive diagnoses. We conclude with a discussion of a number of promising areas for further research and development.

THE STUDENT MODEL

The conceptual basis of an ITS is straightforward. On a general level, it is a computer program or set of programs designed to teach a body of knowledge, monitor what is learned, and adapt instruction to meet the needs of the learner. The AI literature reflects considerable agreement that, in general, an ITS consists of four distinct components: (a) expert knowledge module, (b) student model, (c) instructional module, and (d) user interface (Barr & Feigenbaum, 1982; Burns, Parlett, & Redfield, 1991; Nwana, 1990). The *expert knowledge* module is an organized database of the domain-specific knowledge, both declarative and procedural. The *student model* module is typically designed to build a knowledge base of the student as a learner, and over time the system updates that knowledge as the learner interacts with the expert knowledge module. Pedagogical decisions, in turn, are executed by the *instructional module*. The *user interface* provides a way for the learner to interact with the ITS.

The student model, which encompasses both the learner's knowledge and behavior as she interacts with the ITS, acts as a guidance system that helps navigate the student through the domain's knowledge base. It also serves the instructional module by informing problem selection, providing advice and coaching, often signaling the need for additional explanatory information when cognitive errors or misconceptions arise. It is this component of the ITS that could benefit most from stronger measurement models.

A number of design principles for student models have emerged. Ohlsson (1987) outlined two. The first is the *principle of pragmatic diagnosis*, which states that "the purpose of the diagnostic component of an intelligent tutoring system is to support the execution of its instructional plan" (p. 212). Put simply, the student model should provide inferences that allow for engaging the instructional options available within the ITS. The level and number of inferences about the students' abilities should be aligned with the available instructional options. Ohlsson's second design feature, the *principle of expectation testing*, suggests that "the function of the diagnostic component of the intelligent tutoring system is to test whether expectations presupposed by the tutor's current plan are consistent with its current model of the student" (p. 214). Said differently, the student model, like other forms of educational measurement, is required to have a high degree of internal consistency and should reliably anticipate student responses and behaviors (Gitomer, Steinberg, & Mislevy, 1995; Mislevy, 1994).

Gitomer et al. (1995) recently added yet a third principle, the *principle of appropriate claims of competency*, which asserts that "a function of the diagnostic component of an intelligent tutoring system is to appropriately determine when the student has achieved a specified level of competency" (p. 2). This additional principle references what the student knows or can do. As such the student model is viewed as a module that assigns probabilities of how likely it is that the learner will succeed on a set of problems or task administered as part of the ITS or on criteria external to the tutoring system. This is akin to standard setting, establishing criteria for judging success or achievement.

When viewed in the context of these three design principles, the student model component, as noted earlier, can be seen as a form of continuous educational measurement (Bunderson, Inouye, & Olsen, 1989). As a form of measurement, the student model functions to gather evidence and permit inferences about the level and degree of student understanding of the subject matter. Bunderson et al. (1989) termed this *intelligent measurement*—measurement instantiated in a computer system that interacts with the learner much as an expert advisor. Framed squarely as a problem in ITS design, Bunderson et al. (1989) suggested that . . .

> Intelligent measurement can use machine intelligence to (a) score complex constructed responses involved in items and in reference tasks, (b) generate interpretations based on individual profiles of scores, and (c) provide prescriptive advice to learners and teachers, to optimize progress through a curriculum. (p. 399)

When framed as an ITS design element, these inferences generated through intelligent measurement lead explicitly and directly to a series of pedagogical decisions and activities (i.e., choosing instructional modules [sequencing], redirecting the student's learning, providing explanations or scaffolding learning, etc.). As an assessment method, a student model that is well integrated into the ITS requires attention to the cognitive model of performance within the domain, as well as selection of an appropriate psychometric model to guide the subsequent cognitive diagnosis (Gitomer et al., 1995; Mislevy, Steinberg, Breyer, Almond, & Johnson, 2002).

INTEGRATING COGNITIVE SCIENCE, PSYCHOLOGY, AND PSYCHOMETRICS

Contemporary theories of learning based on work in cognitive science, psychology, and educational measurement provide us with a view of learning that highlights the active role of the learner in constructing knowledge by structuring and restructuring information and automating procedures. This cognitive perspective on human learning is influencing our notions of educational measurement and assessment. Indeed it provides measurement specialists with a scientific basis for rethinking the foundations of assessment (National Research Council, 2001). This array of newer measurement models has direct relevance to the complexity of learning as instantiated in the ITS student model problem. As Snow and Lohman (1993) eloquently stated:

> The possibility now exists to bring new concepts and measures of aptitude, learning, development, and achievement, together with instructional innovations, to create truly diagnostic and adaptive systems. But we must learn how to use the new psychometric, substantive, and technological advances in concert to do it right. This is the main challenge for the 1990s. (p. 1)

Work by VanLehn and Martin (1998) using *Olae*—the On-Line/Off-Line Assessment of Expertise—represents an instantiation of the challenge articulated by Snow and Lohman (1993). For example, *Olae* uses a Bayesian inference network (Mislevy, 1995) to assess students' knowledge within well-specified domains such as physics or mathematics. As such, *Olae* attempts to measure *what* a student knows. This contrasts with more conventional forms of assessment, which gauge *how much* a student knows about a particular content domain. As Martin and VanLehn (1995) noted, in the past most student model designs relied on heuristics to analyze the learner's responses and make instructional decisions. Yet often a heuristic design is not good enough to guide instruction.

Classical psychometric models—those underlying the first generation of student models—were developed largely to permit inferences about how much knowledge, aptitude, or ability an individual possesses. These classical models are useful for inferences related to selection and placement, but they are much less helpful for making instructional decisions. With the emergence of a cognitive perspective on learning and instruction, the emphasis shifts from tests and assessments stressing how much a student has learned, or where he or she ranks on some continuum of achievement, to a focus on the importance of how knowledge is organized and how students reorganize that knowledge to represent and solve problems. That is, they begin to tell us more about *what* students know. More to the point, this shift in perspective moves educational measurement away from models that simply provide ability estimates based on the frequency and number of correct responses to test questions or probes in an ITS. Indeed these theoretical shifts underscore the need for measurement models that distinguish learners in terms of their knowledge states or in terms of their knowledge representations, cognitive processes, and strategies for solving problems. These new measurement models are needed by intelligent tutoring systems as well.

If ITS design is to move into the mainstream along with other instructional delivery systems, it will have to work in situations where its use has increasingly higher stakes for individual students, schools, and training organizations. Building student models based on sound and defensible analytic methods, therefore, is an important goal for ITS designers. Recent developments in cognitive science, psychology, and educational measurement may make it possible to move beyond heuristics to model-based measurement in ITS within the next few years. The dawning of a new age of cognitive psychometrics, particularly at a time when we are witnessing a gradual maturing of instructional science, may provide the measurement models needed to achieve these breakthroughs (National Research Council, 2001).

THE PROMISE OF NEW APPROACHES

In response to the challenge articulated by Snow and Lohman (1993), a number of new and promising psychometric approaches with a decidedly cognitive flavor are being developed. The work by Martin and VanLehn (1995, 1998) referred to earlier is one example. The educational measurement literature and the work currently being done under the general rubric of cognitive diagnosis (see e.g., Nichols, Chipman, & Brennan, 1995) contain a number of examples and approaches. These include, for example, latent trait models (Samejima, 1995), statistical pattern classification methods (Tatsuoka, 1985, 1990), and causal probabilistic networks (Pearl, 1988, 2000). The interested reader can find statistical details of these models and methods reviewed in a paper by Junker (1999) prepared for the National Research Council.

As noted earlier, these approaches do not aim simply to rank students along a dimension of proficiency. Rather these models, albeit in somewhat different ways, attempt to build on detailed task analyses, presumed production rules, representations of knowledge structures, and earlier work on "bug" detection to create cognitively sound assessments with strong instructional validity (Bennett, Enright, & Tatsuoka, 1991). In that sense, these models can be characterized as extensions of earlier work on student models (see e.g., VanLehn, 1988).

A representative set of these new measurement approaches is described in this section. It is helpful to keep in mind that what follows is not intended as an exhaustive review of the various models and their applications. Nor is this sampling intended to represent a full and complete discussion of the available sets of other less measurement-oriented models, which is beyond the scope of this chapter. It may also be useful to note that many other studies could have been included in this review, but for purposes of exposition it may be more informative to focus the discussion on the general classes of available models.

In general, a number of the methods presented next can be viewed as extensions to item response theoretic (IRT) measurement models, including the unidimensional one-, two-, and three-parameter models (Embretson & Hershberger,

1999; Hambleton & Swaminathan, 1984; Lord & Novick, 1968). Others build on the recent work on multidimensional latent-trait IRT models introduced by Samejima (1973), Reckase (1985), and Embretson (1990). Still others, like those growing out of the work on neural networks (Caudill & Butter, 1992) and Bayesian inference networks (Martin & VanLehn, 1995), represent attempts to capitalize on pattern-recognition methods for gathering evidence and supporting inferences. Many of these measurement models assume several solution strategies on the student's part when solving problems. Others, in contrast, attempt to provide descriptions of the students' knowledge or ability structures. If successfully developed and adapted for computer-based instructional environments, these models may in the future be useful for dynamically linking assessment and instruction in ITS.

Latent Trait Models

As psychometric theory advanced over the past three decades, classical test theory—measurement principles and methods based on observed scores—has been supplanted gradually by IRT models (see e.g., Hambleton & Swaminathan, 1984; Lord & Novick, 1968). In general, the IRT family of models attempts to express the relationship between performance on an item (or a problem in ITS terminology) and achievement as a mathematical function, typically approximated as a logistic function. This class of models is appropriate for mapping student performance to an underlying (latent) ability, often referred to as a latent trait. Variations on these models are being developed to model the use of solution strategies in problem-solving contexts (Mislevy & Verhelst, 1990). Others attempt to model shifts in strategy (Gitomer & Yamamoto, 1991). Incorporating these model-based measurement techniques in ITS holds promise for strengthening student models because instructional decisions can be triggered by measurement approaches that characterize solution strategies or signal shifts in those strategies over the course of an instructional sequence.

The development of latent-trait models, which began by modeling performance on test items and extended problem sets that could be scored right or wrong (dichotomously), has advanced in recent years, and models are now available for use with nominal, continuous, and graded response problems. More important, these models are often developed specifically for use in situations where cognitive diagnosis is needed. A series of studies of students' models for electrical circuits (Gentner & Gentner, 1983) provides an example of how IRT models can be applied to distinguish different solution strategies. Gentner and Gentner (1983) suggested that students have differing mental models for how electric circuits are structured and function. Some hold a water flow model with batteries seen as reservoirs and resistors as dams holding back the flow of electricity. Others have a model of electricity that is analogous to a teeming crowd entering a subway, with resistors functioning like turnstiles that control crowd movement into and through the system (Masters & Mislevy, 1993). No doubt, each model is useful for a partial understanding of electrical system. Although better than having no model at all, neither the "water flow" nor the "teeming crowd" model permits a complete understanding of electrical circuitry. To further students' understanding and comprehension of the domain, it may be important for an ITS to distinguish between these two knowledge states and attempt to make repairs accordingly.

Following Masters and Mislevy (1993), an extended IRT model of students' responses on a test of electrical circuits, including knowledge of resistors and batteries, can be employed to make inferences about the nth students' state of understanding (f_n, an integer between 1 and K) and level of proficiency within that state (q_n). Equation 1 gives the probability of a correct response to item i from student n, who has an understanding state of k and a proficiency (knowledge state) of q_{ni}.

$$P(X_{ni} = 1 | q_n, f_n = k, bi_k) = f\, k(q_n,\, bi_k) \tag{1}$$

b_{ik} denotes the difficulty of problem i in proficiency state k, and f_k is a function that relates student and problem parameters to the probabilities of a correct response as they pertain only to students in state k. Many will recognize Equation 1 as a standard IRT model when students are modeled at only one level of understanding. The problem parameters b_{ik} vary from one level of student understanding to another, therefore providing qualitatively useful information to feedback through the ITS as it models the changes in understanding within students over time.

Assuming further that the ITS-based assessment questions or probes are scored right or wrong (although partial credit models may also be used), an extended IRT model can be used to estimate the probability of a correct response given that the student is in k state of understanding. More detailed illustrations of this approach are found in Mislevy and Verhelst (1990), Mislevy, Wingersky, Irvine, and Dann (1991), and Wilson (1984, 1989).

The problem of determining the knowledge space is central to the successful application of measurement models to student modeling. In addition to the approach detailed in the prior example, other researchers are developing measurement models based on latent trait theory, or extensions of it, that may also prove workable for defining the students' knowledge space. For example, work detailed in a series of papers by Samejima (1983, 1995) has led to the development of a *competency space* approach to cognitive diagnosis. Embretson (1985, 1990) developed multidimensional latent trait models for measuring learning in dynamic testing situations. Other cognitively motivated models are under development as well (see e.g., Bennett, 1993), including the Hierarchically Ordered Skills Test (HOST) model (Gitomer & Rock, 1993) and the HYBRID model (Yamamoto, 1987; Yamamoto & Gitomer, 1993). Although different in their measurement approaches, these models all hold promise for further explicating students' levels of understanding as they move through relatively well-defined content domains. For a more thorough discussion of these measurement models, the reader is referred to work by Frederiksen, Glaser, Lesgold, and Shafto (1990), Frederiksen, Mislevy, and Bejar (1993), and Bennett and Ward (1993).

Statistical Pattern-Recognition Methods

Tatsuoka and her colleagues (1983, 1987, 1993) developed a new methodology known as the *rule space* method that provides cognitive diagnoses and classifications. Tatsuoka's work generally builds from efforts to classify students' misconceptions or "bugs" when solving mathematical problems. In that regard, it is not unlike the *DEBUGGY* approach employed by VanLehn (1982) and others. The *rule space* method is based on a statistical pattern-recognition approach that classifies individuals into a number of cognitively meaningful groups established through careful task analysis of a domain. Hence, these groups are referred to as possessing a number of domain-specific knowledge states that are derived by applying probabilistic models to the learners' response patterns and, further, by applying variants of those models to the intersection of the item or problem attributes. Building on IRT methods, Tatsuoka's *rule space* model formulates a knowledge state classification space and uses Bayes' decision rules (Nunnally & Bernstein, 1994) to minimize those classification errors. The resulting classification space(s) are directly related to various knowledge state(s), and forms of misconceptions or bugs in the cognitive abilities are inferred. Thus, Tatsuoka's *rule space* model applies statistical pattern-recognition and classification methods derived from Boolean algebra to provide cognitive diagnoses of the learners' misconceptions or bugs.

The *rule space* classification procedure involves comparing students' score response patterns on a set of problems ($X_i = [x_{i1}, \ldots, x_{in}]$, where x_{in} is the response of the *i*th student to the *j*th problem and *n* is the number of problems in the pool of system) to the patterns expected or specified by a particular knowledge state. Once an ideal response pattern is defined for each knowledge state, and this could be done presumably as the ITS knowledge base for a particular domain is designed and built, the *rule space* classification procedure (Tatsuoka, 1985, 1987) can be employed to classify the students' observed response patterns, and attributions of mastery or competency can be assigned by the method and forwarded to the instructional module of the ITS. This methodology has been applied successfully in the domains of basic mathematics (Tatsuoka & Tatsuoka, 1992), algebra (Birenbaum, Kelly, & Tatsuoka, 1992), architecture (Katz, Martinez, Sheehan, & Tatsuoka, 1993), and document literacy (Sheehan & Mislevy, 1991). In the future, we can expect more refined instantiations of this approach to be applied to computer-based, adaptive testing systems where item or task selection algorithms will include not only rich information about the task, but also more distinct characterizations of the students' knowledge space.

Yet another statistical pattern-recognition method that holds promise for the next generation of ITS employs neural network architectures (Harp, Samad, & Villano, 1993; Kohonen, 1984) in aircraft navigation training. Neural networks—an outgrowth of AI research in the 1950s and 1960s—are a relatively recent development in the information sciences. These methods get their name and biological inspiration because the underlying computational units—networks of processing elements working in parallel—work much like we think neurons function in the brain (Nelson & Illingworth, 1991). In contrast to most computer programs, neural networks "learn" from a set of exemplary data and are not programmed as such. Because neural network learning procedures are inherently statistical methods, they have been applied with increasing frequency to problems of pattern recognition, classification, and psychometric research (Chance, Cheung, & Fagan, 1992; Dickieson & Gollub, 1992; Everson, Chance, & Lykins, 1994; Sands, 1991; Sands & Wilkins, 1991; Shadra & Patil, 1990).

The initial step in applying this approach requires building databases, domain-specific presumably, of students' responses to a series of well-defined problems (or test items). These databases currently exist and can be relatively easily derived from large-scale traditional paper-and-pencil or computer-based testing programs. Once the databases are created, students' knowledge spaces can be mapped using unsupervised neural network methods generally known as self-organizing feature maps (Kohonen, 1984). Repeated iterations of the neural net methods "train" the system, and the resulting feature maps can be used by the computer-based tutoring system as an online knowledge state classification methodology. For purposes of explication, a prototypical neural network architecture is depicted in Fig. 10.1. The students' item or task responses (X_1 through X_n) form the initial input vector for the network. Network architectures similar to the prototype in Fig. 10.1, for example, are used to detect patterns and make classifications (i.e., knowledge states) in large, domain-specific item/task response databases. Currently, these connectionist networks are used in many fields—from psychology to finance to manufacturing—to graphically organize response patterns and uncover relationships in large datasets. Because the networks "learn" from training on these datasets, in theory they could be constrained in an ITS framework to produce multiple output layers representative of students' knowledge space(s).

Although still in the early stages of development, applying neural network and connectionist approaches to the student modeling problem appears promising. Harp et al. (1993) had some initial success in applying these connectionist techniques to the development of a *model of the universe of student knowledge (MUSK)*. Capitalizing on the pattern-recognition strengths of artificial neural networks, *MUSK* learns about the knowledge states of students from analyses of exemplary sets of student performance data. The strategy outlined by Harp et al. (1993) calls for integrating the trained neural nets complete with the feature map-

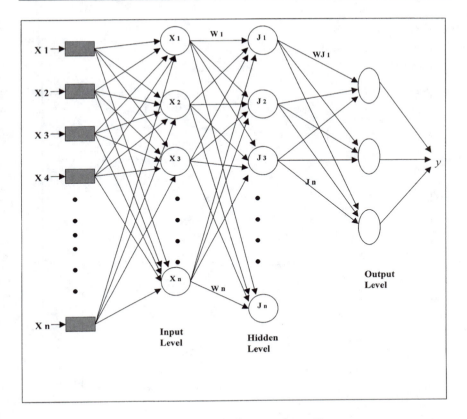

FIG. 10.1.   Neural net back propagation architecture.

ping of students' knowledge spaces. These mapped knowledge spaces, in turn, are used to make predictions and generate inferences about how students will perform on sets of problems stored in the ITS. This integration is represented in Fig. 10.2.

For Harp et al. (1993), the mapping of the knowledge states occurs as the neural nets are trained on response data, as represented by the vector of items on the left side of Fig. 10.2. The networks then monitor performance on the ITS tasks, represented by the vector of tasks or items on the right side of Fig. 10.2. These operations would iterate periodically during the tutoring cycle, and the system would then update its inferences about the student's knowledge state. Thus, the *MUSK* approach is theoretically capable of supporting adaptive assessment, monitoring student progress, selecting and providing scaffolded learning sequences, and providing student feedback. Like the *rule space* method described earlier, the network structure of the feature mapping model is determined analytically and iteratively because the number of knowledge states underlying the database is not initially well defined.

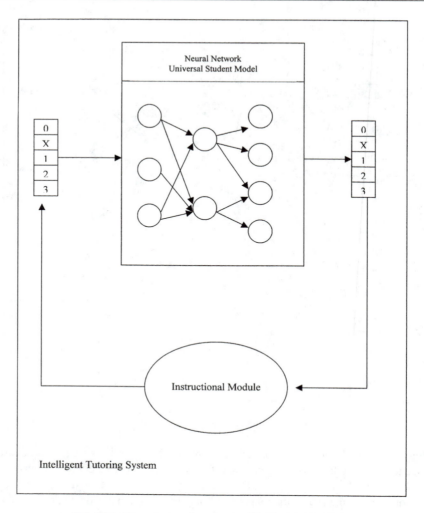

FIG. 10.2.   Neural network student model: The MUSK model.

The work of Harp and his colleagues represents one of the earliest applications of neural network technology to the student modeling problem. Although theoretically rich and technologically promising, the applications to ITS still have a way to go before they can be implemented. Aircraft navigation and performance in mathematics are two domains where work is currently underway. This technology, however, is growing rapidly, and many groups are exploring linkages between neural networks and knowledge-based diagnostic systems. The interested reader can find more details on neural networks and their applications in Caudill and Butler (1992) and Nelson and Illingworth (1991).

Bayesian Inference Networks

As we see from the work of both Tatsuoka (1987, 1990). and Harp et al. (1993), with the statistical pattern-recognition tools now available, it is possible to design and implement pattern-recognition networks in large and complex systems of student response variables, the types of databases typical of large-scale testing programs. The extent of their utility, however, may well rest on how much confidence we have in the sets of inferences drawn from these statistical pattern-recognition methods. Bayesian inference networks or, alternatively, causal probability networks may strengthen the systems' ability to draw reasonably sound inferences about the students' knowledge states. In general, Bayesian networks are complex sets of interdependent variables that provide a statistical framework for reasoning under conditions of uncertainty (Martin & VanLehn, 1995; Mislevy, 1995; Pearl, 1988). These inference networks have been implemented with some success in a variety of fields, including medical diagnosis (Lauritzen & Spiegelhalter, 1988), physics (Martin & VanLehn, 1995), troubleshooting (Gitomer et al., 1995), and proportional reasoning (Bélan & Mislevy, 1992). In all these instances, the inference problem is the same—the system or network must reason abductively from a set of observations (i.e., combinations of known task parameters and response variables gathered in a theory-driven framework) to a student model. Thus, in theory, Bayesian networks are able to build on statistical pattern-recognition methods, extend them to draw inferences about the probabilistic structure of the student model, update the ITS's "beliefs," and diagnose the students' knowledge states.

Mislevy (1994, 1995) provided an illustration of this approach that applies Bayesian inferences networks to data derived from students attempting to solve a set of mixed-number subtraction problems. In this example, 530 students completed 15 mathematical items. Typically, the students used one of two different strategies to solve the math problems. Using *Method A*, students always converted mixed numbers to improper fractions, subtracted, and, if necessary, reduced the fraction. Under *Method B*, students separated the mixed numbers into whole numbers and fractional parts, subtracted one from the other as two problems, borrowing from one whole number if needed, and reduced if necessary. In this application, the student model includes a variable that represents which method the student used, as well as which set of subprocedures were applied. Figure 10.3 provides a directed acyclic graphic description of the connections and interrelationships between and among the skills subsumed under *Method B*.

The boxes in Fig. 10.3 represent the skill sets needed to solve the various math items. These skill sets are arranged somewhat hierarchically and presented to show the relationship of the subsets of skills used under *Method B* to solve the problems at each level of difficulty. The directional arrows signify the dependence of the relationships between and among the skills. Much like the earlier models associated with latent trait methods or statistical pattern-recognition tech-

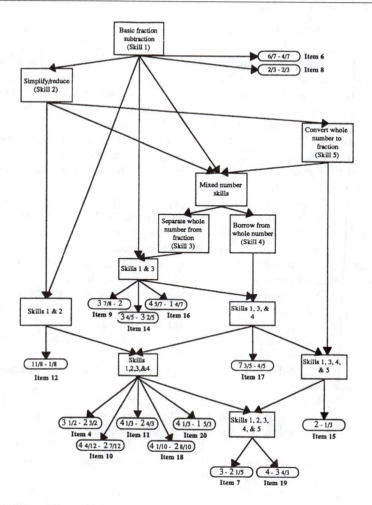

Adapted from Mislevy (1994).

FIG. 10.3.   A directed acyclic graph of a solution strategy for mixed number subtraction problems.

niques, theory-based cognitive task analyses provide the structure of the network
used in this example. Figure 10.4 shows the initial baseline conditional probabilities of possessing the requisite skills and the percent correct on the test items, with
the conditional probabilities derived from prior analyses using Tatsuoka's (1983,
1987, 1993) *rule space* model.

The joint probability distribution of the network of variables in Fig. 10.4 is
simply the product of the conditional probabilities, with individual variables char-

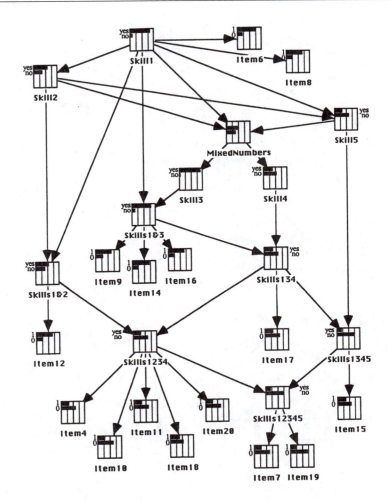

Adapted from Mislevy (1994).

Note: Bars indicate probability estimates, and sum to one for all possible values of a variable.

FIG. 10.4. An initial baseline inference network for solution method B.

acterized by the conditional probabilities of its "parents" (i.e., the preceding boxes in the graph). As Mislevy (1994) described it, Fig. 10.4 represents "the state of knowledge one would have about a student known to use *Method B*, before observing any item responses" (p. 463).

Following Mislevy (1994), Fig. 10.5 shows the inference network for *Method B* once the observational data enter the system. Thus, what we see is how the in-

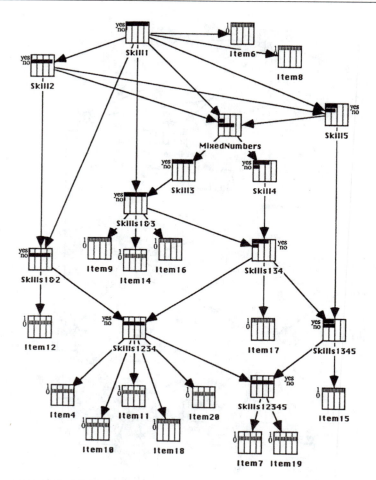

Adapted from Mislevy (1994).

Note: Bars indicate probability estimates, and sum to one for all possible values of a variable. Shaded bars denote certainty based on observed responses.

FIG. 10.5.   An updated inference network for solution method B.

ference networks reflect changes in the "beliefs" or conditional probabilities after students' responses are observed. Again Mislevy (1994) noted, "the updated probabilities for the five skills required for various items under *Method B* show substantial shifts away from the base-rate, toward the belief that the student commands Skills 1, 3, 4, and possibly 5, but almost certainly not Skill 2" (p. 467).

Thus, after gathering observational data and updating the set of conditional probabilities, by comparing the conditional probability estimates in Figs. 10.4 and

10.5 for the use or application of each skill, we begin to detect shifts in the inferences the system makes about whether the student possesses certain skills. The student model is refined and, indeed, could be augmented with additional information about strategy use or supplemented with information about the instructional opportunities students were exposed to prior to the assessment. Obviously, the same inference network approach could be used for *Method A* as well. Further development of these approaches is expected to lead to the creation of extended networks that incorporate strategy switching within and throughout content domains. Indeed following the reasoning of Harp et al. (1993) and others (Martin & VanLehn, 1995), it is not difficult to imagine that these probability-based inference networks will eventually be developed as expert systems and incorporated into ITS in the future.

CONCLUSION

The classes of educational measurement models outlined in this chapter are involved in integrating cognitive psychology and model-based measurement approaches into our thinking about the designs of student models in ITS. By drawing on cognitive theory and analysis, the core idea in the methods and approaches discussed here is to use statistical tools, coupled with psychological learning theory, to define a space representing the student model following Mislevy (1993) and VanLehn (1988). Indeed these various measurement models can all be viewed as forms of intelligent measurement (Bennett, 1993; Bunderson et al., 1989) and as efforts that synthesize methods and techniques from three vital research areas—AI and expert systems, modern psychometrics, and cognitive psychology.

Although I have attempted to introduce intelligent model-based measurement approaches and describe how they can be used to address the issues of student modeling in ITS, many if not all of the areas for future research identified earlier by Martin and VanLehn (1995), VanLehn and Martin (1998) require further exploration. For example, more work needs to be done on the painstaking task analyses that foreshadow model development in various domains. Just how fine grained should the models be? Similarly, the number and quality of the assessment tasks requires attention from researchers. Efforts to map the knowledge spaces in various domains will probably pay large dividends for student model development as well. As computer technology advances, it will bring with it the ability to monitor and incorporate evidence of other cognitively relevant constructs—such as metacognitive abilities, learning styles, and response mode preferences—that in theory could be incorporated into student models and increase their informational bandwidth. As more information becomes available to the system, integrated models of cognition, learning, instruction, and assessment will be needed. The line of measurement research described here has implications for developing assessment methods that incorporate cognitive theory and thereby facilitate instruction, and in the not too distant future it may result in more effective student models for ITS.

REFERENCES

Anderson, J. R. (1993). *Rules of the mind.* Hillsdale, NJ: Lawrence Erlbaum Associates.

Barr, A., & Feigenbaum, E. A. (1982). *The handbook of artificial intelligence,* 2. Los Altos, CA: Kaufman.

Bélan, A., & Mislevy, R. J. (1992). Probability-based inference in a domain of proportional reasoning tasks. *ETS Research Report 92-15-ONR.* Princeton, NJ: Educational Testing Service.

Bennett, R. E. (1993). Toward intelligent assessment: An integration of constructed-response testing, artificial intelligence, and model-based measurement. In N. Frederiksen, R. J. Mislevy, & I. Bejar (Eds.), *Test theory for a new generation of tests* (pp. 99–124). Hillsdale, NJ: Lawrence Erlbaum Associates.

Bennett, R. E., Enright, M., & Tatsuoka, K. (1991). *Developing measurement approaches for constructed-response formats* (ETS Technical Report). Princeton, NJ: Educational Testing Service.

Bennett, R. E., & Ward, W. C. (Eds.). (1993). *Construction versus choice in cognitive measurement: Issues in constructed response, performance testing, and portfolio assessment.* Hillsdale, NJ: Lawrence Erlbaum Associates.

Birenbaum, M., Kelly, A. E., & Tatsuoka, K. (1992). *Diagnosing knowledge states in algebra using the rule space model* (ETS Tech. Rep. RR-92-57-ONR). Princeton, NJ: Educational Testing Service.

Bunderson, C. V., Inouye, D. K., & Olsen, J. B. (1989). The four generations of computerized educational measurement. In R. L. Linn (Ed.), *Educational measurement* (3rd ed., pp. 367–407). New York: Macmillan.

Burns, H., Parlett, J. W., & Redfield, C. L. (1991). *Intelligent tutoring systems: Evolution in design.* Hillsdale, NJ: Lawrence Erlbaum Associates.

Burton, R. R. (1982). Diagnosing bugs in a simple procedural skill. In D. H. Sleeman & J. S. Brown (Eds.), *Intelligent tutoring systems* (pp. 157–184). London: Academic Press.

Caudill, M., & Butler, C. (1992). *Understanding neural networks: Vol. 1.* Cambridge, MA: Massachusetts Institute of Technology.

Chance, D., Cheung, J., & Fagan, J. (1992). *Short term forecasting by neural networks while incorporating known characteristics.* Paper submitted for presentation to the International Conference on Neural Networks.

Dickieson, J., & Gollub, L. (1992). *Artificial neural networks and training. Independent research and independent exploratory development programs: FY91 annual report.* San Diego, CA: Navy Personnel Research and Development Center.

Diognon, J. P., & Falmagne, J. C. (1985). Spaces for the assessment of knowledge. *International Journal of Man-Machine Studies, 23,* 175–196.

Embretson, S. E. (1985). Multicomponent latent trait models for test design. In S. E. Embretson (Ed.), *Test design: Developments in psychology and psychometrics* (pp. 195–218). Orlando, FL: Academic Press.

Embretson, S. E. (1990). Diagnostic testing by measuring learning processes: Psychometric considerations for dynamic testing. In N. Frederiksen, R. L. Glaser, A. M. Lesgold, & M. G. Shafto (Eds.), *Diagnostic monitoring of skill and knowledge acquisition* (pp. 407–432). Hillsdale, NJ: Lawrence Erlbaum Associates.

Embretson, S. E., & Hershberger, S. L. (1999). *The new rules of measurement.* Hillsdale, NJ: Lawrence Erlbaum Associates.

Everson, H. T., Chance, D., & Lykins, S. (1994, April). *Exploring the use of artificial neural networks in educational research.* Paper presented at the American Educational Research Association meeting, New Orleans, LA.

Frederiksen, N., Glaser, R., Lesgold, A., & Shafto, M. (1990). *Diagnostic monitoring of skill and knowledge acquisition.* Hillsdale, NJ: Lawrence Erlbaum Associates.

Frederiksen, N., Mislevy, R. J., & Bejar, I. I. (1993). *Test theory for a new generation of tests.* Hillsdale, NJ: Lawrence Erlbaum Associates.

Gentner, D., & Gentner, D. R. (1983). Flowing waters or teeming crowds: Mental models of electricity. In D. Gentner & A. Stevens (Eds.), *Mental models* (pp. 99–129). Hillsdale, NJ: Lawrence Erlbaum Associates.

Gitomer, D. H., & Rock, D. (1993). Addressing process variables in test analysis. In N. Frederiksen, R. J. Mislevy, & I. Bejar (Eds.), *Test theory for a new generation of tests* (pp. 243–268). Hillsdale, NJ: Lawrence Erlbaum Associates.

Gitomer, D. H., Steinberg, L. S., & Mislevy, R. J. (1995). Diagnostic assessment of troubleshooting skill in an intelligent tutoring system. In P. Nichols, S. Chipman, & R. Brennan (Eds.), *Cognitive diagnostic assessment* (pp. 73–101). Hillsdale, NJ: Lawrence Erlbaum Associates.

Gitomer, D. H., & Yamamoto, K. (1991). Performance modeling that integrates latent trait and latent class theory. *Journal of Educational Measurement, 28,* 173–189.

Hambleton, R. K., & Swaminathan, H. (1984). *Item response theory: Principles and applications.* Boston, MA: Kluwer.

Harp, S. A., Samad, T., & Villano, M. (1993). *Modeling student knowledge with self-organizing feature maps* (Armstrong Laboratory Tech. Rep. AL-TR-1992-0114). Texas: U.S. Air Force.

Johnson, W. L., & Soloway, E. M. (1984). *PROUST: Knowledge-based program debugging.* Proceedings of the Seventh International Software Engineering Conference, Orlando, FL.

Junker, B. (1999). *Some statistical models and computational methods that may be useful for cognitively-relevant assessment.* Paper prepared for the National Research Council Committee on the Foundation of Assessment. http://www.stat.cm.edu/~brian/nrc/cfa/ [April 2, 2001].

Katz, I. R., Martinez, M. E., Sheehan, K. M., & Tatsuoka, K. (1993). *Extending the rule space model to a semantically rich domain: Diagnostic assessment in architecture* (ETS Tech. Rep. RR-93-42-ONR). Princeton, NJ: Educational Testing Service.

Kohonen, T. E. (1984). *Self-organization and associative memory.* New York: Springer-Verlag.

Lauritzen, S. L., & Spiegelhalter, D. J. (1988). Local computations with probabilities on graphical structures and their application to expert systems. *Journal of the Royal Statistical Society, Series B, 50,* 157–224.

Lord, F. M., & Novick, M. R. (1968). *Statistical theories of mental test scores.* Reading, MA: Addison-Wesley.

Lykins, S., & Chance, D. (1992, February). *Comparing artificial neural networks and multiple regression for predictive application.* Paper presented at Southwestern Psychological Society, Austin, TX.

Martin, J. D., & VanLehn, K. (1995). A Bayesian approach to cognitive assessment. In P. Nichols, S. Chipman, & R. Brennan (Eds.), *Cognitively diagnostic assessment* (pp. 141–165). Hillsdale, NJ: Lawrence Erlbaum Associates.

Masters, G., & Mislevy, R. J. (1993). New views of student learning: Implications for educational measurement. In N. Frederiksen, R. J. Mislevy, & I. Bejar (Eds.), *Test theory for a new generation of tests* (pp. 219–242). Hillsdale, NJ: Lawrence Erlbaum Associates.

Messick, S. (1994). The interplay of evidence and consequences in the validation of performance assessments. *Educational Researcher, 32*(2), 13–23.

Mislevy, R. J. (1993). Foundations of a new test theory. In N. Frederiksen, R. J. Mislevy, & I. Bejar (Eds.), *Test theory for a new generation of tests* (pp. 19–40). Hillsdale, NJ: Lawrence Erlbaum Associates.

Mislevy, R. J. (1994). Evidence and inference in educational assessment. *Psychometrika, 59*(4), 439–584.

Mislevy, R. J. (1995). Probability-based inference in cognitive diagnosis. In P. Nichols, S. Chipman, & R. Brennan (Eds.), *Cognitive diagnostic assessment* (pp. 43–71). Hillsdale, NJ: Lawrence Erlbaum Associates.

Mislevy, R. J. (2000). Modeling in complex assessments. *The NERA Researcher, 38*, 7–17.

Mislevy, R. J., Steinberg, L. S., Breyer, F. J., Almond, R. G., & Johnson, L. (2002). Making sense of data from complex assessment. *Applied Measurement in Education, 15*, 363–378.

Mislevy, R. J., & Verhelst, N. (1990). Modeling item responses when different subjects employ different solution strategies. *Psychometrika, 55*, 195–215.

Mislevy, R. J., Wingersky, M. S., Irvine, S. H., & Dann, P. L. (1991). Resolving mixtures of strategies in spatial visualization tasks. *British Journal of Mathematical and Statistical Psychology, 44*, 265–288.

National Research Council. (2001). *Knowing what students know: The science and design of educational assessment. Committee on the Foundation of Assessment* (J. Pelligrims, N. Chudorosky, & R. Gloser, Eds.). Washington, DC: National Academic Press.

Nelson, M. M., & Illingworth, W. T. (1991). *A practical guide to neural nets.* Reading, MA: Addison-Wesley.

Nichols, P., Chipman, S., & Brennan, R. (Eds.). (1995). *Cognitive diagnostic assessment.* Hillsdale, NJ: Lawrence Erlbaum Associates.

Nunnally, J. C., & Bernstein, I. H. (1994). *Psychometric theory.* New York: McGraw-Hill.

Nwana, H. S. (1990). Intelligent tutoring systems: An overview. *Artificial Intelligence Review, 4*(4), 251–257.

Ohlsson, S. (1987). Some principles of intelligent tutoring. In R. W. Lawler & M. Yazdani (Eds.), *Artificial intelligence in education* (Vol. 1, pp. 203–237). Norwood, NJ: Ablex.

Pearl, J. (1988). *Probabilistic reasoning in intelligent systems: Networks of plausible inference.* San Mateo, CA: Morgan Kaufmann.

Pearl, J. (2000). *Causality: Models, reasoning and inference.* New York: Cambridge University Press.

Reckase, M. D. (1985). The difficulty of test items that measure more than one ability. *Applied Psychological Measurement, 9*, 401–412.

Samejima, F. (1973). Homogenous case of the continuous response model. *Psychometrika, 38*, 203–219.

Samejima, F. (1983). *A latent trait model for differential strategies in cognitive processes* (Tech. Rep. ONR/RR-83-1). Knoxville, TN: Office of Naval Research, University of Tennessee.

Samejima, F. (1995). A cognitive diagnosis method using latent trait models: Competency space approach and its relationship with DiBello and Stout's unified cognitive psychometric diagnosis model. In P. D. Nichols, S. F. Chipman, & R. L. Brennan (Eds.), *Cognitive diagnostic assessment* (pp. 391–410). Hillsdale, NJ: Lawrence Erlbaum Associates.

Sands, W. A. (1991, August). *Artificial neural networks: A tool for psychologists.* Paper presented at the 33rd annual conference of the Military Testing Association, San Antonio, TX.

Sands, W. A., & Wilkins, C. A. (1991, August). *Artificial neural networks for personnel selection.* Paper presented at the 33rd annual conference of the Military Testing Association, San Antonio, TX.

Shadra, R., & Patil, R. B. (1990). *Neural networks as forecasting experts: An empirical test.* Proceedings of the International Joint Conference on Neural Networks, Washington, DC.

Sheehan, K. M., & Mislevy, R. J. (1990). Integrating cognitive and psychometric models in a measure of document literacy. *Journal of Educational Measurement, 27*, 255–272.

Sheehan, K. M., Tatsuoka, K. K., & Lewis, C. (1993). *A diagnostic classification model for document processing skills* (ETS Tech. Rep. RR-93-39-ONR). Princeton, NJ: Educational Testing Service.

Simon, H. (1987). Guest foreward. In S. C. Shapiro (Ed.), *Encyclopedia of artificial intelligence* (Vol. 1). New York: Wiley.

Sleeman, & Brown, J. S. (Eds.). (1982). *Intelligent tutoring systems*. London: Academic Press.

Snow, R. E., & Lohman, D. F. (1989). Implications of cognitive psychology for educational measurement. In R. L. Linn (Ed.), *Educational measurement* (3rd ed., pp. 263–331). New York: Macmillan.

Snow, R. E., & Lohman, D. F. (1993). *Cognitive psychology, new test design, and new test theory: An introduction*. In N. Frederiksen, R. J. Mislevy, & I. I. Bejar (Eds.), *Test theory for a new generation of tests*. Hillsdale, NJ: Lawrence Erlbaum Associates.

Tatsuoka, K. K. (1983). Rule space: An approach for dealing with misconceptions based on item response theory. *Journal of Educational Measurement, 20*(4), 345–354.

Tatsuoka, K. K. (1985). A probabilistic model for diagnosing misconceptions in the pattern classification approach. *Journal of Educational Statistics, 12*(1), 55–73.

Tatsuoka, K. K. (1987). Validation of cognitive sensitivity for item response curves. *Journal of Educational Measurement, 24*, 233–245.

Tatsuoka, K. K. (1990). Toward an integration of item-response theory and cognitive error diagnoses. In N. Frederiksen, R. L. Glaser, A. M. Lesgold, & M. G. Shafto (Eds.), *Diagnostic monitoring of skill and knowledge acquisition* (pp. 453–488). Hillsdale, NJ: Lawrence Erlbaum Associates.

Tatsuoka, K. K. (1993). Item construction and psychometric models appropriate for constructed responses. In R. E. Bennett & W. C. Ward (Eds.), *Construction versus choice in cognitive measurement: Issues in constructed response, performance testing, and portfolio assessment* (pp. 238–253). Hillsdale, NJ: Lawrence Erlbaum Associates.

Tatsuoka, K. K., & Tatsuoka, M. M. (1983). Bug distribution and statistical pattern classification. *Psychometrika, 2*, 193–206.

Tatsuoka, K. K., & Tatsuoka, M. M. (1992). *A psychometrically sound cognitive diagnostic model: Effect of remediation as empirical validity* (ETS Research Report). Princeton, NJ: Educational Testing Service.

VanLehn, K. (1982). Bugs are not enough: Empirical studies of bugs, impasses, and repairs in procedural skills. *Journal of Mathematical Behavior, 3*, 3–72.

VanLehn, K. (1988). Student modeling. In M. C. Polson & J. J. Richardson (Eds.), *Foundations of intelligent tutoring systems* (pp. 55–78). Hillsdale, NJ: Lawrence Erlbaum Associates.

VanLehn, K. (1990). *Mind bugs: The origins of procedural misconceptions*. Cambridge, MA: MIT Press.

VanLehn, K., & Martin, J. (1998). Evolution of assessment system based on Bayesian student modeling. *International Journal of Artificial Intelligence and Education, 8*(2), 179–221.

Wilson, M. (1984). *A psychometric model of hierarchical development*. Unpublished doctoral dissertation, University of Chicago.

Wilson, M. (1989). Saltus: A psychometric model of discontinuity in cognitive development. *Psychological Bulletin, 105*(2), 276–289.

Yamamoto, K. (1987). *A model that combines IRT and latent class models*. Unpublished doctoral dissertation, University of Illinois, Champaign-Urbana.

Yamamoto, K., & Gitomer, D. H. (1993). Application of a HYBRID model to test of cognitive skill representation. In N. Frederiksen, R. J. Mislevy, & I. Bejar (Eds.), *Test theory for a new generation of tests* (pp. 275–296). Hillsdale, NJ: Lawrence Erlbaum Associates.

Author Index

Subject Index

CIRCSIM-Tutor, 171
Closed-world domain, 158, 159, 161
Cognition, 21, 39, 62, 101
Cognitive load, 167
Cognitive science
  discipline of, 37
  limited capacity assumption of, 37
  and multimedia learning, 37, 45–47
  and student model, 184
  theories of, 184
Coherence principle, 41–43, 45
Collaboration, 60, 62, 72, 77, 80
  in software design, 77–79, 81, 85, 98
  student benefits of, 60, 62, 63, 65, 78, 80
College admissions, 102
College students, 107, 108
Columbus effect, 133, 134
Community of learners, 55, 64, 65, 71
Community of practice, 63
Competency space, 190
Comprehension, 12
Computer programming, 78
Computer-based instruction, 53, 56, 77, 123,
    126, 130
  history of, 125, 126
  and pacing of learning, 128–130
Computer-based research, 62
Computer-based testing, 112–116
Computer-mediated communication, 143–146,
    148, 150–153
  evaluation, 150
  message types, 144, 147, 148
Computers, 24, 123
  competence with, 64–66
  learning about, 64
  recreational use of, 62
  skills, 53, 55, 59
  as solitary activity, 54
  technology, 3, 53, 123, 124
  tutoring, 158, 171, 183
Constructivist learning, 7
Content screens, 85, 86, 92

D

DEBUGGY, 184
Decision making, 136
Delphi forums, 144
Design-differentiated scores, 83, 88, 89, 95

Digital divide, 53
Discourse prosthesis, 171
Distance learning, 108, 143, 150
Dual-channel assumption, 37

E

eBay, 104, 105
Educational and informational content, 28, 29
Educational aspirations, 64, 67, 68
Educational comprehension, 11
Educational content, 4, 6, 7, 9, 12, 14, 15, 21
Educational measurement, 184–186, 188
Educational media, 3–6, 8–10, 12, 14–16, 26,
    29, 87
Educational technology, 4, 110–112, 121–123
Educational television, 3, 6, 27
Electronic bulletin boards, 63
Electronic toys, 3
E-mail, 143
Employment, 107
Encyclopedia Britannica, 106
Ethnography, 58
Expert knowledge module, 185

F

Fat Albert and the Cosby Kids, 23, 27
Federal Communications Commission (FCC),
    28
Fifth Dimension Program, 57, 58
Formal features, 13, 19, 20, 22, 23, 25, 26, 29

G

Games, 4, 14
Gender, 80
  differences, 80, 90, 92–94, 96, 97
  technological gap, 80
Georgetown Hoya TV Reporters, 28
Ghostwriter, 12
Graphical design, 80
Grolier's Multimedia Encyclopedia, 92, 96
Guided participation, 73